Winter Palace

T. DAVIS BUNN

BETHANY HOUSE PUBLISHERS
MINNEAPOLIS, MINNESOTA 55438

It is important to note that, except as specifically mentioned within the Acknowledgments section, this story is entirely a creation of the author's imagination. No parallel between any persons, living or dead, is intended.

Published by Bethany House Publishers
A Ministry of Bethany Fellowship, Inc.
6820 Auto Club Road, Minneapolis, Minnesota 55438

Printed in the United States of America

ISBN 1–55661–324–5

This book is dedicated to

W. Lee Bunn

Beloved brother.
Trusted friend.

And to his wonderful wife,
Pamela

Books by T. Davis Bunn

The Maestro
The Presence
Promises to Keep

The Priceless Collection

Secret Treasures of Eastern Europe

1. *Florian's Gate*
2. *The Amber Room*
3. *Winter Palace*

T. Davis Bunn, a native of North Carolina, is a former international business executive whose career has taken him to over forty countries in Europe, Africa, and the Middle East. *Winter Palace*, his sixth novel, is based on extensive research as well as recent travels in Poland and Russia. He and his wife, Isabella, currently live in Oxford, England.

"Of all the burdens Russia has had to bear, heaviest and most relentless of all has been the weight of her past."

TIBOR SZAMUELY
"The Russian Tradition"

"When the sun of publicity shall rise upon Russia, how many injustices will it expose to view! Not only ancient ones, but those which are inacted daily will shock the world."

MARQUIS DE CUSTINE
Visitor to the Russian
Nobility
1839

"Everything is collapsing."

MIKHAIL GORBACHEV
In an address to parliament,
August, 1991

"The situation before and after the February 1917 revolution is absolutely the contemporary situation in Russia today. There is still hatred for authorities, the same horror of hunger, the same disorder, and so on. It is the same situation."

EDVARD RADZINSKY
Russian Political Historian
In an interview with the
Washington Post, July, 1992

"The fullness of God's salvation cannot be confined to one or several historical patterns, to one or several Christological titles, to one or several doctrines; it can only be told in a varied multitude of stories which tell us what experiences to expect when trusting in Jesus Christ."

EDWARD SCHWEIZER

"How good and pleasant it is
When brothers live together in unity . . .
For there the Lord bestows his blessing,
Even life forevermore."

PSALM 133:1, 3

Prologue

The loudest sound on the dark Saint Petersburg street was that of Peace Corps volunteer Leslie Ann Stevens' shoes scrunching along the grit-encrusted cobblestones.

There was no movement around her, none at all. Leslie Ann resisted the urge to look upward, to search the blank and darkened windows and see if anyone was spying on her. The sensation of being watched remained with her always, downfall of Communism or not.

Beside her, rusting metal latticework lined the Fontanka Canal. Once this neighborhood had been a most prestigious address, boasting winter homes for nobility from the length and breadth of Russia. Now the royal residences were split into rabbit warrens of crumbling, overcrowded apartments, and the canal itself was nothing more than a scummy pool.

As she approached the end of Fontanka, she thought she heard a murmur of voices and shifting footfalls. She stopped, her heart in her throat, and debated going back. Behind her was the safety of the relatively well-lit Nevsky Prospekt. But the other way back to her apartment meant walking almost a mile farther, and she was tired.

Ahead were the former royal stables of the czars. Once it had been a palace in itself, with quarters both for officers and members of the royal household. Now it sheltered the city's fleet of garbage trucks. Leslie Ann searched the blackness ahead of her, saw nothing, and heard no other sound. She decided to continue on her way.

When President Kennedy had established the Peace Corps in the sixties, the organization was intended to assist emerging nations and to contradict the Soviets' accusation that Americans were only interested in profit, in exploitation. Volunteers had been ordered to go forth and proclaim the goodness of both the nation and the people.

In Leslie Ann's view, the survivors of Russia's Communist era were now accepting that message a little too wholeheartedly.

Her host family tended to take everything she said as coming from the mouth of God. As best she could, Leslie Ann tried to explain that not everything in America was perfect. Not everyone drove a brand-new car. Not everyone had a swimming pool in his backyard. Not all citizens could afford to eat prime beef three times a day.

In her halting Russian, Leslie Ann also tried to introduce the family members to the deeply held faith that had brought her to Russia in the first place. She shared her beliefs, led them through a prayer, and gave them a Cyrillic Bible. All the while, though, she had a nagging impression that they listened because of where she came from, not because of the message she was trying to share.

With every passing day, Leslie Ann also felt a chasm growing between her and the other volunteers assigned to the Saint Petersburg area. Some days, in fact, it seemed the only things she had in common with her companions were her age and her training as an English teacher.

As far as she could tell, none of the others who had signed up for two years' duty in Russia shared her faith. She guessed that believers joined Christian evangelical organizations instead of the Peace Corps. But Leslie Ann did not see herself as an evangelist, at least, not in the normal sense. She was an English teacher who loved God and who intended to carry her faith with her all her life, in everything she did. Yet while the Peace Corps allowed her to practice her chosen profession in an exciting foreign land, it also left her totally isolated in beliefs and motives from most of her companions.

The Peace Corps central bulletin board pretty much summed it all up. About a third of the space was given over to helpful hints on how to survive in the crumbling Soviet empire: which street vendor sold fairly fresh meat, who had a new stock of bottled water, where a trustworthy and affordable Russian language teacher might be found, who was stocking toilet paper. The remainder contained offers of parties, overnight love affairs, companions for cross-country wanderings.

Still, its irreverent humor and homegrown cynicism was one of her few connections to Stateside. Like all the other volunteers, Leslie Ann checked it daily. And just a few weeks earlier, the bulletin board had produced solid gold.

That morning she had come into the office to find a new notice pinned in the bottom left-hand corner, announcing church services in English. Although the card had been up less than twenty-four hours, already its borders had been covered with irreverent scrawls.

The pastor turned out to be an American Baptist missionary, the church a series of interconnected rooms in a filthy back-street building. For Leslie Ann Stevens, entering the newly whitewashed makeshift chapel had been like coming home. And in the space of three weeks, the church had become Leslie Ann's island refuge in a sea of bewildering confusion.

Tonight she had broken one of her own safety rules and stayed at the church until after dark. But it was hard to leave the laughter and the warmth and return to the smelly apartment house where her host family—husband and wife, three children, the wife's mother, and the husband's unmarried sister—lived crowded together into three small rooms. The fourth room had been vacated for Leslie Ann in return for the incredible sum of twenty American dollars per month, more than a professional engineer earned in three.

Saturday evenings, a trip to the floor's only communal bathroom meant struggling down a fetid hallway past clusters of teenagers playing mournful guitars and smoking foul-smelling Russian cigarettes, ignoring the slurred curses of men passing around bottles of vodka, flinching at the screams and shouts that punched through thin apartment walls. For Leslie Ann Stevens, Saturday evenings were the most difficult times for her to recall why she had volunteered for a Saint Petersburg assignment in the first place.

Her feeble flashlight beam played across the rubble-strewn street, and she walked as fast as the darkness and the irregular pavement allowed. She arrived at the end of the Fontanka, turned beside the silent royal stables, and faltered.

Up ahead loomed one of the city's numerous winter palaces, built by royal families who controlled hundreds of square miles of land and thousands of serfs. Now its hulking presence was battered by seventy years of Communism. At the front gate, several men hustled to unload a truck. Over the broad central gates, a single flickering bulb in a metal cage swung from a rusty iron rod. The dim light transformed the men into a series of swiftly moving, softly cursing shadows.

To her utter terror, all movement ceased as she came into view. Leslie Ann turned and started to flee back to the church. Then two of the shadows detached themselves and hustled toward her.

She did not even have time to scream.

CHAPTER

1

Jeffrey Sinclair sat on the hard journey-bench, bracing himself against the furious jouncing and squealing turns by gripping the leather overhead strap with one hand and the cold metal edge of Alexander's stretcher with the other. Their siren's howl accompanied the racing engine as they sped through a London summer evening. The medic bent over Alexander's motionless form while flashing lights painted his tense features with ghostly hues of the beyond.

An entirely alien universe flashed by outside the ambulance. Windows tainted by the multitude of tragedies transported within showed glimpses of a hard, cold cityscape. Jeffrey craned and searched for some sign that the hospital was drawing near and found nothing familiar, comfortable, hopeful. Beyond panic, he wondered at this strange world where it took hours and hours and hours in a screaming, jouncing ambulance to arrive at the emergency room.

Several times the medic raised up from his thrusting and prodding and listening to Alexander's chest to shout in some strange tongue at the two drivers up front. The sounds were then repeated into a microphone and repeated back to them through a metallic speaker. Jeffrey understood none of it.

All he could see was the needle in Alexander's bared arm and the closed eyes and the electric voltage exploding his gray-skinned body up in a pantomime of painful exertion.

Jeffrey felt bleak helplessness wrap itself around his own heart and squeeze. And squeeze. And squeeze.

He gripped the end of the stretcher with both hands, leaned over as far as he could, and screamed out the plea, *"BREATHE!"*

No one even looked his way. His action was perfectly in order with the controlled pandemonium holding them all.

The hospital appeared, announced by a dual shout from both people in front. The driver misjudged the emergency room entrance and hit the curb so hard that Jeffrey's head slammed into the unpadded metal roof. Stars exploded in his head.

The ambulance stopped and the back doors slammed open. Impatient hands threw him out and aside with practiced motions. Through blurred eyes Jeffrey saw the stretcher slapped onto a gurney and wheeled away. He reached forward, but his rubber legs would not follow. They could not.

He did not know how long he stood there before the perky little nurse came out to ask, "Did you come with the gentleman with the heart?"

He nodded, then groaned aloud as the movement sent a painful lance up his neck. He gripped the ambulance's open door for support.

"Don't worry yourself so," the nurse said, misunderstanding his reaction. "You'll only make matters worse, going on like this. The gentleman needs your strength just now."

His eyes did not seem to want to focus. He strained, saw the young woman growing steadily more impatient, then his eyes watered over.

"You'll have to stop that, and right smart," she snapped, and raised her clipboard. "I need some information on the gentleman in there. What's his name, now?"

Jeffrey opened his mouth, tried to reply, wanted to say, that man is my boss and my relative and my best friend. But the blanket of blackness rose up and covered him.

•   •   •

Jeffrey awoke to a blinding white light.

"Don't move, please," a professionally cold female voice ordered. "Can you tell me your full name?"

"Jeffrey Allen Sinclair," he replied weakly.

"Do you know where you are?"

"At the hospital. Is my friend—"

"Just a moment. Look to your left, no, move only your eyes. Now to your right. Up, please. Can you flex your fingers? Fine. Now your toes."

"How is Alexander," he demanded, more strongly this time.

"The gentleman you arrived with? Cardiac arrest? He appears to have stabilized." Fingers probed his head, the back of his skull, his neck, worked down his spine. "Any discomfort?"

"No," he lied. "How long was I—"

"A few moments only." She then spoke to someone Jeffrey could not see. "No immediately visible damage to skull or vertebrae. Possible mild concussion, probable muscle contusion in the cervical area. Have a complete set of spinal x-rays done, then fit him with a neck brace."

"Yes, Doctor."

"You'll be staying with us for a bit, I'm afraid." A tired woman's face came into view and gave him a brief smile. "We'll need to keep you under observation for a day or so. Anyone who passes out at our front door can't be allowed to get off easy."

The longer he was awake, the more his head and neck throbbed. Even blinking his eyes brought discomfort. "All right."

"Popped your head on the ambulance roof, did you?"

"Yes."

She was not surprised. "The casualty department's entranceway is too narrow by half. You're the third one this year who's knocked his noggin. First time we've had one delivered on a gurney, though. You must have caught it right smart. Well, not to worry. Anyone we should contact for you?"

Jeffrey gave the number for Katya, his soon-to-be wife. "Are you sure my friend—"

18

"He's as well as can be expected, given the circumstances. Now, off to x-ray with you." The weary smile reappeared briefly. "And, Nurse, best give our patient something for the pain he claims he doesn't feel."

CHAPTER
2

Ца́рю небе́сний, утіши́телю, Ду́ше і́стини, що всю́ди єси́ і все наповня́єш, ска́рбе дібр і життя́ пода́телю, прийди́ і всели́ся в нас, і очи́сти нас від уся́кої скве́рни, і спаси́, благи́й, ду́ші на́ші.

"Heavenly King, Advocate, Spirit of Truth, who are everywhere present and fill all things, Treasury of Blessings, Bestower of Life, come and dwell within us; cleanse us of all that defiles us and, O Good One, save our souls."

The newly reopened Ukrainian Rites Catholic Church of St. Stanislav sat on the outskirts of Lvov, the second largest city in the newly reinstituted nation of the Ukraine. When the congregation had intoned their amen, the priest continued with the liturgy from John of Chrysostom, reciting the words as they had been spoken in more than a hundred tongues for over fifteen hundred years: "Blessed be our God, always, now and for ever and ever. May the Lord God remember you in His kingdom always, now and for ever and ever. Lord, you will open my lips, and my mouth shall declare your praise."

Ivona Aristonova stood with the others waiting before the bishop's confessional and droned another amen, her thoughts elsewhere. She did not much care for confession to the bishop, and was grateful that the man was normally too busy to

perform this duty himself. Yet today he was here, and as his
private secretary she was obliged to stand and wait; to do
otherwise would have set a hawk among the pigeons.

It was not that the bishop would ever refer to something
from the confessional in their daily life; he was too good a
priest ever to suggest that he even remembered what she
spoke. No, her discomfort came from the fact that inside the
confessional the bishop took his role seriously. He asked
questions for which she had no answer. He probed where she
did not care to look.

The priest conducting Mass stood before the altar table,
separated from the congregation by a frieze of ancient icons.
It was one of only three such tableaus, from over two thousand, which had survived the Communist years. He droned,
"Blessed is the kingdom of the Father and of the Son and of
the Holy Spirit, now and always and forever."

"Amen." Ivona held the prayer book in a limp hand, the
words so often heard that she could recite virtually the entire
book from memory. To take her mind off what was to come,
she cast her eyes back and forth around the scarred and
pitted church. For the past forty years, it had seen service
first as a stable for the horses that drew the streetcars, then
as a garage and oil depot. Only two months earlier had it
been reopened as a church.

"For peace from on high and for the salvation of our souls,
let us pray to the Lord."

"Lord, have mercy." The air was awash in the incense
burning before the altar, the church full to overflowing.
Every seat was taken, the back area packed with those who
arrived too late to find seats. A church made for a maximum
of six hundred now held well over a thousand souls.

"For the peace of the whole world, for the well-being of
the holy churches of God, and for the unity of all, let us pray
to the Lord."

"Lord have mercy." It was like this virtually every service. They were holding seven masses on Sunday, and still
people arrived a half hour early to be sure of a place.

"For this city, for every city and countryside and for the
faithful who live in them, let us pray to the Lord."

"Lord, have mercy." Every side altar was a solid wall of
flickering light, fueled by countless candle flames. Worship-

ers were going through devotional candles at a rate that even two months ago would have been unthinkable. Locating a reliable source was yet another of Ivona Aristonova's unending worries.

"For good weather, for abundant fruits of the earth, and for peaceful times, let us pray to the Lord."

"Lord have mercy." The bishop's assistant had recently departed to study abroad, and to Ivona's mind this was no great loss. The young man was like most of the Ukrainian Rites priests who had been consecrated in secret—poorly trained and suspiciously hostile toward all outsiders, including the bishop, who had recently returned from exile. Still, his absence meant that Ivona and the bishop and the priest saying Mass today were basically alone when it came to coping with the unending problems of resurrecting a church that had been outlawed for forty-six years.

"For those traveling by land, sea, or air; for the sick, the suffering, the imprisoned and for their salvation, let us pray to the Lord."

"Lord have mercy." Ivona chanted the words as she did most things in church—by rote and without feeling. Her mind remained fastened upon the incredible changes that had taken place within the Ukrainian Rites Church over the last few years and the overwhelming difficulties that accompanied them.

When Stalin convened the 1946 Ukrainian bishops' synod and declared the entire church illegal, worship according to traditions founded in the fourth century became a crime against the state. Following the decree, the church's leaders—the Metropolitan and all bishops—were gathered and shipped off to Siberian concentration camps. Only two survived, so battered in body and soul that neither would ever walk again.

All cathedrals and churches were declared state property. Many worshipers followed Stalin's orders and joined the only church officially tolerated within the Soviet Union, the Russian Orthodox Church. Stalin and his henchmen held no special affection for the Orthodox; they simply wished to bring all believers into a single unit so that they might more easily be monitored, dominated, and eventually exterminated. The Russian Orthodox Church had the singular advantage of being based in Moscow, and thus could be more easily controlled.

Josef Stalin harbored a violent hatred for Christian churches, the Ukrainian Rites Catholic Church in particular. It was too nationalistic, and it owed allegiance to a foreign-based pope. As soon as World War II ended and the need for the church members' assistance in defeating the Nazi invaders was over, Stalin began his infamous purge.

In the decades that followed, however, the Ukrainian Rites Church did not die as Stalin and his successors demanded. Despite the harshest possible punishments leveled against convicted believers, the church survived.

It moved underground. Mass was celebrated in cellars. Priests were taught and consecrated in absolute secrecy. Weddings and christenings and baptisms were performed in the dead of night. Bishops lived ever on the run, ever watchful for the KGB, often trapped and tortured and sentenced and imprisoned. The toil and terror and tears of its priests and believers earned the Ukrainian Rites Church the title of the Catacomb Church. Within the Catholic hierarchy, the two names became interchangeable.

Through it all, the Ukrainian Rites Church still did not die. When it again became legal in 1991, four million, five hundred thousand people claimed membership.

"Help us, save us, have mercy on us, and protect us, O Lord, by your grace."

"Lord have mercy." It was Ivona's turn to enter the confessional. She knelt, recited her rehearsed lines, and waited. She dreaded what was now to come.

From behind the intricately carved wooden screen, Bishop Michael Denisov sighed and spoke in his ever-gentle voice, "So, so, dear sister Ivona Aristonova. And have you made peace with your husband?"

But Ivona was saved from both answering and receiving more of the bishop's painful probing by shouts rising above the chanted service. She and the bishop started upright as the priest cut off in mid-sentence.

"Gone, all gone!" A chorus of voices wailed their distress through the sudden silence.

"The treasures have been stolen!"

CHAPTER
3

Jeffrey awoke to find familiar violet-gray eyes peering down at him with a worried expression. "Are you all right?"

He nodded, or started to, then moaned as the pain brought him fully awake. "How?" he croaked, or tried to, but was stopped by the dryness of his throat.

Katya reached beyond his field of vision, came up with a cup. "Don't try to raise up." She fitted the straw in his mouth and said as he drank, "You've had a neck strain and possibly a mild concussion."

He managed, "Alexander?"

"He's alive," she answered, and took a shaky breath. "It's almost ten o'clock. I went to your apartment and waited almost an hour, but when you didn't show up for dinner I went by the shop, and when I saw all the police outside the door . . ." Katya had to pause. "I never want to go through anything like that. Not ever again."

Jeffrey lay still and recalled the events. It had been almost closing time at the Mount Street antiques shop. Just another day. He had been giving the antique table on the front podium a careful polish when the sudden thump had echoed from the back office-alcove. He had called Alexander's name. No response. He had set down his polish and rag and walked back, feeling an icy touch without knowing why. Then Alexander's legs had come into view.

He remembered screaming into the telephone, though he could not recall having dialed a number. He remembered trying to resuscitate the old man for what seemed like several lifetimes, but he had no recollection of the ambulance's arriving or of anyone gathering them up or starting off. Or closing the shop.

"The shop was swarming with the security people from down the street," Katya told him. "You left the door wide open. The security cameras can't see into the back alcove, so they didn't know what had happened until the cameras showed the medics wheel Alexander out on a stretcher."

Alexander's eyes had been open when Jeffrey raced into the alcove. They had pleaded with him, even while one hand tore at the carpet and the other pressed hard to his chest, clenching the suit and shirt with inhuman strength. The power of that gaze was a knife that Jeffrey still felt.

"They almost lost him." She choked on that, swallowed, tried again. "But he's stable now. I've seen him. Twice. He's breathing okay. His heart rate is stable. They say if he makes it through the next seventy-two hours he will probably be out of danger."

"Want to see," he whispered, his voice a rasp.

"You can't move just now," she replied gently. "They've made x-rays of your neck and head. There doesn't appear to be any serious damage, but the doctor wants to check you again. And you have to be fitted with a neck brace."

She stroked a strand of hair from his forehead. "Even if you could move, there's nothing to see. He's in intensive care and heavily sedated. There are all kinds of monitors, and he's being carefully watched."

"Want—"

She shushed him, lowered her face and kissed him softly. "Pray for him, Jeffrey. Speak to him in your heart. He will hear. Now try to rest. He needs you to be strong, and so do I." She grasped his hand with both of hers. "Close your eyes. I'll pray with you."

Despite Katya's entreaties and the doctor's orders, the

next morning found Jeffrey making his stiff-legged way alone to Alexander's bedside. His neck was encased in a white foam vise that smelled like a rubber glove. The soreness had moved lower to wrap around his back and shoot down his legs if he made too wide a step.

Jeffrey entered the hospital room to find the Count Garibaldi di Grupello, an old friend and client of Alexander's, looming above the foot of the hospital bed. The count greeted him with a grave nod, then returned his attention to the bed's silent form. "You positively must not allow me to win our bet, Alexander. You, Jeffrey, what is the word for someone who throws in the towel too early?"

"Wimp," Jeffrey offered, immensely relieved to find Alexander's eyes open.

"Precisely. My dear old friend, listen to me. Behave yourself and do not under any circumstances permit yourself to indulge in any wimpish behavior. We must marry these young people off, then give them a proper start. How on earth do you expect me to do this alone if you insist on wimping away?"

Jeffrey cleared the burn from his throat. "The correct term is wimping out."

"Whatever. I am sure the message has been received. Yes? Nod if you heard me, Alexander. There. You see? He agrees. And now my three minutes are up. Farewell, old friend. Next time I intend to hear you argue with me once more."

He turned away with a regal half bow. "Jeffrey, be so good as to join me in the hallway for a moment."

Before following the count, Jeffrey stood a moment looking down on Alexander and feeling weak with relief to find him alive. The old gentleman's eyes held him in silent communion. Then one hand raised to point weakly at Jeffrey's collar.

"I bumped my head on the ambulance roof," Jeffrey explained.

Alexander released a sigh.

"Hard," Jeffrey added.

Alexander rolled his eyes toward the headboard, gave his head a gentle shake.

Jeffrey watched until he was sure Alexander was resting

peacefully, then slipped quietly from the room.

Once the door was closed behind him, the count said, "Young man, you must be strong for our friend in there."

"I've been told that before."

"Because it is true." The count squinted at the brace and demanded, "What on earth is that ghastly thing clamped to your neck?"

"Long story."

"Not a tiff with the young lady, I hope."

"Not a chance."

"That is good, for she shall also rely on your strength for now." The count held up his hand. "I know, I know. From all appearances she relies on no one but her God. Such appearances are not always true, young man. She has great strength, but not the ability to withstand such blows to those she loves."

"I don't know if I do, either," Jeffrey confessed.

The majestic nostrils tilted back as the count gave Jeffrey his most affronted gaze. "You *must*. You are the bonding force here. Now, go in there and be strong, and bring our friend back to life. The world would suffer too great a vacuum were Alexander to pass out of it."

Jeffrey found it difficult to force words around the thought of Alexander's absence. "What do I say?"

"Talk of antiques," the count commanded impatiently. "What else? Speak about the shop. Feed to him a sense of remaining here with the living. Tell him I have finally agreed to purchase that cabinet, although how you can manage to claim such an outrageous sum for it and still keep a straight face is utterly beyond me."

"Are you?"

"Am I what?"

"Buying the cabinet. You wouldn't want me to lie to him, would you?"

"There, you see? This is what Alexander requires from you. He must feel a part of life. Now go in there and fill the empty house." The count turned his attention to the closed door. "For a man of years, illness brings a new meaning to the word *alone*. Let him live through your strength, Jeffrey, until he is once again prepared to live for himself."

CHAPTER
4

Prince Vladimir Markov, last surviving member of the Markov dynasty, knew exactly what the general was thinking behind his practiced stone mask. No doubt all the former Soviet army officer saw was a beautiful Monte Carlo villa transformed into a vast sea of clutter. The general made it quite clear that he considered the prince an eccentric collector, a magpie in a foppish nest, a pathetic has-been who clung to any object even slightly scented by the past.

It was true that the prince's villa was so full of furniture and paintings and valuables that it looked more like a warehouse than a home. Several rooms had simply been stacked from floor to ceiling and then locked up. The living room alone contained sufficient articles to furnish ten chambers.

But it was not a fanatic's hoarding instinct that drove Prince Markov. Not at all. The articles represented his family's royal past, a past that included a palace large enough to hold all his precious belongings. That palace he intended to have for himself once more.

Prince Markov treated the general with polite disdain. The peon could think what he liked, as long as he helped place the means to the desired end within Markov's grasp.

These days, the prince reflected, retired Soviet army officers were eager for any work that would keep them from the shame of common unemployment. Many of the groups struggling for power and wealth within the crumbling Soviet empire found them perfect as hired hands. Retired Soviet generals, it was said, had years of experience in corrupt activities. They were utterly efficient. They were brave to the point of idiocy. They were weaned of troublesome concern for human life. And they were too dogmatic to come up with independent plans on their own.

These days, it was very easy for such a one to go bad.

General Surikov had a taste for antiques. He stopped several times in his slow meandering walk toward Markov's balcony to examine several of Markov's more remarkable pieces. Markov held his own impatience in check. Barely.

"I know what needs to be done," Markov said, ushering his guest through the doors and out onto the terrace overlooking the Mediterranean and the Bay of Nice.

"Of course you do," his guest replied, giving the spectacular view an approving glance. "You're a professional."

General Surikov was a trim, hard man in his late fifties. He would never allow himself to balloon out as some of his fellow senior officers did. Not for him the triple chins that enveloped his colleagues' collars on parade days, nor the enormous girth that required two towels knotted together in the military baths. Nor did he show the red-veined nose and cheeks of a dedicated vodka drinker. His hair was short, his face as tough as his grip.

"These new Russian politicians," General Surikov complained, accepting the offered seat. "They sit in front of the television cameras and mouth, ma-ma-ma-ma, like sheep. All their lives they've studied butterflies through a microscope or written poetry nobody can read on a full stomach. And now they're running our country."

"Accountants," Markov agreed. "Engineers."

"Civilians and dissidents." The general snorted his disgust. "They tell the people, why do we need a military power? My comrades and I must sit and watch them enact this charade called transition to capitalism. Where is the mighty Soviet state now?"

"Gone," Markov sympathized. "Lost forever."

"These buffoons will not hold on much longer," the general added ominously.

Markov straightened. "You have news?"

"Nothing definite. Nothing except the *Afgantsi* are prepared to move."

Markov nodded. With the growing governmental crisis, the danger of a hardliners' coup grew daily. If one happened, it would no doubt be led by the cabal of officers, veterans of the conflict in Afghanistan, who were known as *Afgantsi*. "Rumor has it that now they virtually control the army."

"For once the rumors are correct," General Surikov replied with evident relish. "The new Defense Minister is one of us. Through him we have secured all but two of the top defense positions. Within the past eighteen months, we have settled the entire senior officer corps in our grasp."

"You served in Afghanistan yourself, did you not?"

"In the early days, yes, before ill health forced me to accept a posting to the Baltic. Were I only ten years younger!" Surikov sighed. "Still, at least I am now again able to stand proud and proclaim that I did my patriotic duty."

And spilled how much innocent blood in the process, Markov reflected. Aloud he commented, "How nice for you."

"Patriotism, yes. It is indeed nice to be among friends who still honor the word, while these idiots called politicians stand around and allow our empire to crumble."

"It appears to be what the people want," Markov observed.

"The people!" The word obviously left a bitter taste in Surikov's mouth. "The people are sheep, to be led astray by the lies of blathering imbeciles. The people will like what they are told to like. Where is their pride now, I ask you. Where is their direction? What has democracy brought except growing chaos and disaster piled upon disaster?"

"A valid point," Markov soothed, deciding not to mention that much of the present chaos was caused by the people who now employed Surikov—they and others of their kind. "When do you think the officers will make their move?"

"Either this winter or the next. When coal and oil run low, and food runs out, and patience runs thin, and fear runs rampant." The words came out as a chant. "Then you will hear the Russian bear howl its demand for change. And we will be ready."

Markov considered the situation carefully and decided a right-wing coup would not damage his objectives; perhaps it could even help things along. An alliance with a former prince of the realm might appeal to the new Russian dictators as a further stamp of legitimacy. "How, pray tell, does all this mesh with your current work?"

The general hesitated, then responded, "A man must eat."

"A good time to have friends, no?"

"I am not made for following a capitalist's orders," Surikov confessed.

"Or for poverty," Prince Markov reminded him. "Which is why you are here."

General Surikov gave an abrupt nod. "To business, then. I am here to report that the time has come to proceed."

Markov struggled to keep the triumph from registering on his features. "This pleases me," he said smoothly.

"As it should. It is seldom that my superiors show such confidence in an, if you would excuse me, outsider. Not to mention one of the former czarist aristocracy."

Superiors. The thought was laughable. The Russian ship of state threatened to sink any day now. Crime filled the current political vacuum, creating vast opportunities for the unscrupulous. Criminals knew sudden power and wealth, and courted those who had lost power with the advent of democracy. Out of the chaos a new alliance had been born.

"Please tell your superiors," Markov kept the irony from his voice, "that I am certain our plans will meet with great success."

"They better," the general replied. "With all due respect, let me assure you that errors of judgment are met with great harshness."

"There is no need to speak in such terms."

"Of course not. I am simply doing as ordered. They, you see, have never had the pleasure of making your acquaintance."

Markov straightened the lapel of his immaculate jacket. "Have they informed you of a time plan for the next stage?"

"Now," the general replied bluntly. "My superiors say the stock has reached capacity. And there have been further developments."

Markov raised an eyebrow. "Developments of what sort?"

"Nothing that affects our plans."

Which means they didn't tell him, Markov guessed, wondering how such developments might affect his own designs. "Then I shall make my contact immediately," Markov replied, "and inform you when events begin to unfold."

CHAPTER

5

Jeffrey arrived at the intensive care unit two days later to learn that Alexander had been moved to a private room. He rushed back down through the central lobby, hurrying because Katya and the doctors allowed him only a few minutes alone with the old gentleman. But as he passed by the main entrance, he nearly ran into his friend Andrew. The antique dealer's face was almost hidden behind a massive bouquet of flowers.

Andrew took one look at his neck brace and commented, "What a loving little company you work for, lad. One gets sick, the others all get sick with worry."

"Worry did not put this thing around my neck."

"No, of course not." He patted Jeffrey's shoulder. "How's the old gent getting on?"

Jeffrey repeated the official, "As well as can be expected."

Andrew nodded his understanding. "Doctors, they all get their lips sewn together at graduation."

"He looked okay yesterday, and I just learned they've shifted him out of intensive care," Jeffrey said.

"Then trust your own gut, I say." Andrew inspected the collar more closely. "So how did you get yourself fitted up?"

"Long story. How are things with you?"

"Oh, I'm suffering a bit. Seem to have swallowed a fire-breathing dragon sometime during the night. Otherwise, I suppose I can't complain."

"Tie one on last night, did we?"

"We?" Andrew looked confused. "Were you there too?"

Jeffrey found it nice to have a reason to smile. "Figure of speech."

"Don't do that to me on such a morning, lad. Makes me worry if I pickled my marbles." He extended the flowers. "Didn't have any desire to bother the old gent. Just wanted you to pass on my best regards and these posies."

"That's very kind, Andrew," Jeffrey said, accepting the sheaf of blooms. "I'm sure he'd like to thank you himself."

"That can wait for when he's dressed in something more than a drafty gown and slippers. Just let him know that I'm thinking of him." He patted Jeffrey's arm. "Take care of yourself, lad. And do let me know if you're ever in need of the old helping hand."

"I believe I have caught my second wind," Alexander declared weakly as Jeffrey entered the room.

"Have you?"

He nodded. "A small breeze, at any rate."

"Your color's better," Jeffrey observed. Alexander still looked very ill, but life was back in his eyes.

Jeffrey lowered himself carefully into the bedside chair. He looked around at the four bare walls, the flickering monitor screens, the hospital bed, the tubes and wires, the starched sheets, the roll-away table with plastic tray and utensils and food. "A long way from Claridge's."

Alexander managed a shaky smile. "You should try the food."

"I already did." Jeffrey returned the smile. "You're resting well?"

"My body draws upon slumber like an elixir," Alexander replied. His voice remained barely above a whisper. "I relish it as I never have before. I slide in and out as one draws a fine silk covering over his body. Sometimes it is so delicate that I am scarcely aware of its arrival."

A gentle knock announced Katya's entry. She walked in, bringing a sense of joyous sunshine with her. She pecked at

Alexander's cheek, gave Jeffrey something more substantial, asked, "How are my two favorite men this morning?"

"Alexander is feeling better," Jeffrey said, giving up his seat and pulling over a second chair.

"Of course he is." She inspected Jeffrey's neck brace. "Did you sleep in it as the doctor ordered?"

He nodded as far as he could. "Turning over has become a major event."

"Better than having to wear that contraption on your honeymoon," she replied primly, then turned to Alexander. "After Jeffrey left to come visit you yesterday afternoon, a Mr. Vladimir Markov called you from Monte Carlo. He seemed most distressed when I said you would be indisposed for the next few days."

"Markov. Sounds more like a spy than somebody living on the French Riviera," Jeffrey commented.

"Hardly a spy," Alexander replied in his hoarse half whisper. "Quite a distinguished gentleman, actually. I believe he may even be some long-lost relative of the Romanovs."

"Romanovs, as in the Russian kings?"

"Czars," Alexander corrected. "Exactly."

"Is he a client?" Katya asked.

"I suppose you might say so," Alexander replied. "He purchased my home in Monte Carlo. I haven't seen him in well over a year."

"Monte Carlo," Katya sighed. "The name alone sounds divine. What was your place like?"

"Quite simple—well, no, I suppose that would be a bit of an understatement." He paused to cough weakly. "It was built of stone, two stories high, and tucked into the hillside overlooking the sea. It had the charm of a Provencal farmhouse, but with these marvelous arched windows."

Slack muscles pulled up in a vestige of a smile. "When Markov walked in, he threw his hands in the air and said, I'll take it. He was perhaps halfway through the entry hall. The real estate agent was as surprised as I. And Markov insisted on purchasing one of my antiques from Eastern Europe. Gave me a bit of a pang, but where was I to place the item otherwise?"

"Perhaps return it to the shop," Jeffrey murmured.

A spark of the old Alexander returned. "So that you might have the pleasure of selling it to someone else? I do so admire your logic."

"So how did this Russian become so rich?"

"It's not that he became rich," Alexander replied. "It is that he held on to a small share of what before was one of the world's largest fortunes. At the turn of the century, the Russians considered it quite chic to travel to France. They positively loved the Riviera, and those who could built magnificent villas there. They learned the language and spoke it with the most atrocious Russian accent. A number of blue-domed Orthodox cathedrals still remain today, quite at odds with the local Provencal architecture."

"But the Revolution changed all that," Katya added.

Alexander nodded. His voice was gradually losing strength. "When it looked as though the Bolsheviks would succeed in overthrowing the government, those of the nobility who did not have their heads in the sand became panic-stricken. Some managed to escape at the last moment, the fires that destroyed their palaces and their heritage and many of their kinfolk lighting their way."

"So Markov's family was in Monte Carlo when the Revolution broke out in 1917?" Katya asked.

"Quite likely," Alexander replied. "He had an amazing house, a palace really, erected by his family around the turn of the century. It looked like an art-deco wedding cake by the sea. It was surrounded by elaborate gardens, with dozens of statues, Greek gods and goddesses. A most remarkable place."

"So he gave this up to buy your home?" Jeffrey asked.

"Yes, I suppose sentimentality can only hold a person for so long," Alexander replied, his eyelids threatening to close of their own accord. "I heard rumors that the place was bought by an Arabian prince for a positively staggering sum."

Katya rose to her feet. "You are growing tired. It's time we let you rest."

Jeffrey stood with her. "I'll be back as usual this afternoon."

"Thank you both," Alexander murmured, slipping away.

Katya held on to her smile until the door had closed behind them. Then she stopped and clung to Jeffrey with fierce
strength, her face buried in his chest. Jeffrey stroked her
silken dark hair. "Alexander's going to be all right," he said,
and for the first time truly believed it was so.

* * *

Alexander awoke in time to watch the afternoon sun
emerge from behind thunderclouds and paint his hospital
room with a thousand rainbow hues. Jeffrey was dozing in
the chair by his bed, his neck still protected by the foam
collar. Alexander stared at him, and saw how the rain-
cleansed light turned the young face into that of a world-
weary king, burdened with the woes of many.

Sleep was a blanket that never entirely left Alexander's
mind, a drug that demanded ever more of him. He had turned
the day into a swatch of gentle breaths, was only halfway
conscious as later the nurse eased him over to bathe a body
that was only partly his. He had slept during the doctor's
afternoon visit, dozed as Jeffrey and the doctor conferred,
caught only snatches of the talk. But it did not matter. It
was enough to lie in a sort of floating awareness and to see
the world anew.

Alexander looked around, taking in as much as he could
while moving only his eyes, seeing everything as for the first
time. There was a glory to each object, a burnished quality,
as though reality had been polished and set on display for
him to savor. But no matter where he looked or what he saw,
always his eyes returned to his slumbering friend. Always.

The sunlight inched its way across the linoleum floor as
Alexander continued his inspection of his surroundings. Bit
by bit, impressions came to him through reawakened
senses—the sharp hospital smells, the dividing lines between pastel shadows and angled brightness, the beep of ma-
chines attached to his body, the squeak of shoes in the hallway, the sound of his own breathing, the memory of how he
came to be here.

Memories. All he had to do was shut his eyes, and the
past rose vividly before him. There was a clarity to his in-

ternal vision that made memories appear as real and fresh and immediate as the world outside. One world with eyes opened, a thousand worlds when the veils fell and his sight searched inward.

Monte Carlo. Monte Carlo. Alexander replayed the morning's conversation as he drifted along the edge of sleep. Monte Carlo. As a young man he had loved the place; the city had made him feel *alive*. All the loss and hunger and deprivation of the war years in Poland had been softened by the thrill of his times in Monte Carlo.

There the senses surpassed themselves. The sea was an impossible blue, fringed with palm trees and sand-castle mansions. Champagne had more bubbles. Just breathing the air made a man feel rich. Alexander had lived for himself there and made no apologies to anyone.

By 1955, Alexander's London-based antiques trade had earned him almost enough money to fit into Monte Carlo society, while his charm and his skill at the gaming tables had made up the difference. Evenings he had enjoyed racing along the lantern-lit Corniche in a vintage cabriolet, taking the scent of night-blooming jasmine in great heady draughts.

Evenings he had wound his way down the hillside to the Place du Casino. He had loved the casino. He had loved to enter late, impeccably overdressed. He had loved the acknowledging nods of the croupiers across the expanse of green felt that separated him from his winnings. He had loved to click his chips into tall stacks, concentrating on the cards and the numbers and the counting. He had loved to drink espresso and tip generously before calling it a night— or a morning, as the case had often been—usually several thousand francs richer for the experience.

When he had finally sold his villa in the late eighties, the magic of Monte Carlo had long since faded. The landscape had changed beyond all recognition. The steep foothills of the Alpes Maritimes had been gouged with dynamite, lined with concrete, and studded with apartment blocks, office complexes, and utterly charmless hotels. A high-rise skyline had been grafted along the rim of the old fairy-tale kingdom.

The people had changed as well. When he finally departed, his neighbors had included deposed African dictators, Arab billionaires, retired arms dealers, and South American drug lords. Hulking bodyguards whose coats pinched around poorly hidden machine-pistols replaced the universal sense of secure comfort. The atmosphere of discreet pleasure once enjoyed by the patriarchs and players had been exchanged for a dismal blend of ostentation and secrecy.

Alexander well understood the secrets of shared confidences between friends, of loyalty to a cause, of wounds kept hidden from the world. But this secrecy took on a conspiratorial quality, serving nothing more glorious than self-interest and bulging bank accounts. Such an atmosphere left him more and more the outsider.

But still, Monte Carlo. The very name continued to hold a power over him. He remembered the place not with regret, but with a bittersweet fondness, as for a childhood sweetheart who had grown up to marry the wrong man. He would like the chance to visit again. There were still a few places that clung determinedly to the old charm. As he drifted toward consciousness again, he wondered if the jasmine was in bloom this time of year.

Even before he opened his eyes, he was cuffed by the offensive hospital odors. This was his reality, being bound to a body that no longer leapt to his bidding. This was his fate, held by his own weakness to a starched white bed in a stark white room. Alexander knew a moment of crushing despair as he realized with the fullness of defeat that Monte Carlo might very well be beyond his reach—now and forever.

He opened his eyes once more to find Jeffrey still seated beside the bed, awake and alert now, waiting patiently for his return. He motioned with his eyes toward the cup.

Once he had drunk, he whispered, "Send for Gregor." Then he closed his eyes once again upon a world where it felt as though he no longer belonged.

•   •   •

When Jeffrey left Alexander's room that evening, he found Katya standing by the nurses' station, deep in conversation with Alexander's doctor. He waited until they shook hands and separated, then walked over and asked, "So, what did she tell you?"

"Well, it is still quite serious. But it could have been a lot worse, especially if you had not reacted swiftly and brought him here as fast as you did."

Jeffrey started to shake his head, winced and caught himself. "It felt like time was standing still."

"I'm sure it did."

"Are they going to have to operate?"

"They don't think so. They need to monitor him for a few days before making a final decision about a pacemaker. But he appears to be in good general health, they say. They are hoping it won't be necessary."

"Alexander would hate having to go through surgery. Anything that reminds him of his mortality is a hard blow."

"He'll probably be insisting that the doctor send him home this weekend." She hesitated. "Especially with our wedding coming up. But the doctors said he will have to be in for at least another ten days. Maybe more."

The wedding. The same thought that had been pressing at him since first looking down at Alexander in the hospital bed rose again. This time it almost broke through to the surface.

Katya caught his internal struggle. "What's wrong?"

"Nothing."

Early on in the planning stages, Jeffrey had learned he had very little control when it came to preparations for the wedding. Over the years, Katya had built up a very definite idea of how she wanted her wedding to be. Jeffrey had learned to look at it as *her* day, and to allow her a free rein in making her dream come true.

Katya searched his face, said quietly, "You are right, Jeffrey."

"About what?"

"I think I have known it since I first walked into the shop and heard you were at the hospital with Alexander. I just haven't wanted to face the truth."

"What are you talking about?"

"You know exactly," she said. "You've known all along."

"Known what?"

"Ten days," Katya repeated. "I can't imagine Alexander not being there."

Jeffrey showed the remarkable good sense of not replying.

"With your family coming from the States, we can't put it off." Katya focused on nothing. "You know he will want to be there, but it would be risking his health for him to try and move across town."

"We can't take that responsibility," he agreed.

"But he has to be a part of this. He's supposed to be your best man." Katya focused on him. "The Bible says we need a faith that can move mountains. Why not a faith that can move weddings? If Alexander can't join us, then we'll have to join him."

"What are you saying?" He waved his arm about as far as he could. "Hold the wedding in the hospital?"

"There has to be a chapel here somewhere. Every hospital does, right?"

Jeffrey blinked. He couldn't believe what he was hearing. Not after the past few months, when an entirely new side to Katya's personality had appeared. Seeing her so happy had granted Jeffrey the patience to withstand an almost hourly barrage of wedding details. But he had wondered about it, wondered how such a practical woman, worldly wise far beyond her years, could become so totally caught up in recreating a fantasy moment dreamed up in her childhood.

And now this.

"I'm sure the chapel isn't anything fancy, but we'll just have to make do," Katya told him firmly. "At least this way Alexander could be with us."

This same woman who was now offering to move their wedding to a hospital had taken a swatch of her wedding-dress fabric to a bakery on the other side of London to make sure that the marzipan frosting was tinted just a shade darker ivory than her gown; she did not want her wedding dress to look dingy by comparison. She had then tracked down the calligrapher for the royal family to ensure that the invitations would be perfectly hand-lettered.

"Don't you think that would be better than not having him share the day with us?"

She had absolutely insisted on Peruvian lilies for her bridal bouquet. Undaunted by the fact that they were months out of season, she had persuaded the director of the Chelsea flower show to have several sprigs shipped by air from Ruritonga, a tropical island somewhere in the Pacific, the day before her wedding. She had also gone to the hairdresser twice for "rehearsals" of her bridal hairdo.

"I would so much rather have it here than have it without Alexander," Katya told him.

She had convinced the Grosvenor House banqueting manager to allow her to attend three receptions, uninvited, so that she could personally sample and *then* decide upon which selection of hors d'oeuvres to serve; despite the fact that there would only be eighteen guests at their reception.

Katya grasped his hand with both of hers. "I know you're disappointed. I am too, in a way. But could we please do it here?"

She had persuaded the Anglican minister at the Grosvenor Chapel to reschedule two christenings so that the church would be available for their early evening vows. After all, she had said, it was so much more romantic to be married by candlelight, and in a church designed by Sir Christopher Wren.

"Please, Jeffrey? For me?"

The preparations for their wedding had been a genuine test of Katya's ingenuity and Jeffrey's patience. Now this same woman was telling him she would be quite content to be married in a hospital chapel. He imagined a small room at sub-basement level, somewhere near the boiler works, painted a shade of off-off-green.

He could not help but love her.

"Whatever you want is fine," Jeffrey said, sweeping her up in a fierce embrace. He released her and started for the main lobby. "Now I have to try to get Cracow on the phone."

CHAPTER
6

Ivona Aristonova glanced at her watch for the hundredth time that morning, counted the people ahead of her in the bread line, and decided she could still make it back to the bishop's tiny apartment in time to prepare his midday meal.

These days she was shopping for two households, both her own and Bishop Michael's. With his assistant studying in the West, there was no one else to make sure the man ate. And unless someone did the cooking and then stood over him, the man would simply forget. He gave little care to the things of this earth, especially to his own well-being. It was one of his traits that left Ivona both a little awed and a little frightened of the man. That and his ability to see much deeper than she preferred.

She took another step in line, maintaining bodily contact with the hefty woman in front. Line breakers hovered like vultures, seeking to swoop down and save themselves the wait. Beyond them rose the cries of beggars, old and young, pleading for the chance to feed themselves another day. The beggars were a recent phenomenon. The line breakers had been with them always.

For a citizen of the former Soviet empire, the everyday components of life were not to be recalled with great fondness. Standing in line for hours and hours was a daily millstone, waiting so long that the back of the man or woman in front became memorized down to the slightest flaw in the weave, the lint on a scarf, the dandruff dusting a collar like miniature snow. Feeling the breath of the person behind was the worst for some; for others, it was breathing the smell of the one before.

Statistics grudgingly released by Izvestia showed that half of Russia's population had fallen below the official poverty level. Helpless to put brakes on the decline, the Russian parliament had reacted by lowering the official level of what it meant to be poor.

Under the Communists, capitalism had been a crime punishable by imprisonment, a stay in Siberia, or treatment at an asylum. Now it was supposed to be the answer to all their nation's ills. But the state foundered in a Communist-made dilemma. Competition remained dampened, if not stifled, for the sake of full employment. People standing in endless lines did not need a degree in business to know that something was not working. Ivona waited alongside her countrymen and felt more than mounting impatience drawing nerves to the breaking point.

After buying bread, Ivona hastened back to the bishop's apartment behind the church and let herself in. She was busy preparing soup when she heard a knock at the door. Before she could set down her work and dry her hands, the bishop answered the call himself.

"Why, my dear brother, what a pleasant surprise," she heard his gentle voice say. "Come in, come in."

The Orthodox priest followed the bishop down the hall and into his cubbyhole of a study with the fearful demeanor of one approaching the gates of hell. She recognized the young man as one of the few Orthodox priests who sought to live in peace with the Ukrainian church. He was an outcast in the eyes of many of his own brethren, but his eyes burned with the fire of abiding faith. Ivona drew back into the shadows so she could see, yet not be seen, certain that if she was spotted she would be sent away.

The young man had a bear's girth and a martyr's openhearted gaze as he faced the bishop. "I had to come."

"You are safe here, brother. There is no need to whisper."

"I am safe nowhere," the priest replied. "But still I had to come."

The bishop sighed. He was by nature a hopeful man, but there were days when the never-ending acrimony between the various factions of Christ's church dragged down his spirit like a lead weight.

Bishop Michael had been a fresh-faced acolyte when he fled the Ukraine directly after Stalin's synod. He had trained for the priesthood in Rome and from there had traveled to serve exiled Ukrainian populations in France, in Switzerland, and finally in New Jersey. He had ministered in lands where religious freedom was a fact, rather than the basis of propaganda. And then, with the declaration of Ukrainian independence in 1991, Bishop Michael had asked to be sent home.

He had arrived to find utter chaos.

More than half the church buildings had been destroyed, often to make way for apartment blocks or office buildings or plazas dedicated to the great Communist uprising. Others had been used as gas and oil storage depots, warehouses, stables, vegetable bins and compost dumps for communal farms, or prisons for the criminally insane. Many had not been touched in any way since the Communists barred their doors seventy years ago. Few remained in any condition to be used as churches.

But now Communist Party members were being tried for crimes against the people, the Soviet Union was facing gradual dismemberment, and the Ukrainian church was once more becoming active. They wanted their churches back. They *demanded* them back.

The government had responded with a paper transfer of the churches that remained. And because they had no interest in tracing the original owners, they had simply given all the properties, six thousand ruined churches, to the only church that had officially existed for the past forty-six years: the Russian Orthodox.

Yet the Russian Orthodox Church could not respond to the Ukrainian church's demands for these properties because they in truth never received anything except a letter. The legislature in Moscow and elsewhere might have acted, but the old Party officials still controlled the local bureaucracies, even within the newly formed Ukrainian republic.

These officials still harbored the same old resentment for anything stinking of church and faith.

Bishop Michael understood all this, and in understanding he was granted patience. Yet he could also understand the feelings of his brother Ukrainian bishops, the ones who had served in persecuted secrecy and who had suffered all their lives under the hands of the Soviet overlords.

These men saw the Russian Orthodox Church as part of the official power structure, the same system that had convicted them of anti-Soviet crimes, imprisoned them, tortured them, chained them into gangs of mine workers, declared them insane, loaded them with drugs for months on end, and murdered fellow believers out of hand. For those who survived the years of fear and persecution and horror, it was very hard to muster patience for anyone, most especially for an institution they viewed as a conspirator to their own oppression.

The bishop led the young priest toward the office's most sturdy chair. "Who threatens you, brother?"

"All who refuse to call you brother in return," the priest replied, his gaze scattered about the room. "All who use their eyes to watch, but not to see."

"Are we not free from such spying times?"

"You, perhaps," he replied, "but not I. Not here. Not ever."

"No, it is my heart's yearning which spoke so, and not truth," the bishop replied sadly. "And yet you came."

"I had no choice," the priest replied. "I saw them."

The bishop stilled in watchful intensity. "The thieves?"

"I was praying a vigil in the side alcove," the other said, his voice lowering to a hoarse moan. "They wore the robes of my order, but they were not of Christ's body."

"I have seen the torn robe and the cross upon the broken chain which someone left lying by the open crypt," the bishop replied. "And now you are telling me that the thieves were Orthodox priests?"

"They wore the robes. And yet, and yet, I saw their eyes. I heard their voices. Their talk was of gain and of death. Their actions were of . . ." He dropped his face to his hands. "What is happening to us?"

"What did they say, brother?" the bishop urged.

"Saint Petersburg," the young priest moaned through his hands. "They have taken your treasures there."

CHAPTER
7

When Alexander's cousin Gregor passed through the gates at Heathrow Airport, most of the waiting crowd saw only a frail old Polish gentleman with a halting, arthritic walk. Jeffrey saw a treasured friend, a business partner, a spiritual teacher. With Gregor's warm embrace he felt the tight knot of anxiety in his chest begin to ease.

Once settled in the taxi into London, Gregor listened carefully to the latest reports on Alexander's condition. He advised gravely, "It is time for you to be strong, my dear young friend."

"I'm trying."

"You will more than try," Gregor replied firmly. "You will *do*. For Alexander. For Katya. And for me. We all require what we know you have."

A distant smudge gradually solidified into the London skyline. Gregor greeted it with a very quiet, "I can scarcely believe I am here once again."

"Forty years is a long time," Jeffrey told him. "The city has changed."

"Of that I have no doubt," Gregor replied.

"You look much better this morning," Jeffrey said to Alexander as they entered his room. A thoughtful nurse had combed his hair and helped him into his robe before elevating his bed to a seated position. The brilliant red dressing gown added to Alexander's natural dignity and lent a bit of color to his pale cheeks.

"Thank you," he said weakly, and focused on Gregor. "Hello, cousin. Welcome."

Gregor leaned over the bed, exchanged the double kiss of greeting, said, "You must be feeling better, if you are able to act the host while in a hospital bed."

Alexander watched his crippled cousin settle carefully into the hard-backed hospital chair. "I confess to a great need for your wisdom, Gregor."

"The Lord is the One to whom you should turn at such times," Gregor said gently, reaching forward and grasping one of Alexander's waxlike hands. "Not another mere mortal."

"I would if I could," Alexander replied.

Jeffrey rose to his feet. "I'll be waiting outside if you need anything."

"Stay," Alexander said in his coarsened whisper. "Please."

Gregor's attention remained fastened upon Alexander as Jeffrey seated himself. He asked his cousin, "You are having difficulty making this approach to your Lord?"

"Never have I felt more alone," Alexander confessed weakly, "or my God more distant. At a time when I need Him most, He is not there. I can no longer find Him."

Jeffrey would often think back to that moment and wonder, not at what he saw, but at what remained unseen. He looked upon Gregor, a man crippled and bent and in pain, his body twisted back and to one side so that the chair took every possible ounce of weight from his disabled frame. Yet that was not what Jeffrey *saw*.

Gregor did not answer directly. Instead, he paused and withdrew to a place Jeffrey could not fathom. He watched a man who lived in perpetual discomfort close his eyes and know a peace so total it shone from his face.

Gregor's creases of pain and sleeplessness and bone-weariness smoothed away in a moment of silent miracle, one so calm and natural that Jeffrey could identify it only by the ache of utter yearning that suddenly filled his own heart.

Gregor opened his eyes, and immediately his features returned to their earthly set. "The sixty-third Psalm was written after David was anointed by the prophet Samuel and proclaimed as Israel's future king," Gregor said in his gently searching manner. "Yet after this promise from the Lord, David was still forced to wait. Wait and suffer and yearn and doubt, straining some forty years before his inheritance could be claimed.

"I have seen you in the sanctuary, David said to the Lord. I beheld you there. He was speaking in the past tense, do you see? It was once so, and now is no more. He saw, he beheld, then again he walked along desert ways. For David, his promised divine inheritance contained vast stretches of isolation and loneliness and want."

Gregor carefully shifted his weight forward, his gray eyes intense with understanding. "My dear cousin, I understand your pain. I too have traveled through lonely, empty stretches. Such an experience is common among believers. It is also common to misunderstand the reason for these periods and to miss the blessings that God bestows in such times.

"You must understand that what is happening to you is *not* punishment. Yes, you face difficulties which you have not brought upon yourself. Yes, you are burdened. Yes, God seems distant. But if you see this as punishment, you set yourself up for assault. Doubts will assail you, and fears, and desires to complain of how you have been unfairly treated by life. Nights are given over to anxiety, when fears chase you back and forth across the floor."

He smiled gently at Alexander's nod of recognition. "At such times, it is most important not to doubt in the dark what you have learned in the light. On the bad days, you must live by the lessons gained in the good times. Remain confident and solid upon the rock.

"The desert, my cousin, is a time of testing. In the eighth chapter of Deuteronomy, the Lord says we are taken into the desert to test our faith and to humble our hearts. He offends the mind in order to reveal the unseen. Your sense of order and balance and symmetry is shaken. You are thrown to your knees. The winds of change blast down from the heavens while darkness blankets your vision, and you *know* your strength alone is not enough.

"In such times, Alexander, you must cling to the rock and cry aloud to the unseen One for strength to cover your naked weakness. And once you return from this testing, you are called to do one thing further: to *remember*. Learn, and then hold on to this gift of learning for all your days."

He touched Alexander's hand. "A fruit tree that remains constantly in the light will never bear fruit. It is the tree that experiences the *normal* cycle of light and darkness that fulfills its divine purpose. Remember that in your trials, my dear cousin. And stay with God."

Gregor rose slowly to his feet, smiling down at his cousin. "Now rest in His glorious peace, my brother in Christ. I will come to see you again this afternoon."

"That was very beautiful," Jeffrey told him as they crossed through the hospital's main lobby.

"Mmmm," Gregor hummed distractedly, then pulled the world back into focus. "I'm sorry. What was it you said?"

"What you told Alexander in there. It was really inspiring."

"Oh, thank you . . ." His mind remained elsewhere. Once through the main doors, Gregor ceased his limping gait to turn and face Jeffrey. "I was wondering if I might ask a favor."

"Anything."

"It is time that I go and visit my Zosha's resting place, but I find myself unwilling to go there alone. Would you be so kind as to accompany me?"

"Of course," Jeffrey replied. Zosha was the name of Gregor's deceased wife.

Gregor offered a distracted smile. "I am indeed grateful, my young friend. This is most good-hearted of you."

Jeffrey left him isolated in his contemplation and joined the ranks struggling to find a taxi in the misting rain. Once in the cab, Gregor gave the driver their destination, then lapsed again into silence. Some moments later he emerged to say, "Forgive me, please. I am sorry for being such poor company."

"There's no need to apologize."

"No, that is the blessing of true friendship in such moments," Gregor agreed. "I was recalling the distant past. Strange how vivid memories can become at these times. I was thinking of our escape from Poland. Or rather, the time leading up to our departure."

"Alexander has mentioned your escape several times," Jeffrey said. "I'm still waiting for the whole story."

"Conversation would most certainly ease the burden of this journey," Gregor assented. There was another long silence as the world shifted slightly to reveal a door long hidden within Gregor's mind and heart. "When Alexander had recovered from his imprisonment at Auschwitz," Gregor then began, "he immediately joined the *Armia Krajowa,* the Polish Home Army, as the underground was called. Of course, he never actually spoke of it to us. The AK, as the army was known, was utterly secret. Even within the ranks themselves, the soldiers were known by code only, and each was sworn never to try to learn another man's true name. This was done so that if they were ever captured and tortured, they had less information to divulge. Of course, with my poor health, I was not permitted to join, much as I begged.

"As with most Poles, I came to know many of the activists within the local AK garrison. There were little signals you could detect if you looked carefully, such as a hint of pride and defiance against the overpowering German might, and the way they stood or looked or spoke. Alexander replaced the horror of his Auschwitz experience with this sense of secret strength, and I saw it in others. But I knew better than to speak of it, even to my dear cousin. I never had the opportunity to tell him how proud I was of him and his actions, or how much I lived through him. Or how, when he slipped away on a mission under the cover of night, he carried my fervent prayers with him. I never slept while he was out. Never. I spent the long night hours praying for his success and his safe return."

The rain stopped, the clouds scattered, the sun turned

the city air dank and sweltering. Traffic held them in a fumy embrace. Gregor seemed scarcely aware of the steamy heat, the beeping horns, or their crawling progress.

"After the Nazis were defeated in Poland and the Russians swept in," he continued, "the AK soldiers began to disappear. Nothing was said, no accusations were made, no evidence was found by anyone who was willing to speak aloud. But one by one, the young men and women I knew to have been in the underground began to vanish. I watched Alexander and saw how distressed he became by this, yet I was unable to broach the subject without his speaking first. And I worried for him more than I ever had under the Nazis.

"Then one night I awoke to the sound of his moving about, the same secret movements that had woken me so often before. This time I went to him. He told me that he and two friends were going to vanish before the Russians made them disappear permanently. Where was he going, I asked. He hesitated, then told me it would be best simply to trust him, and to believe he would one day return. We embraced, and he slipped from the room, and that was the last I saw or heard of my dear cousin for seven long months."

"That must have been terrible," Jeffrey said quietly.

"It was and it wasn't," Gregor replied. "I missed him more than I thought it possible to miss another man. But it was also a time of great beauty, for that was when the Lord brought my Zosha into my life. By the time Alexander returned, I was a married man."

Gregor looked with sad fondness into the distance of his memories. "Perhaps the Lord whispered to our souls that we would only have those two short years together, and so we lost no time in lighthearted flirtation and simple chatter. Perhaps, too, we shared with such desperate openness because of who we were and what the times held for us.

"Zosha had experienced the Warsaw Uprising and arrived bearing the agony of having survived. Despite her past or because of it, we met, and we loved; that is the whole story of our lives together. We met, and the world sang with the tragic beauty of two young people loving each other in a world with little room for love. We shared all we were and all we had and all we knew, and life became so enriched that each new dawn spoke of promises too great for one small day to enclose.

"Zosha was the answer to my every prayer, even the ones which I knew not how to place into words. She drank in the lessons I had learned from my studies of faith, and in taking them so wholeheartedly taught me the heavenly delights of earthly love, of what it meant for two to join as one.

"How Zosha came to be with me, ah, to have a miracle of such joy arrive in the midst of such chaos and turmoil! The trauma of her passage—my boy, you cannot imagine what Zosha went through before she joined me." Gregor sighed and murmured, "Yet she came, my angel in earthly form. And she loved me. Ah, how that woman could love. I saw God more clearly in her eyes than ever in anything else contained within this world."

He was silent for so long that Jeffrey thought his questions would have to wait for another time. But the taxi jolted to a stop at a light, and Gregor stirred himself and continued, "My Zosha spent the war years in Warsaw, until the time of the Uprising. The Warsaw Uprising was one of many tragedies during the war years, yet it held a special bitterness because of the Soviet treachery. The Red Army had promised our underground forces that they would come to our aid and push the Nazis from Polish soil once the battle for Warsaw began. Instead, they massed across the Vistula and watched the Germans pulverize our glorious capital and decimate the population.

"They stood and watched our people die, you see, because they never intended to let Poland be free. Every Polish patriot killed by the Nazis was one less that the Soviets would have to concern themselves with. Neither the promised soldiers nor the arms ever arrived. Half-starved AK soldiers faced the modern Nazi army with petrol bombs and sharpened fence-staves and hunting guns and whatever weapons they could steal.

"The battle lasted two months and was nothing less than sheer butchery. During that time, Warsaw was a city apart. There were no supplies, little water, no electricity or oil. Then, when the city surrendered, the Germans ordered all survivors to leave their homes immediately, taking only what they could carry. Most of these people were starving and weak. They were forced to walk for two days. Along the way they were given nothing—no food, no water. There is no record of how many died in that trek of blood and tears. But my Zosha said that every step of the way was littered with the bodies of those who could not continue and were left where they lay."

Gradually the taxi made its way beyond the cramped confines of central London. Streets broadened and lawns appeared and shops sprouted from low buildings. "German soldiers marched along either side of the road, with perhaps twenty meters between each soldier," Gregor went on, "My Zosha was eighteen, walking with a girlfriend, and their two mothers walked a few paces away. Suddenly a man scrambled up from the hedge and, unnoticed by the Germans, began walking alongside them. He whispered that they had to escape immediately, to go with him right then; there was not a moment to lose. They of course replied that they could not leave their mothers, that they would be all right once they arrived at the prison camp.

"The young man whispered fiercely that they would not be allowed to stay with their mothers. Only the elderly were to be placed in the camp. All young girls were to be sent to the bomb depots near the front. These places were called death factories, the young man told them, because they were being bombed so often. There was no chance of survival. None.

"He was in the AK, this young man. He pulled them from the road, flung them down on the earth, and ordered them to stay there until he returned. He waited for the next soldier to pass, then was up once again and back in line, continuing his death-defying mission of mercy. He never came back, that man.

"Later, once we had all arrived safely in London, we learned that what the young man had said was true. Virtually none of the women sent to the front ever returned. My Zosha never had a chance to thank that young man who had risked his life to save her. She never even learned his name.

"When all the people had passed and the young man did not return, Zosha and her friend walked to the nearest house, where a woman came out, took one look at them, and said, you're from the Warsaw Uprising. That was how strong an impact the events left on the innocent. The woman took them into her house and cooked the only food she had—rancid potatoes and black, grimy flour made into potato pancakes. My Zosha told me it was the finest meal she had eaten in her entire life.

"They stayed with the woman for two days, until the Germans began a house-to-house search for escapees. That resulted in a journey from home to home, village to village, by hay wagon and horse cart and lorry, sleeping in barns or vegetable bins or cellars or open fields, until one early dawn my Zosha arrived at our own doorstep in Cracow. She was so exhausted and weak that her hold on life was a bare thread. My family took pity on the poor girl, and instead of passing her on as would have been safe, they gave her Alexander's room. And I, in turn, gave her my heart."

The taxi turned a corner, and instantly the city was exchanged for a narrow country lane. Verdant fields opened to either side. Wild flowers filled their car with the perfumes of summer. Gregor watched the line of ancient trees parade past their car.

"Alexander had been gone for seven months, as I said," he continued quietly. "He returned as silently and suddenly as he had departed, riding the winds of danger and urgency with a strength and focused power that filled our little world. We had to escape, he said. All of us. There was no time for discussion or debate. The Soviet noose was tightening and soon would close off all remaining channels to freedom.

"We did little to protest, as we could see the evidence of the Soviets' growing might all around us. So that very night we began a journey which took us the entire length of Poland, up to the Baltic Sea and across by boat to Scandinavia, and from there on to England. Every step of the way we were aided by silent, nameless friends whom Alexander had met in his time away from us. Every place we traveled, I saw how those strong men accepted my dear cousin as one of their own, a man who had fought the good fight, and I knew a pride so fierce I was sure it would burn eternal scars in my heart."

The taxi turned through great stone gates into a quiet cemetery, stopping before a tiny chapel. The driver turned off the motor and waited patiently as Gregor sat where he was and went on, "But my darling Zosha had never recovered her strength from the trauma of the Uprising. Her weakness had not been evident when we departed; otherwise, I would never have attempted the journey. But as the days of endless toil and danger wore on, that same look of haunted exhaustion which she had worn upon her arrival at my home returned to her features.

"Still, we survived, all of us. In Sweden we rested, and again I hoped that all would be well. But it was not to be. About a year after our arrival in London, my Zosha went down with a fever, and she never rose from her bed again."

With a long sigh, Gregor eased himself from the taxi. While Jeffrey arranged for the driver to wait, Gregor purchased a map and a great bouquet of lilacs and chrysanthemums from the flower stall by the cemetery chapel. Together they followed the cemetery map past progressively older tombstones, until they arrived at a carefully trimmed plot lined by flowers and bearing a simple black marble marker.

"This is Alexander's doing, bless his soul," Gregor noted quietly. "He has seen to all these details since that very day, when I was too poor and too distraught to manage."

Gregor stood for a long moment in bowed stillness while Jeffrey strolled along ways sheltered by ancient chestnuts. When he saw Gregor wave in his direction, he hurried back.

"It was good to come here once more, before—" He stopped, looked back at the grave site, and concluded. "It was good to come. I have Alexander to thank for this as well. Though I must confess to you, my young friend, that I feel no closer to Zosha at this moment than I have when seated alone in my tiny Cracow flat on many a winter's eve."

Jeffrey thought of his own new love and was brought face-to-face with its fleeting fragility. He found himself with nothing to say as they made their slow way back to the waiting taxi.

CHAPTER
8

The following afternoon Katya walked cheerfully, though somewhat frazzled, into Alexander's room, where Jeffrey was visiting. She bestowed kisses and greetings on both men and asked, "Where is Gregor?"

"Back at Alexander's flat," Jeffrey said glumly. "Packing."

"You couldn't persuade him to stay?"

He shook his head. "I got about as far as you did."

"Oh." Her cheerfulness slipped several notches. "He did warn us. I just hoped—"

"Gregor's place is not here," Alexander said kindly. "You as well as any have the perception to know that."

"But the wedding is just six days off," Katya complained, slipping into the seat Jeffrey offered.

"There is urgent relief work among the Cracow orphanages which simply will not wait," Alexander replied. "He has explained it to us in great detail. And his work here is over."

"You really are feeling better, aren't you?"

"My dear," Alexander said, "Gregor's visit has positively transformed me. This and the news that you are relocating the wedding on my account."

"Jeffrey told you, then." She bestowed the fullness of her gaze on him. "Did he tell you it was his idea?"

"I did not because it was not," he replied.

She nodded slowly. "Yes it was. You were just too smart to suggest it yourself."

"Whoever is responsible," Alexander said, "I thank you both. Your offer has done much to restore me. And I do hope that you still intend to hold your reception in my flat."

"If you really think—"

"Nothing could bring me greater pleasure, except to be there myself," Alexander pronounced gravely. "Know that I shall most certainly be there in spirit. As shall Gregor."

"Well," she said, turning brisk, "my last calm moment before the wedding was shattered by yet another call from our Mr. Markov. Whenever he phones, he seems to grow distressed by degrees. He starts off all cool and polished, ordering me in the most civilized manner to get you on the phone. When I insist that's not possible, he goes bright red."

"You've seen him?" Jeffrey asked.

"I don't need to." She smiled at him. "I'm just glad he waited to call until you had left to collect Gregor. I'd hate you to have a shouting match with somebody six days before our wedding."

"Perhaps I should give him a call," Alexander said thoughtfully.

"From the sounds of things," Katya said, "whatever he has on his mind is quite urgent."

"You do not speak French, do you, my dear?"

She shook her head. "It is a language I have always wanted to learn."

"Well, perhaps the future shall afford you an opportunity. Be so good as to dial for me, would you?"

"Of course." Katya placed the call, then handed him the phone. A woman's voice answered with, "La Residence Markov."

"*Oui. Monsieur Markov, s'il vous plait.*"

"*Et vous etes Monsieur. . . ?*"

"Kantor. Alexander Kantor."

A long moment's pause, then, "*Ici Markov.*"

Alexander switched to English. "Mr. Markov, this is Alexander Kantor returning your call."

"Ah, yes, Mr. Kantor. Thank you so much for responding

so quickly. I understand you have had a bout of ill health. Not anything serious, I hope."

Alexander took in the bleak surroundings in a single sweeping glance, made do with a simple, "Thank you for asking."

"I do apologize for disturbing you."

"Not at all," Alexander replied. "I understood that you were under some time pressure, and I did not wish to delay you further."

"But of course I would expect nothing less than a prompt response from a professional such as yourself."

"You are too kind." For the first time since his attack, Alexander felt a surge of his old acquisitive spirit. The familiar feeling lifted him enormously. "And how are you enjoying your life at Villa Caravelle?"

"Oh, it is a most splendid place. As you know, I fell in love with it the moment I saw it."

"And you don't miss—" Alexander searched his memory for the name of Markov's former residence, one of the largest palaces along the Corniche, and was delighted when he came up with "Beau Rivage? That was certainly a magnificent residence."

"Ah, yes. Beau Rivage. No, I must say I have had quite a number of other things on my mind these past two years. Which brings me to the reason for my call. I have a business proposition for you, Mr. Kantor."

"Well, I don't know, Mr. Markov. Under the circumstances—"

"Mr. Kantor, I need a man of your discretion, honesty, and expertise. This matter positively will not wait and, I assure you, is of the utmost importance." He leaned heavily on the words.

"It is just that I am in no position to be traveling—"

"Oh, I do love the way you play at being shrewd," Markov replied. "Let me assure you, Mr. Kantor. You would find a visit to Monte Carlo most rewarding at this time."

"For any number of reasons," Alexander replied, "I am sure you are right. Regrettably, however, I am ringing you from a hospital bed."

"*Mon Dieu!* It is not serious, I hope."

"This, too, I shall survive," Alexander replied. "The doctors tell me I am on the mend."

"How excellent for you," Markov said, clearly worried. "I must say, however, this is indeed a disappointment. I am afraid my business interests require immediate attention."

"May I ask if this is in reference to buying or selling a particular piece?"

"Buying. Yes. You might say I am interested in acquiring a very special property."

"I see." Alexander hesitated, then ventured, "The only suggestion I might make is for my assistant, Mr. Jeffrey Sinclair, to make himself available to aid you."

Markov showed doubt. "Well, I am not sure, Mr. Kantor. I had hoped—"

It was Alexander's turn to press with all the force he could muster. "He is a young American. Very bright, very perceptive."

"And you trust him?"

"With my life and all my earthly goods," Alexander replied emphatically. "Like my own son."

"Could I be assured of your close collaboration with him on this matter?"

"Absolutely," Alexander replied. "It is one of the aspects of working with him that I find most pleasurable."

Markov permitted himself to be persuaded. Reluctantly. "It is true that I have no one else whom I could trust with this."

"The fact that my body chooses to remain inert," Alexander went on, "does not mean that my mind cannot remain most active. I assure you that I shall take every interest in your affairs, Mr. Markov."

"Fine," Markov decided. "Please have your Mr. Sinclair call me to make further arrangements."

"I shall do so," Alexander replied. "Can you supply me with any details about the item in question? Is this a French acquisition?"

"I believe it is best to discuss such matters in person." Markov hesitated, then continued, "But no, the item is not located here. My proposed acquisition is in former Soviet lands."

"How fascinating." Alexander made do with a minimum of formalities before hanging up.

"Thank you for the vote of confidence," Jeffrey said when the old gentleman turned back to them. "And for the kindness of what you said."

"You are most welcome," Alexander replied. "All the essence of truth, I assure you. I would suggest that you contact Markov yourself first thing tomorrow. He will be expecting your call, and promptness will assist in establishing a positive impression with such a one as him."

"What do you think he wants to talk about?"

"Whatever it is, he wants to discuss it personally. I therefore presume that it must be something quite large. Markov leans toward the extravagant."

Jeffrey smiled. "Like your villa?"

"No doubt the most discreet purchase he has ever made," Alexander replied sharply. "Now, back to the subject, if I may. He would not have contacted me unless his business concerned something out of the ordinary."

"How well do you know him?" Katya asked.

"Not at all well. Primarily from the sale of my villa, and a fair amount based on hearsay. Markov is quite the clever gentleman. Cagey would perhaps be too strong a word, but certainly very clever. The gambler in me would say that Markov is a man with an ace up his sleeve."

Alexander mused a moment, then asked, "I suppose the two of you have already made plans for your honeymoon."

"We're taking our real honeymoon in December," Jeffrey said. "Katya and I are going back to America together. That is, assuming the boss will let us have a month off."

"We didn't want to do it any earlier," Katya explained, "with so many of Jeffrey's family coming over here for the wedding."

"So for right now we are planning a few days up in Scotland." Jeffrey exchanged eager looks with Katya. "I've booked us a room in an inn built in the days of Bonnie Prince Charlie."

"Do you have your heart set on Scotland?" Alexander asked.

"What do you mean?"

"If I may, I'd like to suggest a change of itinerary. That is, if you wouldn't mind combining your days of vacation with one day of work."

"I suppose it would depend on where you want to send us."

"How about Monte Carlo?"

Katya gasped. "Monte Carlo! I hear it's just fabulous." She caught herself, turned to Jeffrey. "Oh, but maybe you had your heart set on Glasgow."

"Edinburgh," Jeffrey corrected.

"Wherever," she said, trying to hide her smile. "Of course, I would miss seeing all those men in kilts. You know what I heard about—"

"A honeymoon in Monte Carlo sounds fantastic," Jeffrey said. "But it's a little out of our price range."

"We're talking business here," Alexander said. "Plus maybe a little extra wedding gift. Believe me, if I could go, I would. As I cannot, I would be most pleased—and grateful—if you could go in my stead."

"I guess I should see to hotel reservations," Jeffrey said.

"The Hotel de Paris," Alexander said firmly. "The only place to stay in Monte Carlo, if you don't mind my saying. It is situated on the harbor, just across the square from the Casino. A marvelous old place, as grand as the Vienna opera house." He smiled fondly at them both. "It should make for a most memorable start to what I have no doubt will be a wonderful life together."

• • •

They went directly from the hospital to Alexander's flat. Katya bid Gregor a sad farewell, then left to resume the complex business of moving a wedding. Gregor followed Jeffrey toward their waiting taxi and asked, "When are you again coming to Poland?"

Jeffrey turned to stare at him. "You can't be serious."

"A shipment is ready for you," Gregor replied. "And the young man from the Ukraine, remember him?"

"I can't leave Alexander alone. Not now."

"The young man's name is Yussef. He is ready to take

you across the border. He says there are some excellent buys waiting," Gregor pressed. "This may be a major opportunity."

Jeffrey remained silent.

"I understand, my young friend. I truly understand. But you must also ask yourself, what would Alexander have you do? Who will pick up the reins if not you?" Gregor gave Jeffrey's shoulder an affectionate pat. "I shall hope to see you before the end of the month. Such urgent matters cannot wait longer than that."

"I'm sorry to see you go back to Poland so soon."

"I have been away as long as my responsibilities will allow." Gregor hesitated, then added quietly, "Not to mention my own human frailties."

"You don't want to go?"

"Want, want, want," Gregor shook his head. "So much of our thoughts hinge on that word, don't they? Especially these days. And yet I must follow the call of my Lord; that is what I *want* above all else."

"But you'd *like* to stay?" Jeffrey persisted.

"Life is very hard in my Poland just now," Gregor replied. He climbed into the taxi, waited while Jeffrey gave the driver directions, then continued, "Change has brought benefits for some, trauma to many. It is easy to forget, while living there, that such places as London truly exist."

"Conditions are growing worse?"

"Conditions, as you say, are chaotic. Robberies and violent crimes are skyrocketing. Most people who have to be out at night have bought the sort of dogs who walk their owners, rather than the other way around."

"So why don't you stay?" Jeffrey tried to keep the pleading from his voice. "Especially with everything that's happening, we'd love to have you here."

Gregor was silent for a time before replying, "Philippi was the apostle Paul's first church in Macedonia. For that and other reasons it held a very special place in his heart. When he was imprisoned in Rome, distant and powerless, frustrated that he could not continue his work, he remained utterly certain that the bonds between him and that church remained strong. No matter that he could not see his friends, no matter that he could not hear of their progress or be a part of it. Always he was sure the church was growing stronger day by day."

"This sounds distinctly like a 'no' to me," Jeffrey said glumly. "Nicely put, but still no."

Gregor smiled and continued, "Such confidence comes from a sharing of the key experiences of life, bonded through shared faith. We yearn for one another in the heart of Jesus Christ. He is the divine link which held Paul together with his distant brethren then, and He will do the same for us now, my young friend. What is more, He will unite us all on His glorious day. What we feel now for one another will then be made perfect in His glory.

"Our fragile strands of feeling are but slender threads constantly snared by the myriad of things left undone, strained by doubt and pulled by earthly hardship. They remain but a hint of what God promises to bring to completion. And this completion is not an end to itself. Not at all. It shall be for us, for those risen above all endings through their love of man's only Savior, just the beginning of all eternity."

Gregor held him with eyes that saw far beyond their earthly confines. "On that day, my dear young friend, at the dawn of our eternal day, we shall rise with the morning star, and with the angels together we will sing our endless, boundless joy."

CHAPTER
9

Jeffrey returned from the airport, stopped by the antique shop to check over the day's proceeds, and read Katya's note to meet her at the church around the corner. He did that often, but he still did so with reluctance.

Katya had been making a widening inspection of the neighborhood that was soon to be her home. In the process she had discovered a church that she pronounced delightful. It served many of the local immigrant communities and held weekly masses in several Eastern European languages. Between masses, the rows were filled with kerchiefed women and old men bowed over canes, murmuring their prayers in a soft tide of foreign tongues.

Upon the great pillars flanking the embossed altar frieze hung two of the largest icons Jeffrey had ever seen. One of the paintings was of a Christ figure painted in the flat two-dimensional style of ancient Byzantium, the other depicted Mary and the holy Child. Both were embedded within frame after frame after hand-etched silver frame. The outermost frames were shaped as peaked medieval doorways and stood a full fourteen feet high.

Beside each of them rose ranks of flickering candles. Often when entering the church Jeffrey's eyes stung from the cloying blanket of incense, and his sense of proper worship felt offended by the sight of old women making exaggerated signs of the cross and then bowing before the icons. Masses were announced by the solemn intoning of great brass chimes hung above the main entrance.

On Sundays he and Katya attended a very evangelical Anglican church in Kensington, and Jeffrey truly felt at home among that congregation. But almost every day Katya insisted on entering this strange world of foreign rituals. She settled herself in the corner of the central side alcove, the only person in the church under sixty. She knelt alongside several dozen old women, who greeted her arrival with smiles that stretched leathery faces into unaccustomed angles. The alcove contained two smaller icons, before which burned rows of glimmering candles. The side walls were decorated with soaring marble angels whose gilded wings stretched almost to the distant ceiling.

As they had left the church after his first visit, Katya had asked him, "Well, what did you think of it?"

"I don't think I like it very much in there."

"Why not?"

He shrugged. "Too many smells and bells."

"Don't get smart," she replied sharply.

"I don't know what to tell you, Katya," he replied. "It just seemed strange to me."

"And I asked you to tell me why," she insisted, a hard light gleaming in her eyes.

"I watched an old woman kiss one of those icons, and I felt pretty sure she did it every day."

"So? Since when did you decide your own faith was so perfect that you had the right to criticize somebody else's?"

He deflected her, or tried to, with, "I just don't understand why you want to go there, Katya. Doesn't the Bible say something about going into your closet to pray?"

"I pray in private," she replied, still hot. "I also like to join with fellow believers in silent worship. This place and what it represents is a part of my heritage, Jeffrey. I feel very close to these people and their lives. I like the sense of communing with them in spirit."

Jeffrey decided it was best not to respond.

She understood him perfectly. "Listen to me, Jeffrey Sinclair. Those people in there may not be doing things exactly right. As a matter of fact, they may be doing a lot of things wrong. But they are worshiping in ways that were designed back so long ago that almost no one was able to read. They were taught rituals as a way of remembering their faith. They have not had a chance to learn different ways because for the past seventy or eighty years anyone who tried to evangelize in their homeland was murdered. They have escaped, and now this church with its 'smells and bells' is the only taste of their homeland they will ever have, because they know they can never return."

"I guess I just don't understand what you see in it," he replied, wanting only peace.

"That is a grand understatement," she said, and strode forth with a full head of steam.

That evening Jeffrey waited by the back wall and bowed a formal greeting to the old women who were coming to know him by sight. He had long since learned to keep his concerns about the church to himself. Eventually Katya stood, crossed herself, folded her headkerchief and stowed it in her pocket, and walked back toward him. Her eyes shone with the soft luminosity he had come to associate with her times of deep prayer. Sensing her inner glow after almost every time of communing here had done much to make Jeffrey more comfortable with the alien surroundings.

They returned to share a quiet dinner at his apartment, content to sit across from each other and drink of each other's eyes. Conversation came and went like a gentle breeze, the food more a reason to sit and enjoy intimacy than to satisfy a need. The hunger that mingled with their gazes of love was one more easily kept in control when not spoken of openly. Instead, they talked about their plans and made little jokes about the piles of boxes that surrounded them.

For the past week, Katya had spent what little free time she had, between helping in the shop and planning a wedding, moving her things into Jeffrey's flat. As a result, the minuscule living space had taken on the look of a refugee center. Every inch of formerly free space was now crammed with her things. Jeffrey had helped carry in cases and boxes and seen them as a herald of deeper changes to come. He had found himself continually inspecting his own internal vistas, discovering fear mixed in with the joyful anticipation.

By agreement, the cramped front hallway would see duty as her future dressing room. The bathroom grew new shelves, which immediately were filled to overflowing. Jeffrey freed up half the closet and all but two of the bedroom drawers, and discovered his gesture had made not even the slightest dent in her seven suitcases. A dozen boxes containing about half of her books—the ones she did not want stored in his minute cellar—were stacked by the window.

They would have to move; he could see that already. But his world would not permit yet another transition just then. Katya had shown great wisdom, and made do in silent acceptance. For the moment.

"What did you and Gregor talk about?" Katya asked over coffee.

Jeffrey found himself unable to tell her he had agreed to Gregor's insistence that he travel soon to Poland and the Ukraine. Instead, he related the experience of watching Gregor's face in the hospital. "He has the most incredible eyes," Jeffrey said. "I've always thought of them as a martyr's eyes. You know, like in the paintings of the saints getting mauled or shot like pincushions, with all the fancy-robed priests standing around and watching."

"Eyes of the soul," Katya agreed.

"They aren't any bigger than anyone else's, I guess. But when I think of them, they always seem twice as large."

"Opened by the wounds of suffering, filled by faith," Katya said. "I don't see how anyone can look into Gregor's eyes and doubt the existence of our Lord."

Laughing at his own embarrassment, Jeffrey said, "Sometimes when I think of Gregor, I imagine him with this light glowing all around, like the old paintings of saints. I know it's not there; it's just this impression I have when I think of our talks. That and his eyes."

Katya was silent a long moment, then told him, "Several years ago, the BBC sent a television team to India to film a special on Mother Teresa. Later they interviewed some of the people who worked on the program, the host and a couple of the technicians. They all talked about filming the hall where the sisters worked with the dying and what an incredible experience it had been for them.

"As they were setting up, they explained, they found that there wasn't enough light for their cameras. The sisters wouldn't let them set up electric lights. There wasn't any electricity, and if they started carting in batteries and cables and stands and lights and everything it would bother the deathly ill patients. So they decided to go ahead and try filming anyway, hoping that they'd come out with at least a couple of clips they could use.

"When they returned to London they found that most of the film they had made in the hall was perfectly clear. Not all of it, though. Where there was no sister, just somebody lying on a bed, you couldn't see anything. Nothing at all. But whenever a sister moved near, Mother Teresa or any other of the sisters, it was all the same. As soon as they came up to the bed, you could see *everything*. The lighting was *perfect*."

Jeffrey fiddled with his cutlery, straightened the tablecloth, placed the salt and pepper in regimental lines, refused to meet her gaze.

"You might as well tell me," Katya said quietly. "It's written all over your face."

"What is?"

"Whatever you and Gregor talked about that has you so tied up in knots."

Jeffrey knew the time had come. Quietly he announced, "I need to go on a buying trip very soon, Katya."

"To Poland?" Her eyes opened into momentary wounds, but she recovered and hid her disappointment behind a brisk tone. "If Gregor and Alexander both agree, then I suppose you must. With Alexander in the hospital, I'll have to stay here and watch the shop, won't I? Mrs. Grayson won't be able to handle it for so long on her own." She folded and refolded her napkin in little nervous gestures. "How long will you be gone?"

"I'm not sure," he said, and forced it out. "Gregor wants me to travel on to the Ukraine. The young man we met at

68

the market in Cracow, remember? He has set up a series of buys for me."

"You'll be traveling to the Ukraine by yourself?" Now real alarm colored her voice.

"With Yussef, that's the man's name. There's no other way, Katya. Gregor can't go. And you've said yourself you have to stay here and handle the business."

"I hear it's like the Wild West over there. Crime is out of control." Her voice took on a pleading note. "Surely you don't really have to go?"

"Gregor thinks so. Alexander agrees."

"How will you get there?"

"Gregor says Yussef will just drive us across the border." Jeffrey tried to make it all sound matter-of-fact. "I don't even need to get a visa anymore. I can arrange it all at the frontier."

"How long will you stay?"

"Gregor thinks about a week."

"That's not too long."

He reached for her hand. "Try not to worry, Katya."

She pulled backed. "What do you mean? Every Polish woman is born with worry in her genes. It doubles with marriage and triples with children." She continued to give her napkin a good workout. "You'll have to get all your shots."

"I'll make an appointment with the doctor tomorrow," he soothed.

"And you'll have to watch yourself every instant. Keep your suitcase locked at all times. Don't go out at night. Don't ever talk to strangers. Carry your valuables everywhere. Watch out for pickpockets. Count your money carefully every time you pay for something."

"Yes, dear."

"I hear there's a terrible drought and heat wave over there right now. You'll need to pack light clothes. And a hat."

"All right, Katya."

"And water. Don't you dare drink any water that hasn't been boiled before your very own eyes, do you hear me, Jeffrey Sinclair? And I'll have to pack you some food. There was a horrible article I saw about—"

"Yes, my beloved."

"Take your own toilet paper. With all the shortages you'll never find any. Don't smile at me, Jeffrey. This is serious." Her features were creased with worry. "Just look at how Western you are. You might as well have it tattooed on your forehead. Every thief within fifty kilometers is going to take you for an easy target. How are you going to communicate anything? What happens if you need help?"

"Yussef will supply a translator," he hoped.

"That's his name? Yussef?"

"I've already told you," he said calmly. "You're not listening, Katya."

"I'm entrusting my husband to a strange Ukrainian called Yussef?" The napkin was balled into a tight little knot. "How do you know you can trust him?"

"Gregor does."

But she was off and running. "What if you get over there and the hotel doesn't have your reservation? It happens all the time. You'll have to go sleep in the train station with the gypsies." Her voice took on a slight wail. "What if there's a coup? What if—"

"The sky falls," Jeffrey offered.

"Don't be silly. There's a drought. How could the sky—" She took on a stricken look. "Hail! What will you do if it hails?"

"Duck," he replied. "You forgot nuclear fallout."

She reached over and took a vice-grip on his arm. "Chernobyl! That's not too far from where you'll be, and it's just the one disaster they've told us about!"

"I think that just about covers it," Jeffrey said, loving her deeply. "Do you feel better now?"

The little girl appeared in her eyes. "I'll miss you terribly."

He walked around the table and embraced her. "I've not had anybody worry about me like this in a long time. Twenty-nine years old and I feel like I'm going out to the playground for the first time."

"This is not a game, Jeffrey."

"I know," he said, keeping his anticipation over the adventure well hidden. "I know, Katya."

CHAPTER

10

Ivona Aristonova walked through the hazy dawn toward early morning Mass. The sky retained the same washed-out blue as every morning for the past four months. The drought was the worst in history, the heat a fierce animal by midday.

Ivona went to church every morning, always for the six o'clock service. Always wearing the black lace head shawl and a coat, even on the warmest of summer dawns. Always clutching a few lilacs from her garden, to be placed before her favorite side altar. And always arriving well before Mass was to begin so as to have time to light a candle and kneel and say the ritual prayers twice through before confession.

The fact that she went to church daily made Ivona Aristonova, in her own eyes, a very religious person. Her neighbors, too, considered her devout because she followed the visible pattern. There was little room in her tightly controlled world for the inner life of faith, but she valued the ritual of the church. Church ritual was understandable. It was definable. It was a visible path to follow. The knowledge that she was walking on the sure path toward eternal rest made the misery of her past bearable.

Ivona Aristonova showed great respect toward all priests, although in her mind not all priests deserved it. She bowed to each one, spoke with reverence, felt keen pleasure when one of God's chosen envoys paid her special attention.

Her prayer time involved a fair amount of breast-beating. She could not aspire to sainthood, so she settled for martyrdom. When she thought of her past, which was seldom and never for very long, she felt the stern satisfaction of knowing that her suffering had earned her God's grace.

She knew, in theory, that God was a God of love. But the reality to her was that the Lord was a wrathful judge. She lived in fear of God's judgment at all times. Forgiveness was something longed for, penance counted out with her prayer beads, salvation left for the life after this one.

After she had lit her candle and dipped a finger in the basin of holy water and crossed herself and knelt in the same pew she occupied every morning, Ivona lowered her head in prayer. But instead of beginning the chant of words that usually came without thought or realization of what she was saying, today her mind moved to the coming meeting with Yussef and the bishop. For some reason she herself could not understand, the topic of their discussion troubled her enormously.

And from there her mind flitted to the past. It was an act that she seldom permitted. But today she had no choice. The memories rose unbidden and refused to go away. Ivona knelt and fingered her prayer beads and struggled to begin her prayers, fighting the images that welled up inside her.

She remembered a white bow for her hair.

She remembered how her father had fashioned the clip from a strand of metal chipped from his saw blade. The ribbon had come from her mother's last petticoat. It had been her twelfth birthday present, a far better gift than the one from the previous year. For her eleventh birthday, the shifting tides of war and men in power had sent her on her first train ride. In an unheated boxcar. For seventeen days.

Ivona Aristonova had spent her early years in Poland, part of the large population of Ukrainians who lived in northern and eastern Poland before the Second World War. When the Russians had invaded Poland at the end of the war, most of her town had fallen victim to Stalin's program of Russification. The objective was to quash patriotism to anything but the great Soviet empire through massive relocation efforts, shifting populations about and blurring borders. Populations who might have a legitimate claim to seized property, such as the Poles and the Ukrainians and Jews, had been sent to projects in the distant north.

Ivona Aristonova knelt with eyes tightly closed and remembered how her family had been deposited about one hundred kilometers from a city called Archangelsk. This was west of the Ural Mountains, still in European Russia. But it was at the same latitude as Asiatic Russia, the region known as Siberia, and less than five hundred kilometers below the Arctic Circle.

Their village had stood at the border of a forest. And such a forest. Primeval. Virgin. Limitless. It stretched unbroken from her village all the way to where the ice conquered all. Other than the one road running from their village to distant Archangelsk, there was nothing but trees stretching to the end of the world.

Her father and mother, along with everyone else, had been put to work in the forest. It did not matter that her father had been a schoolteacher and her mother the administrator of a hospital. In that nameless village, the men had cut down trees and the women had chopped off the bark and the smaller limbs. The children had gathered what they could to supplement a meager diet, learning from those who had come earlier to spend every daylight hour searching for food.

Ivona knelt and fingered her beads and remembered what it was like to watch her parents wither under the strain of simply surviving. She remembered how each passing day became another blow pounding home the lesson that had shaped her remaining days; the lesson that love was a luxury she could not afford.

To her vast relief, the priest intoned the opening words of the Mass. Ivona rose to her feet and managed to push away the unbidden memories. For a few moments she was able to lose herself in comfortable ritual and forget all that lay both ahead and behind.

Her husband went to Mass with her on Sundays, more to keep Ivona company than as an act of faith. Yet he was glad that she went to daily services, for in God's infinite grace he also would be remembered through his wife's penance. He

was an engineer, a steady man, called good by all who knew
him. An honest man. Not a drinker. A man who loved her
dearly and did as well by her as this chaotic world permitted.
A man who never ceased his yearning to have her return his
love.

The women of her circle were certain that Ivona and her
husband were bound in a loveless marriage because her husband could not have children. Ivona was called a saint because she bore the martyrdom of childlessness in silence.
Ivona did not contradict them. She found it best to wrap her
life in layers of secrecy and deny nothing.

After Mass was completed, she hurried back to the church
offices to begin her work as the bishop's secretary. Only the
bishop and his questions in the confessional threatened to
uncover the truth. And she hated the truth most of all.

"There can be no further delay," Bishop Michael Denisov
told the pair. "Every day raises the risk of our treasures'
having departed from Russian soil. If that happens, they
shall be lost to us forever."

Ivona shifted uncomfortably. "I still do not like it. An
unknown man—"

"To you he is unknown," Yussef interrupted.

"—being entrusted with the secret of our greatest treasure," she persisted. "It is too dangerous."

"Not so dangerous as leaving our treasures in the hands
of the Orthodox," Yussef replied. Yussef was Ivona's nephew,
her sister's son, a slender young man of fierce independence.
For their extended family, his trading with the West had
meant the difference between starvation and a relatively
comfortable life. And now he was suggesting they use one of
these trading contacts to assist with the church's most recent
crisis. An American. A dealer in antiques. A man whom
Yussef knew by the name of Jeffrey Sinclair.

"We do not know for certain that the Orthodox are involved," the bishop cautioned.

"We know," Yussef stated flatly. "You are too kind when
it comes to dealing with our enemies."

"Not all Orthodox," the bishop replied, "are such. Not all."

"Enough," Yussef retorted. "And with our treasures most of all."

Bishop Michael waved it aside. "Be that as it may, we need an outsider. Someone who can come and go at will. Who will not be suspected. Who has reason to be asking the questions we ourselves cannot ask. Who can mask your activities as you continue your search."

"Someone we can trust," Ivona insisted.

"This man we can," Yussef replied.

The bishop asked, "And when does he arrive?"

"Nine days," Yussef replied. "We meet in Cracow."

"But an American," Ivona protested. "A Protestant and a stranger to our cause."

"A friend," Yussef countered, "who has proven himself to be trustworthy."

"For the sake of gain," she scoffed. "He does what he says he will because it pays."

"He does what he promises because he is an honorable man," Yussef countered. "I know this. In my heart of hearts I know."

"But how can we be sure?" Ivona complained. "How can we know that he will do as we ask and not work for his own profit?"

"You must test him," the bishop replied simply.

"Test him how," she said, disconsolate. "I know nothing of such things."

"Nor do any of us," Bishop Michael agreed. "And so you shall teach him about us and our past and our ways. You are good at that. Teach, and watch his response."

"I know his response," she replied sharply. "He will be a Westerner. He will smile and nod and say, how nice. He will be naive beyond belief. He will have the face of an infant and a mind like bubble gum."

"This is not so," Yussef replied quietly. "How can you say this when you have never met him?"

"All Westerners are such," Ivona replied, not sure herself why she felt so cross at the idea. "Americans especially."

"Jeffrey Sinclair is an honorable man," Yussef repeated, without heat.

"You have trained our dear brother Yussef yourself," Bishop Michael urged. "A man who feels such a debt to you that he assists us in our quest, although he shares neither our faith nor our needs. A trader who is also the hope of many, because of you, Ivona Aristonova. We rely on him, your very own pupil. Now he tells us that this is the man we require. Should we not give this young man a chance?"

Ivona was silent.

"Teach him," the bishop repeated. "Teach him as much as you can. Shower him with needles of truth about this land of ours. Use your gift to test, and test him hard."

"He will be the sponge I was not," Yussef predicted, grinning broadly, approving the idea. "He will show you his thirst. He will perceive beyond the veil. He will aid us all."

"Go," the bishop urged. "Go and teach and test. You both have my blessing. Only take care, and taste every wind for the first hint of danger."

CHAPTER

11

Andrew arrived to fetch Jeffrey in an enormously jovial mood. "Do hope you won't be giving me trouble today, lad. Hate to have to gather our mates and drag you to the altar."

Jeffrey stepped through his front door and halted at the sight of the vehicle parked outside. "What in the world?"

"It's a boat on wheels, and if you have any doubts, wait till we take our first turning. Lists heavy to port, she does."

The car was a vintage Rolls Royce in burnished gunmetal gray. The fenders reared up and out like a lion's paws. The doors opened front to back. The seats were at a level so as to allow the passengers to look down upon all mere mortals. The hood went on for miles.

"No, no, in the back, lad, in the back." Andrew twisted the old-fashioned handle and bowed Jeffrey inside. "Room to lay back and swoon if your nerves give way."

"This is bigger than a city bus." Jeffrey settled into the plush leather seat and watched Andrew adjust a chauffeur's cap upon his head before climbing behind the wheel. "Is this yours?"

"Only for the day," his friend replied, pulling out the silver-plated handle that started the engine. "As it is, for what I paid I ought to get the Queen's Award for helping the British economy pull out of recession."

Andrew put the car in gear, pressed on the gas, and called out, "Pilot to engine room, all ahead full."

"This is really nice," Jeffrey said, clamping down hard on his nerves. "Thanks."

"Most welcome, lad." Andrew smiled in the rearview mirror. "Think of it as a hearse for your bachelorhood."

"Right. That helps a lot."

"No, suppose not," Andrew replied cheerfully. "Suppose we'll have to call it my wedding gift to the happy couple, then."

Jeffrey wiped damp palms down the sides of his trousers. The dark velvet piping of his tuxedo ran smooth beneath his fingers. "Did you have a case of the nerves before your wedding?"

"Not half. Slept a total of thirty-five minutes the entire last week before taking the plunge."

"What, you timed yourself?"

"Wasn't hard. Tossing and turning as I was, I watched the ruddy clock go right 'round for seven nights in a row. Kept getting up to make sure it was plugged in, the hands moved so slow."

"But still you did it."

"What, walk the lonely mile? Too right I did. Knew the old dear wouldn't even leave a greasy stain if I did a bonk."

"A what?"

"Bonk, lad. Bonk. Head for the hills in Yankish. Do a number. Catch a jet plane. Ride off into the sunset. Take a—"

"I get the picture."

Andrew inspected him in the car mirror. "You're not going to make me pull the manacles from the boot, now, are you?"

"You don't have to say that with such glee," Jeffrey replied.

Andrew laughed and changed the subject. "Been down working on the Costa Geriatrica, I have."

"Where's that?"

"Oh, it's what we call the region from Brighton to Hastings. Bit like your Miami Beach, I suppose. Minus the sun, of course."

"And the crime."

"Well, there you are. That's the price you pay for not enough rain in Florida. Raises a body's temperature, bound to. Turns thoughts to pillage and plunder and other such diversions."

"So what were you doing down in Brighton? Hunting down some new pieces?"

"Too right. Old dear had a houseful, too, she did. Problem was, she'd never taken much notice of their condition, said articles having been in her family since sheriffs were still lopping off heads instead of giving out parking tickets. No, if the worms stopped holding hands, her whole house'd dissolve into sawdust." Andrew permitted himself a satisfied smile. "So to keep the trip from being a total loss, I bought myself a boat."

"You what?"

He nodded. "Almost new. This Frenchie sailed it over, discovered on his maiden voyage that he hated the sight of more water than could fit in his tub. He named the ship *Bien Perdu*. Closest I could come to a translation was 'Good and Lost.' Thought I'd keep it, seeing as how that's exactly what I'll be ten minutes after untying from the dock."

Jeffrey tasted a smile, only to have it dissolve into a new flood of doubt. "Would you do it again? Get married, I mean."

Andrew nodded emphatically. "Long as there's love, lad, even the roughest days are as good as it gets."

Jeffrey felt a settling of his internal seas. "That's reassuring, Andrew. Thanks."

"Think nothing of it." He took a corner wide, gave a regal wave to a group of tourists who craned to search the car's interior for someone wearing a crown. "How's Alexander doing?"

"The doctors seem to be more confident every time I see them," Jeffrey replied. "Of course, they hedge their bets worse than bookies at the track. Getting a straight answer out of them is like trying to squeeze blood from a stone."

"Yes, well, that's why they call it a medical *practice*, isn't it. They're all still studying, trying to get it right." Andrew pulled up to the main hospital entrance and stopped. He turned around and observed with evident pleasure, "I've just enough time to pop around for the bride-to-be and make it back on the hour. If there's even the bittiest chance of your buying passage to Paraguay in the next ten minutes or so, I'll gladly chain you to the nearest tree."

"You're a big help," Jeffrey said, climbing out.

"No, suppose not." Andrew put the car into gear, said through the open window, "Think of it this way, lad. If the old ticker gives way before you make it up the aisle, there's ever so many doctors in there who'd love to practice on you."

Jeffrey's entry into the hospital lobby—dressed as he was in tuxedo, starched shirt with studs, and silk bow tie—caused a suitable stir. Families clustered around patients in robes and pajamas ceased their conversation as though silenced by a descending curtain. Nurses and hospital staff shared smiles and hellos; clearly the news had made the rounds, and the event met with their approval. A few went so far as to offer the thoroughly embarrassed Jeffrey their congratulations and best wishes.

The closer he came to the chapel, the more his fear turned to a barrier against the world. He walked down the long Casualties hall, exchanging numb hellos and handshakes with smiling staff. He forced his legs to carry him down the main stairs and on past signs for Oncology, Radiation Therapy, Obstetrics. He turned a corner and walked by a door labeled Dispensing Chemist, briefly entertaining thoughts of stopping by for a mild sedative, something he could take by the gallon. Next was the Cardiac section—another two beats a minute faster and they'd have their first walk-in patient. A final corner and he had arrived.

Alexander was there by the chapel's closed door, seated in a wheelchair but dressed to the nines, as befitting a best man, heart attack or no. Count Garibaldi, who had agreed to push the best man's chair, was there beside him. In his severe formal wear, the count looked like a black velvet stork, with beak to match. Jeffrey exchanged greetings, shook hands, saw little, felt nothing.

Then a voice behind him said, "Here she is, lad. All safe and sound and pretty as a picture."

He turned, and knew an immediate sense of utter clarity. Of complete and total *rightness*.

Katya bathed them all in her joy. Jeffrey most of all.

Her dress was Victorian in feel, modest and alluring at the same time. The color was called candlelight, the shade of the lightest champagne rose. The fabric was antique satin and lace that her mother had found in a local Coventry market. Together they had oohed and aahed and giggled like schoolgirls as the dress had taken shape, denying Jeffrey the first glance. Until now.

He knew the terms to describe it because he had heard her speak of it in endless detail. It had what was called a princess line, fitting snugly from shoulders to hips, then belling out to a flounced skirt that ended just above her ankles. Her sleeves were tight from wrist to elbow, buttoned with tiny seed pearls, then loose and airy to where they gathered at her shoulders. Her neckline descended far enough to allow an elegant emerald necklace, a sentimental gift from Jeffrey's grandmother, to rest upon her silken skin. She held a bouquet of white roses and Peruvian lilies.

For Jeffrey, the moment was suspended in the timelessness of true love. The others cooed over her dress, her flowers, her hair. Hospital staff gathered in the hall behind them and freely bestowed smiles on all and sundry. The hubbub touched Jeffrey not at all. He stood and drank in the loveliness of her and knew that here was a moment he would carry in his heart and mind for all his days.

Alexander cleared his throat. "Although I lack personal experience in these matters, I believe it is necessary for the groom to parade down front before our festivities may proceed."

"The gent means you, lad," Andrew said, beaming from ear to ear.

Jeffrey shared a smile and a murmured affection with his bride-to-be, then turned and pushed through the chapel doors.

And stopped again.

The room was *filled* with flowers.

The two floral arrangements Katya had ordered stood on

the front altar. The remainder of the room, however, was decked out in vast arrays of cascading roses, lilies, and gladioli.

"A small token of thanks," Alexander murmured from beside him, "for allowing me to be a part of this day."

From the back corner, a trio of ancient-looking gentlemen struck up a stringed-instrument rendition of Chopin's "Polonaise."

Jeffrey looked down at his friend. "Aren't they the musicians from Claridge's?"

Alexander nodded. "They were the only ones I could locate and hire without undue fuss. Now on you go."

Jeffrey made do with a gentle squeeze of the old gentleman's shoulder. He walked to the altar and waited while the trio paused and began the Wedding March.

Then Katya descended.

That was how he would always remember it, how he felt as he stood and watched the moment unfold. Katya descended to join with him in earthbound form, bestowing upon him a higher love.

Throughout the ceremony, Jeffrey remained showered with the light and the love and the wholehearted joy that shone from Katya's eyes.

• • •

Jeffrey stood at the corner of Alexander's living room, amazed at how much noise eighteen people could make.

His eyes moved from one group to the next. He watched his father convulse with laughter over something the count said. He saw Sydney Greenfield chatter through a story, drinking and eating all the while. He knew a momentary pang at the wish that Alexander had been well enough to join them. But his own sense of well-being was too strong just then to grant much room to sorrow.

What had surprised him most during the run-up to their wedding was how well his mother and Katya's had hit it off. Their first contact had been one of genteel inspection, the first few days very formal. By the time of the wedding, how-

ever, they were sisters in all but flesh. His mother helped
Magda to her seat, brought people over to meet her, sat and
chatted with animation. With laughter. And Magda replied
with a smile. Jeffrey watched to see if it would split her face.

Always his gaze returned to Katya. She flowed from
group to group, and wherever she stood, the room's light
shifted to remain focused upon her. She approached someone,
and smiles bloomed like flowers opening to the sun. Men
stood taller, women leaned forward to speak, all were richly
rewarded with a moment of sharing in her happiness.

"This isn't your day to play wallflower, lad," Andrew said
as he approached.

"Just taking a breather," Jeffrey replied, his eyes resting
upon Katya. "And enjoying the view."

"I've never had much respect for a man who's not able to
outmarry himself," Andrew said. "Glad to see you're uphold-
ing my estimation of you, lad."

Jeffrey watched as Katya spoke and laughed and positively shimmered. "I'm a lucky guy."

"You're a ruddy sight more than that. You've the good
fortune of twenty men, lad. Congratulations."

Jeffrey caught sight of himself in an ancient mercury
mirror. Smugness fought for place with wonder across his
features. "I can't thank you enough for the car—"

"Don't give it another thought." Andrew paused, said,
"As a matter of fact, I've got a news of my own. Care for a
glass of something wet?"

"No thanks. What news?"

"My wife and I've decided to adopt a little one," Andrew
said, then, when Jeffrey laughed, "What's so funny?"

"You and your British calm. You'd announce the start of
World War III without raising your voice."

"Having a wee one dribble on your best suit is a trial, I'll
admit, but not quite as bad as that." Andrew grinned. "Life
was bent on sparing us the bother, but my wife and I were
never ones to rest on good sense when we were wanting something. Especially when it comes to kids."

Jeffrey offered his hand. "Congratulations, Andrew. I'm
sure you're going to be a great dad."

"Wish I shared your confidence, lad. The thought is enough to give me a bad case of the shakes, I'll admit." His grip on Jeffrey's hand lingered. "I'd thought of asking you to be his godfather."

"Me?"

"Don't look so shocked. You've got all the right ingredients for a godparent, far as I can see. And in years to come, you'll be able to give the little blighter the kind of gifts he deserves, like a matching suite of Louis XIV furniture." Andrew sobered momentarily. "Seriously, lad. I'd be ever so glad if you'd accept."

"I'm honored, Andrew. Really."

"That's settled, then." Andrew dropped his hand. "You'd be amazed the things you and the little wife will get involved with when your own time comes. Never knew wallpaper coloring was a national priority." He motioned to where Magda waved at him. "You're being summoned, lad. Time to rejoin the fray."

Magda patted the chair next to her as he approached and said, "Allow me the honor of sitting next to the most handsome man in the room for a moment."

"I am only a complement for your daughter's beauty," Jeffrey replied, sitting down.

"For this moment, perhaps." Magda searched out her daughter, responded to her wave with yet another smile. "Yes, it is indeed her day."

"You have raised a beautiful daughter," Jeffrey told her.

Magda turned her attention back to him. "And granted her the good sense to choose an excellent man."

"Thank you, Mrs. Nichols."

"I was so pleased that my daughter was not artistically inclined." She sipped from her glass. "I did not wish the Lord to burden her with this passion."

Jeffrey found her across the crowded room. "She has your passion," he replied. "It comes out in other ways."

"I am glad." Magda inspected his face, asked, "You are worried by this trip to the Ukraine?"

He nodded, no longer surprised by her changes in direction or choices of topic. "Does it show so clearly?"

"No, but I know my daughter. She will have bestowed her own worries upon you. Her life and her heritage has been shaped by one view of the Soviet empire. She sees them as the oppressors. The Bolsheviks. The conquerors. The instruments of Stalin's terror." She waved the past aside. "But this nation no longer exists. Who knows what you shall find?"

"I think this uncertainty is almost as frightening as what you described."

"This too is true." Magda smiled. "Perhaps you are right to be worried after all."

"Thanks a lot."

"When do you depart?"

"Tonight we have a suite here at the Grosvenor House, then tomorrow we leave for five days in Monte Carlo. I travel to Cracow two days later."

"Know that you shall travel with the prayers of at least two women sheltering you."

"Thank you, Magda. That means a lot."

"So, enough of the future. Today we must retain the moment's joy, no?" Magda reached beside her chair and came up with a picture frame wrapped in white tissue paper. "I have made something for you."

"That's wonderful, Magda." He made to rise. "Wait, let me go get Katya."

"My daughter has already seen this," she replied. "She was the one who suggested the quotation."

Jeffrey accepted the package, folded back the paper, and released a long, slow breath.

The frame was simple and wooden. The matting was of dark-blue velvet. Set upon this cloth was a flat, hand-painted ceramic rectangle.

The picture's background was softest ivory. Upon it was painted a man cresting the peak of an impossibly high mountain. With one hand he clutched for support; the other he stretched heavenward. Above him a lamb, shining as the sun, reached down, offering a pair of wings.

Beneath were scrolled the words, " 'Let us press on to know God,' Hosea 6:4."

Jeffrey's mother stepped over to where they sat. "May I

borrow my son for a moment?"

"Of course."

"Did you paint that, Magda? Oh, it's beautiful. May I show it to my husband?" She lifted the picture from Jeffrey's grasp and moved off.

Jeffrey stammered, "Magda, I don't know how to thank you."

She smiled once more. "You shall make a worthy son-in-law, Jeffrey. Of that I have not the slightest doubt."

"Jeffrey?" His mother reappeared. "I do need to speak to you for a moment."

"Go," Magda said quietly. "My blessings upon you both, and upon this wondrous day."

His mother pulled him over to another quiet corner. "Katya is as wonderful as you said."

"You spent a week together and you're just getting around to deciding this?"

She gave him a playful hug. "I've told you that before and you know it."

He pulled a face. "I don't recall."

"You don't recall," she mimicked, rolling the tones. "Listen to my posh son."

Jeffrey was so completely happy he felt he could have skated a Fred Astaire dance step across the ceiling. "You know where that word comes from? In the days of colonial India, people with connections and experience chose the cooler side of the boat for their voyages out and back—port out, starboard home. Posh. Very snooty group, from the sounds of it."

She looked at him with genuine approval. "You're very happy with your life, aren't you." It was not a question.

He nodded. "Other than the odd crisis now and then, very happy."

"These bad things come," she said, her smile never slipping. "If you are strong, and if you're lucky enough to marry a good partner, and if you're wise enough to know a strong faith, the bad things go too."

"They do at that," he agreed.

"Well, I didn't pull you away to discuss the lost colonies of the British Empire."

He played at surprise. "No?"

"Your brother asked me to wait until your wedding day to pass on this momentous news. Don't ask me why. I have long since given up trying to figure out how my sons' minds work." She took a breath, then said, "Your little brother is thinking of becoming a monk."

That dropped his jaw. "Charles?"

"Unless you have yet another brother stashed somewhere which I don't know about, that must be the one."

"Charles a monk?"

"Better than Charles a drunk. His words, not mine. He is very sorry to miss the festivities, by the way. Genuinely sorry. But travel is such a tremendous difficulty for him. We discussed it and decided this was better for all concerned."

But Jeffrey wasn't ready to let that one go. "Charles is going to be a monk?"

"Not only has he convinced me and your father, but the abbot is taking this most seriously as well."

"Abbot?"

"The monastery head. Call him chief holy honcho if it makes it any easier to swallow. Your father does. He's quite a nice man, actually."

"I can't believe it."

"A fairly standard reaction. Charles says to tell you that he has finally recognized himself as a man of extremes. A born fanatic. Either he lands in the gutter, or he takes his religion thing all the way."

"That's what he calls it? His religion thing?"

She smiled, a touch of sadness to her eyes. "My dear son Charles is going to, as he puts it, spend the rest of his life doing a major prayer gig."

She walked over to the gift-laden table, extracted a long slender package, and returned. "He asked that I give you this on the big day when we're alone. I suppose this is as alone as we're going to be. It's a poem. He wrote it himself and did his own calligraphy. You'll be happy to know his poetry doesn't sound like the way Charles talks."

Jeffrey unwrapped the box, pulled out the frame, and read:

Tonight I Hear

Tonight I hear the angels sing
  With ears that never heard this earth,
A gift of grace long undeserved
  From One who longs to grant me wings.

Oh Lord, how long must I remain
  Bound to earth and earthly bonds?
Can my home your home become,
  Your love my love, my life your aims?

I seek, I seek, and cannot find
  A gift which is forever mine,
And in my frantic fury fail
  To hear His voice so softly say,
    Be still.
    Be still.
    Be still,
And know that all is here, and thine.

Salvation, grace, and guiding light
  I know are mine, yet yearn for heights
Which He himself has called me to,
  Far beyond this clinging clime.

Yet perfection shall be never mine;
  Only His, and mine when I can die
To Him, and let Him live through me,
  And know that here indeed are wings
    That soar.
    That soar.
    That soar,
  Beyond earth's stormy shore,
    to Him.

Jeffrey looked back to his mother and managed to say, "Tell Charles I'm proud of him."

"Jeffrey?" Katya came over, rested a gentle hand on his shoulder.

His mother stood, shared smiles with Katya. "If I had ever tried to dream up an image of the perfect daughter-in-law, it would not have held a candle to you, my dear."

They exchanged hugs from the heart. His mother turned

her attention back to Jeffrey and said, "May the Lord bless you and your wife and your lives together, with love and His presence most of all."

Then Katya took her place before Jeffrey, and looked up at her new husband with eyes that flooded his heart with their radiance. She whispered for his ears alone, "It is time, my darling."

CHAPTER
12

Monte Carlo crowned a rocky promontory that descended in steep stages from the Maritime Alps to the Mediterranean Sea. The road running along the coast, the one that linked the tiny principality with such other Riviera resorts as Cannes and Antibes and Cap Ferrat, was called the Corniche. It was bounded on the Mediterranean side by a hand-wrought stone balustrade that gave way first to rocky beaches, then to a sea whose aching blue was matched only by the cloudless sky.

At the heart of Monte Carlo rested its famous port, the waters dotted with the ivory-colored yachts of the international jet set. The surrounding houses crowded tightly against one another, grudgingly permitting only the smallest of spaces for tiny, cobblestone streets. The architecture spanned the years from *La Belle Époque* to ultramodern. Yet somehow it all fit, if perhaps only because of the sun and the sea and the romantic eyes with which Jeffrey and Katya blessed all they saw.

Just off the port rose the gracious and stately Casino. Even surrounded as it was by such chrome and glass apparitions as the Loew's hotel, the Casino remained a regal crown harking back to Monte Carlo's glory days. Facing it across the stately Place du Casino was the wedding-cake structure of the Hotel de Paris, the most prestigious hotel in the kingdom.

The exterior was all honey-colored stone and liveried footmen and wide, red-carpeted stairs and grand towers. The interior was all gilt and marble and Persian carpets and crystal chandeliers. The suite Alexander had arranged for them had a view up over the rooftops to the port and the sea beyond.

It was a magical time, a sharing of happiness that knew no earthly bounds. Nights were too precious to allow for a willing descent into slumber. Exhaustion would creep upon them while one spoke and the other tried to listen, and suddenly it would be dawn. And they would still be together, opening their eyes to another day of shared joy.

They spoke of the serious, the future, the infinite. They dwelled long and joyfully upon the meaningless, the unimportant, and gave it eternal significance with their love.

"I know it's a little late to be worrying about such things," he said the fourth morning, the day of their visit to Prince Markov. "But I've got to ask. Can you cook?"

As was their newfound custom, they took breakfast in their room. They found it all too new, this beginning of their days together, to share it with others. Within minutes of their call, room-service waiters in starched white uniforms rolled in a linen-clad table bearing flaky croissants, fresh fruit, silver pots containing thick black morning coffee and frothy hot milk, and always a rose in a vase. Katya kept the flowers in a water glass on her bedside table.

Katya nodded emphatically. "I make the best gooshy-gasha on earth."

He made a face. "Sounds divine."

"It takes lots of practice. I started when I was, oh, I think maybe two and a half or three years old."

He marveled at the graceful slant to her almond-shaped eyes. "Have I ever told you how beautiful you are?"

She nodded happily. "You take a shiny new kitchen bake-pan and carry it out to the backyard. Then you mix in different things from the garden."

"For taste," he said.

She shook her head, making the dark strands shiver. "For color. Green grass, brown dirt, some water to hold it together, and as many different petals as you could find. Petals are a key ingredient of gooshy-gasha. We had a dozen fruit trees in our backyard. I remember going from tree to tree, picking handfuls of petals off the ground. I called them springtime snow, I can still remember that. It was different from wintertime snow because you could hold it in your hand and it wouldn't melt."

"When you talk like that your face gets like a little girl's," Jeffrey mused, and felt his heart twist at the thought of a child with her face. *Their* child.

But she was still caught in the fun of remembering and sharing. "Gooshy-gasha. I haven't thought about that in years. When it was thick enough you could turn the pan upside down and make what I called a *babeczka*; that means a little cake."

"A garden variety cupcake."

"A baby fruit cake," she corrected him, "with grass and petals instead of fruit and nuts. It was mostly brown, with little bits of green and pink sticking out. I'd serve it to my dolls and our pet bunnies and maybe the neighbor's dog, if I could get him to sit still long enough to put a bib on him. He was such a messy eater." She gazed with eyes so happy they rested on him with a joyous pain. "You're much neater than he was."

"Thanks ever so much." He swung around the table so that he could nestle into her lap, said, "Teach me some Polish."

"Oh no, not now." She almost sang the words. "Nobody can learn it just like this. Not even you. It's the most difficult language in all Europe."

He made mock-serious eyes. "More difficult than English?"

She smiled. "Until you learn. It sounds a lot like Russian to the ear, though the Polish alphabet is not Cyrillic. It is a Slavic language, and all Slavic tongues have similarities, just like all Latin languages."

He traced the line of her chin with one finger, wondered at the pleasure such a simple, intimate gesture could bring. "Teach me something, Katya. Just a couple of words."

"Let's see. *O Rany Boskie* means the wounds of Christ, a favorite remark of complaining grandmothers." Happiness lent a childlike chanting tone to her voice. "*Sto lat* means a hundred years, and is used as a toast and a birthday greeting. *Na zdrowie* is a drinking salute and means to your health. *Trzymaj się* literally means hold on to yourself, but is used to mean hang in there. It's said between friends upon departure or hanging up the phone. *Słucham* means I'm listening and is said when you pick up the phone."

"You have beautiful ears," he whispered, reaching up to kiss the nearest one.

She pushed him away with the backhanded gesture of an impatient four-year-old. "Shush, this is serious. Now the word for hello is, repeat after me, *Cześc*."

"Only if you wait until I need to sneeze," he said, twirling a wayward strand.

"Okay, then *Pa-pa*. Try that. It means goodbye, but you only say it to a close friend."

"That's one thing I never want to say to you," he told her solemnly. "Not ever."

She looked down at him with merry eyes. "*Całuję rączki.* That's thank you in the most formal, flirtatious sense, and really means, I kiss your hand."

He ran his fingers around her neck to mold with the feather-soft hairs on her nape. "How do you say I love you?"

Her eyes shone with a violet-gray light that filled his heart to bursting. She both whispered and sang the words, "*Ja cię kocham.*"

Late that afternoon they took a taxi along the winding Corniche to Alexander's former residence, now owned by Prince Vladimir Markov. Villa Caravelle rose from a steep hillside overlooking the azure waters of the Mediterranean. The walls surrounding the circular drive were of small, round pebbles, overlaid with great blooming pom-poms of wisteria. The air was heavily scented by flowers, especially jasmine. Everything was perfectly manicured—miniature citrus trees, bursts of bougainvillea, magnolia in full bloom. The air was absolutely still.

Jeffrey rang the bell, caught sight of Katya's expression,

asked, "Do you mind having to do this business on our honeymoon?"

"A little," she admitted.

"Sorry we didn't go to Scotland after all?"

"Of course not." She smiled up at him. "Let's just get this real-life stuff over with as quickly as possible and return to fairyland, okay?"

The door was answered by a severe-looking woman in a navy blue dress. "Monsieur et Madame Sinclair? Entrezvous, s'il vous plait."

They stepped into a high-ceilinged marble foyer. When the door closed behind them, their eyes took a moment to adjust to the darker confines. In the distance a voice said, "Mr. Sinclair, madame, please come in."

Electronically controlled shutters lifted from great arched windows. Light splashed into the salon with the brilliance of theater spotlights. Jeffrey was suddenly very glad that Alexander was not there to see what had happened to his former home.

The great room reminded him of a museum between major exhibitions. Antiques and works of art cluttered every imaginable space. Nothing matched. Tapestries from the late Middle Ages crowded up next to Impressionist paintings, which were illuminated by gilded art-deco lamps held by giant nymphs. Persian carpets overlapped one another, with the excess rolled up along the walls. There were three chaises longues from three different centuries, one green silk, one brocade, one red velour. A mahogany china cupboard stuffed to overflowing with heavy silver and gold-plate stood alongside a delicate satinwood secretary, and that next to a sixteenth-century corner cupboard which in turn was partially hidden behind a solid ebony desk.

Prince Markov walked toward Jeffrey with an outstretched hand. "You are no doubt wondering why a man who appears to have everything would be interested in another worldly possession."

That being far kinder than what he was truly thinking, Jeffrey replied with a simple, "Yes."

"Alexander Kantor has spoken so highly of you," Katya fielded for him.

Markov kissed her hand. "Madame Sinclair, enchanté."
A slight blush touched Katya's cheeks, betraying her reaction to both her new name and to his old-world attention.

"Please be so kind as to follow me." Prince Vladimir Markov had the sleek look of a high-level corporate chairman.
He was balding, even-featured, manicured from head to toe,
and frigidly aloof. The results of too many overly rich meals
were hidden by a chin kept aloft and by suits carefully tai-
lored to hide a growing bulge. His lips held to a polite smile
that meant absolutely nothing. Intelligent eyes viewed the
world as a hawk might view its prey.

Katya stopped before the wall beside his desk and said,
"Look at these wonderful pictures." They were enlarged
sepia-colored prints of stern-looking men with square-cut
beards and unsmiling women in bustles and trains.

Markov gave a tolerant smile. "Ah, well, they're actually
what you might call family photographs."

"And is this your father?" she asked, pointing to one of
the figures, which bore a marked resemblance.

"Yes, my father as a young man. He was quite a remarkable gentleman. He loved to hunt. He loved art. And he absolutely loved the classics. He understood the world through
mythology. He was in his twenties when he left Russia, never
to return."

"He left because of the October Revolution?"

"The Revolution, yes," Markov mused, his eyes on the
picture. "The Bolsheviks and their Revolution changed
everything."

"And who is this man here beside him?" Jeffrey asked.

"Ah, yes. That face may indeed look a little familiar. It
is Czar Nicholas the Second. My father and he were distant
cousins and quite close friends in their younger days."

"A prince of the royal family of Russia," Katya murmured.

Markov smiled dryly. "There were any number of princes
and dukes in those days."

"It must have been very difficult for your family to lose
all that during the Revolution," Jeffrey offered.

"At least my father was spared his life," Markov evaded.
"He was passing the summer here on the Riviera, as many

Russians did at the time. He stayed a few weeks longer than most, and that sealed his fate. Word came from his own father not to travel back, that the situation was becoming too dangerous. Shortly thereafter, the czar and his family were taken prisoner. The Bolsheviks had overthrown the government. Nothing more was heard from my father's father or, for that matter, from anyone else in my family."

He motioned them forward. "Shall we sit out on the terrace? Please watch your step here; these carpets were meant for my family's larger estate. As you can see, I have little space here for my remaining possessions."

He led them out through great double glass doors onto a flagstone terrace. Below, the property plunged steeply toward the sparkling Mediterranean. Jeffrey stepped to the edge and took several deep breaths, feeling as if he had been searching for air back in that cluttered room.

"Perhaps Mr. Kantor told you I sold my somewhat larger estate," Markov said, holding Katya's chair and waving Jeffrey to the seat opposite. "The palace was rather old, and required renovations that were outrageously expensive. Quite beyond the reach of an exiled prince, I assure you. What you saw inside, and of course what is contained in the other rooms, is all that I have left now of my family's glorious past."

"Certainly some of your items are quite valuable," Jeffrey ventured, wondering where the conversation was leading.

"It is not a question of price," Markov replied. "I suppose it is a matter of sentimental attachment. There are stories, some shreds of family history associated with each of these things.

"But that is all in the past," he continued, slapping his hand down on the tabletop. "And what matters about the past is the use to which it is put in the future. Which brings me to my reason for asking you here. Circumstances in Russia have changed beyond any of our imaginings. And now the time has come to act."

Markov's every action seemed to have the slightly forced quality of something carefully thought out, impeccably stage-managed down to the last detail. Jeffrey wondered whether this demeanor masked a hidden agenda, or was simply a product of an aristocratic upbringing. He had not met enough princes to know how they behaved under normal circumstances.

"What can we do for you?" he asked.

"I wish you to assist me in reclaiming what is rightfully mine," Markov replied. "The time has come for our Saint Petersburg estate, which the Communists confiscated, to return to its rightful owners."

"That is the acquisition you want us to manage?" Jeffrey asked. "You want us to go into Saint Petersburg and reclaim your family's estate?"

"That is correct. I wish for you to go and evaluate the circumstances, carefully examine and appraise the value of the estate, together with whatever may have remained of the original fittings, then report back to me."

"If you don't mind my asking, why don't you go yourself?"

Markov shook his head emphatically. "Things in Russia are not as simple as they seem. Every local government is desperate for funds. As soon as they hear that a Markov is involved, someone who wants the property for reasons beyond a commercial interest, the price would immediately skyrocket. Not to mention that there is still great animosity toward the old monarchy. I would venture that the Saint Petersburg government would not be pleased with the sudden reappearance of a long-lost prince of the royal family."

"You need a buffer," Katya offered.

"One of the utmost confidentiality," he confirmed. "To make the transaction a success, I must remain utterly unseen."

"We have experience in antiques and works of art," Jeffrey pointed out. "But none at all in international real estate."

"Who has experience in lost Russian palaces? What I need more than anything is someone I can trust." Markov was emphatic. "Your Mr. Kantor proved a most worthy business associate in the past. Since then I have made quite thorough checks into his background and his transactions. He is a man of impeccable standing. His knowledge of Eastern Europe is extensive. And he has recommended you most highly. In my humble opinion, I feel I could not ask for a more worthy representative."

There wasn't anything humble within five miles of this guy, Jeffrey thought, and asked, "So whom do I say I am representing?"

"You shall be the official representative of Artemis Holdings Limited. It is my own company, one I founded many years ago. On its board sit some Swiss and British colleagues involved in international investments and the like. My name appears nowhere."

Jeffrey replied as he thought Alexander would have wished. "I am greatly honored by your confidence, Prince Markov. Naturally, I will have to discuss this with Mr. Kantor, but with his approval I would be happy to act on your behalf."

"Excellent." Markov fingered his tie nervously. "With the Russian economy in chaos, it is hard to say exactly how the privatization of a palace will proceed. However, I understand that approval is most likely to be given to companies planning an ongoing business activity. The documents I have prepared include a business plan for an import-export operation. Associates of mine in the Artemis group are involved in the steel trade. I shall see to details of their business from an office in my palace."

"I understand," Jeffrey said, wishing that were the case.

"Splendid. Your fees will be transferred to you as and when you require." Markov rose to his feet, their audience at an end. "I will send the dossier to London by private courier."

"I can't tell you exactly when I'll be able to travel," Jeffrey warned. "I have another trip planned to the Ukrain and—"

"I shall pay what is necessary to ensure the promptest possible attention," Markov replied in his lofty manner. "This is, as you can imagine, a matter of enormous urgency."

CHAPTER
13

Jeffrey called Alexander from Heathrow airport to report their safe arrival and to see if all was well. Alexander had just that morning returned home from the hospital.

"Thank you, my young friend. And the same to you. Yes, it is indeed wonderful to again be in my own flat. I cannot tell you how eager I am to return to the business of living."

"I cannot tell you," Jeffrey replied, "how great it is to hear you say that."

"I take it you had a successful journey."

"Extremely."

"I was referring to the business matters," Alexander commented dryly.

"Oh, sure. That, too. Is there anything we can do for you now?" he asked, half-wanting to check in on the old gentleman and half-hoping that they could go straight home. *Home*. The word carried an utterly thrilling new definition.

"Most certainly," Alexander replied emphatically. "There is something I have been thinking about every day since my recovery."

"What's that?"

"My dear boy," Alexander said, his tone sharpening. "You really shouldn't offer unless you mean it."

"No, no, it's fine. We both wanted to check in on you."

"Very well," Alexander replied. "Chinese."

"Chinese?" Visions of Oriental mistresses wafted through his mind.

"I have a colossal craving for a Chinese meal."

"I think that can be arranged," Jeffrey said, smiling toward a curious Katya.

"Something that will awaken my taste buds from the insensate slumber induced by hospital fare."

"What did you have in mind?"

"Be so good as to stop by Mr. Kai's on South Audley Street," Alexander instructed.

"At six pounds per egg roll," Jeffrey pointed out, "they're a bit up-market for take-away."

"Anyone returning from a stay at the Hotel de Paris in Monte Carlo has no right whatsoever to make such comments," Alexander retorted. "Now then. I presume that you two shall be joining me."

"Just a second while I ask the wife." *Wife.* The spoken word gave him thrills. He cupped the receiver and said to Katya, "Alexander wants us to join him for dinner."

"Sounds lovely," she said, then blessed him with a look that curled his toes. "Just so we don't stay too long."

"We'd be happy to," Jeffrey said to the telephone. He fished a pen and ticket envelope from his pocket. "Fire away."

"We shall start with shark's fin soup, but only if it has been made today. You must stress that. Followed by their freshest fish cooked with ginger, spring onions, and baby sweet corn. You had best order quite a lot of that."

"You've given this a lot of thought."

"You cannot conceive how much. I am quite certain hospitals make it a habit to lace their meals with mild anesthetic. It is far less expensive than preparing a decent cuisine, especially when so few of their patrons care what they place in their mouths." Alexander returned to the business at hand. "And of course we must have Peking duck. With more than an ample supply of steamed pancakes, mind. Don't allow them to skimp. And plum sauce. Make sure it is fresh as well."

"Sharpen your chopsticks," Jeffrey said. "We'll be at your place by six."

• • •

A cheerful fire dispelled the night's meager vestige of damp and chill, not an unfamiliar occurrence on a London summer eve. Across the polished mahogany expanse of Alexander's dining-room table, Meissen china fought for space with an abundance of aluminum and plastic take-away containers.

"We had a wonderful trip," Katya announced, as everyone began slowing down.

"Amazing," Jeffrey agreed. "No, better than that. What comes after amazing?"

"I'm sure it would do my gradually recovering heart no good whatsoever to imagine," Alexander replied. "Would anyone care for this last pancake?"

"We can't thank you enough," Katya added.

"It was my pleasure," Alexander rejoined. "Words truly spoken from the heart."

"There's a lot to tell," Jeffrey said.

"All carefully edited for my feeble ears, I trust."

"I was speaking of the business matters."

"Naturally." Deftly he reached across the table with his chopsticks. "Neither of you cares for this last bit of duck, I take it."

"Monsieur Markov's proposition is going to require a lot of thought," Katya said.

"You can say that again," Jeffrey agreed.

Instead of replying directly, Alexander set down his chopsticks, pressed a napkin to his lips, and looked around the room. "At times I wondered if ever I would enjoy another night like this," he said quietly.

Katya reached across to take Jeffrey's hand. He found himself unable to look her way.

"There were moments," Alexander went on, a wintery bleakness to his voice, "when I grew utterly tired of it all. The bed became a holding pen, a place to keep my wasting form until it was time to depart."

"I have never prayed so hard in my life as I did for your recovery," Jeffrey managed.

Gray eyes fastened upon him. "Do you know, I believe

there were moments when I could actually feel your prayers.
Not in a physical sense, no. And not just yours. You were
there also, my dear young lady. Gregor, too. The friends who
have enriched my later years gathered there in heart and
spirit and lifted the cloak of darkness and despair from me.
I was able at such times to see beyond the body's defeat and
realize that, in matters of greatest importance, time holds
no boundaries."

Alexander returned his gaze to the room. "All this afternoon I have been content simply to sit and to drink in the
beauty which this realization has granted me. Everything
has taken on the most remarkable sheen. All before me is
crowned in God's great glory. A shaft of sunlight through the
window, the color of light against the wall, your return and
our meal and the discussion yet to come. I do realize that in
time this awareness will dim, clouded over by the cares of
daily life. But for this moment, this glorious moment, I feel
I have glimpsed the tiniest sliver of what it means to be alive.
Thanks to your gift of prayers in my hour of direst need, and
thanks to the Lord above for His gift of salvation, I have seen
beyond the confines of my feeble realm and seen the gift of
life for what it is meant to be. In this moment, this hour, I
feel I have tasted what is yet to come."

CHAPTER
14

A heavy rain streaked the broad patio doors as Prince Vladimir Markov ushered the general into his overcrowded study. As always, the military man unbent sufficiently to cast an acquisitive eye over some of Markov's more valuable items. Markov played the genial host, pointing out remarkable features and describing minor scandals of long-dead relatives connected to the piece at hand. General Surikov seemed unaware of the fact that the names which Markov tossed casually forward had for three centuries ruled the largest nation on earth.

Markov seated them in a relatively uncluttered corner of his study. A silver coffee service was laid out beside the French doors. Beyond his veranda, the blustering rainstorm cloaked the vista of Monte Carlo. All the world was gray and wet. The gloom outside granted their alcove a vestige of coziness.

As usual the general brought with him a complaint. Today it was related to his last posting before retirement—Estonia. As Markov poured coffee, Surikov asked, "You have heard of the Forest Brothers?"

"Of course. Will you take sugar?"

"Two. Bandits, the lot of them. Ought to be rounded up and shot."

"Given the presence of patriots from the old world order,"

Markov soothed, "this no doubt would be occurring."

"Freedom fighters, they call themselves," the general grumbled, slurping his coffee in the way of one used to sucking meager warmth from mugs. "Bandits using chaos as an excuse to incite rebellion."

"None of the Baltic States ever recovered from their brief spate of statehood, I suppose." Freedom had lasted only for the time between the two world wars before Stalin had gobbled up Estonia, along with its two Baltic cousins, Latvia and Lithuania. "Not to mention the fact that Russification replaced over a third of the local population with imported Russians. From what I gather, they became a state within a state. Special positions and better jobs, that sort of thing."

"I do not speak of what is behind us," Surikov barked.

"No, of course not," Markov demurred. "And of course, who could forget the fact that only the presence of our loyal comrades in arms keeps the situation from dissolving into chaos."

"It is chaos already. Unwanted guests, they call Russians who have lived in Estonia for more than forty years. Two generations born on soil they can no longer call their own. Now their so-called parliament has decided to refuse all Russians, even those born in the country, the right to vote." The thought clearly incensed him. "So now we have villages which are ninety-five percent Russian in population ruled by officials elected by the other five percent. Sheer madness."

"Not to mention the revival of the Forest Brothers," Markov offered, deciding to play at patience and let the old boy run out of steam.

"Bandits, as I said. A pity that Stalin halted his purge before the first of them were wiped from the earth."

Stalin did not stop, Markov silently corrected the general. The madman continued creating the infamous Baltic river of blood until his demise. Afterward, the Kremlin wisely gave the project up. For each death, a dozen other Forest Brothers rose to take their murdered comrade's place. "I understand they are operating more or less in the open these days."

"Three days ago they stopped a Russian convoy and demanded their papers," the general huffed. "Imagine, will you? They stood there with their ancient hunting rifles and asked for transit papers and driver's licenses from tank commanders." Surikov shook his head. "I wish I had been there. They would have received the beating they have been begging for, that I swear on my mother's grave."

"One such attack," Markov pointed out, "and the Estonians would force the remaining Russians to make a mass exodus. And that, my dear general, would be a catastrophe."

"Only because the so-called democratic regime that is dismantling my country has the heart of a mouse and the mind of a newborn." Surikov smiled grimly. "Mark my words, they are busy digging their own graves by permitting such impossible situations to continue. My fellow officers are caught in a vise. When they demand billets inside my shrinking homeland, they are forced to stand in line with comrades stationed in Poland, Czechoslovakia, East Germany, Bulgaria, Kazakhstan, Azerbaijan, Armenia, and a dozen other states. There is no housing. There is no money. There is no government strong enough to solve these problems and rescue my country from disaster."

"A powder keg," Markov agreed. "With the fuses burning low."

"There will be trouble," Surikov warned ominously. "Of that I am certain. If the Forest Brothers are not contained, there will be an incident, and one incident is all it will take. My comrades in arms are ready to move at a moment's notice."

"Which is yet another reason for us to move swiftly," Markov countered. "In case your services are required elsewhere."

"Indeed," the general agreed, focusing once again upon the room and the present moment. "I bring a message from my present superiors. We are gravely concerned that instead of the man you told us about, we now are invited to work with an unknown."

"A better choice," Markov contradicted. "An American. A young innocent."

"A wild card," the general replied worriedly. "A loose cannon, perhaps."

"The reason we selected Kantor in the first place," Markov reminded him, "was that we wanted someone totally honest yet utterly inexperienced in such affairs."

"True, true," the general muttered. "And yet—"

"Someone who had reason to go to the East, yet who would have neither the knowledge nor the contacts to dig too deeply."

"And this man Kantor was perfect," the general agreed. "But the new one?"

"Even better."

"You have met him?"

Markov nodded. "This Jeffrey Sinclair wears his honesty upon his forehead, right alongside his inexperience. He is the naive American personified."

"This may suit us," the general conceded.

"He will go and do our bidding and return none the wiser," Markov assured him. "Wait and see."

CHAPTER
15

Jeffrey carried one of the dining-room chairs into the bedroom and stationed himself by the doorway, where he could
watch Katya's every move. He had protested once at the beginning that she did not need to help him pack. Katya replied
that helping him was her way of placing her heart in with
all that he was taking. He sat and watched her move from
bureau to suitcase to closet and back. He replied with simple
nods to her questions about ties and socks, and so forth, his
heart too full to permit passage to many words.

He watched each movement with eyes bound to no memory, as if he were viewing her for the first time. He wanted
to take this moment intact, colored by nothing which had
come before. So he watched her and sought to brand his mind
with the vision. The motions of his wife's lithe body. Soft,
delicate hands that were never still. Violet-gray eyes so full
of his pending departure they could not even look his way
and continue with the packing. Hair tousled by the gentlest
of motions and the faintest of breezes. A heart that filled the
room with love.

As she folded one of his suits, she said, "When I was little,
I thought wearing a suit made men fat. My daddy never put
one on, and he was the strongest man I knew. I never could
understand why any man would wear one."

He pointed at the neck brace resting beside his case.
"What is that for?"

110

"It's for your neck," she said firmly.

"My neck is fine."

She settled it down on top of the clothing in the case. "What if it starts hurting you?"

"My neck is fine, Katya."

Reluctantly she set it aside. "Promise me you'll take care of yourself."

"I promise." Jeffrey swallowed with difficulty. "This is really hard, Katya."

"I know," she said softly. "You'll miss being with me for our two-week anniversary."

"I wish—"

"We must learn to be together even when we are apart. Remember, what's most important remains the same." She walked around the bed to settle in his lap. "We have our love," she said softly. "We have our Lord. We have a life together. In the light of these joys, the momentary fades to nothingness."

They paused for a lingering kiss. Then, "Promise me you won't do anything silly while you're away from me. You know, like three-day drinking contests to prove who's the most macho of them all."

He looked down upon the top of her head. "There's no chance of that, and you know it."

"While we're at it," she snuggled in close to his neck. "Give me your word you'll never, ever start thinking you've got to have a megabuck bank account to be happy."

He tried to back off far enough to look down on her, but she held him close. "What brought this on?"

"Have your cuticles done twice a week, a closet with thirty-six gray suits and a drawer with eleven pounds of silk ties," she said.

"Have you been lying awake at night trying to find something else to worry about?"

"Servants trained to bow every time you burp," she rejoined. "A little silver bell by your bedside for summoning Suzette with morning coffee."

"Suzette?"

"The French au pair."

He let his grin show. "As in Suzette with a too-short uniform and frilly white cap?"

She slapped his chest. "Don't even think it."

"You brought it up."

She looked up at him. "Promise me, Jeffrey."

He turned serious. "There is no one on earth for me but you. There hasn't been since the first day I saw you. I *have* to be careful, Katya. It's part of the responsibility of loving you."

Katya examined him carefully, was satisfied with what she found. She reached behind her, pulled out an envelope that had lain hidden beneath his suitcase. "Here."

"What is it?"

"Just a little something to help you on your way. You have to promise not to open it until you're on the plane."

The thought of what was to come both electrified and hurt. He squeezed her close, whispered, "I promise."

She asked not to have to accompany him to the airport. Jeffrey found he understood. Her love was a very intense, very personal matter. She did not want this first farewell of their married life to be done in public.

A final hug, a caress, a kiss, a look, a word, and he was out on the street, flagging a passing taxi, feeling enormously excited and tremendously forlorn. Jeffrey gave the driver his Heathrow terminal, sat back surrounded by his cases, and knew a keening sorrow that left his insides as hollow as an empty well.

The driver granted him a much-needed silence until they were leaving the motorway at the Heathrow exit. Then he asked, "Where you off to today, then?"

Jeffrey cleared a rusty throat and replied, "Cracow."

The driver pushed his battered cap aside and scratched a scalp wired with a few gray hairs. "Amazing what's tucked away in odd corners of this old world, ain't it? All these places right out of the spy books, now you can just hop on over. That's democracy at work for you. Here, and all them new Russian states."

"They're not Russian anymore."

"No, well, I wouldn't put it past them Russkies to want it all back one day. You ever visited over there?"

"I'm going to the Ukraine for the first time later this week."

"That so? Ukraine, Georgia, Uzbekistan—they made a right mess of the Olympics, all them new countries. And them names, enough to make a body think it's a different planet. Up till not long ago, Lithuania wasn't nothing more to me than an unlucky ship."

The driver pulled up in front of his terminal. "Here you are, then. Hope you get back safe and all in one piece. From the sounds of it, there won't be no holiday camp waiting for you."

As soon as the plane lifted from the tarmac, Jeffrey pulled Katya's envelope from his coat pocket and opened it. Inside was a card featuring a solemn little girl dressed in crinoline and ribbons, her tumbling black curls framing a pair of great dark eyes. Her chubby hand offered out a single red rose.

Jeffrey blinked hard, opened the card, read, "You love me. That knowledge is enough to carry me over any time, any distance, any worry, any event. Take care, my love. You carry my heart with you. Katya."

Jeffrey pressed the card to his chest and turned unseeing eyes toward the airplane window.

Gregor greeted him at the Cracow airport with, "The weather is somewhat unpleasant, I fear."

Jeffrey carried his suitcase in one hand and his jacket in his other as he followed Gregor's swaying gait out of the terminal. "It's like a steam bath out here."

"The longest and harshest heat wave Poland has seen in two hundred years," Gregor agreed. "And it's much worse across the border."

"Thanks for the encouragement." He dumped his satchel

into the back of the little plastic car. "Still driving the same old Rolls, I see."

"It is adequate for my needs," Gregor replied. "As to the weather, I take it as long as I can stand, then I find urgent work at one of my country orphanages. The heat is as bad, but the air is much sweeter."

Their business in Poland progressed on the well-oiled wheels of experience and mutual confidence. Jeffrey threw himself into his tasks with single-minded purpose, using work to soothe the inner ache as best he could. Within forty-eight hours the antiques were purchased, the required paperwork was completed, and the moment of Jeffrey's departure was upon them.

That afternoon, they stood before Gregor's apartment building and waited for Olya, Yussef's wife, to arrive. Gregor told him a little of what he would find across the border. "The Soviets were even less respectful of privacy than the Polish Communists. Their internal spy network was far more vigilant, even savage. And personal wealth has been illegal for far longer."

"So I will be buying mostly small items," Jeffrey concluded.

"Items easy to secret away," Gregor agreed. "That is, unless you deal with former Party officials. They of course seized all the privileges of any ruling despot."

"What can you tell me about the Ukraine itself?"

"Lvov and its surroundings were a part of Poland for almost five hundred years," Gregor explained, "but little evidence remains today. The borders have shifted back and forth, and when Stalin annexed this territory to the Soviet Union after World War II, he immediately began his program of Russification."

"I've heard that term," Jeffrey said.

"Many have, but few can fathom the horrors it involved. Entire towns were emptied overnight, Poles and Jews and Ukrainians all treated with equal brutality. These former citizens were shipped to Siberia or Samarkand or the borderlands of Mongolia, and replaced by Russians brought in and ordered to make the area their home. Any sign of their former heritage was stripped away. Patriotism to any land save

114

the Soviet Union became a crime of sedition, punished by
years of forced labor. As a matter of fact, some of Yussef's
family were Ukrainians who had lived for centuries on Polish
soil. Perhaps you can hear from him a little of what transpired."

"Yussef is Polish?"

"No, our young man is pure-blooded Ukrainian, as much
as anyone can be in a land that has known only glimmers of
nationhood for over seven hundred years. But his mother's
family called Poland home for many generations. His mother
has passed away, but her sister—Yussef's aunt—will be
working as your interpreter, I believe. She has been someone
quite important to Yussef—a sort of lifetime tutor, I gather,
from the little I have been told."

"Sounds like you've spent some time with Yussef."

"Quite a bit," Gregor agreed. "The young man fascinates
me. I fear I have tried his wife's patience quite severely."

Jeffrey recalled the hard-faced woman he had met at the
outdoor market that previous winter. Five minutes of translating into Polish for Yussef, from which Katya had translated into English, had brought her to a boil. "That must not
have taken long."

"No, Olya is not a woman given to idle talk," Gregor
agreed. "In any case, Yussef has remained both independent
and principled in a land which has striven to quash such
qualities. He could never have been admitted to university,
as he vehemently opposed the Communist Party. So this aunt
has tried to teach him, and by all indications she has done
quite a good job."

"I have to admit," Jeffrey said, "he did not seem so impressive when I first met him."

"Do not underestimate our young man," Gregor urged
him. "He has been shaped by a world totally alien to your
own. Yet he has managed to hold on to both his honesty and
his personal integrity in the face of pressures you can
scarcely imagine. He is also most intelligent. He reads and,
what is more, he remembers."

"A scruffy intellectual."

"If you travel this world long enough," Gregor replied,
"you will find that the light of learning burns in the strang-

est of hearts. I urge you to look beyond the exterior and take full measure of this man."

"I'll try," Jeffrey assured him. "So when do we get started?"

"It's all arranged," Gregor said. "You will stay this night in Rzeszow, then at dawn cross the border and begin your journey."

My journey. "Rzeszow is a border town?"

"No, it is a good eighty kilometers from the Ukraine. But Przemyśl, the nearest town to the border station of Medyka, is no longer safe. It has become a campsite for newly arrived Russians and Ukrainians. Those who come over for the first time are said to be the most dangerous, because they do not know how to handle the sudden freedom. All the food they can afford is available. And the liquor. There are constant brawls, with some unfortunate found stabbed in the gutter almost every morning."

Gregor shook his head. "*Przemyśl* sounds like the Polish word that means to think again, or to consider very seriously. Some say it was an ancient warning given to all who crossed the border into the Kingdom of Rus."

"Sounds as if it still applies today."

"Indeed it does. So you shall stay in Rzeszow, where you should be able to have a safe night's rest."

"Should?"

The old gentleman was unnaturally somber. "Such things as should be taken for granted in this world are no longer certain. Not here. Not now."

"It's not safe to be around these traders?" Jeffrey was immensely glad Katya was not around to hear it.

"The men and women who make their living through such international trade live in a gray world," Gregor replied. "What they do is technically illegal, but at the same time the old Communist laws are dropping like trees in a forest being logged. What the traders do is too profitable and too necessary for either the Ukrainian or the Russian officials to close down, so their answer is to squeeze and squeeze and then squeeze even more. The Ukrainian border officials charge fifty dollars for an entry-exit visa. Keep in mind that the current average monthly salary in the former Soviet lands is twelve dollars. Only someone involved in a highly lucrative trading activity could afford to pay such sums just to cross a border. The border guards know this and demand even more in bribes."

"A life that doesn't attract the best kind of person," Jeffrey surmised.

"Pirates, most of them," Gregor agreed. "Our young friend Yussef is truly one of a kind."

Jeffrey caught sight of Olya driving a battered automobile up the street. She approached in a cloud of oily fumes and ratchety noise. He said, "His wife more than makes up for it."

Gregor waved in her direction and hummed a denial. "Olya chose a man with heart. There is much to be said for a person who is capable of realizing her own weaknesses. It is a rare quality, especially in such a land as hers."

Jeffrey watched as the stone-faced woman pulled into a parking space and cut off the motor. He found himself wishing for a chance to see the world through Gregor's eyes. Just once. Just long enough to know what it meant to have the man's wisdom.

"I told them you have only one week," Gregor continued. "I would rather that Yussef worked you hard for a shorter period than expose you to danger for a longer time."

"What danger?"

"Nothing certain, no specific thing you can put your finger on. Just too many problems, political and economic and social, that could become explosive without warning." Gregor saw Jeffrey's worried expression and smiled. "Take comfort that Yussef agrees both that you should be safe and that one week will be sufficient this time."

This time. "You trust them, then."

"So much that I am willing to place your life in their hands," Gregor replied soberly. "Still, I shall not cease to worry nor pray until you have safely returned."

Olya climbed from the ancient car, stomped over, greeted Jeffrey with a curt nod, and poured out a torrent of words that sounded horribly slurred to Jeffrey's ears. Gregor responded in a most courtly manner, bowing and murmuring assent every few moments.

When the woman stopped and turned in dismissal, Gregor said mildly, "You and Olya's husband will alight from the car at the Polish-Ukrainian border and cross by foot. There will be someone to meet you on the other side, I assume Yussef's aunt. Olya will cross over with the car."

"Alone?"

"The wait on the Polish side is well-patrolled and not too long. Only two days, she informs me."

"And on the other side, coming back into Poland?"

"Ah. That would depend on whether or not you are a rabbit, as they call the first-timer. A professional will know whom to bribe and how much and should pass through in six or seven days. A rabbit may wait as long as two weeks and still not pass through."

Crossing the Ukrainian border by foot did not appeal to Jeffrey in the least. "What about just taking a train?"

"The border wait would be longer than going over by foot, at least nine hours," Gregor replied. "This is another hold-over from the Communist days. The tracks are different gauges, you see. The Soviets in their wisdom decided that, rather than allowing passengers to change trains and possibly escape detection, they would seal all compartments and then change the train's *wheels*."

"On every train?"

Gregor nodded. "And every international border crossing. Yussef's ways may seem very strange to you at times, my young friend, but I urge you to trust his judgment. He has had a lifetime's experience at surviving inhuman conditions."

Jeffrey risked a brief inspection of the hard lines upon Olya's face, the determined cast to her eyes, the focused tension that bordered on constant fury. "I hear you."

Gregor patted his arm. "If you will take one additional word of advice."

"Anything."

"Do not fall ill," Gregor said in utter seriousness. "You would do well to guard your health wherever possible. To test the Russian medical system with an emergency would truly be gambling with the rest of your life."

"Katya's already warned me about the water."

"Heed her words well. Drink nothing that has not been taken from a bottle opened before your own eyes or boiled twice within your own sight. And eat only what appears truly clean. And take nothing—"

"You're about to get me worried," Jeffrey protested.

"Better frightened than ill."

Olya barked out an impatient word. Gregor smiled and offered his hand. "You go with my prayers surrounding you, my boy. Take care and return as you are now, only richer. Especially in wisdom."

CHAPTER

16

The road to Rzeszow was decorated with horse-drawn hay wagons and roadside fruit and vegetable stands. The villages were a stream of tired sameness. Forty years of Communist rule, and the Nazis before them, had ground out all charm and individual character. Summertime greenery added splashes of color to the occasional relic of bygone glories—a palace, a vast cathedral, a stolid ministry outpost. All suffered from universal neglect.

Yet everywhere, even in the smallest of villages, were signs of new wealth—satellite dishes sprouting from gray-faced apartment buildings like strange metal flowers, houses under construction, lighted storefronts, billboards, Western cars, fresh paint. They stuck out like beacons of hope for a tired and drained people.

Between the villages, fields bustled with haymaking. Whole families gathered for the task. Grandmothers stood surrounded by tumbling piles of happy infants. Vast spreads of food and drink anchored white swatches of cloth. Crowds of boys and girls labored around horse-drawn rigs while their elders tended machine-driven equipment. Heavily laden carts were pushed and pulled toward distant barns.

On the outskirts of Rzeszow, great black crows began to flock in the freshly cut fields. Their beaks were the largest Jeffrey had ever seen, fully as broad as his hand and almost as long. Olya noticed the direction of his gaze, and said, "Russki." She then clasped hands to her throat and made choking sounds. Jeffrey recalled Gregor's words about a drought and nodded his understanding. The birds had been driven West by thirst.

Their hotel was a concrete clone of the high-rise hotels all over Poland. The foyer was vast and gloomy and lined with fake marble, the lighting distant and dim, the air stuffy and perfumed with cheap disinfectant. As Jeffrey signed in, a bus pulled up outside and disgorged a milling stream of dirty, exhausted passengers. Again Olya offered her single word of explanation—Russki. The bus idled outside the entrance, dusty and swaying in time to the diesel's unmuffled clatter. The vehicle listed to one side. The windows were cracked and stuck half-open, the curtains knotted out of the way. Passengers wearily moved toward the reception desk, free hands kneading overworked backs.

The elevator was loud and cranky and the size of a small closet. Outside his room, Yussef pantomimed for Jeffrey to wash thoroughly. Jeffrey recalled the stories of Russian drought and complied.

Dinner was taken in silence, save for short spurts of conversation between Yussef and Olya. When their food arrived, they ate with great appetite but little gusto. Jeffrey had a mental image of them storing up reserves against leaner times ahead.

When they were finished, he bid them good-night and retired to the cramped confines of his room. He lay in the darkness listening to the sounds of violent revelry that echoed up and down the hallway. Finally he fell asleep, hungry for the feel of his wife's loving arms.

They started very early the next morning. Each Polish village on the way to the border had its market, and at each either Yussef or Olya pointed and announced, Russki. The markets sprouted wherever space was available—on stairs leading to a church, along a wall, in tiny triangular parks, in the middle of parking lots, even on traffic islands. Each vendor sat or squatted before a patch of bright fabric and displayed what he or she had to sell. It was never very much. A few handmade sweaters. Some swatches of cloth. Bottles of shampoo or individual cigarettes or perhaps a liter or two of vodka.

Boredom fought with the heat for domination of the borderlands. A seven-kilometer line of trucks and cars sweltered under a cloudless sky. Olya drove them up to the first fencing and waited while Jeffrey and Yussef pulled their bags from the trunk. She then bid her husband a curt farewell, and deftly swung the car back around to return to the end of the line. Piles of refuse lined the roadside, and bodies sprawled wherever could be found a fraction of shade. Kerchiefed babchas tended scrawny children sucking from soda bottles fitted with rubber nipples. Little wooden huts played old disco hits and plied a booming trade in soft drinks and Western snacks. Beefy truck drivers in filthy T-shirts and shorts celebrated successful entries into Poland with beers drained in one long sweaty swallow.

The border crossing came in four stages. First was a stop at the outpost where arriving trucks and cars had to show their proper documents. Jeffrey and Yussef joined the line of heavily burdened pedestrians and walked on through. Then came the Polish station, a brief glimpse of shade and sultry breeze before the guards passed them along. As they departed, the officer who had inspected his passport muttered something to his neighbor and nodded toward Jeffrey. An American crossing the border on foot. Jeffrey felt eyes on his back as he walked toward the Ukrainian station.

Outside the Ukrainian post, the wait began. Ratty buildings displayed hastily scraped-over Soviet stars replaced by new Ukrainian flags. The air tasted hot dry, metallic, sooty, as if baked in an industrial oven. The breeze was fitful and acrid. People moved slowly to and from the border station carrying satchels and shopping bags scarce inches above the ground. They waited in lines for inspection, waited in line to have their passports checked, waited to pay, waited to complain, waited to move on to wait yet again.

There was a moment at the border when time stood still for Jeffrey. He was shuffling along in line, pressed in on all sides by reeking humanity, when suddenly the world came into sharpest focus. His mind became utterly still, caught by an unseen power as he took in all that surrounded him.

Surly border guards ignored whining pleas as they rifled bags and carry-sacks and demanded customs duties, which were simply stashed away. Other bored soldiers pushed people forward, maintained order, and kept careful watch over how much their fellow guards were pocketing.

As Jeffrey inched forward, he could sense all the wailing cries, all the dust, all the chatter and horns and blaring speakers and thousands of smoldering cigarettes all gathering together and drifting upward as a rank incense on an unclean altar.

He took another step and felt unseen vestments slip from his shoulders. His cloak of security had vanished. Jeffrey's turn came then, and he set his bag down on the long metal bench. He shrugged a reply to the guard's surly bark, heard Yussef reply for him, and thought there had never been a time when he had felt so exposed.

Ivona Aristonova waited beside her car within sight of the Ukrainian border station, smoldering from more than the heat.

She glanced at her watch, sighed, and swiped at a wayward strand of hair. Eight o'clock in the morning and the day was already sweltering. This was by far the hottest summer she could remember. And the driest.

In lands where summer temperatures seldom rose above the mid-eighties, and never for more than a day or so at a time, scores of days came and went where temperatures hit a hundred degrees by three hours after dawn. Weeks melted into months under blistering, cloudless skies. Crops trained to grow on little sun and regular rainfall withered and browned. First streams, then rivers, and finally lakes and seas fell below any levels known in recorded history.

And still the heat continued.

As much talk focused on the coming winter as on the present heat. Babchas told tales of other hot summers, followed by winters where unending snows fell upon an earth hard as iron. Many told stories of hunger as well. Elders argued over whether the famine winters of 1917, 1918, and 1919 had been as bad as those of 1944 through 1947. Younger people wondered if, in their own time, they would sit and argue over the winter that was to come.

Corn rose stunted, with ears the size of middle fingers. Lavender, one of the region's major cash crops, refused to bloom at all. What should now have been seas of ripening wheat were graveyards whose dried husks whispered omens in the arid breeze. Potatoes baked in the ground a month before harvest. Vegetables sent up slender sprouts that wilted and fell in surrender. Village squares became anvils where farmers gathered to be hammered by the merciless sun. They stood and searched the empty sky for clouds. They spoke of omens, and of money and the lack of it, and of governments unable to help in this hour of great need, and of possible calamities yet to arrive.

But more than the heat was troubling Ivona this morning. Something about this whole plan unsettled her, and in a way she could not identify. This unreasoning unease troubled her immensely. She did not like such challenges. Life had trained her to distrust the unseen, for here lay the greatest threats to the established patterns of her existence. She held on to these habits with the same rigid insistence that she had applied to the task of learning languages. Ivona was nothing if not disciplined.

Ivona stiffened as she spotted Yussef's slender form. She returned his wave and scrutinized the tall young man walking alongside her nephew.

The American called Jeffrey was everything she had feared. He was far too handsome for his own good. His face was as fair and fresh and unmarked as a newborn's. His bearing was overly confident, utterly untested.

At that instant, it came unbidden, like a fragrance wafted upon an unseen wind. Once again, against her will, she found herself recalling the past, and the power of that memory stripped her bare.

•   •   •

The cold was indescribable that first northern winter. That she recalled much more clearly than the snow. The week before the first frost, temperatures were as high as forty degrees centigrade. Then one afternoon, the first week in October, winds came down from the north, and overnight the temperature fell to minus fifty-two degrees centigrade, a ninety-degree shift in less than twelve hours. Overnight the ground, the trees, even the grass and leaves turned to stone.

Food was very scarce that winter. To buy it, Ivona's parents sold everything they did not absolutely need. Wives of local Communist Party leaders bought several ball gowns her mother had carried on that long train trip north. After everything was sold and the money was gone, all they had to eat was what the local canteen fed them—porridge in the mornings and in the evenings a stinking fish soup. The smell of that soup, and the rotting fish from which it was made, was so strong it stayed in their clothes and bedding and hands and skin throughout that long, endless winter.

All children were required to go to school in the wintertime. That made the polar winter seem so much longer, sitting in the room next to that stinking kitchen day after day. The sun always rose late and set very early, so they arrived in the dark and left in the dark. All they saw of the day was a line of light that traced its way across the floor. Hour after hour their teachers drilled them in Communist doctrine. Ivona found the lessons a torture as harsh as the cold.

They lived in huts of raw logs with moss stuffed in the cracks. Thankfully, there was plenty of wood, and they kept a fire burning in their little stove day and night. In their settlement were eighty Ukrainian families, over a hundred Polish families, and perhaps half that many Jewish families. Fewer than a handful of those families survived that first winter intact.

In May spring finally arrived. The river outside the village lost its covering of ice in explosions that sounded like a new war beginning. The village was there only because the river was there to float logs down to a sawmill.

Before long, berries appeared; gathering them was the children's job. Those raspberries were their only source of vitamin C. By this time, of course, the whole camp suffered from scurvy. During the winter, they followed the local villagers' example and brewed pine needles in water, letting the concoction soak overnight and then drinking a cup very fast. The taste had been beyond horrible, but it had provided enough vitamins for them to retain most of their teeth.

The children on their gathering trips also found mushrooms and sorrel, from which Ivona's mother made a lovely soup. After a winter of porridge and rotten fish stew, the raspberries and her mother's soups provided a taste of heaven.

Another winter and another spring went by before Stalin proclaimed one of his famous Friendship Treaties with local leaders in the Ukraine. For no apparent reason, Ivona's family received a permit to leave the camp. Most of those who had been forcibly resettled, especially those in the far north, never returned home. Ivona never learned why her family was selected to leave, but they were.

In time Ivona and her family made their new home in Lvov, leaving behind the cold of Archangelsk. But never the memories. Never, no matter how hard she tried, the memories.

As she stood and watched the pair approach, Ivona became certain that the painful act of remembering was somehow tied to the arrival of this young man, this Jeffrey Sinclair. This utterly illogical notion shook her to her foundations. She pushed hard at the thought and the lingering pain that always accompanied her memories. Then she stepped forward to greet her nephew and his companion.

• • •

The car awaiting Jeffrey and Yussef as they came through the borderlands was a boxy, gray-green Lada, the driver an overly thin, gray-haired woman. She replied to Yussef's exuberant greeting with a single word. She then turned to Jeffrey. "You are Mr. Sinclair?"

"You speak English. Great."

"I am Ivona Aristonova. I shall act as your interpreter." She was a prim schoolmarm sort of lady, all angles and thin features. Despite the day's dusty heat, she remained poised and collected. She wore a simple blue skirt trimmed in hand-sewn flowers. Everything about her was old, patched, and immaculate; even her battered purse shone with shoe polish. Slate-gray hair was pulled back into a neat bun. Sky-blue eyes were encircled by deep wrinkles and bruiselike smudges. Her singsong voice, however, sounded surprisingly young. "Shall we be going? We have a long way ahead and much yet to do today."

Jeffrey stored his bag in the trunk alongside Yussef's battered bag, a hand-crocheted satchel which he assumed belonged to Ivona, a case of pepsi, a box of foodstuffs, and canister after canister of gasoline. He sat in the front seat, and felt the car sag upon springs so weary they barely kept his backside off the road.

Yussef grinned at Jeffrey's expression and spoke his off-hand guttural manner. The lady translated, "These days it is best not to draw attention with too new a car or too fresh a change of clothing. Especially with the valuables we shall be carrying."

Jeffrey shifted around to make himself as comfortable as possible. "I can't remember ever feeling this hot before."

"Afternoons are worse," Yussef said through Ivona. "Clouds gather, but it does not rain. The heat is trapped to the earth. It has been like this for over two months."

"How can you stand it?"

Yussef showed his discolored teeth. "This isn't the West. You don't find an answer to every pain here. We do what we have been taught to do by seventy years of Communism. We endure."

Yussef rammed home the complaining gears and said through Ivona, "Welcome to the great Soviet empire."

CHAPTER
17

Mostiska. Javorov. Nesterov.

All of his memories of that time, as they drove from village to village and did their trading and drove farther still, would be tinged by nightfall. Even the brightest day, when the heat was a weight under which their little car threatened constantly to collapse and leave them stranded, the eye of his memory was tinged by unseen darkness.

Just beyond the border zone, the road disintegrated. Cracked and pitted pavement barely two lanes wide slowed traffic to a tractor's crawl. Without warning the pavement surrendered to holes of bone-jarring depth, slid into gravel and dust and rutted tracks, or gave way to ancient octagonal stones that caused their car to drum a frantic beat.

Ivona translated their buying transactions with precision, then maintained a silent distance at all other times. Yussef was content with his own company. Jeffrey found the car's silence as heavy a blanket as the heat.

After their third stop, Jeffrey swiveled around in his seat so as to face her. "Your English is excellent," he asked. "Have you ever traveled in the West?"

Ivona kept her attention fastened on the open window. "I have never left the Ukraine since my arrival."

"Where did you live before coming here?"

"English was my escape," Ivona continued, ignoring his

question. Her voice was her finest asset, so soft and light and musical that if Jeffrey closed his eyes he could imagine its coming from twenty-year-old lips. Her only inflection was a slight singsong lilt. She spoke his name, related the best and worse of news, and translated the most mundane of conversations all in this lilting sameness.

"It was my magic carpet to other worlds. My most special moments were the days I received a new English book. Well, new for me. Old, tattered, pages missing, but still holding voices that called to me. They spoke of worlds where freedom was so normal the people could *criticize* the ones in power. Such stories lifted me above myself, released me from the captivity of my existence."

Jeffrey took in the dull heat-blasted landscape, the poverty-stricken farm hovels, the concrete watchtowers. "I can imagine."

"I love the classics especially. But I also enjoyed your modern novels. Even the trash was useful. Through their pages I watched your world hate a distant war, question God, take drugs, have free sex—make mistakes, yes, but in freedom."

Jeffrey decided he did not understand this prim, undersized woman, with her old face and her young voice, her rigid mannerisms. "It's incredible to think that you could learn such an English from books."

"And radio, of course, when transmissions were not jammed. BBC and Radio Liberty and RFE. All highly illegal. Which made even the British gardening programs exciting." She snagged a wisp of gray hair and patted it back into place. "I taught English, unofficially of course; even when the student was unable to pay still I taught. That gave me hours and hours of practice. Of escape. Of imaginary freedom. For someone imprisoned as I was, such imaginings were as real as life itself."

• • •

Rava-Russkaja. Cervonograd. Sokal.
Every hour or so a tall guard tower sprouted alongside the road. When Jeffrey pointed one out, Ivona explained,

"Before the fall of Communism, cars required transit papers to travel between towns or villages. All exits from main roads were blocked and guarded. Lookouts with binoculars manned the towers and timed the cars' passage. If the drivers moved too fast they were stopped and arrested for speeding. If they moved too slowly, it was assumed that they were trading illegally, and they were stopped and strip-searched."

The smaller villages were rows of squalid hovels lining several crumbling country lanes. Larger towns were clusters of tumble-down factories and high-rise tenements. Always there was a central square, always a squat government building with the charm of an oversized tombstone. Always a patch of parched grass proclaiming itself a park. And always a Soviet statue thrusting aggressively upward in dated fifties modernism. Jeffrey saw concrete pedestals with black iron figures ever pointing to the horizon, steel and cement rocket ships bearing proud Soviet warriors toward lofty heavens, brawny figures marching shoulder to shoulder toward a Communist future that was no more, agricultural images mocking the people's evident hunger.

From time to time the horizon sprouted factories so large they appeared as mirages dancing in the shimmering heat. The closer their car came, the vaster the buildings grew—great monoliths looming up twenty stories and more, bristling with smokestacks, but for the most part standing idle.

"There was a huge defense industry in the Ukraine," Ivona replied to his question. "Now it is idle because Moscow no longer buys anything. Salaries are frozen at the old rate, less than ten dollars a month. People are urged to leave, but no one does because there is no other work to be found."

Within the homes they visited, be they spartan apartments or hovels with splintered boards for walls and newspapers for floor coverings, the hospitality never failed to humble him. The poorest of shanties still offered a standard fare of vodka reserved for guests and fresh bread obtained by waiting in line since dawn. Sometimes there were tomatoes shriveled from the heat, perhaps pickles or a plate of stunted onions. But always there was vodka.

At the first stop, Jeffrey shook his head to the invitation to drink and requested water. The stumpy, middle-aged man recovered from his surprise, went to his kitchen alcove, and returned with a battered cup filled to the brim. Through Ivona he assured Jeffrey that the water had been twice boiled. Jeffrey observed the silt making milky sworls and thanked the man solemnly. He then brought the cup to his tightly closed lips and pretended to sip.

After Jeffrey twice refused the invitation to drink, Yussef began carting in a bottle of warm pepsi at each visit. He set it down in front of Jeffrey and explained to the curious host what Ivona translated as, a vow. Jeffrey swilled the syrupy goo and did not object.

He saw no more water that first day, not even bottled. At most halts, all they had to drink was Yussef's warm pepsi, vodka, and an orange glop that children drank and Jeffrey learned to avoid after the first sip. The heat sucked so much moisture from his body that he felt a constant thirst. He took tea whenever it was offered, which was seldom, and remained bloated from pepsi.

In each village there was some antique or collectible on offer. Many were of considerable value, but a cheap trinket sometimes slipped through. Jeffrey was very concerned the first time it happened, conscious of all the warnings he had received from Gregor before traveling.

A man with a face as seamed as the fields outside his village offered all he had, a tiny pendant set with a few semi-precious stones. He croaked his plea with a voice squeaky from disuse. Jeffrey looked at the pendant dangling from a chain long stripped of all silver plating, held by hands that would never lose their own ingrained plating of grime and oil. Out of compassion, Jeffrey offered him ten dollars. He then returned to the car in shame for being taken.

But there was a new warmth to Yussef's voice, and a strange sense of Ivona being less sure of herself than before.

"Yussef has tried to filter out the useless," Ivona said in translation. "But these people are desperate, and sometimes they make wild promises in hopes of gaining a little something once you arrive."

"And refuse to show the product to anyone but the buyer," Jeffrey said, understanding perfectly. "They say it is too valuable to risk displaying to anyone but the person with the money."

Again Ivona hesitated, as though not sure with whom she spoke. Then, "That is correct. Your ten dollars translates into a fortune for one such as him."

The next village brought yet another worthless item, this time a mercury-backed mirror in a cheap turn-of-the-century frame. The woman watched his inspection with desperate eyes, her silent plea made tragic by the trio of quiet children gathered around her chair. He decided on honesty and told the young mother as kindly as possible why he could not offer more than a few dollars. The woman accepted the money with pitiful gratitude, and Yussef showed genuine approval. As they left, Jeffrey was struck by the thought that respectful honesty from a stranger was perhaps a rare commodity.

Then, in the next village, he encountered a find that made the entire trip worthwhile. The farmer dug up a ragged bundle from the edge of his compost heap, and offered it with hands and arms stained the color of old teak. Jeffrey unfolded the wrappings and extracted a belt of almost solid silver.

The *baldric* was a sword belt worn over one shoulder, diagonally across back and chest, and connected with rope or chain or some frilly foppery to the waist. It was long considered an essential part of a gentleman officer's wardrobe. This particular one was French and dated from the Napoleonic empire. French war-eagles of solid silver rested upon fields of aquamarine. Beside them were rubies carved into stars of rank. Then began a series of silver-framed war symbols done in semiprecious stones, separated from one another by silver family shields set upon mother-of-pearl backing. Jeffrey hefted the belt, estimated its weight at fifteen pounds.

"The spoils of war," he said.

"The French left behind more than their lives," Yussef agreed through Ivona, "when Mother Russia introduced them to a real winter."

Vladimir-Volynskij. Luck. Rozisce.
The people were walking lessons in endurance. Serious,

heavy women wore comically colored hats against the heat—beach bonnets, undersized cotton cones, floppy straw hats with pom-poms and ribbons. Those without hats carried rusty, ragged parasols whose bright polyester colors fought valiantly against the onslaught of dust and abuse.

Old men were either bloated with layers of blubber or shrunk to skin of leather and muscles of wire cable. Everyone, even the young, had features creased by constant squints. Expressions were fixed in a variety of emotions. Anger. Suspicion. Hatred. Fear. Uncertainty. Resignation. Rage.

The children were overly small, overly quiet, overly serious. Young men, many of them strikingly handsome in a rough-cut fashion, clung grimly to seventies disco fashion—elaborate razor cuts, rayon shirts, and oversized bell-bottoms—despite the withering heat. Stunningly beautiful girls showed faces marred by permanent suspicion and hostility. By middle age, men appeared scarred and stone cold, the women faded and overweight. This rapid aging gave the young the air of hothouse flowers, brought to an early bloom that would swiftly fade.

Zdolbunov. Slavuta. Iz'aslav.

It began with the simplest question, the smallest observation. As they left one village, Jeffrey watched a bowed farmer and his wife struggle back from the fields under hand-carried loads of hay. Their backs were bent, their faces warped in a struggle as timeless as a Baroque painting. "I wonder why life is like this here," he murmured almost to himself.

To Jeffrey it appeared as though Ivona stirred reluctantly, drawn into something she did not wish to face. Then she began.

"Our way and yours were divorced in the dawn of modern history. Europe was saved from the savagery of the Mongol hordes, and yet still today they talk of the threat with a thrill of fear. There was no one to save Russia. Russia lived under Mongol rule for more than two hundred and fifty years.

While Europe struggled to cast off the Dark Ages and enter the enlightened Renaissance, Russia remained trapped in darkest night."

"It sounds like a children's fairy tale," Jeffrey said.

"It is from such beginnings, too harsh to be told as fact, that ghouls and good fairies arise," Ivona replied. "But what you must remember is that the Russia of today, along with her sister states such as the Ukraine, still bears the Mongol mark. Look deeply into our society, and you will find roots reaching back over one thousand years. The Tartars, as they were known by the Russians, willed to the people their careless ferocity and utter disregard for the value of human life. They burned into our nation the painful lesson of centralized rule. Our first governments were based upon Genghis Khan's military authority, which permitted no question or doubt or opposition whatsoever."

It hit Jeffrey then. Ever since the border, he had been trying to put a finger on Ivona's attitude toward him. She did not show hostility. Nor did she appear angry. Yet there was something, some barrier she pushed at him constantly. Finally he could name it, though he could still not say why it was there. Ivona *disapproved* of him. She radiated rejection.

"The Mongols' code of law was called the *Yasa,* and it had three underlying principles," Ivona continued in her toneless singsong. "The first was that all people were equal under the law, rich and poor alike. The second was that all citizens were bound to their position in society for life. Ambition to rise above one's station was a crime punishable by torture and death. And third, all people lived in complete submission to the Khan's absolute power."

"Sounds a lot like life under the Communists," Jeffrey observed, and wondered why she bothered to teach if she so clearly wished him elsewhere.

"The parallel continues in many different directions, like roots spreading out from a dark and gloomy tree," Ivona replied. Her quiet, lilting tone carried no sense of enthusiasm. She was like a teacher who was being paid to teach but had no confidence in her student. "All land, for example, was owned by the Khan. It was granted out by title to local princes who ruled in the Khan's name. Those who actually worked the land, the serfs, were bound to it and could not leave. When the Mongols were finally defeated, the czars and their princes continued this practice. To be a serf under czarist rule, right up to the beginning of this century, was to be a slave."

"And then came the Communist state, which owned all land in the name of the people. Whoever they were." Jeffrey shook his head. "But to back up for a moment, how did the Russians get rid of the Mongols?"

"By war," Ivona replied simply. "Three hundred years of war, during which the Russians adopted every despotic tactic of their enemy. The state became all powerful, controlling every resource and person in the country. Men appointed to the military became soldiers for life. There was no alternative except death."

Yussef interrupted with a short query. Ivona spoke to him at length. He was silent for a moment, then responded with a few words. She translated them as, "It also taught the Russians to see all the outside world as their enemy."

"Three hundred years of war would do that to anyone," Jeffrey agreed.

"It was during this period that Russia's rulers learned the power of fear as a ruling force," Ivona went on. "Czar Ivan the Terrible established the world's first political police, called the *Oprichniki*. Sight of their uniforms, with emblems of snarling dogs, became enough to instill terror in Russia's citizens. These six thousand cutthroats employed such savage punishments as impaling, flaying alive, boiling, roasting on giant spits, and frying on great skillets against any man, woman, or child declared an enemy of the czar."

Jeffrey turned around so as to inspect the woman's face. She showed no reaction whatsoever to her own words. Ivona calmly viewed the endless dry-brown vista outside her window, her barrier of rejection keeping him at bay.

The road passed through a copse of brown, stunted trees, then ran straight and true across a flat landscape as far as Jeffrey could see.

"Here begin the Steppes," Ivona told him.

Yussef pointed forward and spoke, his words translated

as, "Up ahead there are hills. But beyond Kiev the road runs straight and true for two thousand kilometers. No rise, no curve, no turning. That, my Western friend, is where the real Russia begins."

They passed a cluster of huts, a meager island of humanity in an endless earthen sea. "I've never seen anything like this," Jeffrey said quietly. "Not ever."

"When the Tartars were finally pushed from Russia," Ivona said, "part of their tribe settled in the Crimea, which lies in the southern Ukraine. They continued to sweep out from time to time, even traveling so far as to sack Moscow three times. But by that time they were no longer interested in conquest and occupation. All they sought was booty, especially slaves. For over three hundred years, until the seventeenth century, Tartar hordes swept out year after year, carrying off the youngest and the best, leaving death and destruction in their wake. Still today this impression of the dangerous Ukraine lingers on in many Russian minds. The name itself comes from the Russian word *Okraina,* or Wild Plains."

At a demand from Yussef, Ivona translated what she had been saying. He nodded and spoke for a time, which she translated as, "The endless land is Russia's greatest wealth and Russia's greatest weakness. There were no natural barriers to stop the foes, and towns here were too spread out to help one another against invaders. I once read a story of an official who counted the slaves as they were herded onto the Crimean boats and shipped to the slave markets of Istanbul. After one raid, the number of slaves topped ten thousand men and women, boys and girls. The official grabbed one young man as he passed and demanded, 'Did they leave anyone there for next year?'"

"It's amazing to me," Jeffrey said, "how you could take a lot of these descriptions, modernize them by three hundred years, and be talking about life under Communism."

There was a moment's silence before Yussef's barked command brought Ivona's translation. He spoke a few words, which she did not interpret. Instead, she paused for a long moment, then asked, "You have heard of Stalin's program of Russification?"

"Yes."

"This, too, came from the czars, and as you have heard, they learned it from the Mongols. In the sixteenth century, Ivan III began the rule of *pomestie*, or state ownership of all land. The czar's army forcibly relocated the princes already in place to new lands far away from their original holdings. These new lands were granted on the condition of loyal service, including delivery of a certain number of new soldiers each year. The people themselves were known as *tyaglye kholopy*, or tax-paying slaves. Their duty was to work the land so that the czarist state could support the army required for its endless wars."

Ivona translated for Yussef, who added through her, "The powerful enemy was defeated only by a powerful central government ruling a powerful army. To draw this power together, they had to learn the lesson of ruthlessness. The importance of individual human life was sacrificed to the needs of the state. It is still so today."

"Over the centuries," Ivona went on, "the same problems that later plagued the Communists choked development of the earlier czarist state. The Russian bureaucracy was staffed by people who by law could never be rewarded for good work by promotion. So they became corrupt and ruled according to who held more power and who paid larger bribes. There was little trade, since no one was permitted to make a profit. Cities remained small and distant outposts, since a serf who left his assigned place was put to death."

She paused while Yussef navigated a series of dangerously dark holes in the pitted road, then went on, "Industry had no labor until the state assigned them serfs, and then companies were forbidden by law to reward skills or performance with bonuses or advances of any kind."

She translated for Yussef, who offered, "You can see the consequences even today. The price of centralized government is death of the individual. The body lingers on, but the spirit is crushed."

"So how did you make it through intact?" Jeffrey asked him.

"By being born when people began to see the lie for what it was," Yussef replied through Ivona. "And by having an aunt who taught me from the cradle to value who I was."

"Couldn't other people see they were trapped by the same forces that held them in the past?"

"Much was made of past horrors," Yussef replied. "But Communism was always painted as the great liberator. Disinformation was a powerful weapon. With their total control over the press and the television and the schools, they could deny that all these problems even existed in modern Russia."

"To deny in such a society means that the problem officially disappears," Ivona continued. "Anyone who discusses it also vanishes. End of discussion."

"This policy dominated contact with foreigners also," Yussef added. "Suspicion of foreigners goes back to the dawn of Russian history. Under the czars, citizens were forbidden to travel outside their country. For over five hundred years, they locked away all foreign visitors who threatened to return to their homeland and criticize the Russian government. Even visiting priests who dared to criticize the czarist rule were arrested and put to death."

"More than one thousand years of serfdom," Ivona continued. "How can the world expect these people to learn new ways overnight?"

"Because there isn't any more time than that," Jeffrey replied. "Either they make the change quickly, or their attempt at democracy will fail."

Ivona was silent a long moment, then translated for Yussef. When she was done the young man removed his attention from the road long enough to grant Jeffrey a look of solid approval. Here at least there was assurance. Yussef was pleased to have him around.

Sepetovka. Polonnoje. Berdicev.

Zitomir. Their evening meal took place by lantern light and was entirely of goose. Nothing else. Just goose. Their hosts, a dumpy woman in clothes hand-scrubbed to ragged limpness and a man who treated Yussef as visiting nobility, apologized continually while the goose was cooking. Jeffrey assured them every time the words were translated that goose would be fine.

While their hosts busied themselves in the kitchen, Yussef spoke in a quiet monotone that Ivona translated as, "In the stores there is nothing to buy. Nothing. Shopkeepers put nothing on the shelves even if they receive a shipment. They hold the merchandise in the back room and sell at the state price plus fifty or one hundred percent. People who can afford it either buy at these prices or travel to big cities and go to the new street markets. The others," he shrugged. "Here you see how the others survive."

Jeffrey glanced around the hovel that was to be their home for the night. He took in the scant furniture, the crude homemade trestle table and benches, the lack of any adornment save a tattered photograph of an icon hung from a cracked and pitted wall.

"Life is not as it should be in my country," Yussef spoke solemnly. "Our world should be otherwise. Someday we will learn that this is a wrongness, and one that must end."

When the goose arrived, the couple paid grave thanks to a gracious Yussef. Then they applied themselves to devouring the lot—skin, entrails, bone marrow, and all. Jeffrey squelched his aversion to so much rich meat washed down with warm pepsi. He stuffed himself with roast goose, goose crackling, goose pate, goose liver fried in oil—so much goose that he smelled the greasy odor in his skin.

As dinner was cleared away, the single bulb dangling from the ceiling came to feeble life. He stared in weary wonderment as it was greeted with cries of pleasure and great activity by the woman and her husband.

"Energy cutbacks," Ivona explained. "Twenty-five percent, the authorities promised, but already it is down to three hours of water and electricity per day."

The old man busied himself filling the sink and bath. The woman brought out a pile of dirty laundry, apologized with a gap-toothed smile and words that needed no translation, and hurried away.

"Cooking and washing often take place in the wee hours," Ivona explained.

"Days without light or power this winter," Yussef said

through Ivona. "The thought gives voice to talk more bitter than the bread lines. Imagine a Russian winter in the dark! Word is, the stock of candles and kerosene lanterns has vanished from every city in the land."

"It must be hard for you," Ivona commented, "imagining how life is here for us."

"It is and it isn't," Jeffrey replied. "I am one-quarter Polish, and over the past year I've been coming to know a little about my own heritage. The hardships I've found here appear to be similar, only worse by degrees. I'm not talking about the system, just what the system has done to the common man."

But Ivona and Yussef were caught by what he had said at the beginning. Yussef asked a question, which Ivona translated as, "You are one-quarter Polish?"

"Yes."

"Which quarter?"

Perhaps it was the fatigue of driving and dealing in the day's heat. Perhaps it was the flickering lantern light, which remained a stronger illumination than the room's single overhead bulb. Perhaps it was the sense of calm that pervaded the crudely chinked farmhouse walls, or perhaps merely the companionable light in Yussef's eyes and the questioning doubt of Ivona's gaze.

Whatever the reason, Jeffrey found the question to be perfectly logical. And he gave what to him seemed a perfectly logical answer.

"The most important quarter," he replied. "The part centered around my heart and head."

Upon hearing the translation, Yussef leaned back and nodded slowly. Ivona, on the other hand, appeared truly shaken. Jeffrey found himself too weary and too full to be concerned any longer, about Ivona or anything else. He stood, bid the pair good-night, and made his way back to the single bedroom, which had been vacated for him. He was asleep before his head hit the pillow.

CHAPTER

18

He awoke the next morning to Yussef's impatient knock. Jeffrey rolled from a bumpy mattress that smelled of sweat and cigarette ashes. He folded the ratty covering and dressed in clothes that reeked from the road; everything in his case smelled from the gasoline canisters in the trunk.

The bathroom faucets were dry. He washed in a bucket of water drawn from the brown-stained bath. He walked into the parlor, greeted Yussef and Ivona, and showed ironclad control when pointed toward a breakfast of warm pepsi and day-old bread. He ate and drank in silence, then carried the last sip of pepsi back for brushing his teeth.

The old couple were moving about in the room where he had slept. While Ivona and Yussef dressed, Jeffrey seated himself at the table and took out his pocket New Testament. Though he did not like reading it in public, and though he had no great desire to read at all that morning, he knew he needed to. Holding to the discipline of daily Bible time was a link to who he was, and who he had grown to be over the past few years. Within minutes of seating himself, Jeffrey was lifted away from all the poverty, all the trauma, all the difficulty, all the discomfort. He read and he spoke a silent prayer and he found a touch of home in an alien world, a taste of peace in a time of upheaval, a time of healing in this wounded land.

He felt eyes upon him and looked up to see Yussef staring. The rail-thin young man bore a look of confusion that bordered on pain. Yussef started to speak, but Ivona chose that moment to step from the bathroom. He cocked his head toward the front door. Time to go.

They drove only a few kilometers before Yussef stopped as close as he could come to a filling station. The line for gasoline was very long.

His eyes on the car in front of them, Yussef spoke in surprisingly hesitant tones. Ivona translated, "I wish to ask you something."

Jeffrey stretched as far as the car's cramped confines would allow. "Fire away."

Yussef spoke again. When Ivona did not interpret, Jeffrey turned around to find her staring at Yussef, a look of bafflement on her features. Yussef spoke to her again, but without his normal brusqueness. Still she did not reply. Quietly Yussef urged her.

Her eyes still on her nephew, she asked, "Are you a devout man?"

For the first time since passing the border, Jeffrey found himself able to ignore the heat. "I think only God can know a man's heart," he replied. "So it is for the Father to say how true to His word a man is. But I try. That much I can say. I have accepted Christ as my Savior, and I try to live by God's Word."

Something in what Jeffrey said agitated Ivona very much. Her voice seemed to tremble slightly as she translated. Yussef then asked through her, "You were reading the Bible this morning at the table?"

"The New Testament. Yes."

"You do this every day?"

"I try to. It is my time with my Lord," he replied simply.

"For this you need no church?"

"A quiet place and some privacy would be nice," Jeffrey replied. "But no, nothing special is required except a prayerful heart."

Yussef said through a very subdued Ivona, "I watched you. I think I could see this prayerful heart on your face."

"I would be happy to read with you some morning," Jeffrey offered.

"You would do this?"

"Of course."

Yussef rubbed a hand down the stubble on his cheek. "I thank you for the invitation. I will think on it."

When they finally arrived at the pumps, Yussef motioned for them to stay inside. He climbed from the car and spoke long and hard with the attendant. Money was exchanged at intervals after pleading arguments. Gasoline was doled out in twenty-liter lots. When the extra canisters in the trunk were finally revealed, the attendant replied with frantic hand waving and head shaking. Yussef made certain no other car could see and revealed American dollars. The atmosphere magically changed. The tank was topped off, the canisters filled, and the attendant saw them off with a wave.

Once they were again underway, Jeffrey said quietly, "I sure would love a cup of coffee." And a bath, he added to himself. And a bed with clean sheets. And food that doesn't have me crunching on grit. But he would settle for a coffee. "Or tea."

"Coffee is hard to find outside the big cities' black markets," Ivona replied. "Tea is a different story. The former Soviet Union grew quite a good tea in the Muslim states and imported more from China and Vietnam. But the new states are desperate for hard currency and refuse to accept the ruble in payment. Now we receive only what we can barter for, and as our industrial base falters, it becomes increasingly difficult to find things they wish to buy."

They pulled into a dusty square left breathless by the heat. There was not the first hint of breeze. A pair of trees stood with leaves glued to an empty sky. Jeffrey eased from the car, his shirt welded to his skin with a coating of dried sweat. It was nine o'clock in the morning.

Their destination was an apartment in an older building which, before the Communists chopped it up, had been a village manor. Their hostess was a small, swarthy woman who kept the night's coolness trapped within closed windows and drawn curtains. A beautiful teenaged girl ignored the visitors as well as her mother's repeated screams, sulking off to whichever room they were not using. But when the woman brought out her parcel and unwrapped the multiple layers, the teenager was immediately forgotten.

The snuffbox was dated 1782 and stamped with the royal crest of Catherine the Great. Catherine ruled all of Russia for thirty-four years, after deposing her own husband in 1762. She was a ruthless libertine who plotted her husband's assassination with a favorite lover—one of over two dozen. She was also an extremely efficient ruler who founded universities and museums with the same free-wheeling verve she applied to her private life. And Catherine loved her snuff. She was known for keeping jeweled snuffboxes in every chamber of her vast palaces and for passing them out to favorite subjects as the fancy took her. It was her habit to dip only with her left hand, so that the right would always be clean for her visitors to kiss.

This particular snuffbox depicted her predecessor, Peter the Great, mounted on a proud war horse. The box was wrought of enameled silver, the emperor and his horse were gold, standing on a boulder of mother of pearl. Thirty matched diamonds encircled the scene.

From a queen's palace to a dusty backwater village. With a silent sigh Jeffrey handed back the parcel, began the lengthy purchasing discussions, and wished that the box could tell its tale.

Thus was the pattern for their days established—up at dawn, a quick breakfast, a hasty wash, a brief time of prayer and study for Jeffrey. Then they would be under way, driving through scalding heat toward another gray-washed village.

Several times Jeffrey invited Yussef to read and pray with him. Yussef always responded with the same reply: he was not yet ready. And yet he continued with his hesitant questions. Ivona translated, although their discussions clearly disturbed her.

Katya's absence was a wound inflamed by every motion, every experience. Each breath of feeling that drifted through his heart was accompanied by the thought that he was incomplete without her. Life was not as it should be unless she was by his side.

Yussef had done his work well. There were very few unimportant items, very few wasted visits. He had also succeeded in reducing the number of icons offered to just one. This was a relief to Jeffrey; by now, most London antique shops had sprouted walls of ancient holy images. Russians fleeing to the West had brought them in droves, and the flood of merchandise had dropped the price to one twentieth of what it had been before glasnost.

Their icon appeared on the fourth day. It was an *Elevsa*, the form that showed Mary embracing the Christ-child, usually with their cheeks touching. The other major form, known as a *Hodigitria*, depicted Mary and the Child separate; usually the baby was painted in the act of blessing the viewer, sometimes holding the holy Book in his left hand. This particular icon was encased in three overlapping silver frames. Enameled into the silver, to either side of the central figures, were paintings of two Russian saints, their names etched in Cyrillic above their heads. The item probably dated back to the late sixteenth century and was clearly of value to a collector.

Yet another item found that fourth day would have brightened the eyes of Jeffrey's friend Pavel Rokovski, an official of the Ministry of Culture in Poland. It was a silver casket, about ten inches square and eight inches high, whose entire exterior was decorated with gold wire woven into an intricate Oriental motif. It clearly dated from the late sixteenth century, when this part of present-day Ukraine was Polish soil. The styles of that era were largely drawn from Persia, which at the time bordered the empire's southern reaches. Floral patterns twined their way about hexagonal shapes, in keeping with the Koran's prohibition against depicting the human form. Along the front, golden pillars supported a domed and sweeping roof, as found upon Persian palaces of that day. The casket was supported by four balled feet of gold-studded lapis lazuli.

After each visit, as they returned to the car and the heat and the drive, Ivona continued with her endless instruction. As the hours and days dragged on, Jeffrey found it increasingly difficult to feign an interest in her lessons. But still she continued. She hammered at him with soft-spoken chisel strokes of her tongue, pressing and pressing and pressing him to learn.

By the sixth and final day, however, Jeffrey found it almost impossible to listen to Ivona's droning lessons. He was exhausted by the heat, the constant stop-and-go driving, the unpalatable food. He was tired of wearing dirty clothes, tired of trying to do business in a foreign tongue. He missed Katya fiercely. And on top of these irritants, the barrage of bounces in a car utterly lacking in shocks had brought on a recurrence of his nagging neck pain.

That afternoon they were cruising along at a modest speed when the car dive-bombed off the end of the pavement. The road went on; the pavement simply ceased. No warning, no markings, just a razor-cut across the road and a ten-inch drop from asphalt to gravel. Jeffrey felt the jar right down to his toenails. His neck and back began complaining in the strongest possible terms.

By evening his patience was worn thin as tissue paper. They were staying in a faceless apartment block, their dinner punctuated by a continual racket from the hallways and other apartments—music blaring, babies crying, adults screaming, children shouting and playing tag up and down the stairs. No one else paid the slightest attention to the babble. The middle-aged couple who were hosting them looked too bowed down by their own internal troubles to pay anyone or anything much mind. And throughout the meal, Ivona continued her endless recital of facts and data.

Finally he had had enough. Too much, in fact. Jeffrey set down his fork and demanded, "Why are you telling me all this?"

His was the one question she did not expect, and it stopped her cold. "I—What?"

"All this information. Why are you telling me?"

"I—" She stopped again, blue eyes blinking hugely behind heavy frames. "To help you."

"To help me what? Buy antiques? That's what I'm here for, isn't it?" His neck's throbbing pain felt as though it hacked at his brain. "How does it help, can you tell me that?"

"You don't want to know?"

"Of course I want to know. But this—" He waved his arm to take it all in and winced as the movement sent a lance through his back. "You're going to all this trouble, force-feeding me information all the time, nonstop, for what reason?"

Ivona faltered visibly, and her English slipped a notch. "Is not good information?"

"Of course it's good. It's great. It's incredible. I've been given a six-day university course. But why? For Yussef, sure, it's fine, he's your nephew, you teach him. But why me? You don't know me, you may never see me again, and yet you never let up teaching me. I can see you're absolutely exhausted. We all are, yet still you go on. Why?"

She did not reply. Jeffrey watched her face and decided he'd insulted her so badly she would depart right then and leave him to fend for himself in a foreign tongue. He searched for an apology, but could not think past the pain. He stood and left the silent room for bed.

• • •

"What did he ask you?" Yussef demanded.

Ivona replied, her habitual lilt muted by shock.

"Naive, you called him," Yussef scoffed. "A mere boy in a man's body. A Westerner who sees nothing but gain."

"How could an American be so suspicious?" Ivona asked.

"I'll tell you how." Yussef rose to his feet. "By being twice the man you give him credit for. Ten times."

"I was so sure you were wrong," she said.

Yussef barked a short laugh. "Go. Go and speak to your bishop. Tell him I have found the man who will help us."

CHAPTER
19

Once they were under way the next morning, Ivona announced, "There has been a change of plans."

"Fine," Jeffrey said. "Listen, I need—"

"There is someone we wish for you to meet. His name is Bishop Michael Denisov. He is one of the leaders of the Ukrainian Rites Church."

"Sounds great," Jeffrey replied. "But I'd just like to apologize—"

"There is something I must first tell you, however," Ivona continued in her softly warbled drone, unwilling to hear what he had to say. "You need to know a bit of the background to what we face here."

"Fine." Jeffrey leaned back in defeat. "Let's hear it."

"During the Communist era," Ivona explained, "the Russian Orthodox Church was the only church recognized by the Soviet state. The Ukrainian Rites Catholic Church was outlawed in 1946. Stalin saw the Ukrainian church as too patriotic. Nationalism to anything but the Soviet state was in Stalin's times one of the gravest crimes one could commit. Stalin needed the Ukrainians' assistance in fighting the Germans, so he did nothing until the end of the war. But in 1946 he convened a synod of all Ukrainian bishops. He gave them two choices. Either they would disband the church and instruct all believers to become Orthodox, or Stalin promised to exterminate every Ukrainian Catholic—man, woman, and child."

"The Orthodox church was under Stalin's control?" Jeffrey asked, and swiped at his forehead. Only eight o'clock in the morning and already the breeze through the car's open windows was hot as a blow dryer. Outside, the landscape crawled by in unrelenting sameness.

"There is no way to be certain," Ivona replied. "What is sure is that the Orthodox church has been a part of the Russian state government for centuries. It was more centrally organized, and it was more controllable than something based in Lvov or Kiev and owing allegiance to a nation that would never again exist, if Stalin had his way."

Yussef gave his quiet command, and Ivona translated for him. He shook his head, gave a few sharp words in reply. Ivona translated them as, "The Ukrainian church has suffered as the Ukrainian people have suffered. And now the Ukrainian Catholic church and the Russian Orthodox are locked in a very serious struggle. That is all you need to know." She watched the young man driving, and continued, "The young have little time for discussion. The Communists fed them a lifetime of twisted words, words warped into lies. Now the young wish to act. I cannot fault them for this lack of patience."

"So Stalin tried to wipe the Ukrainian church off the map," Jeffrey said, wondering anew how she managed to stay so intact in this heat.

"The Communists tried to extinguish the fire in the hearts of Ukrainians," Ivona replied. "They sought to crush all that was great. In these many decades, people here have learned to live with the worst. Few can even remember the time when their church was not something hidden in cellars and their faith not practiced in secret. Fewer still know of any great Ukrainian saint or artist or king or poet, because the Soviets sought to erase all memory of their names. This was what it meant to live under Soviet domination. This was the punishment of the innocents."

·   ·   ·

Bishop Michael Denisov greeted Jeffrey with an appearance that was the only falsehood about him. He looked so gentle, so frail, so helpless in the face of all the turmoil and hardship that surrounded him. He beamed pleasant defenselessness to all he surveyed, displaying a weakness that Jeffrey sensed was not the least bit real.

"Last year, I am letting my assistant go off for a doctorate," he said, ushering Jeffrey into a cramped little flat owned by two local church members. Jeffrey showed no emotion as Yussef planted yet another warm pepsi on the table in front of him, then retreated to the sofa beside Ivona. "Can you believe?" the bishop continued. "Who is needing a doctorate here? But, okay, there is no excuse for me, selfishness is not a holy virtue, I have to let him go. And now I am alone."

His face was aged, yet strangely unlined. His hair was snow-white and so very soft, like his gaze, which blessed everything it touched with humble peace. He moved not with an old man's shuffling gait, but rather like a balloon tethered to an impatient hand, bouncing here and there, attracted to all it saw but returning to its original path with little jerky motions. His English was somewhat mangled, but delightfully so, and his accent strong but understandable.

Jeffrey motioned toward where Ivona translated quietly for Yussef. "You don't look too alone to me."

"Yes, friends. Thank the God above for friends, no? But I tell you, brother, what we are needing more than all else is priests. First priests, then money. We are drowning in work. Drowning! And my assistant, where is he? Studying for a doctorate in Rome. But the walls, they have all come down. How can I refuse my assistant his lifelong dream?"

"I think you did the right thing," Jeffrey replied.

"You think yes?" The bishop gave a happy shrug. "Thank you, dear brother. Maybe. Maybe. But what you don't know is my church, it is having no doctorates. Not even the bishops! The apostolic delegate, yes, he is having such a title. But my assistant, he is studying Petrology. You know what is this?"

"No idea at all."

"No, nor I!" The bishop seemed delighted by the fact. "He will return and I will be having an assistant who is knowing more than his bishop. What do you think of that?"

"I think there are all kinds of wisdom, most of which does not come from books," Jeffrey replied, liking him. "Where did you learn your English?"

"Oh, dear Jeffrey, life is so full of moments that you don't expect. I am having big experiences in Newark, New Jersey. Big experiences! I was there two years, can you believe that? After I escape from the Ukraine, I am studying for priesthood in Rome. Then I am working in France, always with refugees from our homeland. Many, many people escape. So many. One million flee in 1920 alone, oh, yes, and even with so many difficulties and hardships, still there are people escaping over years, just like me. We are having our own diaspora, just like the Jews into Babylon. Yes, so many tragedies. So, I am sent to the United States for two years, and still my English, it sounds like I am learning last week."

"Your English is fine."

The bishop wagged his finger. "Now, now, dear Jeffrey. You must not tell falsehoods, are you not knowing your Bible? Look at Ivona here, never out of the Ukraine since a child, and still she speaks perfect English, does she not?"

"She speaks better English than I do."

"Oh, no, no, dear, no. There you are, falsehoods, falsehoods. This will not do, brother Jeffrey. We must have truth even in compliments, yes? So. I am without an assistant, and I must use my very poor English to ask help from a brother in Christ, yes?"

"Yes," Jeffrey agreed, letting his smile loose.

"So. How to explain, how to begin." The bishop sighed happily. "The Ukrainian Rites Catholic Church is in communion with the Pope, while the Russian Orthodox is not, do you see?"

"I think so."

"Excellent, excellent." The bishop beamed his approval. "Ukrainian Catholics are therefore called Uniates, because we are united with other Catholics. But our liturgy, dear Jeffrey, our services, are very much Byzantine. Uniates, yes. And then there are the Orthodox. Ivona has told you of them?"

"A little."

"They have many problems, dear Jeffrey. Oh, so many

problems. Now they are having Orthodox believers in many cities who want to make a new church, separate from Moscow, separate from Rome, separate from everybody. And not just here. Just like the Soviet states, how they are dividing, right now, right now, this very moment the church is in explosion after explosion. Estonia, Latvia, Belarus, Georgia, Lithuania, everywhere there is problems with nationalism and patriotism and Orthodox faith."

"And with your own church, if I understood Ivona correctly."

The gentleman's gaze dimmed. "Ah, dear brother, what problems you cannot imagine. Last year, we had a synod of our bishops. You are knowing this word, synod?"

"A conference," Jeffrey offered.

"Yes, a conference of bishops. The first true synod in one hundred and one years exactly. The Synod of Lvov, pronounced *Livief* in Ukrainian. Many of my brothers, almost half, they were consecrated in hiding. You see, brother Jeffrey, in 1946 Stalin was outlawing our church. Yes. But many people did not wish to become Orthodox, they are staying to the faith of their fathers, and their fathers' before them.

"Yes. Back thirty generations, this tie to the Ukrainian church. Stalin hated this. Our church was a threat to his one great Soviet state. So our priests and bishops, they only worked in secret. Great danger, dear Jeffrey, such danger you cannot imagine. They gave Masses in cellars and they christened in trucks and they met only in night. Still there were the spies and the informers, and many died. Believers and priests and bishops, many suffered. But many still believed, dear Jeffrey."

"And now it's all changed."

"Not changed, my brother. Oh, no, no. *Changing*. All is still difficult for us. Our churches, take our churches for example. Last year, we are finally receiving our cathedral, the St. George Cathedral here in Lvov, and the archbishop-general, he is now residing there. But the others, oh, Jeffrey, you cannot imagine."

"I've seen a few," Jeffrey replied grimly.

"For seventy years they have been stables. They have been warehouses. They have been crematoriums and laboratories and homes for the insane. Whatever the state could do that was bad to God's house, they did. Then in 1991, under glasnost, all the churches are being given back. More than six thousand churches, Jeffrey, can you imagine? Six thousand churches, and most of them in ruins. But this is not the problem, dear brother. No. The problem is who *received* these churches."

"The Orthodox," Jeffrey guessed.

The bishop clapped his hands. "Precisely! And do they want to share with us? No! Will they even speak with us? No! So now the Ukrainian government, first it declared independence on August 24, 1991. Then the new parliament, it *ordered* the Russian Orthodox Church to give back our churches. And still, dear brother, still they are doing nothing. But we, dear Jeffrey, we cannot wait! We have people calling to us in the street, begging us for Mass and schools and, oh, they ask for so much, and we have no place, no place! So do you know what we are doing?"

"Taking over the unused churches?" Jeffrey offered.

"If only, dear brother. If only we could. But an unused church, what do you think of a building that was seven hundred years old, and then was a stable, and then was a garage for trucks, and then was left without doors for thirty years?"

"Rubble."

"No roof, no windows, rain and snow and dirt. Oh, my brother, you cannot imagine how it pains me to go into our churches." He shook it off. "No, we *share* churches with the Orthodox. And what sharing! We hold Masses at different times, yes, but our priests, they pass like strangers down different aisles. They do not speak, they do not see each other. And what are we teaching the people who come?"

"Not love, that's for sure."

"Yes! You understand!" The bishop cast a look back toward Ivona. "So now we decide, we call them brothers. Yes. Now we are having the freedom with the religion, with our faith, so now we must show ourselves as Christians. We begin. We take steps. We are blind to anger. We give in Christ's name and see only that they are Christians. Human, yes, but brothers in our Lord. Only the heart we see. Only the good. And slowly things change. Not with all priests, no, dear brother, not theirs, not ours. But many. We see smiles. We share what we have. We *pray* together."

He stopped.

"And then?"

"Yes." Bishop Michael sighed the word. "There must be a then, no? I am here, I am asking for help, so change has come. A bad change."

"Something was taken," Jeffrey guessed.

When Ivona had translated for Yussef, the young man rewarded him with an approving look. Bishop Michael nodded. "Of course. You are intelligent man. You are *perceptive* man. But are you honorable? That is what we must know. Because, dear brother Jeffrey, this is a problem of great importance. Oh, so great. Yes, so I must ask, and then I must answer all the others who ask the same question. Is this American honorable?"

Jeffrey found himself with nothing to say.

The bishop nodded from the waist, bobbing back and forward in time to his words. "Yes, you are right, dear brother. There is no answer you can give. Not in words. Just in action. So. Do I trust you or not?" Still giving his gentle body motion, he closed his eyes, waited, then said, "I am thinking yes. So. Yes, dear brother. You are right but not right. Not something was taken, but *things*. Many things."

"Antiques," Jeffrey hazarded.

"Treasures," Bishop Michael corrected, then settled back as to begin a tale. "There is a street in Lvov, dear brother, called Ameryka. It was lined with great houses. People in last century went to the United States, they worked, they came home, and they built great houses with their money. There was a church. A beautiful church. Church of St. Ivana, yes. The Communists, they made the front hall into Party offices and the back into oil storage depot. But you see, dear Jeffrey, it had doors. It had windows. Bad smell from oil, yes, but we could start there. So what we do, we *invite* our Orthodox brothers to come with us. Yes. Come and pray, we say. There are also Orthodox who need priests here. Come and share. And they do, dear Jeffrey. They come. But some people, they do not like this."

"People in the Orthodox church complained about the two

groups working closely together?"

"Their church, our church, government, everywhere there are people who like and not like. Big problems, dear brother. So big. And then, we discover the crypt. No, not discover. You know that word, crypt?"

"Yes."

"A few know of crypt. Not many. One priest now in Poland, he was told by another priest, who was told—" Bishop Michael waved it aside. "No matter. We know. The church was built on older church. No, not on."

"The church was erected on the foundations of an earlier church," Jeffrey offered.

"Exactly, dear brother. You are seeing churches here. Christianity is old here, oh, so very old. The first churches, they used for building wood and the old bricks, and they crumble. With time new churches of stone were built, yes? But the foundations, dear brother, they remain. And crypts, yes, some were old. More than old. Ancient. From the great Kingdom of Kiev. Yes. Before Mongols, before invaders from Asia. Before power moves to Muscovy. Old."

"And forgotten." Jeffrey nodded. "A perfect place to hide treasures."

"Exactly!" The bishop began his nodding motion once more. "So when the Revolution starts, you know, in the twenties, up come the stones, these heavy stones in the floor, up they come, and church treasures from all over Ukraine, those they could bring in time, they are placed inside crypts. Inside coffins. Quickly, quickly, because outside there are fires and riots and battles. Chaos everywhere, dear brother. Churches full, people pray to be taken away. People are searching sky for Christ. With so much chaos, many people are saying *must* be Second Coming. But Christ is not coming, only Communists. Battles are coming closer, and the stones, you know, they were put back and the rings were cut out, so no one could see where was the stairs down."

"And then the Communists arrive," Jeffrey said. "And you wait. Amazing."

"Yes, dear brother. We wait. All over world we wait for time to come home. And now we are here. And we have people starving and churches ruined, oh, so many problems. So we open the crypt, yes, and the treasures, they are still there. Amazing!"

"And then they were taken."

"Stolen," the bishop agreed. "The crypt is opened, and after two nights it is empty."

"Do you know who did it?"

"I know what people *say,* dear brother."

"The Orthodox?" Jeffrey stared at him. "Orthodox priests stole from you?"

Bishop Michael spread his hands wide. "Is not strange? Strange they would come in robes to steal? Strange they leave Orthodox cross on broken chain? Torn robe?"

"Those are the clues you have? It sounds almost as though they wanted you to think it was them," Jeffrey said.

The bishop clapped his hands in agreement. "So do I think also! And others! Orthodox also! We have new friends, dear brother. Friends in Christ, they pray with us, and they are friends. They look. They go where we cannot. They tell us, yes, there are whispers here and there of treasures. Big gathering of treasures in Saint Petersburg. Too great to leave Russia easy. Icons and altars and miters and oh, so many things."

"And they sound like your pieces?"

"Some, yes. Some not sound, *are.*"

"A big city like Saint Petersburg, close to the sea and having strong ties to the West; it would be a perfect gathering point." Jeffrey thought it over, glanced around the impoverished apartment, reflected on how much the bishop was struggling to accomplish with so little. He reached his decision and said, "So you want me to go to Saint Petersburg as a buyer."

The bishop weighed the air in open hands. "Is little chance they sell to you, brother. They are finding better prices in West, less problems with money. But yes, you have *reason* to be in Saint Petersburg. You go, Yussef goes as your hunter, like here, and Ivona goes too."

"As my translator, just like here." Jeffrey nodded agreement. "Where do I start?"

Bishop Michael examined him. "You are helping us?"

"I am helping you," Jeffrey confirmed. "If you like. I will

have to speak with my boss in London before saying for sure, but I think he will agree."

"You take care? Great care? There is danger, dear brother. No treasure worth life."

"I have already promised my wife to be extra careful."

Bishop Michael nodded as though this made perfect sense. "Then you must know all."

"There's more?"

"Oh yes, dear brother." The bishop took a careful breath, then continued. "We are also needing help for finding what was there *before*."

"You're telling me," Jeffrey said, once they were underway, "that the priests found other treasure already in the crypt when they took their own valuables down?"

"It was a good hiding place when the Communists arrived," Ivona replied. "It had been so before. Long before."

They made their rocking way back toward the Polish border, the car's windows opened wide in a futile effort to reduce the heat. The air blowing in felt drawn from a blast furnace. The sweat dried as fast as it poured from Jeffrey's body.

"How long?" he asked her.

"No one knows for certain," she answered. "Perhaps as long as a thousand years. Long enough for all records and all memories to be washed away in the sea of time."

"So they opened up this ancient crypt to put in the church's valuables and found somebody else had the same idea a couple hundred years before." Jeffrey smiled at the idea. "Bet they were surprised."

Ivona translated for Yussef, who replied, "They were too busy to be surprised for long."

"So you've got two sets of treasures that have been taken together to Saint Petersburg—you hope." Despite the heat, Jeffrey felt the faintest surge of adventure thrill. "Do you know what the first treasures were?"

"Not for certain," Ivona replied, "but perhaps an idea. In the ninth century, Lvov was the provincial capital of the Kingdom of Kiev. Sometimes it is also called the First Kingdom of Rus. It was a great center of learning in those days, and of tremendous wealth, especially within the house of Rurik. One of the Rurik princes ruled Lvov when the first Asian hordes swept down out of the Steppes. Khazars, Pechenegs, Polovtsys—historians argue over which tribe finally defeated the First Kingdom. But in the twelfth century first Kiev and then Lvov were sacked, and the center of power in Rus shifted to the more easily defendable Muscovy."

She dabbed the perspiration beading on her temples with an embroidered handkerchief. "The Rurik crown jewels were never recovered. Legends abounded, but nothing was ever located."

Jeffrey twisted in his seat and examined her impassive face. "Treasures have lain hidden under this church for over seven hundred years?"

She translated for Yussef, who replied, "A wooden structure burns and falls upon a stone floor. Records burn with the rest of the city. All the city's noblemen and priests are murdered." He shrugged over the steering wheel. "A river of blood and a mountain of ashes. Those were the only records the invaders left behind. It would be easy to lose a world of secrets beneath them."

Jeffrey Allen Sinclair arrived back at the border feeling as though he wore a second skin of grit. He climbed out of the car with the stiffness of one several days in the saddle. Yussef came around and asked through Ivona, "How is your neck?"

"Still there."

Yussef gave his discolored smile. "It shouts to you, does it?"

"Only when I blink," Jeffrey replied. "No, seriously, it's much better. And it's been worth it."

"No doubt you will enjoy a bath tonight."

Jeffrey looked down at his rumpled form. "I've probably been dirtier," he replied, "but not since I was five years old and rolled around in mud puddles."

Yussef grinned. "There is a certain flavor to friendship

after a week of such work, yes?"

"Flavor and aroma both," Jeffrey agreed. "It's been great, though. Really."

Yussef spoke again. Ivona's internal struggle and hesitant voice returned. She gave Yussef an affronted stare before translating, "Can you tell me, where did you learn to read Bible?"

"I've studied with some different people," Jeffrey replied. "And I've read some books. But the most important lessons for me have come through God showing me some special message in His Word. I know that's hard to understand, but it is true."

"Yes," Yussef responded once Ivona's flat-toned translation was completed. "I see that you speak what is truth. For you."

"For anyone," Jeffrey replied. "For anyone willing to read God's Word with a listening heart."

"I have watched you," Yussef said, as though trying to convince himself. "You live what you believe."

"I have doubts," Jeffrey countered. "I have difficulties. But I try to do as He commands."

"Well said." Yussef scuffed his shoe in the dust, studied the road stretching out before him, decided, "I will think on what you say."

"And I will pray for you," Jeffrey replied quietly.

"A kindness for which I am grateful." He straightened from his thoughtful slouch. "Now, to business."

Yussef motioned toward fenced pens where crowds of exhausted-looking people stood in the dust and the heat. "Usually there are between three and four thousand people in the holding areas, waiting to cross from the Ukraine into Poland. They are treated horribly by the guards because they're the poorest. They can't afford cars, so their bribes will be small. Give me thirty dollars, and I'll take care of your way out."

"All right." Jeffrey handed over the money. "How will you get the items we've purchased across the border?" he asked, and instantly regretted the question. "Sorry."

When Ivona had translated, the young man laughed. "You will not pass it on to other dealers?"

"I need no other dealer in the Ukraine," Jeffrey replied simply. "Not ever."

Yussef grinned at the translation and then explained. "According to the law of today, what I take out of the country is not illegal. But yesterday it was, and tomorrow again, perhaps. Besides, such wealth is an invitation to every dishonest guard at the border, yes? So I stock heavy items that will require a large bribe. Automobile parts and wrenches are the best. Underneath is a false bottom to both the trunk and the backseat. It is too much trouble for the guards to shift all that weight, and too unlikely that a simple trader would carry anything else." He showed his gap-toothed grin. "Sometimes it is best to look the peasant, no?"

"Yes," Jeffrey agreed, and offered his hand. "These were the longest days of my life. I can't say it was fun, but I learned a lot, and I am grateful for the company."

Yussef accepted the hand. "You share your Cracow friend's honesty." Ivona hesitated a moment, then continued translating, "Bishop Michael was right to trust you."

"I will try to help."

"You *will* help, of that I am sure." Yussef pointed beyond the border station. "There is a bus just across the frontier at Medyka which leaves every two hours for Cracow. With luck, you will arrive at the Hotel Cracovia before midnight."

Making for another very long day, Jeffrey thought, and said, "Fine."

"You will travel to Saint Petersburg tomorrow?"

"If I can get a flight, yes." And if Katya doesn't mind too much, he added to himself.

"Then we shall see each other in the big city." Yussef grinned. "I will keep looking for antiques there through my contacts, and I will bring you anything I can find of value."

"Great."

"It is indeed our good fortune that you have this other business to take you to Saint Petersburg." He examined Jeffrey, added, "You would call it a miracle, no?"

"I find God's hand in almost every part of my life these days," Jeffrey replied. "Will you consider praying with me when we meet there?"

"It is so important? That I pray with you?"

162

"It is important that you pray," Jeffrey replied. "With or without me."

Yussef nodded and changed the subject. "You will come to the Ukraine again?"

"If you like."

"I like very much. Your coming has enriched our lives as well." He clapped Jeffrey's shoulder, then said, "Wait here while I arrange your passage through the border."

When he was gone, Jeffrey turned to Ivona and began, "I can't thank—"

She handed him a slip of paper. "This is the name of a small guesthouse run by Ukrainian friends of ours in Saint Petersburg. They are people you can trust. You will be much safer there than in the larger hotels."

Jeffrey nodded his acceptance, both of the news and of her barriers. "All right."

"I will depart from Lvov by train before dawn," Ivona told him. "I should arrive in Saint Petersburg that afternoon. As the bishop explained, I will act as your interpreter whenever you need me. If anyone asks, you should explain that we worked together here and that you asked me to join you. With work in dollars so hard to come by, there should be no questioning of this."

"I understand."

"Yussef will travel as your buyer. When you do not need us, we will continue with our search for the missing church treasures." She nodded to where Yussef was motioning for him to come, and said, "Goodbye, Mr. Sinclair. Until we meet in Saint Petersburg."

CHAPTER
20

Jeffrey watched his plane descend through smoggy Saint Petersburg skies and missed Katya with an ache that had settled in his bones. The very fiber of his being knew the need of her. That his heart continued to beat so steadily baffled him.

Their telephone conversation had been surprisingly smooth and intensely painful. Katya had listened carefully as he described the trip, the problem, and the need for him to travel on to Saint Petersburg immediately. "Five days," she had said quietly when he was finished. "Five days more is all I can bear."

"I miss you," he said, feeling the words carried by a wind that scorched the heart's lining.

"I woke up this morning and reached for you," she said, her voice a sorrowful tune. "When I realized you weren't there, and how far away you were, I started crying."

"Katya," he whispered.

"I couldn't help it," she said, the words trembling like leaves in rainfall. "My heart wasn't there where he was supposed to be."

"Five days," he agreed. "I'll confirm the reservation from Saint Petersburg back to London before I fly out tomorrow."

• • •

Only one shuttle bus was there to meet the plane from Cracow. It was too small and soon full. Jeffrey came off the plane too late to have a place. He milled about with a hundred or so other passengers until a militiaman finally arrived and escorted them to the terminal on foot.

The hall was vast, as high as it was long. On the distant domed ceiling, ornate cupolas and gilded wreaths surrounded square paintings of bombers flying overhead and releasing scores of paratroopers. Jeffrey joined the jostling throng and filled out the required currency declaration form, listing his watch and wedding ring as instructed. He fought his way through the worried passengers calling in a dozen different tongues as bags were tossed carelessly onto the single revolving band. After a wait, he picked up his bag and headed through customs.

The exit was a squeeze. Currency traders and taxi drivers jostled one another and called out offerings of business. A harried Intourist guide shouted warnings to avoid unofficial traders because many were giving out counterfeit bills. Her voice was drowned out by the clamor.

Three paces later a leather-jacketed young man approached Jeffrey and insisted, "Ten dollars, six thousand eight hundred rubles. Bank only give you five thousand nine hundred. You change, yes?"

"No thank you."

"Why you not change?" The man moved to block his progress toward the taxi rank. "This good rate. You save big. You change how much?"

"*Vsyo, vsyo!*" A driver ran up and shooed the man away, then led Jeffrey back toward his taxi, a relic from a bygone era. He was a little man with pudgy features creased into a worried frown. He accepted Ivona's slip of paper, read the address printed in Cyrillic, said something Jeffrey could not understand. Then he gunned his motor and they sped off.

Saint Petersburg wore the air of a queen in a royal sulk. The city remained dressed in the imperial finery decreed by Peter the Great, founder of the Russian empire. Yet eight long Communist decades had left her sullen and slightly wilted. Buildings cried out for a good cleaning. Filth clogged every pore. Dust erased the sea's perfume and choked the air.

The city was rimmed by water and laced with canals. Narrow cobblestone streets opened suddenly into great thoroughfares, which emptied into sweeping royal plazas, then closed again into cramped alleys. Bridges were poorly preserved works of art.

The guesthouse was located on the Nevsky Prospekt, one of the city's main thoroughfares. No sign announced its presence. The taxi driver stopped in front of what appeared to be storefront windows masked by heavy drapes and pointed down a set of stairs leading to an entrance slightly below street level. Jeffrey paid him and motioned for him to remain while Jeffrey made sure the place was open for business. The driver nodded as though he understood, but as soon as Jeffrey had pulled out his suitcase and closed the trunk, the driver was away.

Jeffrey turned to find a tall, dark-haired man come bounding up the stairs. "You Sinclair?"

"Yes. Is—"

He was about Jeffrey's age, but his face appeared to have lived through twice the number of winters. "How much you pay that driver?"

"What he asked. Twenty dollars."

The young man shook his fist and shouted abuse after the rapidly vanishing taxi. Then he turned and grinned. "Is okay. You rich American, yes? You pay four times cost for taxi, maybe ten times cost for room."

"No. That is—" Jeffrey stopped. "Four times what I was supposed to pay?"

The young man laughed. "Hey, is no big problem. He bring you where you want to go, not to place where gang wait and take everything, maybe your life." He reached for Jeffrey's case, hefted it, said, "Welcome to Saint Petersburg, Sinclair."

The stairs led down to a glass-door entrance that still bore faint remnants of its former business. "This old butcher shop," the young man said. "We buy lease from city. First make mountain of paper. Send paper to everybody in whole world. You get your paper?"

"Not yet," Jeffrey replied.

"It come, no worry." The young man wore faded jeans and a Harley-Davidson T-shirt under a form-fitted leather jacket. "You my first American guest. This special day. I love America. So great there. So free. Can do anything, no rules. Nobody looks down your back all the time. You work hard, you make good money, you keep it. Is dreamland, yes?"

"America isn't perfect," Jeffrey replied quietly. "A lot of people have it tough there." The young man chose not to hear. He opened the doors and ushered them into what clearly had once been the main shoproom and was now a ceramic-tiled parlor, sporting threadbare furniture and brightly colored Kazakh carpets. A waist-high stove was decorated with cheerful hand-painted tiles. Through the rear doors, Jeffrey could see a neat dining area leading into a large kitchen. A set of wooden stairs climbed the side wall and disappeared into a hole in the ceiling that appeared to be lined by an old door frame. Jeffrey squinted and decided it was indeed a door frame.

"This place is great," he declared. "A thousand times better than some faceless hotel."

The young man puffed out with pride. "I am Sergei Popov. Welcome to first Popov Hotel."

"The first of many," Jeffrey assured him.

"That is dream." He turned to a doting old lady seated by the stove. "This is grandmother," he said fondly.

Jeffrey gave a formal sort of bow and motioned toward the intricate hand-crocheted tablecloth on which she was working. "That is truly beautiful work."

The old lady replied with a smile that revealed a mouthful of gold teeth. She spoke to her grandson, who translated, "She asks if you are one buying old estate for Artemis company."

Jeffrey assumed Ivona had already been at work, setting their cover in order. "I won't be acquiring it myself. I am just representing a buyer."

"Grandmother not happy with this. She wants all old palaces to go back to proper families," Sergei translated. "My grandmother's mother used to work at palace, before Revolution. Grandmother was there often as little girl. She remember old family very well from this palace you buy."

"How interesting," Jeffrey said politely.

"My grandmother," Sergei continued, "she survives the Nine Hundred Day Siege. You have heard of this, yes?"

Jeffrey nodded. It was the name given to the Nazis' attempt to bomb and starve Saint Petersburg into submission. "It must have been horrible."

The young man translated and was given a few creaky words in reply. " 'The hardest time is now.' That is what she says. That is what many of the people are saying. The hardest time is now. I tell you, Sinclair, if many more people begin to say the same, you will see change from your darkest dreams."

"My name is Jeffrey," he corrected. "The people are growing angry?"

"My people, their anger is like wave," Sergei replied. "Up and down, up and down. All their lives they wait, wait, wait for change. Now change comes, but so slow it touches grandchildren's lives, not theirs. And the new government, now they say, you must wait some more. And the people are saying, no. No more waiting."

He picked up Jeffrey's bag. "Come, I show you room."

As they climbed the narrow stairs, Jeffrey said, "I love the way so many of your buildings are painted with bright colors."

"Yes, is pretty. You see, Russian winters are hard. Many days with gray skies. Much snow and ice. Colors important then."

"I've seen a lot of buildings being reconstructed. I hope they keep to the old color schemes."

"Yes, maybe." He opened a door onto a small room equipped with a sagging bed, a nightstand, a chair, a table, a tiny window, and frayed curtains. It was spotlessly clean. "But the reconstruction, it is almost all stopped. The city has no money. The city tries to teach people to pay taxes. You can guess what the people say back, yes?"

"I sure can," Jeffrey replied.

"Sure. So the city asks bank for loan. You can guess what says the bank. So the city is broke. Police, they stop cars and say, I give ticket. People say back, no, here is money. Police say good, no salary, so I take. This new style of Russian government. You like?"

"Not really."

"No. I am also not liking. Is chaos." He set down the suitcase with a thump. "Room okay?"

"It's fine, thanks."

"Not first class Paris-style, but clean. And my grandmother, she good cook. You see." He clapped Jeffrey on the shoulder and turned away.

"Wait," Jeffrey said. "Do you think there's any hope that Russia can make it work?"

"Sure, is hope." The man exposed a stained grin. "You know Russian folk songs? Balalaika and accordion and mandolin?"

"I've heard a few."

"So many songs, they start slow, very soft and slow. Then a little fast. Then more fast. Then very fast and boots stomping and hands clapping and everyone shouting and boom! All the people are laughing and singing so fast, like storm of music. The Russian people, they are like song. Slow at start, then boom! You watch. The boom soon come. Either they race to be good capitalists, or they race to darkness. But my people, soon they race."

Ivona Aristonova arrived in the early afternoon. She acknowledged Jeffrey's greeting with a brief nod and allowed Sergei to show her to her room. The stress of her long train journey was etched deep on her face, but she swiftly returned and began the trial of telephoning around for appointments.

An hour later she announced, "We are in luck. The director responsible for applications to acquire property is available this afternoon. We have an appointment to present your request. You cannot imagine how fortunate you are."

"Great," Jeffrey replied, and wondered why she sounded as if she were accusing him of something. "Could I perhaps book a call to my wife?"

Again there was the sense of unbalancing Ivona with his

words, again for no reason that he could understand. "Your wife?"

"In London," Jeffrey replied. "I would just like to let her know I'm all right."

"How long are you staying?"

"Five days. Why?"

"It will not be long enough to obtain a connection." She collected herself. "Shall we be going?"

Basil Island was connected to what now was Saint Petersburg's center by the Palace Bridge. It was the largest of the forty islands in the Neva Delta that made up Saint Petersburg, Ivona explained as their taxi drove them to the meeting. Jeffrey showed polite interest, wondering if the lessons were intended as anything more than a shield. A shield against what, he could not determine.

"Originally," Ivona continued, "the region belonged to the Novgorod principality. In the time of the Tartars, that principality was the only one in all Russia strong enough to resist their onslaught. It remained a free city throughout that dark time. But in the sixteenth century, Czar Ivan the Terrible decided that Novgorod was not loyal and succeeded in doing what the Mongols could not; he slaughtered the inhabitants, then put to the torch what before had been Russia's most active port. The region was then too weak to withstand the Swedish invasion and remained under Swedish rule until Peter the Great retook the area and declared it the capital of the new Russian empire."

She pointed to a red-brick castle wall fronting the river. "Czar Peter's first residence was the St. Peter and Paul Fortress, which in later years became the most infamous and gloomy prison in all Russia. Not far beyond that is our destination, the Smolny Convent."

"We're meeting with government officials in a convent?"

"Most of the city's old winter palaces, including the one you are interested in, are the responsibility of the Ministry of Culture," Ivona replied. "The ministry's central offices are located in the convent's outbuildings."

The taxi turned into a garden fronting a vast series of Baroque buildings. Their exteriors were painted a bright robin's-egg blue and were graced with dozens of white pillars and porticos. A series of gold-decked onion domes crowned the roofs.

Ivona waited while Jeffrey paid the driver the agreed-upon fare of two dollars. As they walked toward the side entrance, she continued, "Smolny Convent literally translates as the convent of the tea warehouses. Peter the Great placed the city's main spice and tea docks on this point. When the harbors were moved farther from the growing city, the Empress Elizabeth established a convent here. Her successor, Catherine the Great, turned it into the nation's first school, and it remained a school until the October Revolution. Now the main church is a hall for city recitals and speeches, and the outer buildings house the city's Ministry of Culture."

They entered doors embossed with the standard red-and-gold Cyrillic sign denoting an official government building. Ivona gave their names to the blank-faced receptionist seated beside the hulking militia guard. Soon a heavyset woman appeared and motioned for them to follow her.

The reason for the officials' willingness to see Jeffrey on such short notice was evident the moment introductions were concluded. "It is a tremendous strain to maintain these places," the senior official explained through Ivona. She was a dark-haired matron with piercing green eyes. "We now are required to pay the going commercial rate for all materials. The cost of upkeep for several hundred such old palaces is enormous."

"So you are willing to sell us the palace in question?" Jeffrey asked, pleased with her direct approach.

"Under the proper circumstances," she replied, an avaricious gleam to her eyes. "Some of these places will be retained for state use, but there are so many of them right now that it really doesn't matter which ones are sold."

Her associate, a bearded gentleman seated beside her at the oval conference table, spoke. Ivona translated, "For what purpose did your group wish to use this building?"

"Artemis Holdings is a Swiss trading company with an international board," Jeffrey began, reciting directly from the papers Markov had supplied. "They deal primarily in construction metals. They want to use the estate as a base for business operations in Russia, and maintain residential flats there for local managers."

"Good," the woman director replied. "We are most eager to see more international companies coming in and making such investments."

"Given that Artemis proves to be an acceptable company," her associate agreed, "this should be no problem. Especially since their activities in metal trading will help stimulate our economy."

The director consulted a paper before her. "The property appears to have been well maintained over the years. The house was formerly used as office space by a government-owned company which went out of business with the advent of perestroika. Then last year a local company took a short-term lease on the ground floor." She peered at the next page. "They list their purpose as warehouse and distribution."

"With the enormous rise in costs," her associate said apologetically, "we have been forced to accept whatever offer comes our way."

"This is not necessarily all bad," the director offered. "Having an occupant means that vandalism is kept down. This has been quite a serious problem recently with vacant buildings."

"All renovation must maintain the external facades," her associate continued. "No expansions will be permitted unless they retain the original architectural style and are accepted by the local council. You would be amazed, some Western groups have wanted to transform our priceless heirlooms into warehouses."

"That won't be a problem here," Jeffrey murmured. Ivona did not translate.

"Here is a list of all the documents we require, legal and financial, before the purchase can be cleared," she said, handing him a two-page register. "And this is a translated description of the main house."

"What about the evaluation of the property from your side?" Jeffrey asked, folding the papers and sliding them into his pocket for future examination. "Can you give me some idea of the price you'll be asking?"

She smiled for the first time. "What is the value of such

a property in the Russia of today? Do we take the cost of building another, the cost when it was built, the value today in rubles, the value ten years ago, or the value tomorrow?"

She shrugged. "It is up to the potential owners to make a bid, and that bid will be taken into consideration by the privatization committee. On the basis of the financial documents and proposed purpose, the committee will decide if the bid is acceptable. A formal notice will be posted in the *Saint Petersburg Gazette* and at the mayor's office, and thirty days will be allowed for any other parties to submit a competing bid. At the end of that thirty days, if no other bid is received, the notaries are instructed to draw up the lease documents."

Jeffrey sat up. "Lease?"

"Lease-purchase," the associate corrected. "The new Russian parliament has still not passed the necessary laws to allow us to sell these properties outright. At the same time, our city government is fighting off bankruptcy, and we cannot afford the upkeep."

"So we have reached a compromise solution," the director continued. "We are offering thirty-year leases with the proviso that the tenant has the first right of purchase at the stated price, with all rent payments going toward the purchase, once the ruling is made law."

"That sounds more than fair," Jeffrey said. "I guess the next step is for me to take a look around."

"My assistant will take you over immediately," the director replied, rising to her feet and offering Jeffrey her hand as Ivona translated. "She speaks some English and will be your contact here if there are any questions. I shall await word from you."

Once they were back downstairs and waiting for the assistant to locate the necessary keys, Ivona said, "If you will permit, I shall leave you here."

"Of course."

"The bishop has arranged an appointment for Yussef and me this afternoon. I know the gentleman's family, and Yussef does not."

"No problem," he said.

Ivona continued her scrutiny of the gardens beyond the door. "I shall be taking whatever time possible to continue our search. Naturally, I will be available whenever you require my assistance."

"Naturally," Jeffrey replied dryly. "I am most grateful."

"Until later, then," she said and strode away. Jeffrey watched her hasten toward the taxi rank, wondered if it was just his imagination, or if she really was running away.

CHAPTER
21

The same woman who had brought them upstairs appeared soon after Ivona had departed and announced in heavily accented English, "I am responsible for your file."

"Great," Jeffrey replied.

"Come," she said, heading for the door. "We take taxi."

She led him out to the taxi rank on overly tight, high-heeled shoes, her feet crammed in so that the flesh puffed out around the edges and threw her weight forward. She slid into the taxi with difficulty, her dress being far too tight for her girth.

"Bottom floor of palace was warehouse for metal pipes," she said, propping the folder open on her knees as the taxi drove them to the estate.

"So they told me." He watched a throng of people moving slowly past a group of old ladies selling everything from cold potato pancakes to shoe polish on the street curb. "I wonder what happened to all the people who worked for the company that was upstairs."

"Who's to say?" She did not raise her head from the file in her lap. "Now is no more socialism. Now all is private initiative. Fine. Let some private initiative find people more work."

The taxi turned from the main thoroughfare onto a boulevard lined with old apartment houses and shadowed by the past. They swung around the corner and stopped beside a small caretaker's lodge. It was built into an outer wall constructed of brick and hand-wrought iron. Huge, rusty hinges, now broken and twisted, had probably once held impressive gates. Through the sweeping entrance, Jeffrey could see what once must have been a formal garden and now was little more than a jungle.

His attention was caught by the sight of a large American car parked along the curb opposite the estate. The black Chevrolet totally dwarfed the little plastic cars near it, including their own taxi. Jeffrey paid the driver and got out in time to see a tall, lanky man with a blond buzz-cut, his tie at half-mast, saunter out through the main gates.

Jeffrey's guide did not like this development at all. She clambered from the taxi and paraded toward the blond man. Jeffrey was right behind her. The woman shouted a full blast of rapid Russian.

"Sorry, lady," the man drawled in English. "I don't speak the lingo."

Jeffrey stepped forward, unaccountably irritated by the intruder's air of nonchalant superiority. "She wants to know what you're doing here," he said. "And so do I."

That startled him. "You American?"

Jeffrey nodded. "I asked what you are doing here."

The guy flicked a glance at something behind them, and sidled swiftly back into the estate. "What's it to you?"

"He official bidder," the woman answered, following the man's backward movement, her tone rising indignantly. "He have right to ask. I am ministry official. I have more right. Now you say, what you are doing here?"

"Just having a little look. No harm in that, is there?" Keen eyes flickered back from their inspection of what was behind them and rested on Jeffrey. "That right, what the lady said? You want to buy this place?"

"I don't see how that's any business of yours," Jeffrey retorted. "And you still haven't said what you're doing on this property."

He shrugged. "Maybe I'm thinking about buying it too."

Just as Jeffrey had feared. A competing bid. "Who for?"

The guy shook his head. "You first."

"This private property," the woman said sharply, almost dancing in place. "You must have proper authority to enter. Mr. Sinclair has authority. You have nothing. You leave. Now."

"I was just on my way out," he replied. "That your name? Sinclair?"

"Who else wants to buy this place," Jeffrey demanded.

"See you around, Sinclair," the guy said, and ambled off.

"Come," the woman insisted to Jeffrey. "We go."

"I don't like the look of him," Jeffrey said quietly, watching the man's slow progress down the street.

"I am also not liking," the woman agreed. "Is much in Russia today I am not liking. People with no proper authority do much, too much. No respect for anything."

Jeffrey followed her down the drive. "Have you had other bids for this palace? Any from Americans?"

"No, no bids from anywhere. Is just another winter palace, one of thousand. More. City full of old palaces." The woman walked the rubble-strewn path on feet that clearly pained her. "We need many buyers with proper authority. Not men who walk where they like and speak without respect."

She fished through a voluminous purse and came up with a series of heavy, old keys wired to a piece of cardboard. "How long you take?"

"This afternoon," Jeffrey mused, craning to get a look at the exterior above his head, "three or four hours. I suppose I might as well start on a floor plan, then finish that up tomorrow. And I'll need a local architect to look over the foundations and the roof."

"Yes, yes," she said impatiently, climbing the rough stone stairs. "But such time I don't have. I give you keys, yes?"

"That's fine with me."

"You let no one in without proper authority?"

"Not a soul," he promised.

"I come and check on you," she warned.

"I will look forward to it," he replied.

She harrumphed, unlocked the door, pushed it open, and handed him the set of keys. "You now responsible."

"I'll guard them with my life," he replied. "Thank you."

• • •

Everywhere were remnants of the past, whispers of the mansion's former glory. The dual entrance halls were floored with marble mosaic, now cracked and pitted and dulled by ingrained dirt. Hallways were floored with rough-worn hardwood overlaid with cheap, peeling linoleum.

The ground floor chambers had been whitewashed, but so long ago that the paint was falling in a slow-motion snowfall upon the pipes and sheet metal and bent steel rods scattered over the scarred floors. The back garden doors had been enlarged with a sledgehammer, then fitted with a rusting warehouse-type truck door.

Upstairs the linoleum gave way to laurel-wreath carpet that smelled of damp and age. The first great hall was lined in what once had been royal-red silk wall covering and now was a dull pinkish-gray. The fireplace was large enough to stand in upright and was flanked by two ancient Greek statues. This had been a common practice in many great royal houses, when conquerors returned home with spoils that were then fashioned into their villas as decoration. The ceiling was a full thirty feet high and decorated by a handwrought wooden frieze, now completely covered with water stains and mold.

Opening from the hall's far end was a smaller room that testified to Russia's former love affair with the Orient; it was a gilded chamber in the best Islamic style, the intricate geometric designs on the walls rising to lofty heights, where they joined to a gold-leaf ceiling shaped like the dome of a mosque. Beside the main doors, where the family's crest had once been carved, former Communist occupants had painted crude hammers and sickles.

Beyond this chamber began, if Jeffrey correctly read the cursory description supplied by the ministry, the rooms of the head of the house, Prince Markov's grandfather. As befitted a distant member of the royal family, the suite consisted of a dozen chambers—billiards, music, library, reception, study, and so on. Across the main hall, his wife had struggled to make do with a mere seven rooms of her own. His work set aside for this first viewing, Jeffrey walked through the rooms in a reverie of what life in this great house once might have been.

The third floor was an almost endless series of connecting rooms for younger children, with separate halls for honored guests. After a brief inspection, Jeffrey returned to the ground floor. The kitchen and galleys had been stripped and filled with the warehouse's rubbish. Jeffrey went back to the central room, which clearly had been sort of a glorified waiting salon, not nearly as grand as the upstairs chambers. Leading from that was the apartment of the family's eldest son, Markov's father. It consisted of a large sitting room, a study, a dressing salon, a bath, a toilet, a second private salon, a long hall lined with closets and wardrobes, and a bedroom.

Four hours later, Jeffrey had completed the initial floor plan and seen about all he cared to for one day. He left via the front entrance, carefully locking the door behind him.

A voice from the bottom of the stairs asked, "Is the dragon lady still around?"

Jeffrey bristled at the conspiratorial tone. "Whether she is or she isn't," he retorted, "the situation's the same. You have no right to be here."

"Proper authority," the young man scoffed. "What a joke. Proper authority's sent this country to the bottom of the economic scrap heap."

"So why are you here?" Jeffrey stalked down the stairs and strode up close to the other man, trying to make him give ground. "Better still, why don't you leave?"

The man backed up a step. "Hey, did it ever occur to you that maybe we got started on the wrong foot?"

Jeffrey pressed forward. "Now."

Another step. "I got a better idea. How's about you ask me one more time who I'm with?"

"I don't care anymore."

"Hey, but you should."

"I just want you—"

From the other side of the high outer wall came the sound of several men's voices approaching. The man's casual attitude vanished. Quick as a cat, he grasped Jeffrey by his shoulder and arm, pushing him across the driveway and up against the wall. There wasn't much force behind the movement, and the contact was softened by a thick overgrowth of hanging vines. Still, the jolt was enough for his neck to give a lancing ping. Jeffrey groaned, or started to, but the man stiffened and hissed and silenced him.

The voices receded. The man released Jeffrey, craned to see through the open gates, said softly, "You ever heard the name Tombek before?"

Jeffrey rubbed his neck. "Would you mind telling me what's going on?"

"I asked you a question, Sinclair." His attitude was casual again, but his voice was distant as last winter's frost.

"I couldn't care less. Who are you?"

A swift motion brought forth a leather ID, which was flashed open so fast that Jeffrey only caught sight of a photograph and official printing. "Name's John Casey. I'm here with the U.S. consulate. Cultural Affairs, if you want to be technical, which I'd advise you not to be. Now, Sinclair, have you ever heard the name Tombek?"

"No." Consulate. It didn't make sense. Jeffrey felt his anger subsiding into embarrassment. "Why push me around like that?"

"A couple of their goons followed you here." He watched Jeffrey continue to massage his neck. "Hurt yourself?"

"No. You did."

"Sorry." He eased into the gateway and searched the road outside the gates. "I think it's okay."

Jeffrey remained unconvinced. And hot. "If they were already following me around, why try and hide me?"

"Can't say for sure that they were. But their car pulled up right as you and Miss Proper Authority got out."

"And?"

Casey shrugged. "Why take chances?"

His neck subsided to a dull throbbing. "So who is this Tombek?"

"Tell you what," Casey replied, leading Jeffrey over to the large American car. "Why don't we take a little drive and let the Consul General decide how much you ought to know."

"The place you've been looking over backs up on the Fontanka Canal; that's the water trough running down the middle of that street over there," Casey said as he navigated the heavy car along the rutted pavement. "Used to be one of the best neighborhoods the city had to offer. Over across the street is the former royal stable. It runs a full city block and has an interior courtyard over two acres in size. Now it houses the city's garbage trucks, police vans, and some of the smaller buses."

Jeffrey reached past his growing annoyance and confusion in an attempt to gain more information. "How do you know so much about this area?"

Casey shrugged in reply. "Boredom, I guess. Had to have something to do in my off time, so I studied some of the local lore."

"Off time from what?" Jeffrey probed.

"That's for the Consul General to say." He pointed through the front windshield at a beautifully restored church with six multicolored onion domes. "That's the Church of the Resurrection. Alexis II, the czar who abolished serfdom in 1861, was assassinated on that spot by nobles who weren't too happy to lose all their slaves. The local folk, though, they wanted to honor the guy who gave them freedom. After Alexis was killed, it became a crime to speak his name. So they always called that church the Cathedral of the Spilled Blood."

"I'm not in any trouble, am I?" Jeffrey demanded.

"You might as well save your breath," Casey replied. "Why don't we just give it a rest and enjoy the ride?"

The United States Consulate in Saint Petersburg was built to fit within the hollowed-out shell of a once prestigious city dwelling. Set upon the fashionable Furshtadtskaya, the outer stairs were as worn and pitted as the rest of the city. Beyond the double set of bulletproof doors and past the watchful Marines on guard duty, however, all was pure Americana—plush, neutral-colored carpets, warm wood-veneer walls, fluorescent lighting, decent air conditioning, color photographs of the President.

Jeffrey waited in a cramped security lobby while Casey went elsewhere and reported in. Eventually the Consul General's private secretary arrived, introduced herself, and led him into an elevator operated by a key suspended from her belt. Jeffrey tried not to gawk as he was led down a bustling corridor past ranks of bombproof filing cabinets stamped "Top Secret" and clamped with combination safe locks.

The Consul General's office had once been the house's central drawing room, and no amount of bland paint and dull-colored carpet could completely erase the chamber's former splendor. As Jeffrey was ushered inside, a vigorous-looking man rose from his desk and walked around it with hand outstretched. "I'm Stan Allbright. Good of you to stop by."

"Jeffrey Sinclair," he replied. "I didn't have much choice."

"Casey didn't get too carried away, I hope." Allbright's softly measured midwestern twang had been polished by distance and time and foreign tongues to the point that the accent seemed to come and go at will. "Why don't you take a seat over there in the comfortable chair, and let's talk it over. You like a coffee? Maybe a pepsi?"

"I'm fine, thanks."

Even when the Consul General was seated, he appeared to be in motion. He was a wiry bundle of energy, the sort of man who brought people to attention just by turning their way. He was dressed in what Jeffrey had once heard described as diplomatic fatigues—dark suit, white shirt, black shoes, bland tie. His gaze was intelligent, cautious, measuring. "What brings you to town, Mr. Sinclair?"

"I'm working on a project."

"Mind if I ask what sort?"

Jeffrey explained the Markov estate purchase. "This is the first assessment."

"You have any idea what's behind the interest in that particular project—what'd you say their name was?"

"Artemis Holdings Limited. And no, I'm not sure what they want to use it for, besides something to do with their company's operations. Exporting metals, I think."

"The name Artemis is new to me. The international corporate community is still small enough for us to have a handle on most movers and shakers, especially somebody big enough to go for a winter palace backing up on the Fontanka. You know that's what it used to be, don't you?"

"I figured it had to have been somebody's private residence," Jeffrey hedged.

"Yeah, these royal families, they all had their estates out in the back of beyond, and believe me, you can't get farther out in the sticks than some of these places in Russia. So off they'd all go and rule their serfs and farm their lands and make their money during the summer, then hightail it back to the capital and civilization before the first snows. A winter out in the boonies meant eight, maybe nine months without contact to their nearest neighbors. Taking care of the estates during the cold, lonely days was what overseers were for, right?"

"I suppose so," Jeffrey agreed, wondering where the man was headed. Wishing he would get there.

"These people, their holdings were *big*. Twenty, thirty, even a couple of hundred square miles. Tens of thousands of serfs. Folks like these, they'd have their family castles back on the home range, then set up a second winter palace here in downtown Saint Petersburg. Most of these houses are in pretty bad shape after seventy years of Communism, but the ones that haven't been trashed would make your head spin. What's the condition of the one your people are looking at?"

"Stripped bare," Jeffrey replied. "But otherwise not too bad, considering."

"And they weren't interested in any other property but this one?"

Jeffrey shook his head and winced at the motion. "Why are you so concerned about this?"

"I'll get around to that in just a minute. What's the matter with your neck?"

"Your man Casey pushed me into a wall."

"Yes, he told me. I'm sorry about that, but he assures me it was important to get you out of view. You say you've never heard the name Tombek before?"

"Not until this afternoon. Who is it?"

"Local trouble." The tone turned deceptively easy. "How'd you get involved in this project, Mr. Sinclair?"

"My boss in London and the head of Artemis are business associates."

"Mind if I ask who's behind the Artemis group?"

"Sorry, I can't answer that."

"No, of course you can't." Long legs stretched out in a parody of calm. "I have to tell you, Mr. Sinclair, I get the impression you're not telling me everything."

"You haven't told me anything at all."

"No, suppose not. We've got ourselves a problem here, you see, and it must be kept quiet. I'm tempted to go against the grain and let you in on it, but I can't get a handle on whether or not I can trust you."

"If you mean trust me to help, I can't answer that unless I know more," Jeffrey answered. "But if you mean trust me to keep my mouth shut, I guess the way you feel about the answers I've given so far are the best response you could have."

Consul General Allbright gave a genuine smile. "You know something? I do believe if we ever had the time we could get to be friends. Mind if I call you Jeffrey?"

"I guess not."

"Fine. What we're facing, Jeffrey, is one utter mess. We had someone kidnapped a little over a week ago." Allbright opened the file in front of him, extracted a photo, handed it over. "Young lady by the name of Leslie Ann Stevens."

Jeffrey inspected the picture, saw a fresh-faced young woman in her early twenties with auburn hair, alert eyes, and a sweet smile. "An American?"

"Peace Corps volunteer," Allbright confirmed. "Picked up right in front of your little palace too, far as we can tell. A couple of neighbors didn't actually see the girl get snatched, but did spot a truck parked outside the manor late that same night. Only activity on the whole street. Crime's so bad these days, you don't see much moving after dark except on the main boulevards—which this isn't, not anymore. Everybody we talked to agreed on one thing; they were unloading something from that truck. A lot of boxes."

"Into my palace?"

Allbright nodded. "That's why I was asking, Jeffrey. You sure you didn't find anything that could have been packed inside boxes and shuttled inside?"

"Not a chance." Jeffrey was emphatic. "The place looks furnished from a jumble sale. And all the warehouse section has in it is a lot of rusting pipes and sheet metal."

"You've been all over the place?"

"Top to bottom."

"Casey's been all through the grounds, says the house must be all of ten thousand square feet. Big house like that, you might have missed a room."

"Not unless there's a hollow wall. I've already worked out a basic floor plan."

"Mind if Casey takes a look around inside?"

Jeffrey hesitated, then decided, "I suppose not."

"Thanks. Any way we might be able to get in without attracting attention?"

"I've got a key. Why would somebody want to kidnap a Peace Corps volunteer?"

"Can't say for certain. We do know she's been kidnapped, though." Allbright rubbed a hand through thinning hair. "We know because we've received a ransom note and her Bible. The pastor at the local English-speaking church identified it as hers. Seems she was returning home from a prayer service."

"And the palace was on her way home?"

"It was if she took the shorter route, which she wouldn't have if she'd showed the brains given a very small rabbit. She could have walked on down Nevsky Prospekt, which she didn't, according to one of the people who saw her off. It was twice as long that way, and maybe she was tired. Maybe she thought she'd be safe, that close to home. Maybe she just didn't think." Allbright managed a weary smile. "My biggest concern right now is whether the lady's still thinking at all."

"Have you been to the police?"

Allbright grimaced. "Any crime involving a foreigner is still the KGB's bailiwick. They're a strange bunch to work with these days, let me tell you. Always have been, of course, but before at least you knew where you stood. With the changes facing everybody these days, you can't be too certain they won't turn around and bite off the hand you're offering."

"So you're going to pay the ransom?"

"Washington is busy giving me the royal runaround, but if we could have some assurance the lady's still alive and kicking, yes, we'll pay."

"So what can I do to help?"

"That's what I like to hear. No beating around the bush, just straight up and straight out." The Consul General rose to his feet. "Tell you what. We're having a little reception for some people tonight over at my residence. Why don't you stop by? We'll discuss it then."

"All right, thanks."

"Good. What we could do is have Casey come by for you."

"At the palace," Jeffrey said, understanding. "An hour or so early, and I could just offer to show him around."

"See? Just like I said." He extended his hand. "Nothing like a man who knows how to get things done."

CHAPTER

22

St. Isaac's Square was dominated by St. Isaac's Cathedral, which had been the largest church in Saint Petersburg before the Communists declared it a museum. Its marble exterior still bore the scars of Nazi guns; it had been bombed almost daily during the Nine Hundred Day Siege. The high gold cupola had remained visible to the German gunners stationed across the Baltic even when everything else in the city had been masked beneath the smoke from bombs and countless fires.

Across the square, by the Blue Bridge, was the Marien Palace, the home of the new city government. Between them and slightly to one side was the newly renovated Astoria, one of the city's two exclusive hotels. Room prices were higher than a five-star hotel in the heart of Paris, meals more costly than a restaurant overlooking New York's Central Park. By Western standards neither were worth half their cost—especially the meals. But the hotel was clean, and visitors could be fairly assured that what they ate would not make them sick. Western businessmen kept it booked solid six months in advance.

The young man leaned across the coffee table and asked, "You're absolutely certain they can't trace this back to me?"

He wore a rumpled suit in the latest Western fashion. His hair was carefully trimmed, his shoes softest Italian leather.

He looked like an up-and-coming young executive exhausted from a hard week's work—which he was, after a fashion.

He was also extremely frightened.

"You have our word," Yussef replied for both himself and Ivona.

They were seated in the lobby of the hotel's ruble section, where their language and appearance drew fewer stares. The Astoria was in effect two hotels—one for rubles and one for hard currency—with different entrances, reception desks, key systems, gift shops, and restaurants. Staff relegated to the ruble hotel were perpetually disgruntled, barred as they were from ever seeing dollar tips.

"How was trading today?" Ivona asked.

"Like always." He stood and cast off his jacket. Dried sweat stained his expensive shirt in darkened splotches. He could not have been over twenty-five years of age, but his eyes held the blank confusion of a tired old man. He lit a fresh cigarette from the ashes of his last and drank thirstily from his beer.

"Buy, sell," he rattled. "Took fifty thousand pairs of stockings in exchange for a hundred personal computers this morning. You like a pair?"

"You are very kind to ask," Ivona replied. "But no."

Before, when a Russian company needed something—anything, no matter how small or large—it would place a requisition through the Moscow-based central planning agency called Gosplan. Gosplan would then, hopefully, approve the request and forward it to the appropriate supplier, who could sell nothing unless Gosplan first approved the order. The product would inevitably arrive late and be of poorer quality than requested, but to a point the system had worked.

All that had vanished with the fall of Communism.

In an attempt to stifle an inflation rate approaching fifty percent per month, the government had dried up the source of rubles. Companies with products to sell suddenly found themselves either without buyers, or with buyers who had no hard cash. So they had begun to trade.

By the second summer after Communism's fall from grace, the government owed two hundred and twenty billion

rubles in unpaid salaries. Cash-starved factories paid workers with truckloads of fresh oranges and ton-lots of clothes.
Company apartments were completed by trading steel wire
for concrete, then having skilled machinists work overtime
as plasterers and carpet layers. The world's largest steel
works, the Metallurgical Complex in Magnitogorsk, was reduced to paying workers with fifty-pound sacks of sugar and
pieces of steel that their employees could then resell.

The fastest growing industry, in a country whose economy had contracted thirty percent in a two-year period, was
the commodities exchange. Russia resembled a vast factory
in a panic bankruptcy sale. The commodities markets sold
everything from vodka to new MIG jet fighters.

Whenever the government told the commodities brokers
that selling a certain item was against the law, that item
was simply removed from the floor and offered on the street
just outside the exchange. New laws were tossed out as easily
as the floor sweepings each evening. Computerized barter
houses overloaded the outdated phone systems and took a
taste off the top from every deal cut.

The majority of dealers were under twenty-five. They had
been born at a time when their culture was coming to realize
the Communist social structure was based upon a lie. Thus
the propaganda and brainwashing had not stuck so well.
Initiative had not been stripped away nor traded for the
promised security of socialism.

Ivona received the nod from Yussef. "Could you please
tell us what you have learned?"

The frightened look returned. "I need to know I'll be safe."

"We seek only for ourselves," Yussef soothed. "What you
tell us will go only to the bishop, no further. He will treat it
as though it came from the confessional."

The young man leaned forward, said quietly, "There are
rumors of a *matrioshka* shipment."

"This is news," Yussef said, clearly pleased.

Russia's *matrioshka* dolls were known worldwide: a series
of smiling wooden figurines in graduated sizes, each figure
nesting in the next larger size. A *matrioshka* shipment
meant hiding an illegal product inside a legitimate export.
The technique was normally used for transporting heroin

from the Asian states to the West.

"This is mafia work?" Yussef asked.

"Who knows? But that is how it sounds, and what the rumors say. The bribes are too high for anyone else to use the transport route, and the mafia controls the docks." He looked from one to the other. "It is the mafia you are up against?"

"We do not know who was behind the theft," Ivona replied.

"We know," Yussef retorted, his face like stone.

"We are not sure," Ivona insisted.

The young man flashed a weary smile. "Confusion is a sign of the times."

"What will the outer shipment be, do you know?" Yussef demanded.

"Hard to say, but my guess would be raw metal. There is more of this than anything else going out just now. One group I know does forty tons per week to Estonia. They're hooked up with Western buyers who like the Russian prices but don't want to have to bother with Russian bureaucracy. The group clears four thousand dollars a week."

Yussef whistled softly. "They're mafia?"

"Not the group themselves, but anything this rich will have the mafia circling like vultures around a kill. They take a taste, never fear." The young man stubbed out his cigarette with jerky motions and lit another with a gold Dunhill lighter worth more than the average Russian's annual salary. He snapped the top shut, said with the smoke, "Copper, bronze, zinc, titanium, strategic metals—we see the trades every day, and we know the end buyer is in the West. The factories are crumbling, they have no money to pay salaries, and the Westerners are ready to pay in real dollars. Anything the companies can smuggle out, they do; it's the difference between life or death for many of them."

"Big business," Yussef agreed thoughtfully.

"Listen, I'll tell you how big. Estonia has no metal resources at all, and only a handful of factories. But this year Estonia became the sixth largest exporter of copper in the world. There is one trial before the courts right now, where a group was caught trying to ship *five thousand kilometers* of aluminum irrigation tubing from Saint Petersburg. One deal."

"We think this would be shipped from Saint Petersburg," Yussef replied. "Have you heard of anything here?"

"A new player?" He flicked his cigarette in the ashtray's general direction. "They come and go like the wind. But something this big would require big financing, maybe more than one shipment if what you say is correct." He thought a moment. "There is word of a new metals dealer with backing from a Swiss group. Nothing definite. Nothing on the market. But big enough to attract interest. Traders are like wolves. They sniff the wind and travel in packs."

Ivona concluded, "So you think the mafia might handle such a deal—"

"They handle nothing," the young man said impatiently. "They *control*. They falsify the export documents. They pay bribes. They frighten. They threaten. They eliminate all that stands between themselves and profit."

"And they tell the suppliers what will be hidden inside their metal for shipment," Yussef finished.

The look of genuine fear returned to the young man's face. "You now have my life in your hands."

"We will guard it well," Yussef promised, rising to his feet. "We thank you. All of us."

CHAPTER
23

Casey arrived at the palace exactly on time. He shook hands with Jeffrey, and said, "No hard feelings, I hope."

Jeffrey found the man's casual attitude as fake as his smile. "I still don't know what it was all about."

Casey motioned toward the door. "Mind if I have a look around?"

"That's why we're here." Jeffrey led him into the central foyer. "Do you even know what you're looking for?"

"Tell you what," Casey replied in his lazy drawl, looking over the papers jumbled on the trestle table, "why don't you just keep on with your business plan or whatever it is you've been doing and let me mosey about on my own."

Jeffrey waved a free hand. "Be my guest."

Ninety minutes later, Casey interrupted his continued sketching of the floor plans with an abrupt, "Guess I've seen all I need to. Matter of fact, we were due at the Consul General's a half-hour ago."

Jeffrey stacked up his work. "Find anything?"

"Like you said, a lot of dust and steel. Nothing else. Come on; this place's got too many dried-up memories for my liking."

Jeffrey followed the man down to the waiting car. They drove through the gathering dusk in silence.

The evening's beauty rekindled his yearning for Katya.

The blankets of smog and airborne soot burnished the sky a hundred fiery hues. He wished for her to share this night, when only main streets had lights, and former palaces had their wounds soothed by soft illumination. During the day he had been sorry to be alone, yet glad she was not there. This world was too harsh. The people were drawn with jagged lines. Safety was a word with little meaning. This evening, however, as he sat in the American car's plush luxury and watched the silent orchestration of colors, he ached for her with a longing that scarcely left him room to breathe.

As they turned onto the Nevsky Prospekt, Casey interrupted his reverie with, "How's the neck?"

"Better, but still sore."

"Didn't mean to handle you so rough."

"I hurt it a while back, I guess it's not completely healed." His hand went up automatically to massage it. "Who is this Tombek anyway?"

"The bad guys."

Talking to Casey was like drilling through stone with a toothpick. "What makes you so sure somebody was following me around?"

"If you don't know," Casey replied, "don't ask."

"What kind of answer is that?"

"A smart one." Casey hesitated, then went on, "There aren't a lot of black and white lines to be drawn around here right now. Too much gray in this country for my liking. But Tombek's all black. Not anybody you want to mess with. Definitely not."

Jeffrey thought of Yussef and Ivona's work, asked, "But why would Tombek want to have me followed?"

"Brother, that's the million dollar question."

"I've got another one for you," Jeffrey said. "Why does a local consulate official know this much about the Saint Petersburg bad guys?"

"Like I said, there's too much gray in this world. Not many people we can rely on. Best way to get things done is to do it ourselves."

"Consul General Allbright indicated the KGB weren't much help."

"You said it. These days, the KGB's like a dead elephant

lying in the middle of the Russian road to progress. All that
weight is hard to shift, and it stinks to high heaven. But it's
blocking traffic something awful, and sooner or later it's got
to go."

"Have they done anything for you at all?"

"Lot of paper flying back and forth, lot of telephone calls
asking these double-edged questions. But we haven't seen
much in the way of real results. No, this thing's gotta be
baked at home." Again Casey hesitated, as though debating
something internally. Then he went on, "There is hope,
though. Maybe. We've made contact with a sort of subgroup,
a new offshoot within the KGB that appears to mean business. They've offered to help us on this."

"And you think this guy Tombek might be involved in
your kidnapping?"

"Tombek is not a person; it's a gang," Casey corrected.
"They're involved in just about everything else. Might have
their hand in this as well."

The Consul General's official residence was located in a
short alleyway off one of the city's main thoroughfares.
When they arrived, the cul-de-sac was filled with late-model
Western cars and grim-faced Russian bodyguard-chauffeurs.

The residence still maintained a vestige of its former
glory. High ceilings supported brilliant chandeliers whose
light shone down upon chambers of vast proportions. The
well-dressed crowd milling about the carpeted expanse could
have been lifted from any major international community.

Jeffrey circled about the trio of rooms filled with the city's
movers and shakers. He paused beside a group paying careful attention to a heavyset Russian who spoke with authority: "Step by step we make progress. It is a long voyage from
Communism to liberty. Very long. No one expects to make
it overnight. But if I have one criticism of my countrymen,
it is that they concentrate overmuch on the unsolved and do
not take hope from the successes. Yes, the positive aspects
are small when taken against all that is left undone. But
these are steps in the right direction, and for this reason it
is most important that they be given a place in the lime-
light."

"I guess seeing goods on the shelves has helped reassure
the people," a listener offered.

"Yes and no. Appearance of Western goods and high-priced foods is pleasing to those who can afford them, but a source of great tension to everyone else. Most people find these products completely beyond their reach. They see them, but cannot buy them. This is like one of our ancient fables." He shrugged. "We are a patient people. We are very hard to get moving, but once we are going, we are very hard to stop."

Somebody asked, "How does the situation look for this winter?"

"Difficult, but we hope not dangerous." He tossed back the remainder of his drink. "So long as there is not a coal or rail strike and the roads stay open, we will make it. Famine combined with no heat would end everything."

"At least there is some help coming from the West," another offered.

"Not enough, and too slow," he replied. "We are starving on the West's cautious assistance. The biggest lesson we have learned recently is that capitalist money is a coward. The spenders hear the word risk and they zip up their pockets. We are fed with words, when what we need is the machinery to make our own bread."

"Speaking of bread," someone asked, "is there any hope that Russia will ever be able to feed itself?"

"At the turn of the century," the Russian replied, "my nation was exporting more food to England than it consumed itself. In the years before the October Revolution, after the system of serfdom was abolished and Russians worked the land as free men, the farming villages had a higher level of income than the cities. But the Bolsheviks feared the peasants' power and smothered the villages with their policy of collectivization."

"Not to mention the pricing structure," another offered.

The Russian nodded his agreement. "A loaf of bread cost the same in 1987 as it did in 1925. The situation was so catastrophic that farmers found it less expensive to feed their pigs with fresh bread than with raw barley. Communist pricing structure was a lesson in insanity."

The Consul General appeared at Jeffrey's elbow. He pulled him away from the crowd and said quietly, "Sounds like Casey wasn't able to find anything more than you did."

"I wouldn't know," Jeffrey replied. "He made it clear he'd just as soon not have me around."

Allbright smiled without humor. "In these parts it's hard to find people to trust, and harder still to trust them once you do. Casey's got the eyes of a hawk, though. Doubt seriously if he missed anything." He nodded a friendly greeting to a passing face and said more quietly, "I hope."

"You took quite a risk in telling me about the kidnapping, didn't you?"

"Not if you're as honest as you look."

"Still, I imagine you had some disagreement from your staff," Jeffrey ventured. "Disapproval, even."

"Comes with the job. You develop a thick hide or you retire and grow flowers," Allbright stated flatly. "Might surprise you to know that Casey felt we could trust you as well. I put a lot of value on that man's opinion."

Jeffrey hid his surprise. "I imagine you learn to trust your own judgment, too."

"Makes a lot more sense than asking the advice of somebody behind a desk in Washington, six thousand miles from the action." Allbright faced him. "What are you getting at?"

"You were right when you said I hadn't told you everything," Jeffrey replied. "I think I ought to exchange honesty for honesty."

"That's all a man can ask for." He took Jeffrey by the arm. "What say we find us a quiet corner."

They left the main suite of three public rooms and passed the central staircase where Casey stood watching everything and everyone with his deceptively easy gaze. Allbright motioned for him to join them. Together they ducked into a small guest apartment.

"We call this the Nixon Rooms," Allbright explained. "He used to stay here when he visited during his presidency."

Once they were seated in a small alcove, Jeffrey related what he knew about the stolen articles from the Ukrainian church. "One of the priests overheard the thieves say something about the treasures being headed for Saint Petersburg. There was also evidence that the thieves were from inside the Orthodox church."

Allbright mulled this over, asked, "You're not alone on this, are you?"

"There are two others here from Lvov, sort of using me as a cover while they check things out."

"And you think you can trust these folks?"

Jeffrey shrugged. "All I have to go on is their word, but I believe they're telling me the truth. If so, the stolen items would be worth millions in the West. More."

"And the Orthodox might be behind the theft," Allbright mused.

"Nothing definite," Jeffrey replied, "but according to what I was told, there is at least the possibility."

"From the tone of your voice, I'd say you don't believe it."

"I guess I have trouble accepting the idea that one church would steal from another," Jeffrey confessed.

"Are you a believer yourself?"

"Yes."

"Protestant?"

"Baptist," Jeffrey affirmed.

"Well, there are a few bad apples in every barrel, even in a church, I'm afraid. But like you, my first reaction is to treat this with skepticism. Still, Russia's not like any place you've ever been before, and that holds true for the Orthodox church as well." Allbright exchanged a glance with Casey. A moment's silent communication passed between them, then Allbright said, "Have you spoken to anyone within the church here?"

Jeffrey shook his head. "I don't know a soul."

"Something as serious as a possible theft of another church's treasures should certainly be discussed with a senior authority. Let me make a couple of calls," Allbright offered. "Maybe I can help you out there. If so, I'll make the connection with someone who will be sure to give you a fair hearing."

"That would be great, thanks."

"Hard to tell what happens these days when you pull a string. Might come up with gold. On the other hand, so much changes every hour, you might come up with something that'll try to eat both the string and the hand that's pulling it." He gave his best effort to produce a reassuring smile. "But maybe it's time to take that chance. If not for your sake, then for the sake of our lost lady friend."

CHAPTER
24

The Alexander Nevsky Lavra was surrounded by wide thoroughfares. The streetcars and trucks created a continual barrage outside the high stone gates. In his conversation that morning, Allbright had explained to Jeffrey that a Lavra was a large monastery whose enclave had been granted independence by royal decree, a sort of miniature city-state. The early morning light treated the ancient structure with a gentle hand. The roughened walls were smoothed, the flaking plaster polished, the colors restored to their brilliant past. For a brief instant, Jeffrey was gifted a glimpse of what once had been.

The high outer walls contained an area so vast that two great cemeteries, a canal, and a forest surrounded the seminary and cathedral. The walls and first line of trees muted the barrage of traffic noise to a distant hum. Pensioners and cripples lined both sides of the central cobblestone way, their chanted prayers and soft pleas a murmur as constant as the wind.

Inside the dual cemeteries rested the remains of Tolstoy, Dostoyevsky, Tchaikovsky, and other greats of Russian arts and literature. Yet what caught Jeffrey's eye as he headed for his meeting was how many of the old gravestones had been defaced, their crucifixes damaged with savage strokes. Over more recent Communist remains rose simple marble pyramids topped with a single red star, stone fingers pointed toward a heaven whose existence they eternally denied.

"Go see Father Anatoli," the Consul General had told him that morning over the telephone. "He's personal assistant to the Metropolitan of Saint Petersburg, though for how much longer is anybody's guess. The ultraconservatives are sharpening their knives. He studied in England for a couple of years, which leaves him tainted in the xenophobes' eyes. Anatoli doesn't have time for their 'Russia for the Orthodox' nonsense, and he'll say so to anybody who listens. Not a way to make friends in this town."

Jeffrey stored away his questions about xenophobia, took down the address, and asked, "What's a Metropolitan?"

"Local church leader. In the Orthodox church, the Patriarch in Moscow is the head. Metropolitans run the different regions."

"The Patriarch is like the Pope?"

"Yes and no. There's no such thing as papal infallibility in Orthodoxy. The Patriarch's called 'the first among equals.' "

"What should I tell Anatoli?"

"That's for you to decide. If I were in your place, though, I think I'd trust the man."

Following the Consul General's instructions, Jeffrey turned right by the outer canal and followed the walkway to a tall, freestanding structure enclosed within its own fortified wall. Jeffrey walked through the copse of tall birch, entered the broad double oaken doors, and loudly pronounced the priest's name to the elderly gentleman acting as both guard and receptionist. The man rose from his stool and shuffled down the long hall, motioning for Jeffrey to follow. They passed through an outer alcove fashioned as a private chapel, where the man made a sign of the cross using large, exaggerated gestures. He opened tall inner doors and pointed Jeffrey toward a dark-haired man seated at a massive desk.

"Mr. Sinclair?" The voice held a rich depth, the eyes great clarity. As he rose, the silver cross hanging from his neck thumped against his chest. He walked forward with hand outstretched. "I am Father Anatoli, the Metropolitan's personal assistant."

"Nice to meet you." Jeffrey felt his hand engulfed in a bearlike grip.

"Please take a seat." He motioned Jeffrey toward the conference table at the room's far end. "I have spoken with Mr. Allbright this morning. He said you had something of possible importance to the church which you wished to discuss with me."

"Yes, that is, I—"

"The Consul General also informs me that you are a Christian." A peasant's hand, flat and broad as a shovel blade, began stroking his broad curly beard where it collected upon his cassock. "And a Protestant. Is all this true?"

Jeffrey listened behind the man's words and heard the same measuring tone he found in almost everyone in this alien land. The need to assess, to test for truth and strength, before trusting. "I know Jesus Christ as Lord," Jeffrey replied. "I hope and pray that on the day when I stand before Him, He will know me as well. And yes, I am a Baptist. My wife and I currently attend an evangelical Anglican church."

"This is all most interesting," the priest said, his lazy hand motions belied by the intense gleam in his eyes. "I seldom have an opportunity to meet with Protestants from the West. Tell me, Mr. Sinclair. Have you visited one of our churches?"

"I have not yet had an opportunity, but I would like to."

"You know, Mr. Sinclair, many of my fellow priests within the Orthodox faith are quite opposed to the Protestant revivals sweeping our country. I do not agree with these men, but still they are a force to be reckoned with."

Jeffrey met the questing gaze square on and replied, "In America there is room for many different kinds of churches."

"Some of us believe the same is true here in Russia. But not all, I am sorry to say. There are those who say the Orthodox way is the only way for Russians. Such men claim that the Orthodox church alone has been invested with spiritual responsibility for this nation. Such declarations in my opinion are as great an error as it would be to say that only

Protestants hold the keys to heaven."

"I always thought salvation rested in Jesus Christ," Jeffrey said.

"A profound statement." A glimmer of approval showed on the heavy features. "But unfortunately, not a truth the church always remembers. The first Protestant churches arrived in Russia toward the end of the nineteenth century, established by German and English missionaries. There was horrible persecution in those early days, both by the state and, tragically, by my own church. Both saw it as an invasion of the spirit. They accused the outsiders of weakening the Russian nation. In the smaller cities and villages there were massacres. Then in 1905 the czar issued a manifesto that legalized all evangelical churches. There was a truce of sorts until the Bolsheviks swept to power. In the persecutions of 1917 to 1930, as the Communists solidified their position, the churches learned to band together in order to survive. This lasted until the onset of perestroika."

"So now that the state persecutions are over," Jeffrey concluded, "the old feuds are surfacing once more."

"And with great ferocity," Father Anatoli agreed. "You see, under the Communists every person was taught that he or she was an element of a unique social system. Their nation was destined to teach the world not the better way, but rather the *right* way. The *only* way. The entire Communist method of education for the young and indoctrination for adults is based upon this principle." He paused. "Or was, I suppose. If the beast has truly been laid to rest for all time."

"You don't think it is?"

"I see problems everywhere," he replied, "with no solutions, only empty promises from our politicians. I hear questions being raised and no answers being offered, only arguments. I do not know how much more my poor nation can take before panic drives them back to the known, to the familiar. At least under the Communist dictatorship they were granted a sense of security." He spent a moment delving inward in weary resignation, collected himself, and asked, "Where was I?"

"Conflict among believers," Jeffrey reminded him.

"Thank you. The Communists taught people to live in

enmity. They taught that progress for the socialist society was possible only if all who were not Communists, all who resisted their doctrine, were eradicated. They pressed the people to live in perpetual suspicion and violent hostility toward 'the other.' You know, of course, who this 'other' is."

"Anybody who does not believe as they do," Jeffrey offered.

"Exactly. Such a mind-set does not disappear simply because the government changes. Four generations have been taught since the age of three, when public schooling begins here, to hate anyone who does not conform.

"Today, the newcomers who fill our churches may indeed be sincere seekers of truth, but many retain vestiges of the old Communist psyche. They see other people going in a different direction with their faith, and the old attitude surfaces: Is the other person correct in their beliefs? Do they worship the *true* Christ? If not, punish them. Lock them up. Declare them criminals. See them as the enemies they are."

Father Anatoli sighed with regret. "Such people insist that every letter of every page of every doctrine be checked and rechecked. Such people have a new name for the incoming Protestant ministers: 'the wolves from the West.' Such people fear that this new invasion will tear down what few walls of Russian Christianity the Communists left standing."

"But you disagree with this."

"I and a number of my fellow priests, although we are a minority and at times find our voices drowned out by the others," he replied. His gaze evidenced a grim memory of former battles. "With us, the problems are all tangled together like a ball of yarn. For example, there are one hundred and eighty parishes in Russia. Twenty of these, some the size of an American state, have no priest at all. All parishes are short-staffed. We need a minimum of twenty more priests in Saint Petersburg alone. There are not enough priests to staff even *half* of our churches. Many of the priests we do have should not be priests at all. They have little training; they have less faith. There are only seven seminaries in the entire country. There are only twelve church-run schools."

He shook his head. "Problems, problems. We drown in problems. I close my eyes and watch them dance before me in the darkness, and I find no solutions. None."

Jeffrey hesitated, then ventured, "You could ask the Protestants to take over ministries that your church can't staff."

The explosion he feared did not come. Instead, the priest sat with head bowed low. "In a perfect world," he murmured. "In a world that truly followed the teachings of Christ . . ."

He lifted his head, the gentle light back in his eyes. "You have a gift of simple speech," he told Jeffrey. "It makes the hardest challenge something I can bear to hear. For this, I thank you."

"I haven't done anything," Jeffrey replied.

To his surprise, the father smiled broadly. "No, perhaps not." He leaned back in his seat. "So what was it you wished to discuss with me?"

Father Anatoli listened carefully until Jeffrey was finished with his account of the missing Ukrainian church treasures. Then he turned away and sat in utter stillness. Eventually he murmured, "A letter. Such a simple affair. Who could think that it would create such problems."

Jeffrey showed confusion. "I don't—"

But Father Anatoli was already on his feet. "Come. Let us walk together to the cathedral. I must prepare for Mass. What are your own plans for the next week?"

"I leave for London the day after tomorrow, Monday afternoon," Jeffrey replied, rising with him. "I'm not sure exactly when I will be back in Saint Petersburg, but it shouldn't be too long."

"Then I suggest you leave this matter with me until your return. I will see what I can learn."

The cathedral interior was rich with the cloying flavor of incense, and Jeffrey instantly felt a familiar unease. There were no seats within the vast hall. Icons were everywhere, rising in great gilded frames ten and twelve high upon the walls. They rested upon the central pillars, they stood on huge bronze altars in the many alcoves, they bedecked the screen before the nave. Candles burned before them all. Hundreds of people were deep in prayer—standing, kneeling, laying prostrate upon the worn marble stonework. Each began and ended their petitions with multiple signs of the cross, some resting their foreheads upon the icons' glass enclosures.

Jeffrey and Father Anatoli paused together at the high-arched entrance to the central chamber. Eyes turned their way, examining the black-bearded priest standing beside the Westerner. Father Anatoli kept his attention focused upon Jeffrey. "You are uncomfortable with the concept of our icons," he observed.

Jeffrey nodded. "It's something I just don't understand, I guess. Maybe it's my Baptist background."

"The arguments and the issues and these icons date back almost two thousand years," Father Anatoli explained, his voice pitched low. "The problems arose when some Christian first painted a picture of Christ in the catacombs and another called the painting an idol. Your word *iconoclast* came from that time and described one who destroyed icons. They also had a name for those who wished to see no picture of Christ, or even crosses. They were called puritans."

He lowered his head so that the black beard fanned out and molded to his cassock. "There was a time in the eighth century when people found with a painting or tapestry depicting the Lord Jesus, or even a cross with a man's figure carved upon it, were tortured and put to death."

"All in the name of love," Jeffrey said quietly. "The same love that drives this wedge between us today."

The light of approval was strong in Father Anatoli's eyes as he continued, "The Orthodox concentrates upon the *mystery* of faith. The *wonder* of the liturgy. Great emphasis is placed upon experiencing union with God. We seek constantly to remind all believers of their responsibility to seek knowledge of the glory that comes through complete and utter surrender to Christ."

"Everything I see here seems so alien," Jeffrey confessed.

"Icons are not idolatry," he stated flatly. "They are not the object of veneration, but a reminder. They point the direction only."

208

Jeffrey watched a woman complete her prayers by leaning forward and kissing the jewel-studded icon's lower frame.
"I'm afraid it looks awfully like idol worship to me."

Black eyes leaned close and drilled him with their intensity. "Now who is the one who condemns with judgment?"

Jeffrey tried not to flinch under the man's gaze. He kept
his disquiet hidden until the father nodded and said, "I must
go. Come to my chambers immediately upon your return to
Saint Petersburg. I should know something by then, if there
is indeed anything for me to know."

Two cultures moved within the church, the tourists and
the penitents. Jeffrey felt like a stranger to both.

Those who came in prayer remained utterly blind to the
others, displaying a single-minded focus that Jeffrey found
awesome. They represented every age, every walk of life. The
young and successful in suits or fresh new dresses. The old
and bowed, clinging to canes and crutches. Mothers with
children, husbands with wives, teenagers in groups and
alone. And as he watched their coming and going, Jeffrey
found a trait utterly lacking in the outside world of Saint
Petersburg. Here were gentle smiles and unstrained voices.
Eyes held a simple, open quality. Hearts could be seen in
many gazes. Not all, but many.

Jeffrey stood beside a pillar, out of the way of those kneeling in prayer. As he stood and watched, a pair of male voices
began a chanted prayer from somewhere above his head. The
first, a light tenor, sang a swift chant upon one single note.
The second voice was very deep and very rich. His words rose
and fell in slow, steady, deliberate tones, like the tolling of
an unseen bell.

Jeffrey found the atmosphere utterly alien, yet comfort-
ing, like the making of a new friend who somehow greeted
him with the ease of a trusted brother.

As Jeffrey turned and left the church, it was this feeling
of calm acceptance that troubled him most of all.

CHAPTER
25

Peter the Great housed his art collection in one small extension of his winter palace. His successor, Elizabeth, gave little thought to art, and left the collection where it was. The next ruler of Russia, the Empress Catherine the Great, found it necessary to build an entire new palace to contain her acquisitions. Yet she continued the practice started by her great-uncle Peter of allowing only a privileged handful of outsiders to view her collection. Over the years, the halls of art and treasures became known as "The Dwelling Place of the Hermits." As French became the language of royal culture, the name was translated to L'Ermitage.

Ivona entered the Hermitage museum and walked down the long Hall of Eighteen-Twelve, lined with over one thousand portraits of officers who had fought in the war of that year. Those who had died in the field and left no record of their faces had empty frames, with their names embossed beneath, to commemorate their sacrifice.

The hall gave way to the Outer Chamber, where dignitaries had waited—sometimes for weeks, sometimes for years—before being escorted into the smaller Throne Room beyond.

Ivona then entered the Pavilion Hall, and found her contact awaiting her beneath one of Russia's few remnants from the rule of the Mongol Khans. Eight centuries before, the

Khan had traveled to Poland on a diplomatic mission, fallen in love with a beautiful Polish princess, and made her his fifteenth wife. The first wife, bitterly jealous of the Khan's evident love for his new bride, had arranged for the girl to be murdered. In her memory, the Khan had designed a pair of matching wall fountains where water trickled down in unending streams, from one onyx half-shell to another, representing the continual cascading tears of his heart.

Ivona strode toward the slender man who stood beside that weeping fountain. "Ilya, I bring the heartfelt greetings of Bishop Michael, as well as those of your beloved parents."

He said nothing, only took her hand and guided her away from the tourist hordes. Twice he paused and scanned the crowd while pretending to point out treasures for her inspection. The third time she asked, "Is there something wrong?"

"If there is," he replied, sweeping his hand out in a grand gesture to present a treasure neither of them saw, "you will know of it when I disappear."

The Hermitage administrator seated her in an unobtrusive corner and searched the throngs once more with worried eyes. "Tell me why you are here."

"Word has come to us of your difficulties. The bishop asks for details."

"Word?" He showed real alarm. "What word?"

"Through your mother," Ivona soothed. "She told us only after hearing of our own troubles. And only after the bishop gave his solemn word that the information would go no further."

The Hermitage administrator subsided. "You, too, have something missing?"

Ivona nodded slowly. "Tell me. Please."

Ilya was quiet for a very long moment, then said, "There are so many treasures on display here that no one thinks of what remains hidden. So much rests in our warehouses, more than you can ever imagine. The authorities just leased to us the former Military College to use as storage space. This is distant and harder to keep secure, but anything is better than the damp confines of our basements. I have six hundred thousand etchings baled together and stored in closets."

"And in the process of this transfer," Ivona guessed, "you have found items missing from your inventory."

"Not for certain," Ilya replied. "Certainly none of the most valuable articles, for which we have records in duplicate. But every day another three or four articles are not to be found—sketches, *objets d'art,* small paintings, religious artifacts, anything."

"You are sure?"

"I am sure of nothing anymore," he replied resignedly. "Even within the museum itself, the halls closed to visitors are stacked with boxes. The papers listing their contents are lost. Security is declining as the government allocates us fewer and fewer militia guards. Do you know what we are paid?"

"I know," she replied quietly.

"Twelve dollars per month," he persisted. "The most qualified museum staff in all Russia, and we can barely feed ourselves and our families. How can you blame those who turn to accepting bribes and looking the other way?"

"I blame no one," Ivona replied.

"There is more. The Golden Treasury has been closed for renovation. We are not sure," he said, then hesitated.

"Sure of what?"

"There are over twenty thousand items in this collection alone," he continued. "If it were one crown, yes, of course, we would prize it. But with seven hundred? So what if one is lost? Could we not have loaned it to a regional museum? Twice we have almost sounded the alarm for missing items, only to find records that twenty, thirty, forty years ago they were loaned to a provincial museum for some exhibition."

"And never returned," she finished.

"Why should they be, when we never asked for them back?"

"But you do think items are missing," she pressed.

"Nothing certain, and nothing of first order."

"Relatively speaking."

"Exactly."

"Their value?"

"In the West?" He pursed his lips. "Who can say? And

once again, the museum is not even sure that anything is gone at all."

"We speak not of the museum," Ivona replied. "Official announcements can be kept for the press. I ask for your opinion."

"Candelabra," he relented. "Gold chains, emblems, boxes, a few icons. From the other departments, any number of items. Possibly. I repeat, nothing is certain."

She thought in silence, then asked the inevitable. "The same is occurring in other museums?"

"Rumors," he replied. "We are feeding on rumors only."

"Yet again—"

"What could they do with so much?" he demanded, his voice rising in painful frustration. "If even a tenth of these rumors are true, we are speaking of thousands of objects."

"Perhaps a bit more quietly," she cautioned.

"*Tons* of valuables," he continued. "Where could they be taking it all?"

"There is no reason to shout," she said.

Ilya sank back. "There are too many rumors for the stories to be smoke alone. There must be a fire. A hundred fires. Yet the government refuses to listen."

"They have other problems," Ivona stated. "Other crises."

He nodded. "You realize, of course, that such thefts have occurred before."

"Yes." Such stories had circulated for years.

"One of the largest collections of Impressionist paintings in the world currently occupies the Hermitage's former attic servant quarters," Ilya went on. "It was collected by two merchants. They presented these treasures to the czar as a bribe for safe passage when they and their families departed westward the year before the October Revolution."

"This much I have heard," Ivona said.

"When the Communists came to power," Ilya continued, "the paintings were condemned as degenerate and made to disappear. For decades it was rumored that Party officials had destroyed them all—Matisse, Van Gogh, Degas, Pissaro, Monet, Renoir, Cezanne, Gaugin, three *rooms* of early Picasso. Then in the late fifties the Party line changed, and Impressionists were declared to be compassionate painters of the common man." Ilya snorted. "The exhibition then reappeared without fanfare, as though closed only for cleaning. Yet dozens of the paintings, perhaps even hundreds, were not to be found. Investigators were met with unofficial warnings, and the persistent found themselves granted postings to museums in Siberia. Eventually all records of the missing pictures also disappeared."

"Who do you think is responsible," Ivona pressed. "Not for the paintings, that is history. For your current thefts."

Ilya shrugged, despondent.

"Are there stories to be heard on this as well?"

"Rumors," he muttered. "Of what worth are they to a custodian of Russia's treasures?"

"The Orthodox church," she demanded. "Could they be involved?"

"Of this I have heard nothing," he replied, definite for the first time that day, "although there are rumors of items missing from this quarter as well."

"From within the Orthodox churches?"

Ilya showed wry humor. "You would think they had already lost everything of value, no? Fifty thousand treasures we have here in the Hermitage alone from the churches, all listed as voluntary gifts. Very generous with the new Communist state, these churches were."

"Mafia or KGB," Ivona pressed. "Do you hear anything unofficial? Could one or the other perhaps be behind the thefts?"

He looked at her. "Why do you suggest they are separate? As far as I am concerned, nowadays they both function outside the law. Why should they not operate together?"

"So there *is* word of this," Ivona said.

"Suddenly the air in here is stifling." Ilya stood. "Come. I will walk you out."

Reluctantly she allowed herself to be led forward. "There is nothing more to say?"

As he walked he drew her closer with one hand on her elbow. He asked in a small voice, "Tell me, Ivona Aristonova. What rumor is worth getting killed over?"

"I seek information for our use only," she replied just as quietly. "Tell me what you know."

"I know nothing."

"What you guess, then."

They entered a vast chamber in the original palace, one whose ceiling and pillars were gilded with more than seven hundred pounds of gold. Excited clusters of tourists milled about, jabbering in a dozen alien tongues. Ilya slowed his pace, pointed to a chest made in the time of Peter the Great from sixteen tons of pure silver. He pitched his voice so low that it was lost at three paces. "The KGB is selling its only remaining assets."

"Information and access," Ivona offered.

Ilya nodded. "Still there are moles on my staff. Only now the KGB bosses are no longer interested in dissidents. They seek only to pad their nest. With dollars."

"These moles are making it easy for certain items to vanish," Ivona helped him with guesses of her own. "They are pointing out what articles to take, then making the records disappear."

They stopped before a massive display case containing religious artifacts appropriated from the nation's churches. A handwritten sign stated that it was a sample from the Hermitage's Golden Treasury, which was now closed for renovation. The case contained gold plates for sacramental bread, the handles fashioned like crowns. Gold and silver chalices, embossed with diamonds and rubies the size of quail's eggs. A Bible with a cover of solid gold, the depiction of Christ framed by a hundred matching emeralds. Yet another chalice, the entire exterior embossed with diamonds. An incense burner in the form of a holy shrine, an empty tomb at its heart, all in gold.

"There are several articles I know in my heart are missing," Ilya murmured, "though I can now find no record of their ever having existed. I am beginning to suspect that a drop has been arranged. Outsiders dressed as security or transport workers come for shipments, or to move a case, or to relocate a picture. All the documents are in order, all the proper answers prepared for anyone who asks."

"Mafia," Ivona repeated.

"Wolves in sheep's clothing," Ilya replied. "They devour our nation's greatest treasures. They have the pity of carnivores for their prey."

They entered the exit hallway. Ilya swept a despairing hand at the surrounding boxes. "This passage is used by thousands of visitors every day. Yet we line it with the beautiful and the valuable, the returned foreign exhibits. Why? Because we have no place else to keep them. Look at the addresses. Brisbane, Australia. Long Island, United States. Turin, Italy. Seoul, Manila, Tokyo, Sao Paulo. What you see is the smallest example of this national crisis."

She stopped at the exit doors, tried to put her own worries aside. "You are a good friend, Ilya. In the name of our bishop, I thank you."

"Bring back my treasures," he replied quietly. "Return my nation's pride."

CHAPTER
26

The general arrived in a very worried state. "Your naive young American is causing my superiors great concern."

"How is that possible?" Markov seated the general at the rosewood table in the most comfortable corner of his cluttered parlor and personally poured tea for them both. "The boy has only been in Saint Petersburg for a few days. Don't tell me he's already made a drunken fool of himself in public. There is nothing more ridiculous than a young man with a bellyful, don't you agree?"

General Surikov was not amused. "He arrived in Saint Petersburg with Bishop Michael Denisov's personal secretary as his interpreter."

"Bishop who?" Markov seated himself. "I don't believe I know that name. Will you take sugar?"

"Denisov. He's one of the leaders of the Ukrainian Rites Catholic Church."

Markov sipped at his own cup, gauging the man across from him. "Please forgive me, but I fail to see—"

"Let us just say that Denisov is someone we wish to have as far removed from this entire process as possible."

Markov nodded slowly, his mind working hard. Clearly something had been taken from the Ukrainian church. Something valuable. But that the young American with whom he met might be—no, no, it was simply too preposterous. "My dear fellow, you and I both know that one reason we selected this particular individual was his established links to Eastern Europe."

"Such links as these to the Ukrainian church are utterly unacceptable," Surikov barked.

"Please calm yourself. The American mentioned that he already had a trip planned before coming to our meeting. He said this to explain why he would be unable to travel immediately to Saint Petersburg."

"He said that?" The general relaxed by degrees.

"He did, indeed. Now think for a moment. How on earth could he have planned a voyage to ally himself with such a group before he even met with me and learned of my requirements?"

"That is true," the general murmured. Still he remained troubled. "With all due respect, Prince Markov, you had best be right."

"I am quite sure it is mere coincidence," Markov declared. "Mr. Sinclair traveled to the Ukraine, he worked with a good interpreter, he asked her to assist him in Saint Petersburg. Nothing more, nothing less."

"My superiors will no doubt be pleased to hear of your news. It was a most unpleasant moment when they learned of your man's choice of interpreters."

"May I ask why?"

"You may indeed," the general replied sharply. "But I am not sure you would wish for my superiors to know that such questions were being posed."

"An idle remark. Please disregard it," Markov said. General Surikov's superiors were not the type to displease with unnecessary probings.

But the general was not finished. "You have not seen, as I have, how curiosity is dealt with. And mistakes."

"I am quite sure—"

"The Chechen clan were not selected for their manners," the general pressed on. "They are the cruelest of the cruel. And they are always hungry for more."

Chosen by whom, Markov wondered. And for what? But he quashed such curiosity flat and chose the wiser course of a personal question. "Tell me, general. Why do you consort with such as these?"

For once the general did not retreat. "I was offered a job in the ministry last week," the general confessed, but without enthusiasm. "Done out of respect, however. Not out of real need."

"You are too modest," Markov protested. "No doubt they see in you a treasure trove of experience."

"It was made out of loyalty," the general countered. "A job without meaning or purpose. And the payment is paltry, made with currency that grows more worthless with each passing hour. Still, I have been considering it."

"Perhaps it would be wiser to wait until the course of events is more certain," Markov offered, and thought, or at least until our own business is concluded.

"Perhaps," the general agreed dismally. "And yet I was ordered—" There he stopped.

"Ordered?" Markov's interest overrode his better judgment. "By whom?"

But Surikov shook his head. "I have my reasons."

Could it be, Markov wondered, that the military cabal and their Party minions maintained a shaky alliance with the Russian mafia? Markov inspected the general as he sipped his tea, and decided the idea had merit. In the present vacuum, the mafia had risen faster and higher than anyone could have imagined. In such a case, Surikov would be far more valuable as a liaison than as simply another retired officer cluttering the ministry's hallways.

"A senior Soviet officer, now serving a cabal of criminals," Markov hesitated, then guessed, "perhaps with connections to the KGB—you must admit that is, well, rather remarkable."

"Former officer, former KGB, former Soviet empire," Surikov corrected. "The world has tilted on its axis."

"The KGB still exists."

"Not as it once did," the general amended. "And not as it still should." The bushy eyebrows tightened. "Nor as it shall again, you mark my words."

Absently Markov stirred his cup. If it were true that Surikov was being used as a liaison with the increasingly powerful criminal elements, that meant the general would be an even more valuable contact for himself. He ventured, "I have heard that parliament almost managed sufficient backing for a no-confidence vote. Our leaders must be quaking in their boots. No doubt you are pleased with these developments."

The general returned to his habitual bearlike rumblings. "I will be pleased when the whole circus is over, when such nonsense is put back in the only place it belongs—the theater."

Markov nodded sagely. "The delegates who would most likely support a coup are led by the Speaker of the House, are they not? A Chechen, if I recall correctly. Of the same tribe as your superiors."

Surikov responded with a stony silence, then, "Perhaps we should return to the matter at hand."

"Certainly," Markov agreed, satisfied that his guesses were correct. "Please assure your superiors of my wholehearted support."

"Your support, yes. They will be most pleased to hear of this." General Surikov's gaze was bleak. "Let us also hope that you can assure them of success. Because if not—"

"There is no chance of anything other than full success," Markov replied hastily. "We need not even discuss such a contingency."

"That is good," Surikov replied. "As to the American, my superiors are not as trusting as you appear to be."

"On the contrary," Markov countered, "I trust only myself. This American, however, is of no great account. A pawn in the great game of power and wealth. He knows nothing and understands less."

"It is indeed good to hear that you have no great affection for the man."

"Affection?" Markov lifted his eyebrows. "What has that to do with anything?"

"Because if there proves to be a problem," Surikov answered, "there will soon be no problem."

A chill wind wafted through the chamber. "What will they do to him?"

"Better to ask," General Surikov replied, rising to his feet, "what they will do to you."

CHAPTER
27

"Good morning, Sinclair," Sergei Popov greeted him cheerfully as he descended the stairs the next morning. "How you sleep?"

"Great, thanks."

"Your lady translator, she leave early. I have message." He handed over a slip of paper, then a second. "And this come too. American in big car. Maybe gangster, yes?"

"Doubtful."

"Yes, you right. Russia has too many already, no need to import from Chicago. You like breakfast?"

"Please." Jeffrey seated himself at one of the little tables and opened the notes. The first was from Ivona, whom he had not seen since their meeting the day before. "We meet with Yussef tomorrow before your departure. He has news and antiques." No greeting, no apology for leaving him high and dry, no nothing.

The second was from the Consul General, and more positive. "If you can spare the time, I have a conference this afternoon which you might want to be in on. If so, I'll pick you up at three in front of your winter palace. And in case you are interested, there's an English-language church service this morning at ten and a second service at twelve. If you want a seat, you'll need to get there a half-hour earlier. They fill up fast. Allbright." Below the Consul General had written an address for the service.

Sergei came back with coffee, bread, and jam. He glanced at the New Testament Jeffrey had brought downstairs with him and asked good-naturedly, "You are religious man, yes?"

"I try. I think I fail more often than I succeed, but I do try."

"That is answer of a good man," Sergei decided. "I have friend, he is religious man. He believes."

"And you?"

"Maybe someday," he replied cheerfully. "Now life too full."

"Perhaps faith could help you handle your problems more easily," Jeffrey offered.

"Maybe," he said doubtfully, then added, "Good to be religious. Give you something to fight about, now that Soviets gone. Man must fight or die, yes?"

"I hope not."

A forefinger as rigid as a broomstick poked the table beside Jeffrey's Bible. "You Christians, you talk peace and fight all same time. Go in church, shout love, love, love to everybody, yes? Then go out, shout hate, hate, hate to all other churches. Protestants, Catholics, Orthodox, all same." The finger retreated to tap the side of Sergei's head. "Christians, they smart. They know. Man needs enemies. Keeps him strong."

"I try never to condemn anyone," Jeffrey replied quietly, remembering yesterday's experience in the cathedral, wondering if he spoke the truth.

"Then you very strange man, Sinclair," Sergei declared, and changed the subject. "You know, now Russians, they go to church, but many not go for God. Before, nobody goes. Now is fashion and people with no belief, they go. But this stops soon, I think."

"Why do you say that?"

He shrugged. "Church asks too many questions. People who not believe, they don't like these questions. Soon they will stop going, and the church will be for believers."

Jeffrey shook his head. "I know a lot of people in the West who go to church, hear the questions, and just decide they apply to everybody else but themselves."

Sergei showed surprise. "This problem is in West too?"

"Maybe less than here, since churchgoing isn't such a fashion anymore. But yes, we have it."

Sergei thought it over. "Yes, is true. People turn from questions they don't like. So. Maybe churches stay full but not full of belief. What is answer?"

"I think it lies in searching your own heart," Jeffrey replied. "Searching with honesty and prayer."

Sergei turned serious. "I think maybe you know many questions. Hard questions. You know answers too?"

"Only a few," Jeffrey replied. "The most important one is Jesus Christ. You need to know that he is your Savior, to know His presence in your heart."

Sergei mulled that over in silence until Jeffrey finished breakfast. As he stood, Sergei said, "Listen, Sinclair. My grandmother, she collects things."

"What kinds of things?"

"From other lands." He gave a cheerful shrug. "What no matters. Her room a museum of all what you never want to see."

"You mean tourist souvenirs."

"Look." He reached in his pocket, came out with crumpled dollars. "I have twenty dollars. You take, buy for me. Buy things for tourists. Things so she can look and think of lands she will never see."

"No, I can't accept your money."

"Take, take. Is good money. Not stolen. You buy with this, yes? You bring back next time. Please. You do this. Friends, yes? You help me. Please."

"All right."

"Is good to help. I know. Touches heart. Gives much freedom to soul, this help of friends. You have strength, you share."

"What strength?"

Sergei showed great amusement. "You have so much, you don't understand. Freedom is strength, yes?"

"I suppose so."

"You free to choose. But to choose is hard. You learn to be strong because you learn to choose. You act. In Russia, we strong in talk, not in act."

"You can learn."

He shrugged. "Maybe yes, maybe no. Who can see? We have big experience in talk. Too big. Centuries and centuries. Action dangerous. Get you killed. Talk our only freedom. But my people, they forget how to act."

Jeffrey accepted the money. "I'll bring a little something back with me next time."

"Good, good. You earn thanks. You see, I pay. I pay back big. Someday you need, I give." He extended his hand. "You watch."

Jeffrey grasped the firm grip and agreed, "Friends."

The church was located in a series of interconnected storefront rooms just off a main thoroughfare and not far from the Markov palace. Jeffrey found it wonderfully refreshing to enter, be greeted in English, exchange the sort of smiles and greetings he was used to in his own church. After a few minutes, he found himself relaxing in a way that had not been possible since his arrival.

The church was *very* full. Every seat was taken. People stood four and five deep along the back and side walls. Jeffrey listened as first the greetings and then all songs, prayers, and the sermon itself were given in English, then translated into Russian. He looked around the crowded chambers and guessed that perhaps half those attending were locals.

According to the program handed him as he entered, the pastor was a Reverend Evan Collins. He was a scholarly sort, not in the least what Jeffrey might have expected in the rough-and-tumble of post-Soviet Russia. He was a middle-aged gentleman with sparse graying hair. Collins viewed the world through kindly, inquisitive eyes. There was no righteous anger, no domineering salesmanship. He spoke with a voice that invited listeners to lean closer, relax their guard, draw near. Here is safety, his voice seemed to say. Here is rest.

When the service was over, Jeffrey joined the congregation for coffee. He bided his time until the pastor was free, then walked over and introduced himself. "I have a problem

I was wondering if I could ask you about."

Reverend Collins shifted over one chair and invited him to be seated. "How did you find out about our church?"

"Through the American Consul General."

"Oh, yes," Collins said, quickly sobering. "Stan Allbright has proven to be a good friend to us. We have been confronted with a very serious problem, and had it not been for his assistance, quite frankly, I don't know what we would have done."

"As a matter of fact," Jeffrey replied, "the work that's brought me to Saint Petersburg might be connected."

"How is that?"

"I'm not sure I should say." Or could, he added silently.

"No, of course not." Reverend Collins paused to greet a passing friend, then continued, "But I take it you know about Leslie Ann Stevens."

"A little."

"She was returning from a prayer meeting at our church when she was kidnapped. I suppose you know that, too. We have done everything we can think of, spoken to everyone we could approach, and the only vestige of hope we've found has been from the Consul General."

"He appears to be taking the matter very seriously."

"That girl was an absolute godsend for my wife and me," Collins said, his eyes reaching out over the crowd. "Often we feel we are trying to run a church on the outer edge of civilization. The problems have been impossible to describe, truly impossible. We are growing at an incredible rate, utterly understaffed, more crises than you could ever imagine. And then up pops Leslie Ann, always willing to help out, never complaining, always taking over at the last-minute—"

A gray-haired American gentleman breezed over and cheerfully shouldered his way into the conversation. Collins introduced him as a deacon. Jeffrey shook hands and settled back to wait. Eventually the pastor turned back to him. "Sorry about the interruptions. Was your question about Leslie Ann?"

Jeffrey shook his head. "It wasn't anything urgent. I can see you have a lot of more important things to tend to right now."

"Nonsense. I'd be glad to help if I can, and now is as good a time as any. Do you mind talking about it here in public?"

"No." He related the discussion with the Orthodox priest and his feelings upon entering the church. Reverend Collins listened in silence, his eyes never wavering from Jeffrey's face, his depth of listening resembling the hidden reserves of a quiet, slow-moving river.

"Unity among believers is based on a twofold process," Reverend Collins said when Jeffrey was finished. "In the Book of Peter, we are told that all of us, once Christ has entered our lives, participate in the divine nature. Christ is in me, and I am in Him. A glorious reassurance. And throughout the New Testament, we are declared joined to each other. A *body* of believers. The bride of Christ. A hint of the divine in earthly form. I think that we owe it to our Father to behave as He commands, don't you?"

Jeffrey nodded. "In principle, I agree totally with what you say. I guess my question is where to draw the line. At what point does a practice become unacceptable?"

"Who are we to judge what is and is not acceptable? In Proverbs we are told that one of the seven things God truly despises is a man who sows discord among those whom God loves. Why on earth would anyone wish to take that risk?" He paused to sip from his cup. "The Bible says that all the world is in the hands of darkness. Conflict between believers is for me the greatest evidence of this dark presence within the earthly body of Christ."

Jeffrey took a breath. "I lost my faith a while back and only recently found it again. Or it found me; I'm not so sure about that part. What I'm trying to say is that the experience is still really fresh with me. I can remember how it felt to be without faith—boy, can I ever. And I can still feel how it was to return to the fold. Such a *powerful* moment."

"The moment of earthly rapture," the man agreed. "An earth-shattering experience."

"I think a lot of people," Jeffrey went on, "mix up the *path* that led them to this moment with the *goal*."

Gray eyes fastened him with an intensity that suspended time. "Fascinating."

"I wonder if maybe people think that because their particular church brought them to Christ, it is *the* church of Christ. The *only* church. The *right* church."

"And what, pray tell, keeps you from making the same mistake?"

Jeffrey had to smile. "A Baptist loses his faith, falls in love with a devout Anglican, and is guided back to the Lord by a Catholic brother. Who do I give the credit to?"

"The good Lord Jesus," Collins replied firmly.

"And yet," Jeffrey added, "I have these strong feelings of discomfort with the way the Orthodox worship. Actually, I guess it's the way a lot of the Eastern churches worship. It's not anything I've thought out. In fact, it bothers me to feel this way. But I do, way down at gut level."

"Their ways are different," Collins agreed. "But so is this entire world. What troubles me about the Orthodox church is their view toward evangelism here. They tend to see themselves as guardians of the country's spirituality. As a result, many are uncomfortable with anyone else coming in to do direct evangelism. They tend to identify the church very closely with their national heritage, you see."

"What about the icons," Jeffrey asked. "Don't they bother you?"

"It's interesting," Collins replied. "One objection the Orthodox make about us is that Western religious art depicts saintly figures in contemporary form. Do you understand what I'm saying?"

"Yes." As styles of art and even fashion had changed with the centuries, Western religious paintings had done so as well. Biblical figures had been painted using local models and had often been dressed in clothing from the period in which the painter lived. Jeffrey had laughed when he first learned of this habit, until another dealer had pointed out that even today, actors in period films had their clothes and hairstyles adapted to modern styles and tastes.

"But we don't kneel before Western art and pray," Jeffrey protested.

"Certainly not in the same way," Collins agreed. "But you see, the Orthodox *deliberately* make their paintings more abstract, exactly because they are used in the worship service. They do not wish to depict people, but rather religious principles."

Jeffrey thought this over. "I still don't get it."

"Perhaps you are right," Evan agreed. "Perhaps I am trying too hard to show compassion and fellowship with people who make real mistakes in their form of worship. But so long as there is this tiniest room for doubt in my mind, I hesitate to condemn. There has been so much condemnation between Christians over the centuries."

Jeffrey recalled lessons about the Reformation wars. "And so many bloody mistakes."

"Exactly. So I tend to search for harmony rather than judgment, even if that may mean erring on the side of tolerance. I still feel more comfortable leaving the condemnation up to God."

He shrugged and added, "The Orthodox are facing problems which we in the West have enormous difficulty even imagining. Not enough priests, and those they have are often undertrained. Large numbers of believers who cannot read. And even if they could, for seventy years it has been virtually impossible for them to have Bibles."

Jeffrey struggled to understand. "So they use pictures to remind people of lessons?"

"Here again, the Orthodox would say we are making a typical Western judgment," Collins replied. "They do not see icons as pictures at all. They exaggerate hands and eyes and features because they intend to communicate truth *through* the painting. Attention should not be on the painting, but rather on what stands *behind* it. The worshiper must be pushed by the painting to see *beyond* the picture to the spiritual reality itself."

Jeffrey shook his head. "But how do you separate the concept of icons from that of idolatry?"

"Well, maybe you shouldn't," Collins allowed. "I'm not saying what is right or wrong here, you understand. I'm simply trying to understand what they think. That was a central question I had when I arrived: was I facing a nation that, like the early Israelites, had fallen away to follow other religions? As my Russian improved, I listened as best I could, and I came to believe that those who had refused to follow the idolatry of Communism had remained Christian, at least in their own eyes."

"And so?"

"And so I'm still not sure," Collins replied. "What I *think* is that it is one thing for informed priests and theologians to *know* the difference, and *maintain* the difference, and so look through an icon to the truth beyond instead of worshiping the icon as an idol. But it seems to me that maybe ordinary folks haven't been able to maintain that distinction. They end up identifying the Spirit's power with these icons and images. In the worst of cases, perhaps they do follow the idolatrous path.

"They make offerings to shrines—we see this all through the poorer lands where illiteracy is a big problem, not just here. Mexico is covered with them. The impression you get is that people identify the source of power as the object itself, not something beyond the object. So I think—and it's just one person's thoughts here, all right? But yes, I think that the way priests explain the icons is often quite different from the way a lot of the people here understand them, and the way they understand salvation. These distinctions are lost on a lot of them."

The troubled look firmed into a clear-sighted determination. "So I take it as my own personal responsibility to remind everyone with whom I have contact of the Lord Jesus' saving grace. I do *not* condemn. I simply remind. I point to the Bible. I teach from the Bible. I teach as I myself was taught. I pray with them. I encourage them in the Lord. And I hope that all who seek shall find the one true Answer."

"What I'm about to tell you is documented fact," Consul General Stan Allbright told Jeffrey that afternoon when he and Casey picked him up at the Markov palace. They were driving toward an unidentified appointment, with Casey at the wheel. "But it's also highly confidential, so I want you to keep it under your hat."

"I understand."

"For the moment, we're going to assume that even if there's no connection between our two dilemmas, they are at least not in conflict, and possibly in parallel. You have any problem with that?"

Jeffrey shook his head. "Not that I can think of."

"Okay, here's the picture." Allbright crossed his legs in the Chevrolet's roomy interior. "Everything we've been able to uncover points toward the Orthodox church not being directly involved in anything going on here. The mafia clans—and they call themselves that, by the way, mafia, even spell it out like that in Cyrillic. So the mafia and the Orthodox, they occupy two totally different worlds. What makes your story interesting is the suggestion that maybe, somehow, there is a bridge between the two."

Casey spoke for the first time. "All those unemployed spies got to have something to occupy their time."

Jeffrey looked from one to the other. "You mean the KGB?"

Allbright nodded. "You've probably heard stories about how some of the priests used to spy for them. That's true. But what is not true is this assumption some people make that because a few of the priests were twisted, everybody in the church was on the take. That is plain nonsense."

"A minority," Casey interjected. "Powerful, dangerous, deadly. But still a minority."

"Now, these Orthodox priests who were controlled by the KGB," Allbright went on, "they've lost their power base. Just like the KGB itself has."

"Can't say I've ever had a chance to talk with one," Casey offered. "But I kind of doubt that they're real happy about the current state of affairs."

"What this means," Allbright continued, "is that there are two struggles inside the Russian Orthodox Church. One is between the devout and the xenophobes—that's what I call the ultraconservatives who believe that only the Orthodox should tend to the spiritual needs of Russia. You get this struggle in a lot of churches, sure, but not like here, where the lid's been screwed down tight for over seventy years. Anyway, the one point these two groups agree on is the second contest, which is in effect a major house cleaning. And guess who's on the way out."

"The priests who spied on their own church."

"Right the first time," Casey said.

"I bet that's easier said than done."

"Absolutely," Allbright said. "The KGB infiltration goes right up the ladder, although it's not as complete as you might expect. In some places, though, like in the Ukrainian Orthodox church based in Kiev, the power structure's pretty much rotten to the core. So instead of obeying the commands of the Patriarch in Moscow, they just broke away entirely."

"And where does that leave us?"

"The only people these soon-to-be outcast priests can rely on," Allbright responded, "are their old buddies over at the KGB."

"Who are in a pretty shaky position themselves," Casey added.

"Exactly. But the KGB hasn't been sitting around on its hands while its power vanished. On that point you can bet your whole bundle. Part of the organization is digging in its heels and shouting doom and gloom at the top of its collective voice. The radicals are working hard as they can to bring down the democratic government and replace it with a dictatorship. Some of these are diehard Communists, some are right-wing military fanatics, others are just out to feather their nest."

"A real mixed bag," Casey said. "They'll stay together only as long as they don't have power. Right now, though, you'd think they were all long-lost brothers."

"This faction also contains the KGB department that used to control the flow of black-market goods," Allbright said.

"Which was where the mafia gained their first foothold in the Russian power structure," Casey explained.

Jeffrey asked, "So you really think the mafia's involved here?"

But Allbright was not to be hurried. "Any place as tightly controlled as the former Soviet Union needed a safety valve for illegal goods, especially for items the bigwigs wanted, like Western radios and cameras and such. The KGB was the guy riding shotgun on the stagecoach. Only now, with their power structure in shambles, the horses are in control and the shotgun riders are hanging on for dear life."

Allbright began drumming his fingers on the car window. "Over in the Asian part of Russia there's a saying that goes, 'A man needs two legs to stand upright.' A lot of people feel like Russia's trying to make headway with only one working leg. This newest Russian revolution has made great political strides, but from the legal side there's total chaos. Economically too. The mafia's taken a long look at this situation and decided to fill the vacuum and their pockets all at the same time."

"How does this tie in with your missing girl?"

"This is pure conjecture," Allbright replied, "but I think maybe our lady just happened upon something she shouldn't have seen. They took her because she was there."

"If it's the mafia in control," Casey said, "our only hope is if they figure she's worth more alive than dead."

Allbright pointed to the blank-faced building up ahead, a concrete and glass structure not far from the Neva River. Uniformed policemen flanked the entrance, stood sentry at either corner, and arrayed themselves in silent ranks across the street.

"KGB headquarters," he said, then went on with his explanation. "There's a second group emerging in there. Been hard at work over the past few months, made a strong impression on me and some others. Real law-and-order team. They're trying to adapt to the new world order, become a sort of super-police, kind of like our FBI."

"A definite minority," Casey added. "Powerful, though, and growing stronger every day. They're about our only hope when it comes to problems like ours."

"Follow our lead here," Allbright ordered. "Don't open your mouth until we're in the group's offices and the door's locked. As far as they're concerned, their most dangerous enemies are people under the same roof."

"The mafia in Saint Petersburg is just as powerful as the city government," the scruffy young man declared. "Here and every other major city in Russia."

When Jeffrey, Casey, and the Consul General had entered

the main doors, their contact had been waiting for them. He had exchanged harsh words with the sullen guard behind the protective glass barrier, refused to sign his guests in, then led them down a grimy hall lined with closed, unmarked doors. The only sinister element to the entire building had been the silence.

The man led them into a large office containing a dozen battered wooden desks pushed into a trio of square groupings. A punching bag hung over the entrance. At their arrival, the other four men and two women stopped their work and gathered near. Clearly they had been expecting the visitors. The outer door was quickly shut and locked.

They were all young, all hard-faced, all armed. They listened in silence as the Consul General related his own findings in surprisingly fluent Russian. Jeffrey spent the long minutes looking around the room. It was as cluttered and faceless as any American big-city bullpen. The biggest difference was the lack of electronics. There was no trace of a computer, nor any of the normal background radio static. He saw only one prewar telephone for the entire room. It did not ring the entire time they were there.

One of the young men spoke fluent English. When the Consul General was finished and they had conferred in quiet, clipped tones, he said to Jeffrey, "There are almost three thousand gangs operating in Russia, and another thousand or so from other states that work here from time to time. The markets are coming more under their control every day. Doing business means finding the right connections and paying them a share. If somebody doesn't pay on time, the answer here is to shoot him."

"This group is Saint Petersburg's main anti-mafia squad," the Consul General explained. "I've worked with them on a couple of items before, and think you should trust them. I do."

"Hits go for about two hundred dollars these days," the young man continued. He was dressed in rundown denims and a shirt that had seen better days. He needed a shave and a month of dedicated sleep. But his voice carried the authority of hands-on experience.

"Soakings, they're called. We get seven to ten of them a

day just inside this city. The Azerbaijani mafia is battling
for control of the central markets, so right now we're seeing
a lot of intergang killings, more than usual. The Uzbekis are
big in the local hash and marijuana trade. The Chechen control most roads and harbors. The Georgian mafia controls
most of the restaurants. The Siberian clans control the flow
of gold and diamonds and furs. The Ingush are big in pro-
tection and shakedowns."

"What about kidnappings?" Allbright asked.

A flash of grim humor circled the room after the young
man had translated. "Everybody," he replied flatly.

"And treasure?"

A glimmer of new interest surfaced. "Stolen?"

The Consul General turned to Jeffrey and waited. This
was his ball to play as he chose. Jeffrey hesitated, knowing
for certain what Yussef would think of his sharing the information with the KGB. Finally, he decided to go with his
gut. "In the Ukraine. From a church."

Swiftly the information was translated. Then, "Value?"

"Big. Very big. Hard to say without having seen it, but
from what I've heard, well over a million."

"Dollars?"

"Yes."

The group exchanged glances, and one of them released
a silent sigh. "We have been hearing rumors," the young man
explained. "A couple of pieces missing here, more there, little
bits and pieces that alone are not too much, never too much.
Never as much as what you are saying, not apart. But together?" He shrugged. "A fortune."

"Any idea who's behind it?" Allbright demanded.

"We don't know if what we hear is true at all. But we hear
there is a gathering of pieces."

Allbright shot Jeffrey a quick glance. "Here in Saint
Petersburg?"

The young man shrugged. "Rumors only. But we think
yes."

"It would be logical," the Consul General speculated.
"The ports around here have the greatest amount of traffic
with the West. And Saint Petersburg is the city closest to the
Finnish border."

The young man shook his head. "Something this big, I think by sea."

Casey spoke up. "What about the Tombek clan?"

The room's atmosphere instantly rose to a new level of intensity. Even those who spoke no English reacted to the sound of that name. The young man asked, "What about them?"

"Are they involved in kidnappings?"

"They are involved in everything," he replied flatly. "Especially things that make big money."

"Like kidnapping foreigners," Casey persisted.

"Maybe. Why do you think they are involved?"

"Casey thought he spotted a couple of their men following Mr. Sinclair," Allbright explained. "Near to where Miss Stevens was taken."

"Not think," Casey corrected. "Know."

Alert gray eyes focused on Jeffrey. "You were followed by Tombek?"

"So he says."

Glances were exchanged with other members of the team. "You are still alive?"

Jeffrey fought off a sudden chill. "As far as I can tell."

"Tombek is Chechen," the man said, as though that were all the explanation required.

Casey explained to Jeffrey, "Chechen is a tribe from the Caucasus region of southern Russia. They are winning the bloody gang war for control of the Moscow markets."

"Here, too, they are a problem," the young man added. "Very dangerous. Very deadly. Many killers."

Allbright asked, "Have you heard anything about them moving into stolen treasures?"

There was a moment's quiet discussion, a chorus of head shakes. "Nothing," the young man replied. "But Chechen control much of the ports and international harbor traffic."

"Like drugs," Casey explained to Jeffrey. "Raised in the southern reaches of the country, then exported to Western Europe and America."

"Big in trade," the young man continued. "Like importing stolen cars or exporting Russian factory goods. We have heard they are making big contracts with Western companies to supply steel. They have plans to make everything look legal."

"Front," Casey offered. "They have a Western group that is going to front for the gang."

"Yes. This we have heard. There is much money in such trade, especially if they can make it look all legal with such a front."

"But no treasures?" Jeffrey asked.

"Or kidnappings?" Allbright added.

"Who knows with Tombek? They are always hungry, always growing. Never enough. And always danger. There is great danger with all Chechen, but especially Tombek. Their only answer to a problem is to kill."

Allbright demanded, "So you'll check it out?"

There was a brief discussion, then, "We will see if we can learn anything." To Jeffrey, he asked, "Where do you stay?"

"A small guesthouse off the Nevsky Prospekt, near Kirpichny."

"Run by the Ukrainians, yes? It is nice?"

"It's fine."

"And if you happen to find a missing American lady while you're looking," the Consul General added, "I'd sure appreciate hearing about it."

The young man stood and motioned toward the door. "We'll be in touch."

As they passed through the entrance, the Consul General drew the young man over to one side. Jeffrey took the opportunity to tell Casey, "It looks like I've misjudged you."

Casey shrugged it off, his eyes on his boss. "It happens."

"I think I owe you an apology."

"Takes a good man to be willing to change his mind." Casey turned toward him and stuck out his hand. "Pals?"

"Sure, thanks."

"Just be sure and watch your back. If the Tombeks or any other of the Chechen clans are involved here, the stakes are high. Winner takes all."

CHAPTER
28

On Monday morning, Ivona stepped into the guesthouse's cramped parlor. She spotted Jeffrey Sinclair seated in the corner waiting for her, but she hesitated before approaching him. Somehow, for reasons she could not yet understand, everything about the young American was a challenge to her, a threat. Even before she had first met him, she had feared the meeting.

It was here again now, this challenge. He sat in a quiet corner of the crowded lobby, the jangling noise and the milling people touching him not at all. Amidst this clamor, the young man sat quiet and still. His attention was focused on the small book in his lap. His entire *being* was drawn into the act of reading.

As she stood just inside the entrance and watched him, once again the unbidden memories arose to add to her disquiet.

Her family was given transport passes to leave Archangelsk, but that did not mean they could leave the frozen north. Not yet. First they had to obtain train tickets. The very same night the passes were handed out, her parents sold whatever they did not need to wear or eat or drink. The next morning, they all went together to the station. And there they found a scene straight from hell.

Thousands of people fought and screamed and wept and pleaded for seats on the one train leaving for the outside that week. There was much fear that the policy would be overturned before the next train arrived, and so everyone fought for a ticket. Somehow her father managed to battle his way through the crowd and buy seats.

The train trip to the southwest of Russia, to near Kiev, lasted three weeks. Fifteen people and all their belongings were crammed together into a compartment meant for six. Three of these were men from the gold mines of Vorkuta, a place so awful that Ivona's parents refused to speak of it around her. They looked like walking skeletons, these men. Two did not survive the journey.

For Ivona, time simply ceased to exist. She sat and she lay and she watched the same endless landscape of mud and trees and primitive villages move slowly by. She sank into a feverish, half-awake state and came to see the train as a new prison, one from which they would never escape. They were destined to drift for the rest of their lives, with no money and little food, on tracks that led nowhere.

And then, finally, they arrived in Kiev, the capital of the Ukraine. Their long journey came to an end, and the ordeal of beginning a life in a strange new land, with neither family ties nor work nor money nor a place to live, began. As Ivona struggled to disown the past and put down roots in new rocky soil, she learned the lessons of self-discipline and determined concentration and fierce independence. And the seed of love within her heart remained stillborn.

•   •   •

Jeffrey was seldom able to lose himself in the Scriptures. Most days the words remained silent upon the page. He had sometimes come upon Katya during her times of prayer and felt the silence and power that surrounded her. The intensity of her stillness humbled him and mirrored the tenuous hold he felt he held upon his own faith.

This morning he was forced to do his morning study while

seated in the lobby, waiting for Ivona to arrive. He had awak-
ened late and rushed through breakfast, only to realize he
had forgotten to pray. So back he went for his Bible and,
ignoring the people and the noise surrounding him, he sat
down and bent over the Book.

He prayed silently, his eyes open yet not seeing the page,
the words a tumble in his mind. He then focused upon the
verses there before him, struggling hard to hold on to this
fragment of daily spiritual discipline. Although he was unable to admit it even to Katya, these moments were the an-
chors that reminded him of just how important faith was to
him. He saw these brief periods as a much-needed expression
of belief in a world that granted little room for anything of
the Spirit.

But today, without warning, his inner world changed.
Somehow, surrounded by the cramped parlor's noisy clatter,
he felt an enveloping peace. The same thing had happened
once or twice on his trip through the Ukraine. Why this sense
of gathering calm would appear in the midst of such chaos,
he could not say. He just knew a sense of being utterly protected, separated from all the world by a divine sea.

He read and reread the passage, searching for something
that would tell him why here, why now, why today. He found
nothing.

So he let the moment go and drifted back across the sea
of silence to join with the world once again.

· · ·

Ivona circled the lobby so as to come up from beside and
behind. She looked down, and saw that it was the same Bible
the American had carried with him throughout the Ukraine.
She couldn't escape the fact that he was encircled by an immense stillness. It called to her. It touched deep. It left her
troubled.

All her life she had heard the tales of holy men and
women who through great trials and sacrifices had approached God. Yet here was a young man, coddled by the
West, his face as smooth and unlined as a newborn babe. He
followed no tradition that she could see. He practiced no rit-

ual. He bore no marks of suffering. How was it then that even in the act of reading he knew the stillness of abiding prayer?

Jeffrey stirred, straightened, and shifted the muscles of his shoulders. With a guilty start Ivona stepped into view.

Jeffrey was instantly on his feet. "Good morning. I'm sorry, I didn't see—"

"We must hurry," she said, more sharply than she had intended. "Yussef is expecting us."

* * *

The apartment where Yussef waited was located off a side street near the hotel. It was reached by passing through a long tunnel lined with the rotting blankets and newspaper padding of several homeless people. Wires sprouted from rusting fuse boxes to run in slack confusion overhead. The passage opened into a courtyard, which led to another courtyard and after that to another and then another still. All were surrounded by faceless apartment buildings and lined with dead grass and a few stunted trees. Jeffrey followed Ivona up a set of crumbling stairs. She stopped and spoke to a bloated middle-aged man who occupied a glass-enclosed room; the man waved her on without turning from his flickering television.

In contrast to Ivona's silent resentment, Yussef appeared genuinely glad to see him. He clapped Jeffrey on the shoulder as they entered, led him toward a trio of threadbare settees, and asked through Ivona, "You have had a successful trip?"

"Very," he replied. "Yesterday afternoon I completed the preliminary work. Now I have to make the presentation and have my client complete all these forms and give me a figure for the formal bid."

"And you leave today?"

"In," Jeffrey glanced at his watch, felt an electric thrill at what awaited him, "about three hours."

"We have no right to ask," Yussef said delicately, "but your presence here is our best possible cover."

"I can't say for certain when I will be back," Jeffrey replied, understanding perfectly. "I will have to discuss it with my boss and my wife."

Yussef grinned at the translation. "There is a difference between the two?"

"Maybe not," Jeffrey agreed. "I will explain the situation to them, though, and try to be back before the end of the week."

"The sooner the better," Yussef said. "We can only stay so long here without you."

"You really think there is so much danger?"

"The more I learn," Yussef replied seriously, "the more certain I become of that."

"You haven't found anything, I take it."

"Nothing definite. Only trails." He pushed the gloom aside, and went on, "Ivona has told you that I came here to visit my fellow countrymen and ask if they had anything to sell. At least, that is what everyone is hearing."

"Are you sure we should be talking about it openly?" Jeffrey warned.

"Here we are safe," Yussef stated flatly. "Within these doors you may rest easy."

"That's good to know," Jeffrey said doubtfully.

Yussef watched him with evident humor. "You are learning the lesson of distrust, yes? We'll make a Russian of you yet."

Gingerly he lifted a heavy, wrapped object from his carryall and set it on the table, then swept aside the covering with a flourish. "Tell me what you think."

The object's beauty as well as its surprise appearance caused Jeffrey's heart to stutter. The *coupe en cristal* was a sixteenth-century drinking basin that usually served a decorative purpose. The goblet, fourteen inches long and ten high, was carved from one solid piece of rock-crystal. The face elegantly concealed the stone's single flaw by incorporating the milky-white vein into a bull's head. The horns bore intricate crystal floral wreaths and were sturdy enough to be used as handles. The base was of solid silver, delicately carved as a series of matching wreaths, and the center of each held a ruby the size of Jeffrey's thumbnail.

"This is fantastic," Jeffrey murmured.

"There is more," Yussef announced, enjoying himself immensely. A smaller package was produced, the wrappings unfolded. "In the company of wolves, a hungry man needs to find those he can trust. The bishop's word has opened many doors for us here."

Jeffrey scarcely heard him. The cigarette case had a facing of a sunray pink enamel usually referred to as *guilloché*. On this background, intricate work had been done *en plein*, which meant different colored enamels had been applied in such a refined manner as to appear like carved gemstone. Along the sides was a chasing of white gold, swirling in a complicated union at the catch, which was set with a large, rose-colored diamond. Jeffrey thumbed the clasp, found a scrolled interior of *quatrecouleur,* or blue-tinted metal formed by combining gold with copper, steel filings, and arsenic. It was signed in fashionable French hand plate by Court Jeweller Carl Blanc, Saint Petersburg, and dated 1899.

"Now, one last item," Yussef announced, playing the conjurer a final time, "at least for now."

The ebony-backed case was the size of a book. Within was an early Limoges ceramic altar of the kind used in private chapels or as adornment in the houses of wealthy believers and dating from the early fifteenth century. The interior scenes were startlingly vivid, the colors made by pounding jewels and semiprecious stones to dust and mixing them with resin. The picture frames were of solid silver.

After the business was concluded, Jeffrey watched with pained reluctance as Yussef rewrapped the items and made them disappear once again. "You'll have plenty of time to enjoy them in the West," he said through Ivona.

Jeffrey nodded, offered, "I've been trying to help you with your search for your church treasures. I haven't accomplished very much, but I've done what I can."

"For this we are grateful," Yussef replied, his eyes on a downcast Ivona. "Tell us what you've learned."

All lightheartedness vanished as Jeffrey described his contacts with the Consul General. With his description of the Orthodox priest, Yussef's face became an immobile mask. By the time he had completed describing the meetings with the KGB organized crime squad, the atmosphere had turned frigid.

"You are taking risks," Yussef muttered. "Such risks you cannot understand."

"I think it was correct," Jeffrey said stolidly. "Each step felt correct at the time, and still feels right. By the way, have you ever heard the name Tombek before?"

After the translation, Yussef and Ivona exchanged glances, then, "The name means nothing. Why do you ask?"

"They are a gang. Part of a tribe called Chechen from a region in southern Russia. I was told they were following me the other day."

"Again, why?"

"That's what I can't figure out," Jeffrey replied. He related what had happened at the winter palace. "All I can say is, from the looks of things I'm doing what you and the bishop wanted. The attention is on me, not you."

"My blood runs cold at the risks you are taking," Yussef said worriedly. "Risks with our lives as well. The Chechen mobs are animals."

"I haven't mentioned your names to anybody," Jeffrey countered. "And I am convinced the people I spoke with are on our side."

To his surprise, Yussef did not disagree. Instead, he searched Jeffrey's face with a probing gaze. "I see you truly believe this."

"With all my heart," Jeffrey replied. "I am certain that they are allies to your cause."

Ivona said something sharply in Russian. Yussef did not respond. Instead, he kept his gaze centered on Jeffrey. "I cannot tell if your bravery comes only from innocence, or if you are truly guided by a greater hand."

Jeffrey could not help but grin. "Both come in handy. At least I can sleep at night."

"In four days Bishop Michael is visiting here to meet with fellow Ukrainian priests. He will help in setting up home churches, taking care of problems, serving Mass, christening newborns. He must hear of this."

"Give him my regards," Jeffrey said. "He is a good man."

"So are you, Jeffrey Sinclair," Yussef replied, "though

what you have done is touched by the brush of madness."

"I don't think so."

"No, this much is clear, that you believe strongly in what you have done." Yussef pondered this a moment longer, then went on, "I would ask you something."

"Anything."

"Though I remain troubled by what you have done," he went on. "I wish to speak on something else while you are still here with us. I have thought much on what you have said to me about faith, and there is much I do not understand."

"I'd be happy to help you any way I can," Jeffrey replied. "But for answers to many questions you simply have to turn to the Father."

"You make that sound so simple."

"It is and it isn't." Jeffrey tried hard to overcome Ivona's cryptic, singsong dullness with heartfelt sincerity. "To make the turning called repentance, to admit to past errors and sins, to ask for Christ's gift of salvation, is probably the hardest step a man can take. But the *gift* of salvation, and the growing wisdom which comes through prayer and daily Bible study, is there for anyone who asks."

Yussef's brow remained furrowed with the effort of concentration. "And God speaks with you?"

"He does," Jeffrey replied. "Only not always in words."

"You have visions?"

"No." Jeffrey was surprised by the absolute clarity that filled the moment. He looked about the room and knew he would never forget any of it—not the smell of old smoke and unwashed bodies, nor the filth cluttering the floor, nor the taste of the air, nor the stubble on his companion's cheeks, nor the sense of divine presence that presided over it all. "But when I feel the Spirit, then sometimes I can read God's Word and know that it continues to live for me here. Today."

"The way you say this," Yussef shook his head. "You make it sound possible."

"A person is either willing to listen to God or he is not," Jeffrey said. "If he is, he will hear."

"Yes? You can be so sure of this? That I will have such a gift as well?"

Jeffrey nodded. "Sometimes the most powerful of messages cannot be placed into words at all."

"Yes? And then how can the impossible be stated?"

"With love," Jeffrey replied simply, awash in the reality of faith. "And the gift of peace that surpasses all understanding."

"I wonder if what you feel is truly peace," Yussef countered, "or just a resignation."

"I think it would probably depend on whether the Spirit of God was at work, or just my imagination," Jeffrey replied.

"A worthy answer. So tell me. How do you ever know the difference?"

"Only from within," Jeffrey replied definitely. "Only by personal experience. Only if you go and try for yourself." He paused, then offered, "You could try praying with me. It's the only way you'll know if God is trying to speak to you right here, right now."

Yussef shook his head. "I'm not ready yet for that."

"For myself," Jeffrey replied, "I've found that to be the best time to act."

CHAPTER

29

When the flame of his homecoming had cooled to warm embers, when he could bear to loosen his embrace for an instant, when the painful release within his heart had soothed to a murmur, when he finally could accept that he was truly home and truly with Katya and truly held by arms who craved him more than anything else in the entire world, Jeffrey lay with his head nestled in her lap, his face turned upward so as to search deep into her eyes. And he loved her with the fullness of a gradual awakening.

They joined for a kiss, a lingering vow beyond words, a tasting of each other's love with their lips. The fullness of the moment left them silent for a time, until there was again the time for heart to know heart through words as well as eyes and touch and taste.

He stirred and asked, "What is your earliest memory?"

She cocked her head to one side. "Where do you come up with these questions?"

He gave an easy shrug. "I just want to know."

"Know what?"

"Everything." He reached up to caress her cheek. "I want to know everything, Katya. I want to know how you think when I can't see your thoughts on your face. I want to hear your heart speak to God. I want to know how you became this person I love."

Her touch was as gentle as the sighing music of her words. "I have missed you so much."

He sifted the silk of her hair with gentle fingers. "I want to *know* you, Katya. I want to fill myself with your love and your words and your touch, so that when I go away somewhere, I can take all these memories with me and keep me warm."

Katya held him with a strength meant to weld them together, and said, "Cherries."

"What?"

"My first memory is of getting dizzy on candied cherries."

"You're kidding."

She shook her head. "Do you remember me telling you about Chacha Linka?"

"The old woman who kept you when your mother went back to work. Sure. She taught you Polish."

"She was a real Polish country woman. Her days always started before dawn, and everything in her kitchen was homemade. She had a cellar full of canned mushrooms and jams and pickles and vegetables. Her house always smelled of fresh bread. I can't go into a bakery without being back at, oh, I must have been around two, holding myself erect with one hand on a chair leg, surrounded by the smell of baking bread."

Jeffrey let one finger trace its way around a perfect ear, then down the line of her neck. "I wish I had known you then."

"Chacha Linka kept this enormous jar on her kitchen counter, filled to the brim with fresh cherries floating in pure grain alcohol and sugar," Katya went on. "The adults would eat them for dessert, sometimes a couple with afternoon tea."

"Pure grain alcohol." Jeffrey smiled. "Must have packed quite a wallop."

"It did for me. Sometimes Chacha Linka gave me one to suck on when I was teething. I still remember rubbing that cherry back and forth across my gums, and how good it felt." She looked down at him, the little girl in her reaching across the years to gaze at him through Katya's grown-up eyes. "Sometimes I told her I had a toothache when I really was okay."

Jeffrey backed off in feigned shock. "You didn't."

She gave a little girl's solemn nod. "They tasted so good, those cherries, and I knew she wouldn't just let me have one. So I pretended."

"You fibbed," he corrected.

The two-year-old Katya thought about it for a moment, decided, "Only a little bit."

"You absolutely must return," Alexander declared over breakfast the following morning. "And at the first possible moment."

The old gentleman was up and about, but at a pace markedly reduced from his earlier days. Still, Jeffrey was immensely pleased at his friend's evident improvement. In the days since Jeffrey's departure his color had improved, his voice had gathered strength, his gaze had become more alert, his hands had steadied. The doctor had expressed satisfaction with his progress and predicted that he should be able to return to a relatively normal, if somewhat reduced, routine within six weeks.

Katya had insisted that Jeffrey take this morning time alone with Alexander; the old gentleman had been so looking forward to seeing him again. Jeffrey had complained about being apart from her even for that long, but not too loudly.

"This was not exactly what I had hoped to hear," Jeffrey replied.

Alexander's gaze showed a glimmer of humor. "You must take solace from the fact that you and Katya shall have the rest of your lives to enjoy each other's company, then be prepared to go when and where the call is made."

Jeffrey reached across the table, poured each of them a fresh cup of coffee. "You really think it's that important."

"I know that it *may* be important, yes. Here you are, back from your first venture into what for you were two unknown territories. And if your descriptions are correct, you have come upon a number of world-class finds. And only because of the efforts of this one young Ukrainian and his aunt."

"All true," Jeffrey agreed.

"So your new ally finds himself in a position where he urgently requires your assistance," Alexander went on. "Of course you must return. And immediately. Certainly no later than the end of the week. You are building powerful alliances, Jeffrey. Go. They need you. Upon such actions a lifetime's trust is founded."

"Do you think there is any real hope that they will find this treasure of theirs?"

Alexander waved the subject aside. "That is immaterial. What matters, my young friend, is that this search is important to *them*. They are trying. They request your help. I urge you to give it to them. Immediately."

"Markov will be pleased to hear he's receiving such prompt attention," Jeffrey said. "It has been an interesting project."

Alexander shrugged. "A one-time deal, quite removed from our normal activities. That the gentleman agreed to my rather exorbitant fee without a whimper is surprising, but there is no accounting for the impulses of these royals. No, my young friend, the potential for future business rests not with the likes of Markov, but rather with your scruffy Ukrainian. I agree wholeheartedly with Gregor. This young man is indeed a find."

"Well, I'll talk to Katya about it this afternoon," Jeffrey promised. "There shouldn't be any problem about my traveling so soon. She figured out last night that I had to go back."

"Of course she did. You have found a woman who matches intelligence with a very keen perception. A worthy combination."

Jeffrey gave his friend a frank inspection. "It's great to see you looking so well again."

"Thank you, Jeffrey. Yes, it has been a long struggle, and far from an easy one. But I do feel as though the worst is behind me. For the moment, at least."

"What is that supposed to mean?"

"It is most distressing to confront the time pressures set by an ailment for which there is no cure," Alexander replied.

Jeffrey knew a keening fear. "I thought the doctors said everything was all right."

"I was not speaking of an affliction in the traditional sense," Alexander answered. "No, I meant the ultimate of ailments for those privileged to lead a full life—old age."

"We've been through this before," Jeffrey pointed out.

"Spare me the record-keeping when I am attempting to unburden myself," Alexander replied sharply.

"I don't like to hear you talk about this," Jeffrey complained. "It really makes me uncomfortable."

"Not half so much as it does me, I assure you. But despite our mutual loathing for the topic, we shall nonetheless have discussions. I insist upon it."

"You can't expect me to sit here and listen to you talk about growing old and whatever comes next—"

"Death, my boy. Death. You might as well say it. We all knock at death's door sooner or later."

"Alexander, can we please stop this?"

"Death is not my concern. Not any longer. Not now, when I have come to know the Savior's eternal blessing. No, what I find most distressing is a possible slow descent into permanent ill health. That prospect, I must confess, absolutely terrifies me. As far as death goes, I have busied myself seeking a peace with Almighty God. Although I admit to more confusion than illumination, I still feel a solace that is far beyond anything I could ever have offered myself. This is most reassuring, both when thinking of what lies beyond death's door and when wondering at this path I have chosen for my latter days."

Alexander crossed arms determinedly over his chest. "I do not intend to slide reluctantly into old age. I shall march into it vigorously, taking these last years of life with great strides and departing with a wealth of fanfare and farewells."

"From what you said a moment ago," Jeffrey replied, "I thought it was out with the wheelchair and shawls."

"Tears," Alexander doggedly continued, a warning in his visage. "I should like a few tears at my passage. Enough to know there remain at least a few true friends who shall remember my name with fondness and miss me at least a little."

"And a nurse," Jeffrey continued just as stubbornly. "A

battle-ax with the face of a gargoyle, the sort of nurse old-timers get when they can't manage a sterling beauty."

"I shall thank you to never refer to me as an old-timer," Alexander snapped. "Not ever again."

"A nurse built like a tank and dressed in a starched white bunny cap, support hose, and marching boots," Jeffrey persisted. "Voice like a foghorn. Good for getting through when you lose your hearing aid."

"Are you quite through?"

Jeffrey subsided. "You scared me back there."

The old gentleman permitted the bleakness to show. "At least you were frightened here in a well-lit room, with a comfortable chair and a friend to keep the shadows at bay. My own fears arrive in the dead of night, when loneliness drapes itself around me like a shroud and my prayers exit as dust from my mouth to blow listlessly through my heart's empty chambers."

Alexander inspected Jeffrey gravely. "I shall need to share these fears with you from time to time. Bringing them out in the open, you see, helps mightily."

Jeffrey nodded his assent, not trusting his voice just then.

A hint of the old fire returned. "And I shall expect you to answer with your jabs and jests, young friend. Continue to remind me of the folly of self-pity."

He cleared his throat, managed, "I'll try."

"Splendid. Far be it from me to spend my remaining hours planning the one celebration which I know in utter certainty that I shall not be allowed to attend." Alexander tasted his coffee, said, "One other item which I have found most remarkable during this entire period is how vivid my recollections have become."

Jeffrey found immense pleasure in changing the subject. "Gregor said the very same thing."

"Did he, now. When was that?"

"While he was here in London."

"And what was it that he found so riveting about his past?"

"He was recalling your escape from Poland after the war," Jeffrey replied.

Gray eyes sparkled brilliantly. "Did he, indeed?"

Jeffrey nodded. "Could I ask you something?"

"Anything."

"I was wondering what happened when you disappeared like that toward the end of the war."

"That is just like Gregor. He knows the story well, unless his memory is fading with age."

"His memory is fine. He was involved," Jeffrey hesitated, then finished, "in another story."

Alexander sobered. "Zosha?"

"Yes."

Alexander sat in reverie for a long moment, then drew the present back into focus and asked, "It was hard for him, going back to the grave site?"

Jeffrey nodded. "But he was glad he did it."

"That is good. I would not like to think I asked him back to London, then forced upon him yet another painful duty. So. What did he tell you of those days?"

Jeffrey related the story. "I was wondering what happened when you disappeared for so many months before returning home. All he said was that, with the Red Army's arrival, one by one the AK soldiers began to vanish."

"Indeed they did." Alexander settled back in his chair, his gaze centering upon the distance of vivid memories. "Our officers said nothing outright. It was all still too new, and the full extent of our betrayal during the Warsaw Uprising was as yet unknown. The Germans remained our primary enemy, and although they had been pushed from Polish soil, the battle for Berlin still raged. But within a few days the evidence was too stark; we were forced to accept that the Russians had begun eliminating the Polish Underground's survivors.

"I decided, along with three of my closest friends, that we needed to beat them at their own game. The Soviets had begun recruiting Poles to join them in the battle for Berlin. We signed on, under false names, for Red Army training."

Alexander's voice held a mere shadow of his former strength, yet some of the old determination and drive came alive through his recollections. "After just eleven days of the most rudimentary training imaginable," Alexander continued, "we heard that we were to be shipped to the front. My friends and I realized that we were meant to serve as nothing more than cannon fodder. So using that most universal of Soviet currencies, vodka, we bribed our way into the tank training school. We hoped that those six weeks of further training would be enough to see us through in safety until the end of the war.

"But it was not to be. The conditions at the camp were horrid, worse than anything I had known since my imprisonment at Auschwitz. Our food was watery gruel for breakfast, gruel for lunch, and gruel for dinner, served with whatever insects and filth happened to land in the pots while it was being cooked. Our second week, the entire camp refused to eat a particularly bad breakfast. There was no discussion; the food was simply inedible. We were then marched out onto the parade ground, where the commanding officer accused us of mutiny and ordered that every tenth man be taken off and shot.

"A few days later, or nights rather, I was waked from a deep sleep by a bright light in my face and the order to dress and follow in silence. I did not need anyone to tell me that this was the work of the NKVD, as the Soviet secret police were then known. I was taken to a metal-lined room and subjected to a most brutal interrogation. They had word that some of the new recruits were former AK, and they wanted names. I somehow managed to convince them that I knew nothing about the underground army, and I was eventually released.

"The next night, my friends and I escaped under the wire and joined up with an AK outfit operating from the forests not far from the training camp. I stayed with them, fighting the invasion of this new enemy, until it became evident that the struggle was in vain and that to remain meant certain death. I then decided to leave my beloved Poland behind. I returned home for Gregor and my family, and there I met Zosha.

"I wish you could have known her, my young friend. She was truly not of this world. The first time I met her was the night of our escape, I suppose Gregor told you that. Yes, after a seven-month absence, I arrived back to my family home in the dark hour before dawn, chased by any number of ghosts, both seen and unseen. Gregor was there to meet me, as I hoped, and with him was a woman. At first sight I thought she was an angel who somehow had hidden her wings. After all these years, I am still not sure I was wrong.

"Her face was luminous, Jeffrey. Lit from within by the love she held for my cousin. She would look his way, and the room was bathed in a light that touched the farthest recesses of my cold heart. I have never in my life felt unworthy, save for that moment. I watched them share their glances of otherworldly love, and I knew that here was something that was forever beyond me.

"Still," Alexander continued, his voice filled with gentle yearning, "I was blessed to know her as I did. The ruling force in my life at that time was a desire for revenge. Then I would speak with her, or see her with my cousin, and I would know that if I were to be worthy of even the smallest place in her life, I would have to cast my hatred aside. It was hard, so very hard, but even so I did it. For her.

"Zosha, Zosha," he sighed, his vision cast to another time, a different world. "Even to be loved as a friend by her was more than one man deserved. I suppose she was beautiful, but I am not sure. I believe her hair was somewhat dark, and perhaps a bit long, but it matters not. Even then, when I was away from her, I could not recall how she looked. Her heart gave off such a blinding light that I was unable to see anything else about her very clearly.

"When she died—" he began, and had to stop. After a moment he went on, "When she passed on, the world's light was dimmed. A candle passed from this earthbound home to burn more clearly in a heavenly sanctuary. Although we never discussed it, my cousin and I, this thought held me intact through those first dark days after her departure: that she was never meant for this world. Her place, in truth, was elsewhere. Her heart was made by heavenly hands to serve in other, more holy lands. Angels such as Zosha possessed hearts too great to ever be held for long in a fragile earthly vessel."

CHAPTER
30

Ivona stopped outside the Kuznetahny Market's main entrance to button her purse inside her jacket. As she rejoined the jostling crowd, she passed a relatively well-dressed young man who stood on an empty wooden crate and called to the crowd in an official-sounding voice, "Watch out for your valuables. There are pickpockets at work in the market."

Ivona watched as men patted their pockets and women clutched tighter to their purses. Out of the corner of her eye she spotted two other youngsters who noted the motions and passed the information on to a series of runners. They in turn sped off to tell the pickpockets which newcomers looked to be paying less careful attention and where their money was kept. It was a ploy introduced several weeks ago by the Uzbeki mafia, who now controlled Saint Petersburg's largest market. She had been warned of the danger by the person she was here to meet.

There was now an alternative to the endless Russian food lines. At least, there was an alternative for those with money. Free-enterprise markets, they were called, stalls tended by greedy babushkas and unkempt men charging vastly inflated prices. An average Russian's weekly wage for a bag of lemon-sized oranges. A pensioner's entire monthly check for five kilos of beef. Meanwhile, rats feasted on refuse at the stallholders' feet.

Health regulations were becoming the source of numerous jokes, humor remaining the populace's safety valve when facing problems out of their control. Out of anybody's control, in truth. The government remained in a state of flux, with inspectors' wages set at the old levels and prices now out of sight. Most could be bought with a pittance.

Stallholders sold food tainted with salmonella, used contaminated chemicals for canning, mixed poisonous mushrooms with safe, offered botulism as a main course. Cats and dogs were disappearing from the streets. Butchers dangled lit cigarettes over their work and used ashes as a universal spice. People bought meat pies from street vendors, then waited for them to cool before taking the first bite; if it was a genuine meat, like beef or lamb, the fat solidified and became visible. Food poisoning was so prevalent in hospital emergency rooms that orderlies were taught basic treatment. Outside the major cities, epidemics of hepatitis and meningitis and amoebic dysentery worsened daily. Authorities were powerless to take protective measures.

Laws were left at the market gates. Restaurants and bars did a booming business in empty whiskey and brandy bottles, which enterprising stallholders purchased and refilled using grain alcohol colored with old tea.

The word for street market was *tolkuchka,* which translated literally as "crush." The word applied as much to the trash that formed borders around the poorly policed areas as it did to the hordes that crowded the rickety stalls. Chinese brassieres, French cosmetics, Russian T-shirts, Spanish faucets, German shoes—the wealthier stall owners offered smatterings of whatever they had managed to pick up from unnamed sources. Hunting knives glinted beside stacks of disposable diapers. Plastic cola bottles shouldered up to rat poison.

Next to the professional stallholders crouched old-age pensioners, whose social security payments no longer kept body and soul intact. With the ruble's tumble from financial power, Russian old-age support was set at forty-seven U.S. cents per day. The result was a forced sale of whatever was not desperately needed. They at least escaped the mafia's control, at least so long as not too many of them appeared.

Ivona passed an old woman crouched on the curb, offering two rusty cans of imported hot dogs. An old man sold sweaters not required in the summer heat; winter worries could be left until after today was survived. An elderly couple offered cracked flower-pots, a container of oatmeal, three boxes of matches, and a pair of expressions locked in silent desperation. A woman held up a second pair of shoes with her only pair of laces; the ones on her feet were roped to her ankles and lined with newspapers. One offered a half bottle of old hair dye, another a ratty pullover with one sleeve unfurled, yet another a battered kitchen pot. The meager possessions on display were a loud condemnation of the crumbling regime.

Years of chronic scarcity had taught Russians to barter whatever was not needed. But today was different. The tone of pleading was not one of simple need. Despair and panic overcame the shame of begging. Hunger contaminated voices. Men and women alike shouted silent accusations with rheumy eyes. Medals tarnished with bygone glory hung listlessly from lapels in a declaration that here, this person, this one who had sacrificed and risked all, now deserved better. Was owed more. No matter what the regime, they should not be left to know such shame.

The stallholder Ivona sought sold fresh fruit, the produce of fine Ukrainian orchards brought here because, even after the mafia took its share, the profit was ten times what the husband-and-wife team would earn at home. They paid the mafia's price and counted themselves lucky to have a place in the market at all. Ivona picked up and examined beautifully fresh apples. "Yours are the nicest in the entire market."

"You touch, you buy," the woman declared harshly. "Four hundred fifty rubles a kilo."

Ivona could not help but gape. "That's twenty times what the state stores charge."

"You want state produce, go stand in line," the husband said loud enough for the benefit of passersby. "Here you pay the price."

Ivona fumbled inside her jacket for her purse. "A half kilo, then. It is all I can afford."

"More than most," the man replied, more quietly now as the crowd before them thinned out. "You see what they did to Tortash?"

"Who?"

"Next stall but one. The man with the bandaged face." Ivona spotted a man bearing a heavy white gauze strip running from eye to chin. Around the edges of the bandage peeped a violent rainbow of blue and black bruises. "He had two bad days in a row, sold almost nothing, and didn't pay on time," the shopkeeper told her softly. "They have men who like that kind of work. Call them brigadiers."

Ivona accepted the package. "I understand. Your information is safe."

"Nothing is safe," his wife grumbled as she stacked fruit. "To live in these times is dangerous, to say what you know is worse. Better your eyes do not see than to speak."

"Yet I have seen," the husband said, placing a trio of pears upon the weighing machine. He waited for a shopper to pause and ask prices and shake her head and walk on, then said, "I saw a crate of paintings at the warehouse when I went for my fruit."

"When?"

"Four days ago. And another of icons. In gold. Old, or so they looked."

"And did your mind not scream danger?" His wife crumpled an empty packing crate with violent motions. "Did you not have a care for your children?"

"There were more boxes, but smaller and closed," the man went on, twisting the bag closed and handing it over. "And in the office when I went to pay there were people. Dangerous people."

"And still you speak," his wife hissed, her eyes darting everywhere. "Still you risk speaking. And for what?"

"For the church," Ivona said softly, handing over money her eyes could not even count. "For us. For our children and their heritage."

The woman faltered, turned sullen. "Say it then. Be swift."

"Southerners," the man said. "Some of them, anyway. Of the Chechen clan. From the Tombek family. Senior men."

Ivona thought of what Jeffrey had told them before his departure. "Tombek is mafia?"

"Tombek is death," the wife declared. "Even their shadows are poison."

"They are here from time to time," the man went on. "There is some agreement with the people who control the market. Transport, probably. Tombek controls the roads into Saint Petersburg."

"And the harbor?"

The man shrugged. "I have heard so, but cannot say for sure. We have no dealings with the sea."

"Better we had dealings with none of this," his wife retorted. "Not ever again."

Ivona stowed her purchases in a shopping bag pulled from her pocket. "I and all who cannot be seen thank you for this gift," she said, and turned away.

CHAPTER
31

"I express-mailed all the completed bid documents to you yesterday," Jeffrey reported to Markov by phone. "Along with a copy of my report."

"How long have you been back in London?" The man's voice sounded decidedly strained.

"Three days. I waited to call until after I had the photographs and had worked through the documents with your lawyer. Everything looks in pretty good shape."

"Excellent." Markov was decidedly less than enthusiastic.

"The documents, I mean, not the house," Jeffrey added. "Well, the house is in fairly decent shape as well, all things considered. A group's been using your ground floor as a warehouse for the past few months. The floor's pretty badly scarred."

"You don't say."

"There was also a company with offices upstairs, but they've gone bust. They seem to have left everything pretty much intact. All the ornate fittings have been stripped, of course. And there's virtually no furniture left anywhere, so there was nothing for me to evaluate within my own area of expertise. Basically, all that's left are some wardrobes."

"What?" He turned positively alarmed.

"They're in the suite of rooms that I believe were your

father's chambers," Jeffrey said, wondering where he might have made a mistake. "His dressing room has some really nice built-in mahogany wardrobes. They've been painted this awful matte white, but you can tell that they would be worth fixing up."

"I see," Markov said, subsiding.

"The garden is overgrown, and the outbuildings have pretty much surrendered to the march of time," Jeffrey persisted. "You'll probably have to gut them and start over."

"Quite, quite." Worriedly.

"I have an architect going over everything right now. Which brings us to my next question. The architect won't have his blueprints and repair estimates done for another week, maybe two. But the Saint Petersburg authorities are pressing for some kind of formal bid. They're really eager to see this manor taken off their hands. So I was wondering if you'd review the package and give me a figure I could use as an opening bid. I'll make it contingent upon the architect's finding no serious structural damage, of course."

"Fine, fine."

"You need to make your bid for the actual sales price, but they will only be able to offer you a lease for the moment. I guess you already knew that."

There was a heartbeat's pause, then a shrill, "A *lease*?"

Jeffrey explained the current legal situation. "The contract with the city authorities will state that they will sell the palace to you once the laws have been passed. Until then, you will have a thirty-year lease, with all payments going to the eventual purchase price."

There was the sound of breathing, then, "I shall look forward to receiving your report and then will come back to you immediately. Until then. Goodbye."

•   •   •

"Someone who nobody in Russia knows, you said," General Surikov told him. The man's guttural voice was flat as an empty barrel. "Somebody with a name in Eastern Europe, yet unknown in our area."

Prince Vladimir Markov shifted uncomfortably. "It could be just a fluke."

"Indeed. A fluke that the young man arrives in Saint Petersburg with Bishop Denisov's secretary, then proceeds to make contacts with a series of people who have nothing whatsoever to do with his assignment. A fluke. Indeed."

"Speaking of flukes," the prince countered, "you said that if I were to cooperate with you on this, the palace would be mine once more."

"Once more?" The general showed frosty humor. "It has never been such."

"Mine, my family's, there is no difference." Markov hated the way his voice sounded to his own ears. This was too much like begging. He hated not having the money to simply go in and purchase the palace on his own. But that was completely beyond his reach.

Almost all the family's wealth had been tied up in land and houses and possessions in Russia, every cent of which had vanished with the Bolsheviks' arrival, along with every member of his family save for his father, who had been saved simply because he had been in France at the time of the October Uprising. The same father who had squandered away almost all their remaining funds upon mistresses and drink and gambling and entertainments the family could hardly afford. The same father who had left him a crumbling Riviera palace he had not been able to keep up, along with burning desire to see his family's position restored.

Markov had been forced to accept the reality that, given his own financial situation, he would never be able to afford the repurchase of his family's Saint Petersburg estate. The sale of his current, smaller Riviera home would barely cover the cost of renovation. No, Markov had decided, the purchase funds would have to come from elsewhere.

And then the general had appeared.

"The agreement," Markov reminded him, "was that my palace would be used as a warehouse for your goods. My company would be granted your required export licenses, your shipments would be made, and I would be left in peace to restore my family's name and honor. And home."

Markov had struggled long and hard before agreeing to

allow himself to be used as a front. Front for what, Markov did not ask nor care to know, but he assumed it involved drugs or something equally dangerous, illegal, and expensive.

Surikov's group had initially approached Markov solely because of his name. They had seen the prince with his gradually declining wealth as a perfect front for their export activities. Markov had then responded with the plan that was now unfolding. In return for allowing his palace to be used as a warehouse, his company as a basis for the export of their goods, Markov would be granted the return of his old home.

It was the sort of work that Markov felt was not beneath his station. All was to have been kept at arms' length, and his hardest task should have been to wait for all to unfold. Until now.

"Such loyalty is to be admired," the general said dryly. "In any case, the holdup is a mere formality. Parliament will pass the required laws any day now."

"That may well be," Markov replied. "But what of my home?"

Surikov showed confusion. "What of it?"

"Your group will pay the required lease amounts until your shipments are completed," he said bleakly. "And then you will leave me with a debt I cannot pay, for a palace I will not be allowed to keep."

"Ah. Now all is clear. Rest assured, Prince Markov, this too can be arranged in a manner acceptable to all concerned. An account opened with the sales figure deposited before the first shipment is completed."

Markov nodded his acceptance, yet somehow knew in an instant of startling pain that the moment would never arrive.

"What should concern you just now is remaining healthy so that you may enjoy it." Eyes the color of old Siberian ice plunged deep. "To whom have you spoken of our little project?"

"To no one, of course."

The general snorted his disbelief and declared, "A payment will be demanded for this error."

"I have made no error," Markov protested, his heart fluttering like a captured bird. "I did only as we discussed. As we agreed. And there is still nothing certain to indicate that the American is anything more than he appears."

"Let us both hope that nothing incriminating is ever discovered," the general said, then subsided into brooding silence.

"You will be moving your articles to another location?" Markov asked, half-hoping that it would be so. At this point, he wanted nothing more than to be rid of the general and his invisible superiors and the whole stinking mess.

The general shook his head, his eyes focused elsewhere. "Not just now. There is too much attention placed upon it. By too many. Including the Americans."

"You stole from the Americans?"

"No. Well, yes, I suppose. In a sense."

Markov could scarcely believe what he was hearing. "But why?"

The gaze sharpened. "Shall I pass that question on as well? Allow my superiors to hear that you are now questioning their judgment?"

"No, of course not. It is just—" Markov backed off, wiped a clammy forehead. "What do you wish for me to do?"

"Send your American antiques dealer back to Russia."

"That is all?"

"For the moment. My superiors have decided to take matters into their own hands."

"The American has just informed me of his intentions to travel at the end of this week."

"Excellent. Whether or not he is simply a casual bystander, a mere pawn, the risk has now grown too great. The chance that he might be other than he seems is now too dangerous to permit. This chance must now be eliminated."

"And for myself?"

"Know I shall argue on your behalf," the general assured him. "Still, if I were in your position just now, I should have long and serious discussions with whatever gods might be at my disposal."

CHAPTER
32

"First the United States Consulate, then the Russian Orthodox Church, and now the KGB." Bishop Michael Denisov gave his head a merry shake. "Our young American friend has proven to be quite a surprise."

It was a rare ability, this talent of his for enthusiasm. He delighted in all, showed compassion with humor, brought even the bitterest of babushkas a moment of peace. This reaction to all that the world brought his way caused Ivona equal amounts of awe and frustration.

"You cannot possibly be pleased with his actions," Ivona protested.

They were seated in the kitchen of what had been the central Ukrainian Rites Catholic Church in all of Saint Petersburg—a converted cellar in a nameless high-rise apartment block. Now that the church was permitted to work above-ground, now that Mass could be held without the threat of arrest, the cellar had been split. Half had been converted into a Bible school for children, and the other half served as a small apartment for visiting church officials.

"Well, he most certainly has been active. You must say that for him." Bishop Michael looked to Yussef. "Has he told you why he chose to disclose our loss to them?"

"He thought he could trust them," Yussef replied, and shook his head. "It chills the blood."

"Yes, quite so," the bishop agreed, although he did not appear the least concerned. "Still, he has avenues open to him that we do not."

"The KGB?" Ivona's voice had a shrill catch to it. "The Orthodox? You call these avenues?"

Yussef released the briefest of smiles. "My dear Aunt Ivona, were you not the one who refused to accuse the Orthodox church of being behind it all?"

"But to turn to them, to confess our secrets," Ivona protested. "This is madness!"

"He thinks not," Yussef countered.

"And what has he learned," Bishop Michael demanded. "Has he told you that?"

"It matches what we ourselves have discovered."

"Does it indeed?"

Yussef nodded. "And adds some missing pieces."

"You approve of the American's actions?"

"The better I know him," Yussef confessed, "the more I approve."

Bishop Michael examined him closely. "You are not speaking just of our mission."

"Not only, no." Yussef took a breath. "He has a way of bringing the impossible within reach."

For some reason his words appeared to shake Ivona to the very core. Her hand trembled as she set down her tea and muttered, "Madness."

Bishop Michael paused to inspect her face, then turned his attention back to Yussef. "You think that he may lead us to the missing treasures?"

"I think," Yussef said carefully, "that he will do his very best to assist us. And I believe that all his actions are meant to further this aim."

"Then his coming is indeed a miracle," Bishop Michael declared. The expression that flashed briefly across Yussef's features caused him to pause. "What is it?"

"He . . ." Yussef hesitated. "I do not know how to say this."

"He speaks to Yussef about faith," Ivona said bitterly, "and Yussef listens."

Bishop Michael's eyes widened. "This is true?"

"He challenges my heart," Yussef confessed.

The fragile, gray-haired man gave a faint smile. "Indeed a miracle," he repeated.

Ivona was dumfounded. "You can't possibly mean that you approve of this outrage."

The bishop gave her a long and thoughtful stare before telling Yussef, "When he returns to Saint Petersburg, share all we know with the American. Let him apply his heart and mind to solving our puzzle. And guard yourselves as best you can, both of you. Danger stalks behind every shadow."

CHAPTER

33

The night before Jeffrey's departure, they held each other close and long, speaking little, sharing with their hearts. If truth be known, if night whispers were to speak in human tongue, it might be found that he wept a bit that night. For he was much in love, yet the wind called out to him, and he knew it was to sweep him away with the dawn.

He knew, but did not let the knowledge rise. He wept, and thought the tears were hers. Which they were. He gave them to her, and she accepted them with her heart and with gentle lips that tasted their saltiness and the love that lifted them from his eyes.

She cried as well, trying to lower her head so that he would not see how his tenderness opened her soul. She with a woman's wisdom could, in the moment of their first true confession of spirit, see all that was already gone from her life, all that he and his love was to change, all that she was called to leave behind. That was the price of this adventure called lifelong love.

The next morning she clung to him with bonds that went far beyond the tender caresses, the soft words, the yearning eyes. Her heart held his, filled him with a light and a joy that caused real pain as his own heart grew and expanded to accept her gift. They watched the dawn with eyes sharing an inner light more majestic than the cloud-flecked sky, more glorious than the symphony of bird-song outside their window.

"You can't just treat this as a game," she said over coffee.

"It's tempting," he confessed.

"Not anymore," she went on. "Not when my life is in your hands."

He reached for her, said the words that seemed ever new no matter how often they were repeated. "I love you, Katya."

"There is responsibility with that, Jeffrey."

"I know."

"If something happened to you, I could not go on." Her eyes were violet wells into which he plunged and wondered at the depth of love he found there. "I'm not saying that to scare you, but just to make you understand. You have to be careful. For me. You have to take care."

"I will, Katya."

She searched his face, found enough reassurance there to taste the smallest smile. "You're too handsome by half, Jeffrey Sinclair. Don't you dare look at another woman until you get back, do you understand?"

"I've already packed my club."

"I never thought I would fall for a handsome man. Never in my wildest dreams."

"Sorry to disappoint you."

"My dreams were always of a man with pretty eyes. I indulged myself that much. Pretty eyes and a good heart. A minister, maybe, or a doctor who spent his free days working with poor children." She stared up at him and repeated with wonder in her voice, "Never in my wildest dreams."

"Are you sorry?"

Jeffrey decided hers was the way all smiles should be, beginning at the heart, brimming up through the eyes, finally touching the lips. She said, "Now you're fishing for compliments."

"A shopkeeper who sells used furniture—"

"A fine young man with the face of some famous explorer," she corrected, and traced the line of his jaw with one fingernail. "You really do, you know. Full of strength and bravery and courage."

"Makes up for a heart the size of a lemon, I guess."

"Stop it, Jeffrey," she said mildly. "I think that's what frightens me, how you take this strength so much for granted. It makes me worry you might try something foolish, not even thinking it through, just because your strength's never really been tested."

"You're beginning to get me about half-scared."

"Good." Her smile took on a hint of sadness. "You are precious to me, Jeffrey Allen Sinclair. More precious than my own life."

His eyes burned from the honesty in her words. He leaned forward, tasted her lips, whispered the promise, "I'll be careful, Katya. For you."

•   •   •

Jeffrey stepped off the plane to find Saint Petersburg sweltering under a mustard-yellow sky. The air stank. Each breath burned his nostrils and coated his tongue. While waiting for his suitcase, he overheard another passenger say that the city's garbage dump had been burning out of control for nine days. Because of the drought, there was no water available to put out the fires.

The streets, such as they were, belonged to the pedestrians. Few people could afford cars, fewer still the bribes required to obtain gasoline. Streetcars were jammed, the metros eternally overcrowded and stuffy. Gypsies worked the crowded pedestrian ways, surrounding their chosen victim, wailing in a dozen voices, and pressing cranky babies up to the victim's face, while nimble fingers used the confusion to pick the victim's pocket. Street kids rode buses and trams for kicks, clinging to the rear guide wires that led up to the overhead power cables. They swung by one hand, smoked cigarettes with the other, dangled their bodies over the cars behind, laughing all the way.

Jeffrey watched the street scene from the backseat of a jouncing taxi and nursed a sore neck. Perhaps because of missed sleep or anticipated stress, perhaps because of missing Katya, his back was once again complaining loudly. The taxi driver did not help matters. He drove too fast down pot-holed streets, slammed on brakes at the last possible moment, raced his motor at stoplights, wove in and out of traffic, used elevated tram tracks like ski jumps, and generally drove like everyone else. Jeffrey braced himself as best he could and hoped the pain would not worsen.

After dropping his case by the guesthouse, Jeffrey continued on to the Alexander Nevsky Lavra. When he arrived at the monastery's office building, Jeffrey was escorted immediately into Father Anatoli's office.

"I have some information for you," the priest reported, motioning him toward a seat. "But first it is necessary to explain the background. Earlier this year, the leader of the Ukrainian Rites Church wrote a letter to our Patriarch in Moscow. I suppose you are familiar with the history of the Ukrainian churches?"

"Just the bare bones," Jeffrey replied.

"In his letter, the Ukrainian wrote and said, let us be brothers in Christ's name. Let us work as one for the salvation of our Russian and Ukrainian brothers and sisters. It was a glorious moment for people within the church who feel as I do. Glorious.

"Patriarch Alexis did not wish to reply with words, but rather with deeds. He ordered the Metropolitan of Kiev, the head of the Orthodox church in the Ukraine, to accept the offer and to return the Ukrainian churches that were given to the Orthodox after Stalin's infamous synod of 1946." His expression turned bleak. "You can guess what happened."

"The Metropolitan refused."

"Exactly. Patriarch Alexis used this refusal as an opportunity to convene the first synod of all Russian Orthodox bishops in over ninety years. Evidence was brought against the Metropolitan of Kiev and others who had been raised up within the church hierarchy under pressure of the former regime."

"The Metropolitan of Kiev worked for the KGB?"

Father Anatoli nodded. "This we knew for a fact. And now that the KGB no longer held the reins of earthly power, he worked for the new Ukrainian government. For the Communists turned capitalists. At any rate, the synod stripped the Metropolitan of his titles."

"Something in your face tells me the story didn't end there," Jeffrey observed.

"Indeed not. The man replied by breaking the Ukrainian Orthodox church away from Moscow."

"Trouble," Jeffrey offered.

"Chaos and danger. Our priests within the Ukraine who condemn this action are now beginning to disappear. He has the backing of the Ukrainian government, you see, who wish to have the religious ties as well as the political ties to Moscow broken." The priest looked infinitely weary. "It is a problem like that of the Communists all over again."

"The Consul General mentioned the church's tie to the KGB," Jeffrey said. "It amazes me that they could infiltrate the church's hierarchy to such an extent."

"It is indeed so easy to judge the ways of others," Anatoli replied coolly.

"I'm not judging anybody," Jeffrey countered. "I just don't understand."

He examined Jeffrey closely. "Very well, I shall explain. There can be no question that many of the clergy worked closely with the KGB. Not just from our church, but *every* church allowed to operate within the former Soviet Union, including the Protestants. The question we face today is, when did the necessary contact with the Communist authorities become collaboration and betrayal? In some cases, it is almost impossible to determine. In others, there is no doubt."

"Like with the Metropolitan of Kiev," Jeffrey offered.

"Exactly," Anatoli agreed. "You see, under the Communist system, *every* priest and *every* Protestant minister required government permission to preach, to organize a parish, and to hold church office."

"Did you also have to have permission to enter the priesthood?" Jeffrey asked.

He hesitated. "Officially, no. In practice, yes. No one could be admitted to a seminary or theological college without the government's permission. Why? Because it was necessary to apply for travel permits to journey from one city to another. And once there, it was necessary to have a residence permit in order to stay and study."

"A legal straitjacket," Jeffrey said.

"In effect," Father Anatoli confirmed. "In the first year

at seminary, all students were then ordered to visit the local KGB official responsible for church activities. He was always a senior officer. The pattern was well known. At this first meeting, he would be quite kind, quite friendly. There would be no threats. He would say, there is of course religious freedom in our country. We in the government are merely anxious to see that the church function in its proper way.

"But, the KGB officer would continue, there are some elements within our society who are opposed to the great Soviet system. They seek to use the church for ulterior motives. It is essential that we identify these people and protect our nation from harm. If you see among the staff or students at the theological college any anti-Soviet attitudes, we would be grateful if you would inform us. Just to ensure that the church functions smoothly, you understand. Such people can do a lot of harm to everyone."

"It chills the blood," Jeffrey declared.

"As it did for many students, especially those young ones from small villages who had no way of preparing for this contact," Anatoli replied. "Now in the second year, the interview would be much tougher. The KGB agent would say, we were looking for your cooperation, but you haven't offered it. This does not bode well for you. It is a dangerous direction to take, and it makes me question your patriotism. Here, I have a list of names. We want you to report back to us in two or three months with any information you might be able to gather on them."

"And there it starts," Jeffrey said.

"If you were a person of strong moral character," Anatoli continued, "you could get through your four years of training without giving anything of great importance away. But even so, the seeds of distrust and fear were sown among the clergy. There was never any assurance that someone might not inform on you, if ever you were to speak too openly or trust someone too deeply."

"And those of weaker character?"

"Exactly. Inevitably, among two hundred students or so, there were some who were unstable."

"Or scared," Jeffrey added.

"Or who fell into moral difficulty," Anatoli finished. "The

KGB were most eager to use honey traps on any of the weaker priests. This granted them a weapon they could wield against the priest for his entire life. And so a network of spies was established within each seminary class."

"And once that first step was made, the next step was much easier."

"The downward path quickly became very steep," Anatoli agreed. "Among my own classmates there was the saying, give the KGB the first knuckle of your little finger, and they will soon take the entire body, the entire mind, and the entire soul. Once the weaker priests were hooked into the KGB machine, the state used its influence to push forward these people's careers."

"Through these permits."

"For a start. No priest or bishop could serve anywhere without first receiving permission to live there. Then, of course, once a person they controlled was in a position of responsibility, the KGB would instruct them as to which priests they should bring in or assign elsewhere."

"The way you describe it," Jeffrey said, "it seems amazing that any believers at all were brought into senior positions."

"It is indeed a miracle," Anatoli agreed. "A testimony to the power of God that despite these pressures, the majority of priests and bishops remained steadfast in their refusal to compromise their faith and their church."

"So where does that leave us in regard to the missing treasures?"

His manner turned grim. "Some of those who compromised themselves under the old regime continue to do so today. They have either chosen to do so willingly or have been forced to continue their unholy service. Their masters have simply traded one cloak for another."

"They told the KGB about the treasure hidden in the Ukrainian church crypt," Jeffrey said.

"Who in turn sold it elsewhere," Anatoli finished. "To some group who, in my opinion, has also been responsible for thefts of church treasures and artifacts from museums all over the country."

"You mean the government is involved in repeated thefts?"

"The government is involved, but not involved. Just as six thousand churches taken from us by the Communists are returned, but *not* returned. The laws offer the bureaucracy room to abuse us."

"Which they do."

"Which they have done, and continue to do at every opportunity. This was a favorite Communist trick. Now it is a favorite trick of Communists turned capitalists. The deal is done, but not done. The church property is returned on paper but not in fact. So there is a vacuum. Museums which supposedly have released church artifacts show us directives to return confiscated treasures and icons, but the church has never received them." He spread his hands in resignation. "We are forced to grasp a double-edged sword by the blade."

"You believe treasures from your own church have also been stolen in this way?"

"We know, but we have no proof. When we question others about this, we receive no help. The bureaucrats recall the orders of their former Communist masters and shun us. The police pocket the mafia's bribes and offer only words, never action. The museum directors stand under leaking roofs and shrug their lack of concern."

"I have a friend I would like you to meet," Jeffrey said. "That is, if he's still in Saint Petersburg. And if you wouldn't mind meeting someone from outside the Orthodox fold."

"He is Ukrainian?"

"A bishop," Jeffrey agreed. "Actually, while we're discussing this, there's a Protestant minister here in town whom I'd also like to introduce. Has the Consul General told you about the kidnapping of Miss Stevens?"

Father Anatoli nodded. "A tragedy. I continue to pray for her safety."

"Reverend Collins is the minister at her church and has spent a lot of time in the search. He probably won't be able to help with your thefts, but he could possibly assist with some of your other problems. From what he told me, I'm pretty sure he would like to try. Plus, I think you'd enjoy meeting him."

"Enjoy," the priest mused. "I can scarcely imagine using such a word when describing such a meeting." He focused his attention on Jeffrey. "But I agree. It is an opportunity to express my own feelings with more than words."

"So where does that leave us as far as the thefts in Lvov are concerned?"

"I have alerted my friends throughout this region," Father Anatoli replied. "They shall speak with our brothers, and they in turn with those they trust. So it shall spread, in ever wider circles, reaching out through the faithful until, I hope, an answer is found. It is by far the safest road for us to take, and one that has brought great results in the past."

He rose from his chair and extended a broad peasant's hand as he added, "You must take great care, my brother. There are wolves who hunt under the darkness of our nation's gathering night. They are without mercy. Do not fall into their clutches, I urge you. Do not relax your vigil for an instant."

As before, when Jeffrey left the priest's office, he walked back through the monastery grounds and entered the main cathedral. Mass was being celebrated, and the cathedral was packed. Jeffrey found a spot near the back and looked out over the throng.

Upon the ceiling, a burnished sun rose above an earthbound cloud, and golden light streamed out from the all-seeing eye of God. From every wall, at every height and angle, flattened two-dimensional figures within ornate frames stared down at him. Their hands held open Bibles, or pointed toward a lamb wounded on one side, or beckoned for the beholder to look up, up, up toward a bejeweled city descending from on high.

Each worshiper in that vast, chairless space appeared intent on his or her own inner world. They converged, yet remained separate, each wholly involved in the individual act of worship. Even the priests, when intoning prayers, turned and faced forward with all the others. There were five priests in all, chanting prayers and moving about in ancient formality. Yet attention did not remain on them. No person held center stage. Attention was *elsewhere*.

Signs of the cross were grand gestures, often utilizing the entire body. Up to the forehead went the right hand, then below the heart, then shoulder to shoulder before clasping the other hand in an amen. Sometimes they genuflected, bending and touching the floor before repeating the gestures again and again and again.

Aspects of the church still disquieted Jeffrey. The icons remained alien presences to his mind and heart. Yet as he stood and felt the peace of worship pervade him, surrounded by the incense and murmured prayers and beautifully chanted verses, he made a conscious effort to set his judgment aside. For the moment. For this instant of seeing an unknown culture. He shut his eyes and prayed that he be able to see as he should, to understand with compassion, to witness the lives of others who struggled under burdens he could not fathom.

Jeffrey stood and watched, and for the moment was content in the enigma of all that remained unknown. And in that moment when judgment was suspended, there came a gift. A mystery. He stood in this alien world and became somehow united. Not to the others gathered here, not directly. Simply joined. His body no longer seemed to mark the boundaries to his life.

He listened, and for a brief instant he felt his heart to be listening also, hearing a voice not spoken to his ears. He heard the choir intone prayers his mind could not fathom and felt a union with the mystery of the sacrament. A communion.

The prayers rose to a crescendo, the priests' deep basso drones punctuated by lofty calls thrown heavenward by the choir. Jeffrey stood isolated within the glory of this moment and yet felt less alone than ever before in all his life. He prayed, and felt his words rising as incense to the heavenly throne room above, and truly felt as though his heart soared upward with his words.

Boundaries he had not even known existed suddenly melted to reveal vistas that called to him, challenged him to rise beyond the confines of logic and realize the deeper mysteries of living in faith. Of following the commandment to *love*.

CHAPTER
34

The Hotel Moskva was an enormous structure designed to process tourist groups with factory precision. Built in the early seventies, this hotel of a thousand rooms stretched out rather than up. Because the city rested on what formerly had been swampland and marsh islands, buildings were restricted to nine floors or less. The hotel made do with seven, but extended around a full city block.

Outside the main entrance, Yussef pushed through a crowd representative of Russia's progress to capitalism. Beggars in rags and crutches skirted the parking lot. Police mingled with illegal money changers. Crowds of hard-faced men gathered and smoked and talked and eyed passersby with the gaze of carnivores. Western tourists huddled in tight clusters and tried to hide their fear.

Directly in front of the entrance doors, dealers had pulled up four full-sized Cadillacs and two Lincolns. They dwarfed the plasticized Ladas and Muscovites parked to either side. The eventual buyers would be after symbols of the American good life as much as transport, an important fact in a land where legal gasoline purchases were limited to four gallons per month.

The crowd shoving good-naturedly about the cars consisted of the traders who filled the hotel's third and fourth floors. By day they bribed the mafia for market space; by night they filled the city's *Valuta* bars, which took only American currency. These traders came mostly from southern lands—Kazakhstan and Georgia and Uzbekistan and the Crimea—and were flush with sudden wealth. All their lives they had dreamed of the day when their fists would close around dollars, and now that day had come. They paid more than a month's average Russian wage for one night in the hotel, then spent five times that amount each night on food and vodka. They bought the most expensive items they could afford—radios, televisions, suits, jewelry, cars, prostitutes—giving not a thought to the days to come. The barriers had come down. Their years of waiting were finally over.

Yussef took one of only four elevators to the third floor. Narrow hallways extended the length of a football field. Carpets bunched and threw out nylon tentacles. The walls were falling apart, with panels simply propped up against their frames. Lights were dim and intermittent. The sound of drunken revelry floated from nearby rooms.

Like all Russian hotels, the front desk did not issue keys, only a hotel ID card. This was taken to the appropriate floor, where a hefty woman known as a key lady inspected all arrivals. In the past, all comings and goings had been carefully noted in a multitude of books—part of the continual surveillance of all foreigners. Now, she sat alone and bored behind her desk, her power lost with the gradual dismemberment of the KGB.

Beyond the key lady's desk was a small, poorly lit lobby with a "dollar bar." Its prices were slightly lower than those of the main downstairs bar, and it attracted a crowd of hard-drinking guests.

Kiril was there waiting for him, along with a trio of his associates. To Yussef they seemed so *young*. Barely escaped from their teens. Wiry with the unfinished lightness of youth. Yet their eyes bore scars of seeing too much too soon.

"I bring greetings from your father," Yussef began.

Kiril was clearly their leader. When he showed no reaction to Yussef's greeting, the others remained mute. All four smoked their cigarettes to nubs. No paper-tube *papyrosi* cigarettes for them. They pulled Dunhills from a communal pack in never-ending turns.

Yussef drew up a chair, seated himself beside Kiril. He reached over and fingered the young man's shirt. Silk. "Very nice," Yussef said. "And is that a gold Rolex? Business must be booming."

Kiril puffed a series of casual smoke rings toward the ceiling and asked in bored tones, "What do you want?"

"Information."

"I sell cars. You want information, the KGB has opened their files. Go talk to them."

Yussef made no complaint over Kiril's attitude. Anyone who had survived what he had survived deserved the right to choose whatever attitude would see him through.

Changing borders and conquering armies had struggled over Kiril's birthplace for centuries. Lithuania, Russia, Poland, and Prussia had all at one time or another dominated his home region. And through it all, Kiril's family had declared allegiance to only one country, one that had rarely existed save in the hearts and memories of its citizens—the Ukraine.

When Stalin's army drove through what before had been a border village of East Prussia, the entire population had been collected—Poles, Ukrainians, and all the Prussians who had not fled westward—and sent off to a city on Russia's southeastern border. Semipalatinsk, the largest city in Kazakhstan, had earned its first notoriety in the last century, when Fyodor Dostoyevsky had been exiled there. Then, as Stalin had continued his Russification program, Semipalatinsk had become a favorite dumping ground for Poles and Ukrainians taken from the newly Sovietized western lands.

Kiril's parents had been shipped to Semipalatinsk in the late fifties. By the time Kiril was born ten years later, Stalin had selected the area as the testing site for the Soviet Union's nuclear weapons. As a result, that city became the only place on earth where the majority of its living population witnessed a nuclear explosion with their naked eyes. Not just once, but as many as one hundred and twenty-four times.

Semipalatinsk pharmacists had experienced the same trouble stocking up-to-date medicines as the rest of the Soviet Union, but they had always managed to keep Geiger counters in stock. Families had used them daily to test their bodies and their food. By the late seventies, when even more acute shortages had hit the nation's medical system, Semipalatinsk hospitals had begun turning away all terminally ill radiation patients because of a lack of essential medicines, including anesthetics.

In the eighties, the biggest killer had been a wasting disease that locals called Semipalatinsk AIDS. It was a radiation sickness with all the symptoms of sexually transmitted AIDS. Around that same period, the region had earned the highest suicide rate in the world; the victims had mostly been young men rendered impotent through radiation. A large number of local babies had simply disappeared at birth.

Kiril's father had been one of the fortunate ones, an engineer whose skills had required resettlement in Lvov when Kiril was fourteen years old. Kiril's father and mother had returned with the faith that had sustained them through all their difficulties. But the years Kiril had spent in Semipalatinsk had left him unable to believe in anything save the cruelty of man toward man.

"I need your help," Yussef replied quietly. "Not the government's. I talk to you."

"Then we talk cars. You like a nice Audi? How about a Renault?"

"I saw the Cadillacs parked out front. Are they yours?"

Kiril cast a lazy eye down Yussef's scruffy form. "You're not the Cadillac type. Too expensive. Maybe a Lada."

"Thanks. I have one." Yussef leaned forward. "Have you—"

"Cars," the young man stated flatly. "That is all I know. How about a Skoda? You like a souvenir from Prague?"

"I come with a request from your family," Yussef persisted.

Kiril stood, lifted the trio with his eyes. "My family is a thousand kilometers and a thousand years from here."

Yussef willed himself to nod acceptance. "You were good to see me. For this I offer thanks. I will tell your family I found you well."

A flicker of something else passed in the flat depths of the boy-man's gaze. Kiril slowly drained his glass as the other young men moved a few steps away. Then he shrugged on his doeskin jacket, allowing the cigarettes to slip from his grasp and fall to the floor. He reached to the floor beside Yussef's chair and asked with the motion, "What?"

"Treasure," Yussef murmured. "Are the big men moving any? Your bosses, or anyone else's clan?"

"I am my own boss," the young man said loudly, slipping the cigarettes inside his jacket. As he turned, he quickly whispered, "Kazan Cathedral. Midnight."

CHAPTER

35

It was late afternoon when Jeffrey arrived at the United States Consulate, and the long day was taking its toll. Jouncing taxi rides from the airport to the guesthouse to the Lavra to the consulate had left his neck and back complaining loudly. Casey arrived to find him rotating his head, trying to work out the kinks.

Casey stuck out his hand, asked, "Hope you're not still suffering from our run-in with the wall."

"No," Jeffrey said, shaking hands. "Still having problems from that earlier accident."

"Sorry to hear that. Well, the Consul General's got a free minute or two, so let's go on up."

In the elevator Jeffrey asked what he had been wondering since their first meeting, "Are you with the CIA?"

"My brief says I'm assigned to the cultural attaché," Casey replied with a perfectly straight face. "And there are some questions you just don't ask. Not ever."

Allbright tossed his reading glasses onto the pile of papers scattered across his desk as the pair appeared in his doorway. "Good to see you again, Jeffrey. Come on in."

"I tried to call you from the guesthouse when I arrived," Jeffrey apologized, accepting the man's firm handshake. "But all I got was the sound of a war zone."

"Yeah, this city has a phone system that would do Beirut

proud. Have a seat in the comfortable chair there by the window." He motioned Casey into the seat alongside his desk. "When did you get back?"

"This morning." Jeffrey related what he had learned from Father Anatoli. "Have you had any word about the missing girl?"

"No, afraid not. But I may have picked up a little something for your Ukrainian friends. Have you seen them yet?"

"They weren't at the guesthouse when I went by, so I left a message."

"Casey's buddies over at the KGB," Allbright began, permitting himself a small smile. "Boy, I can hardly believe I'd ever say such a thing. Anyway, they've been scouring the earth. Came up with a lot of evidence—nothing solid, mind you, but enough to convince them that something big is going down."

"Like what?"

"Like an organized effort to make a fair-sized killing in one fell swoop," Casey replied. "Appears they've been skimming bits and pieces from a lot of different museums. Probably churches as well. Small pieces, mostly. No centerpiece, no pride of the collection, nothing that would attract too much attention, except in your case. The anti-crime squad say the thieves probably figured your Ukrainian treasure wasn't supposed to be there in the first place, so they'd be fairly safe just taking it all."

"Who are they?"

Casey shrugged. "The lines separating the KGB, the mafia, and the old Party bosses are pretty much nonexistent these days. Looks like they've pooled their muscle and knowledge and gone for the big one."

"That's what these people are saying, anyway," Allbright added. "And others, too, some of whom I would tend to trust when it comes to observations like these."

"There may be some kind of holdup with the transaction," Casey went on. "Exactly what, nobody seems to know. But something's kept the thieves from moving the goods out of the country, or so everybody's hoping."

"It appears they decided it would be safer to stockpile everything here," Allbright explained, "instead of exporting it in dribs and drabs."

"And risk having a small consignment be discovered and alert the authorities," Jeffrey guessed.

"Exactly. They have supposedly collected everything at a safe house here in the Saint Petersburg area. From there they were planning to make one massive shipment."

"Only they haven't done so yet."

"Not according to rumors. Which is all we've got to go on right now."

"My friends will be glad to receive this news," Jeffrey said. "Thanks."

"Don't mention it."

Allbright leaned forward. "Two things, Jeffrey. First, I think it is time you told them about Leslie Ann Stevens and ask them to keep an eye out. If the big boys are involved here, her disappearance may somehow be connected with the thefts."

Jeffrey nodded, then winced as the motion sent the familiar lance of pain up his back. "Sure."

Allbright was immediately solicitous. "What's the matter?"

"Nothing."

"Man's still got trouble with his neck," Casey explained.

"I'm all right, really," Jeffrey protested. "It's just been a long day."

"Well, let's finish this up so you can get back to your hotel. The second thing is, tell your friends to be careful. You, too. These boys don't play by the book."

"I understand," Jeffrey said. "So what do we do now?"

"Wait. Patience is a virtue in this business, and a necessity if you're going to work in Russia." Allbright rose to his feet. "Go get some rest, son; you look done in. As soon as we hear anything more, we'll be in touch."

•　•　•

When Jeffrey arrived back at his hotel that evening, he found that his message for Ivona and Yussef had not been collected; Sergei had not seen either since early morning. Jeffrey went to his room, lay down, found himself too wound up to rest. The pain in his neck pounded in time to his heartbeat, and he was not quite weary enough to sleep through the discomfort. Jeffrey rose from his bed, opened his case, swallowed a couple of aspirin, and drew out the pair of gifts he had purchased with Sergei's money.

Back downstairs, the grandmother beamed her toothless thanks when Jeffrey presented her with the pint-sized copperplated model of Big Ben and the Beefeater guard doll. Sergei was moved beyond words, making do with a series of shoulder pats and handshakes. Then he went into the kitchen and returned with two heavily laden plates. He set them down, moved behind the bar, and pulled out a bottle of vodka.

"Come, we drink to your return."

"Thanks, but I'm not a drinker."

"Usually, yes, this is fine. But tonight very special."

"No, really—"

"You new in Russia. Vodka old Russian tradition. You take."

"No, I—"

"Yes, yes, Yussef explain vow. Make sure we have much pepsi. But this good Russian vodka. Best in world. You—"

The grandmother lashed out with a shrill volley of words. Sergei raised his hands in submission. "Grandmother, she say more Russian men should take such vows. Wait. I get you pepsi."

He went out to the kitchen, and handed Jeffrey the warm drink. "Take. Please. Friends, yes?"

Jeffrey took the glass, agreed, "Friends."

Sergei motioned toward the gifts, said, "Thank you, friend." He drained his glass and gestured to the food. "Is for you. Another thanks. Good Russian food. People come now, easy to see only bad—bad people, bad danger, bad food. But Russians have art of food. Very old. Very good. Here. You try."

The plates held a variety of miniature cold cuts, Russian style. Caviar and sour cream on cold *blinis,* or thin potato pancakes. Salty fish on dark bread, smoked fish on light, both with heavy dollops of butter. Thinly sliced nuggets of roast beef with homemade mustard. Mushrooms, both fresh and pickled. Tiny cucumbers, spring onions, and baby tomatoes sliced and served in iced vinegar and pepper. Jeffrey tasted one of the fish, pronounced it delicious.

The grandmother said something which her grandson translated as, "You are again here for work on the winter palace?"

"Yes." He reached slowly toward the plate—gradual, deliberate motions were easier on his back. He then sat and ate and held his head carefully still as he listened to them go back and forth in Russian.

"Politics and romance," Sergei said suddenly.

Jeffrey worked to focus his attention beyond the pain. "What?"

"My grandmother, she used to visit Markov palace. Back when a little girl. Her mother was Markov's number-two chef." Sergei poured himself another shot. "Once she even saw the czar."

He took another miniature sandwich, this one containing a slice of smoked sausage topped with fresh horseradish. Chewing made his muscles ache more, but the food was delicious. "I've got enough romance in my life just now, thanks."

The grandmother laughed like an old woman, a dry remnant of what once probably had been light and musical. "Young prince Markov," Sergei translated. "So handsome. And so naughty."

"You mean the current Prince Markov's father?" Jeffrey asked.

The young man's interest sparked. "You know Markov?"

"I've met him," Jeffrey replied, deciding there was no harm in discussing it among friends. "Once."

Sergei turned to his grandmother, who chomped her toothless way through one of the delicacies. When Sergei translated the news she became even more voluble. "Yes, this was in 1916, so must be father. The young prince," Sergei said for her, "he was engaged to girl from big family. Girl very nice, but Markov, he have other girlfriends. Many, many girlfriends. He, how you say, make wedding wait?"

"Postpone," Jeffrey said, massaging his neck with one hand.

"Yes. But father old, sick. He worried about family. Then

girl's family start saying they stop wedding, young prince
never marry. So they make day. But young prince, he still
have many girlfriends, only secret. Except servants, of
course, they know everything. They know of secret stairs to
cellar, and door from cellar at back of garden."

Jeffrey smiled politely, sipped at his pepsi without raising
his head.

The grandmother misunderstood his lack of interest.
"She thinks you not believe," Sergei reported.

"That's not it," he protested. "It's just that my back—"

But she was not listening, and the grandson did not dare
stop with his translation. "I know exactly where was secret
stairway. They go from young Markov's chambers down to
cellar."

Jeffrey played at wide-eyed interest while his nerves continued to throb.

"Grandmother spent much time there when she was little
girl. Servants showed her everything," Sergei continued,
drinking and translating with equal verve. "Markov chambers have long hall for clothes. Doors have paintings. Paintings were from old Russian fairy tales. Box with lever for
stairs was behind one of troika. You know troika, sleigh with
three horses?"

"Yes," Jeffrey replied, and decided he had sat as long as
he was able. "Please thank her for me and say how fascinating it was to hear of Markov's father as a young man. But I
think I need to get a breath of air."

Gingerly he stepped outside, climbed the six stairs, and
stood leaning on the metal banister. He could go no farther.
His pain hung like a veil across his brain, and through it he
suddenly felt danger everywhere.

He gripped the railing and breathed metallic-tasting air.
The pollution turned passing headlights into gleaming pillars as solid-looking as the cars. Jeffrey felt the same sense
of descending into agony that had marked his dinnertime
confrontation with Ivona back in the Ukraine. For the moment, it dominated his world.

Impurities hung so thick in the air that streetlights wore
golden globes twenty feet across. As he watched, these globes
seemed to pulse, driven by the unseen beat of the city's heart,

pacing in time to the late-night trucks and cars thundering by. He seemed to see shadows coalesce into dark shapes that slipped among the throngs of hard-faced people to whisper words of rage and hopelessness into unprotected ears. He stood there helplessly, his mind too foggy to pray, as the lights coalesced and clustered around him as well, mocking him with words that pierced his heart and mind.

We are the legacies of centuries past, they chanted, and in his deepening gloom Jeffrey knew the words to be true. Look and see those for whom you pray, they cried. And he did, and he saw the chains of history and the manacles of fatigue and the shackles of darkest despair. Go home, the shapes mocked. Your place is not here. We are many, and you are nothing. Go home and leave us to our work. Pray not for those already lost.

Jeffrey turned and fled as fast as leaden feet would carry him, through the lobby and up the stairs and into his room and away from their mocking tones. As he carefully lay his head upon his pillow, he knew an instant's gratitude that at least this time he had managed to suffer through the moment of pain alone.

CHAPTER
36

Under the Soviet regime, the Kazan cathedral had been renamed the Museum Of The History Of Religion And Atheism, a suitably bulky Communist title. Yussef remembered seeing its graceful colonnade in his childhood textbooks, the same books that had classified Christianity as a dangerous Western cult.

Only two of Saint Petersburg's multitude of churches had been allowed to remain open as houses of worship during the Soviet years—serving a population of five million people. A few had been closed and then reopened as meeting halls or recital chambers or museums—always with great fanfare and, according to the propaganda releases, always at the request of the Soviet people. Others had been used for less noble purposes; the Cathedral of the Holy Trinity, for instance, had become one of the city's three central storehouses for potatoes. The Cathedral of the Holy Spirit had been razed to make way for the Finland train station. Most others had faced with a similar fate, blown up and bulldozed and rebuilt as apartments or offices in the blockhouse style known as Stalinist constructionism.

Yussef kept away from the romantically entwined couples and the home-going revelers and paced impatiently along the colonnades, waiting for Kiril, the car dealer, to appear. Overhead the sky was cloudless, yet so laden with

298

pollution that the stars remained lost behind a copper-colored veil.

The kid slid from the surrounding shadows and sauntered toward Yussef. He was perhaps nine years old, but it was hard to tell. Despite the heat still trapped and held firmly to the earth by the pollution, the kid wore a man's sweatshirt that fell to below his knees. Beneath that were threadbare jeans and ancient sneakers secured with binder twine around his ankles. The outfit made him look more undersized than he already was. His scrawny face had the unwashed leathery cast of a full-time street kid, and he took Yussef's measure with a professional gaze.

His appearance made his words even more startling as he recited in English, "Postcards, you buy postcards, yes? Look. Leningrad, Hermitage, Fortress. Twenty postcards, one dollar. You buy?"

Yussef was genuinely offended. He replied in Russian, "Do I look to you like a rich foreign tourist?"

"You look to me like the trader Yussef from the Wild Plains," the kid retorted. "And the price is now five dollars American."

"For postcards?"

"You buy, you see." The kid was having a good time. "You know somebody who likes silk shirts?"

Yussef reached into his pocket. "One dollar. No more."

"Ten."

He peeled off three, punched the air between them. "Add this to what Kiril already paid you."

The kid grabbed the money, tossed over the cards, retorted, "Go back to the country, peasant. City streets are dangerous for the likes of you."

Yussef nodded. "His words?"

"And mine." The kid added a rude gesture and scampered off.

Yussef strolled carefully back along the lighted way until he was well and truly lost within the nighttime crowd. He then flagged a taxi, gave his address, and released the postcards from their band. A tiny piece of paper fluttered free. He picked it up, read, "The storage point is a winter palace somewhere in Saint Petersburg."

CHAPTER
37

Jeffrey awoke to the glory of no more pain.

His neck and back remained stiff and quietly complaining as he washed and dressed and prepared for the day, but the overbearing discomfort of the evening before had vanished with the night. Gone, too, was the depression that the pain and the city had visited upon him.

As he shaved, a tiny cymbal jangled in his mind, nagging him that something important had been overlooked. But the internal voice was not strong enough to disturb his great good humor. Jeffrey descended the stairs, resisting the urge to break into song.

He accepted a note Sergei gave him from Ivona, saying that she and Yussef would be coming by soon and that he was to wait for them. He made sympathetic noises over Sergei's ashen expression, watched Sergei gingerly set his coffee cup down on his saucer and wince at the noise it made. He asked, "What did you do to yourself last night?"

"Vodka," Sergei whispered hoarsely, measuring the coffee out with bloodshot eyes. "Too much vodka."

The grandmother moved over from her customary position by the ceramic-lined stove and chattered away. Sergei translated dully, "Grandmother, she wish to thank you once more for her gifts."

"Tell her it was my pleasure."

Sergei shuffled back to the kitchen. While he was gone, Jeffrey found that the language barrier between him and the grandmother had begun to dissolve; he understood a surprising amount of what she had to say. He sat and sipped his coffee as the old woman first described her vast collection of memorabilia, then bemoaned the sad state of affairs in her fair city, before launching into a detailed analysis of her own aches and pains, then finishing off with a rip-snorting dissection of the present government.

When Sergei returned bearing breakfast, Jeffrey told him, "Your grandmother is a truly fascinating woman."

Sergei struggled to exhume a smile, set down the platter at Jeffrey's elbow. "Here, friend. Eat. You need, believe me, you need."

During breakfast Jeffrey continued to be pestered by the sensation that there was something which he had overlooked. It occurred to him that he had not contacted the Protestant minister, Evan Collins, so after breakfast he made the call. Jeffrey explained the reasons behind his meetings with the Orthodox priest and the Ukrainian bishop. The preacher showed the same quality of patient listening he had displayed in person.

"Any time, any place," he replied when Jeffrey asked if he would be interested in such a meeting. "The sooner the better, as far as I'm concerned."

"That's great, thanks."

"No sir, I thank *you*. This is an opportunity I've been wanting ever since I arrived. You're to be congratulated."

"I haven't done anything."

"If nothing else, you've allowed yourself to be used as the Lord's willing servant," Reverend Collins replied. "And I appreciate your filling me in. I don't suppose there has been any further word about Leslie Ann."

"Not that the Consul General mentioned to me."

"She is a very fine young lady. We all miss her terribly, and her parents are beside themselves with worry. You be sure and let me know if there's ever anything we can do to help you out."

"I will, thanks."

"Fine. And give me a call when you've fixed the meeting,

Jeffrey. Like I said, any time, any place. I will look forward to hearing from you."

Jeffrey set down the phone, still beset by the feeling that there was something important he had left undone. He searched his mind once more, came up blank, then returned upstairs for a Bible reading and prayer time while he waited for Yussef and Ivona.

•   •   •

Yussef entered the miniature hotel lobby, greeted a sub-dued Sergei, and sat down to wait while Sergei went to tell Jeffrey of their arrival. Ivona sat beside him, consumed by the unease she habitually showed around Jeffrey. He under-stood the reasons, yet could find nothing to say that might improve the situation, so he remained silent.

Yussef had never had time for religion. It had called to him, but he had not responded. He had not *cared* to. Until now.

Yussef was too honest to ever deny the interest in his heart. But not every hunger was good for a man with goals, not every craving a call to be answered.

During his younger years, religion had meant guilt and fear and danger. It was laced with mumblings in old Russian, intoned by bearded strangers dressed all in black. He found the incense suffocating, and loathed the taint of superstition. In faith he saw only a prison of memorized prayers and end-less masses and feast days and hopes that if he did as the priest wanted, as the rituals demanded, he would be granted some poorly defined eternal release. No, religion was not for the likes of him.

His desire for a doorway to God was not so great as his demand for freedom. He had fought too hard, sacrificed too much, to accept chains from heaven.

Yet this baffling Westerner challenged him. Not with words, however. With silence. He pointed a way Yussef thought could not exist, and he did so not with demands, but rather with his life. Here was a man who spoke directly with God. Not through a church or a ritual or a chant or a priest. By himself. For himself. Jeffrey was strong in the world of business, yet somehow he also remained above the world. He demanded nothing of Yussef. Yet by his life he pushed Yussef to question everything he had ever assumed of belief in God. He was a *man*. Yet he was also a man of *faith*.

Jeffrey clattered down the stairs, looking both relaxed and happy. He patted Sergei on the back, said something that made them both smile, giving the young Russian a gentle push up the stairs and pointing toward his room, as though urging him to go lie down. Then he turned and greeted them both.

As soon as they were reseated, knowing he needed to do this while his resolve still held, Yussef took a breath. "I wish to speak with you about your Christian faith."

• • •

"Nothing could bring me greater joy," Jeffrey replied.

"I wish to know God. Yet I find no comfort in ritual," Ivona translated, her voice a dull monotone. "I find no hope in tradition. Only chains."

Jeffrey winged an instant of prayer upward and spoke from his heart. "Since beginning my travels in Eastern Europe, I've seen a lot of church rituals that are totally different from what I was brought up with. I suppose a lot of the people I've met here would find the rituals in my own Baptist church pretty strange, too. What I think it comes down to, though, is that everyone needs to make an honest examination of his own heart. If the ritual itself is their way of earning salvation, then the Bible says this is wrong. Ritual empty of living faith is dead religion."

He waited as Ivona concluded her shaky, hesitant translation and marveled at the intensity with which Yussef listened.

"But every church I've ever been to has ritual," Jeffrey continued. "We come at a certain time. We stand. We sit. We greet others. We sing from a book. We hear the minister pray for us. We listen to our preacher give a sermon. And so on.

"When we follow this pattern," Jeffrey went on, "I think we are trying to give definition to the Invisible. We are setting a form to the formless. We are giving an earthly structure to our worship of the Almighty Lord. So long as the ritual remains just that, nothing more than a means of guiding us and focusing our attention on Him, then what we do in the form of rituals is probably okay. Maybe necessary. It is part of being human. But I like to think that when we reach heaven, we will find that all ritual vanishes, because we won't need it then. We will be part of God's eternal home."

Yussef continued to nod slowly as Ivona reluctantly completed her translation. "Then what is the purpose of your worship?"

"The central purpose for all Christian worship," Jeffrey replied, "is salvation."

"And how is this mine?"

"By accepting Jesus Christ as your Savior," Jeffrey replied. "By accepting that you are a sinner who has fallen short of God's glory, and then by recognizing Jesus as the Son who came to die in your place, so that you might have eternal life."

"That is all?"

"It is the bridge of salvation. It is the first step of a walk leading toward the Father, a walk that will continue all your life." Jeffrey searched his face, asked, "Do you want to pray with me now?"

Yussef thought a moment, then decided, "No. This first time I would like to do so alone. It is not required for me to do this with another, yes?"

"Just you and God," Jeffrey replied. "Nobody else is necessary."

"Then I shall do it," he said, his voice as determined as his expression. "I shall speak with God as you say. Perhaps later we can pray together, yes?"

"I would like that," Jeffrey said, "more than I know how to put into words."

Yussef released an explosive breath. "I thank you, Jeffrey Sinclair."

"It is my honor," Jeffrey replied, "and my greatest pleasure."

"It would be good if we could now speak about other things."

"To business," Jeffrey agreed.

Their discussion took the better part of an hour as they compared notes and revealed their discoveries. Ivona never returned to her habitual singsong, however. She remained locked within some internal struggle that left her with barely the strength to translate, much less join in the conversation with her own ideas.

Yussef checked his watch and rose to his feet. "I have to check with someone before he begins his lunchtime work. There is only a very slim chance that I shall learn what I need to know, but it is the only other possibility I can think of just now."

"Perhaps the anti-crime squad will come up with the missing link."

"Perhaps," Yussef agreed doubtfully, "but it would be far better to bring them in once we have the answer ourselves, rather than wait at the door and beg for crumbs. If they find the treasure first, we have no guarantee that what was taken from us will be restored to us."

"Good luck, then."

Yussef extended his hand. "You are a good friend."

Jeffrey saw him through the door, then felt an invisible hand drawing him back toward where Ivona sat downcast and silent. He lowered himself into the seat and asked, "Is something wrong?"

"I do not understand you," she said, exasperated almost beyond words. "The church is a sacred place. Yet you never even mention it. But this is where we have a relationship with God."

"I really believe our relationship with Jesus should be contained in every hour of every day," Jeffrey said quietly, "not restricted to a certain time and place."

"Christ established the church to be the center of worship," Ivona replied heatedly. "Over the centuries it has been the church that has drawn men to God."

"The church as a body of believers," Jeffrey asked calmly, "or the church as a building?"

"It is in the church that we have priests who can assist us in understanding spiritual matters," she said, so angry the words tumbled out upon one another. "In the church we have traditions handed down over centuries that maintain our sense of community and of faith. Where would the church be if everyone was like you? You pray at the table, you pray in the car, you pray on the street corner. Where is the sacred place where you go to meet God?"

Jeffrey responded calmly, "Ivona, the ritual will never save you."

"I—" She stopped in midsentence. "What?"

"Jesus Christ does not reside in ritual. He resides in your heart."

The faltering confusion returned to her eyes, but not the hostility. Now there was only naked anguish. "You are wrong. Simplistic and wrong."

He shook his head. "This truth is both simple and eternal. You either have a personal relationship with your Savior or you do not. If you don't, no ritual on earth will bridge that gap."

He leaned forward, filled with a certainty that surprised even him. "Unless your ritual is done for Christ and toward Christ, unless it is truly Spirit-filled, it has no meaning. If not . . ."

Jeffrey stopped, searched her aching gaze, wished there were some way simply to give her the peace himself. "If not," he continued softly, "then you need to go before the Lord on your knees. In solitude. In humility. You must ask Christ to fill your life with His everlasting love. And meaning."

CHAPTER
38

Sadko's was a restaurant favored by the city's underworld bosses, a smoke-filled din of imitation Western elegance and outrageous prices. Hard-faced men in tight-fitting suits cut deals in quiet voices while dining on Frenchified dishes. Hired muscle slouched around the room's periphery, decked out in dark colors, sporting a variety of weapons, and holding their bosses' portable telephones like badges of honor.

Yussef pulled his rusting car up at the far corner of the street, away from the early arrivals' Mercedes and BMWs and Volvos. He hustled down the filthy alleyway leading to the service entrance and hoped that he was not too late.

The average Russian wage was 450 rubles per month, less than one American dollar at current exchange rates. With the new power of *green money,* spoken in English and denoting dollars, all rules were off. When one dollar could buy eleven pounds of fresh meat in a starving land, and two dollars could purchase an air ticket from Moscow to Saint Petersburg—farther than from Boston to Washington—all barriers were down.

The result was visible everywhere. A surgeon became a doorman at a restaurant catering to foreigners. An avionics engineer became a hotel bartender. Bars and restaurants and nightclubs sprouted leather luxury, were guarded by former KGB officers dressed in evening wear, and over their door bore the single word *Valuta*. It was a world within a world, open only to those who found a means of obtaining *green money*.

A *valutnaya*, a currency girl, earned four years' average earnings in one night. A black-market tout gained eighteen months' salary with each scalped ticket to the Kirov or Bolshoi. Taxi drivers shunned anyone who did not dress in Western style. Eyes on the street hunted out wandering tourists and hungered for the immeasurable wealth they carried in their pockets.

Yussef opened the restaurant's back door, spoke in most respectful tones, asked if he might have one word with a friend about a most urgent matter. Then he waited, the scar-faced back-door bouncer watching him with eyes the color of a very dark pool.

His friend blanched when Yussef came into view, recovered quickly, came forward with hand outstretched, and said loudly, "Yussef, so kind of you to bring word personally. How is my brother?"

Yussef allowed the man to guide him back outside into the alley. He answered quietly, "Your brother the bishop needs your help. Badly."

"So badly that he would wish to see me dead?" The man hissed his words through teeth clenched in fear. "What is it that could not wait for a more private meeting?"

"I tried your apartment," Yussef replied. "I was told you had moved, and I knew nowhere else to go."

"This is true," the man subsided slightly, but his eyes continued to dance their nervous gait up and down the narrow way. "Business has been good. The pay is nothing, but the tips are sometimes in dollars. I have been able to take a larger flat."

"I am happy for you," Yussef replied, and lowered his voice even more. "The Tombek clan. They come here still?"

At the name the man's face turned the color of old bone. "Do not ask, Yussef."

"I must."

"Horrid things happen to people who ask about such as them. Things from your worst nightmares."

"Still, I must. Have you ever heard mention of a winter

palace? It would be a place where things are stored."

The man wiped a face damp from more than just the day's gathering heat. "I waited on them three nights this week. Enough to make me wish for a government job that paid in rubles. I hold my breath and pray unceasingly whenever I approach their table."

"And you heard something," Yussef said, tensing in anticipation.

"It is a place on the Fontanka," he replied, the effort of forcing air through over-tensed muscles causing his whispers to rise and fall in power. "Near the old royal stables."

Yussef jerked as though slapped. Hard. "It can't be."

"People like that can't be," the man hissed. "But they are. Now go. If the walls have ears, my children will starve."

CHAPTER
39

Jeffrey was out the door, his hand raised to flag a taxi, when he realized what it was that had kept nagging at him. He dropped his arm, turned, and raced back into the hotel.

Sergei was less than excited to see him again. His eyes resembled eggs fried for several hours on a very hot stove. But Ivona was nowhere to be found, and Jeffrey knew no one else to translate. So he grabbed the young man by the shirtsleeve and dragged him complaining to where his grandmother sat knitting by the little parlor fireplace.

"What, what," Sergei complained, then raised a hand to the side of his head. "Ah, too loud. I speak too loud. What you want, Sinclair?"

"Your grandmother," Jeffrey puffed, suddenly out of breath. "She said something last night about a cellar in the Markov palace."

With a martyr's long-suffering expression, Sergei translated, listened to her reply, told Jeffrey, "She say, of course there is cellar. What you do in that house for so long?"

"How big a cellar," Jeffrey demanded.

"Size of whole house," he translated, as puzzled as the old lady. "Bigger. Run back under garden."

Jeffrey smacked the table beside him. "It's there," he breathed. "It's been there all along."

"Of course it's there," Sergei replied, misunderstanding.

"Big house like that, have cellar for food, wine, heat, maybe treasure room. How you miss such a thing, my grandmother wants to know."

But Jeffrey was already moving. He ripped a sheet from the note pad by the telephone, scribbled furiously, flung it at Sergei. As he raced for the door, he shouted over his shoulder, "Give this to Ivona or Yussef, whoever shows up first. Tell them to meet me there as soon as they come in. Tell them I think I know!"

The architect was bent over his blueprints when Jeffrey arrived. He had made a trestle table by taking a door off its hinges and laying it across two sawhorses. The entire front hall was awash in partially uncoiled drawings. Jeffrey flung a greeting toward the bespectacled man as he raced on past.

First the kitchen, just to be sure. He tore through the main scullery, scrambled down the feeble stairs, carefully searched the cramped storage room. The walls were filthy with the dirt of ages. If anyone had erected a false barrier it was impossible to tell. Tapping on the walls yielded nothing but a shower of dust.

Back up the stairs, down the hall connecting to the ground-floor parlors, scrambling over the pipes and steel sheeting and rod-iron, thinking all the while how easy it would be to disguise a former cellar entrance under all this junk. Just as Yussef had said about hiding contraband in his own car; it was all too heavy to lift unless there was a very good reason.

Through the smaller private parlor, the one formerly belonging to the young prince, Vladimir Markov's father. Through the dust-blanketed study, his footsteps skidding as he took the turning into the hallway leading to the bath and the bedroom and the dressing salon. And the wardrobes.

There were six of them, lining both sides of a chamber made into a hallway by their size. They rose from floor to distant ceiling, each door a full four feet wide. Jeffrey opened each door in turn, the massive hardwood frames groaning with disuse but swinging easily, testifying to the quality of their original workmanship. Even through the heavy white-wash, it was possible to trace the wood's grain, to see where the full-length mirrors had hung, to see how the drawers had been fitted and the shelves made to swing out so that even the item farthest back could be easily retrieved. It was also easy to see where the framed paintings had been placed.

Jeffrey searched each of the small shadow-frames in turn, his heart beating a frantic pace. Not until he had worked his way past the first wardrobe did he realize that in order to have a box behind it, the painting Sergei's grandmother had spoken of would have to be set upon something other than a door.

There were four painting-shells not on the doors them-selves, two set at either end of the long chamber. Jeffrey struck gold on the third try. At his gentle pressure the wooden block squeaked aside on hidden hinges, revealing a hiding space perhaps a foot square. His hand scrabbled in and back, his lungs chuffing like an ancient locomotive as he found the knob. And pressed. And felt the wall beside him tremble as something unseen gave way.

He pulled his hand out, looked into the closet next to him, and saw that the back section had swung out and away. Lead-ing down into the gloom was a set of ancient stairs.

A shout from the front hallway made him jump two feet in the air. Carefully he sealed the little box, then spent a frantic minute trying to figure out how to close a door that had no handle. The shouting continued unabated as he set-tled on a hairsbreadth of breathing space, sealed all the closet doors, and raced back to the front hall.

Sergei was dancing a full-throated, panic-stricken two-step when Jeffrey appeared. "They come! They come! My grandmother, she speak with them. I escape through kitchen! They know your name! They come for you!"

Jeffrey fought for meager breath, asked, "Who has?"

"They! They! Who needs a name for terror?"

His heart tripped into a higher beat than he thought pos-sible. "You mean the mafia?"

"Mafia, KGB, who knows the name these days? They seek you, Sinclair. That is all you need to know."

His mind froze, unable to move beyond the point of, I've found it! "But what for?"

Sergei turned, exasperated. "What do you think for, to dance? They come to make you disappear!"

His legs grew weak. "What do I do?"

"You wish to live? Yes? Good. Then leave, Sinclair. Go to consulate. Run. Fly. Go now."

A car scrunched on the gravel lining the main entryway. Sergei swung around at the sound, backed away from the door, groaned, "My head hurts too much to die."

Jeffrey's mind raced into high gear. He turned to the panic-stricken architect. "Tell them this. You let yourself in with your own keys, as usual. You were here alone. You haven't seen me since yesterday."

The architect yammered in fear, "But I—"

Sergei hissed a soft scream at him in Russian. Footsteps sounded along the drive.

Jeffrey grabbed his friend's arm, pulled him back through the main hall and into Markov's private salon. Jeffrey moved in frantic haste as Sergei scrambled and drew short chopping breaths. Together they raced back through the private rooms. Sergei stopped at the dressing chamber, saw a bathroom with barred walls, a shuttered bedroom, moaned, "We shall soon be corpses."

"Not yet," Jeffrey urged. He flung open the closet, pushed out the back wall, asked, "Do you have any matches?"

"What?"

"Never mind. Come on, come on, down the stairs."

Sergei took in the secret doorway and the darkened depths beyond with eyes the size of dinner plates. "What this is?"

"Compliments of your grandmother. Down the stairs."

Jeffrey followed him in, pulled the closet door closed behind him, stepped down three stairs he could not see, fumbled and pushed the back wall-door shut on muffled voices.

As quietly as they could in utter blackness, they hustled down the stairs. When they stepped off onto cold concrete flooring, Jeffrey heard Sergei fumble about. There was a click, a spark, and a small flame pushed the gloom back three paces. What stood revealed was enough to rob Jeffrey of his last remaining breath.

Treasure.

• • •

A lifetime's experience had trained Yussef for this moment.

The instant he spotted the car outside the guesthouse's front entrance, Yussef hunched his shoulders and continued steadily around the corner. There he parked his car, weighed his choices, and decided he had no alternative but to see if there were any chance, any chance at all.

He made his way through the interconnecting *dvurr*— the cramped apartment-lined courtyards—until he arrived at the back of the guesthouse. He glanced through a ground-floor window and was both reassured and mightily worried. The guesthouse kitchen was empty save for the old lady, who sat in a chair by the unlit stove and wailed a constant note of wordless pain.

Yussef glanced about, tapped softly, then raised the glass farther and stepped through. "The American. Where is he?"

"Gone," she keened. "First I tell him where to dig his grave. Then I send my grandson to join him."

"Where? Where did they go, old woman?"

"The palace, the palace," she moaned. "Had I never opened my mouth, oh, my beloved grandson."

"Markov's palace?" Yussef resisted the urge to shake her. "He's been working there for more than a week. What could you tell him that he did not already know?"

But the old woman would say no more. She simply held out an arthritic fist, which clutched a crumpled, tear-streaked paper. Yussef pried open the fingers, saw the writing was English. He shoved it in his pocket.

Quietly Yussef moved forward at a crouch, peered through the doorway, saw nothing, no one. This was a guesthouse for citizens of the former Soviet empire. They could smell such trouble a world away and knew precisely when to be away. Anywhere would do. Just away.

He raced through the lobby and up the stairs, then stood at the landing, wishing he had thought to ask which was her room. "Ivona," he hissed. Then louder, "Ivona!"

A door opened to reveal a rumpled Ivona, a cold compress applied to her forehead. "What is it?"

"A day for pain," he replied, grabbing her arm. "You have on shoes? Good. We go. Now."

"What? Why?" But something in his tone and tension made her follow without question.

Straighten up here, now, yes, calmly reaching the landing and walking past the window that looked out over the idling car where two hard-faced killers waited, waited, like carnivores tracking their prey. Back through the kitchen, pause for a word of comfort to the old woman, a pat on her shoulder, a promise he hoped he could fulfill. Open the window and help Ivona through, then himself. Now straighten and hurry and hope that ever-curious eyes would just this once be searching elsewhere.

When they were back in his car and underway and both were able to breathe again, Ivona said, "Tell me."

"First read this." Yussef plucked the note from his pocket and handed it to Ivona, who translated, "It is all in the palace. I know where. Jeffrey."

She looked at him askance, demanded, "He has found the treasure?"

"And perhaps his own death. We must hurry."

She repeated, "Tell me."

He did, in the fewest possible words. "I will drop you by a taxi stand. Go to the bishop. Tell him our only hope is to gather at the palace."

"Who should gather?"

"Everyone. Any call that can be made must be made. Any friend who is near must come. *Must* come. Our only hope, our only safety, is in numbers."

"But we know nothing for certain." Softly. Without the strength to truly protest. "And he has been working there for over a week. How could he have missed something so important until now?"

"This I feel in my gut to be the place and the time," Yussef said, pulling up to a rank of taxis. He turned to Ivona. "I have no answers to your questions, no way to be sure except to go back and ask the men sitting out before the guesthouse. Shall I do that, Ivona Aristonova? Shall I?"

Ivona remained silent.

"No, I thought not. Go. Tell the bishop. For the life of my new friend, tell him to hurry."

Ivona climbed from the car, asked, "And you?"

Yussef put the car into gear, spoke through the open window, "Do you remember if Jeffrey said the American Consul General speaks Russian?"

•   •   •

Stacked from floor to an arched ceiling lost in darkness were boxes and sacks spilling treasure. Piled in careless heaps. Tied in frantic bundles. Wrapped in packing blankets and sealed with tape. Spilling from overstuffed crates. Jeffrey and Sergei did a dual open-mouth spin of the room until the lighter heated up enough to burn Sergei's finger. Then a stifled curse, a clatter, and darkness.

"You dropped it," Jeffrey moaned, immediately on his knees and fumbling in the utter black.

"Here, I have." A rustling, tearing sound, then light once more, with Sergei's hand protected by a segment of his shirt. Jeffrey looked about, spotted the remnants of several candles, plucked them from the jutting stone shelf. He held the longest shred up for Sergei to light.

"What now?" Sergei asked.

"Your grandmother said something about another exit at the back of the garden," Jeffrey said, concentrating as he struggled to get his bearings, then pointing down a shadowy passage that mawed before them.

Sergei hung back. "That was long ago, Sinclair. Seventy, eighty years."

"So what would you rather do?" Jeffrey was growing frantic. Now was not the time for debate. "Sit around until we're hungry enough to eat gold? Maybe form a two-man reception committee for the next crew that comes down here?"

Sergei nodded. "You are right. We go."

They made their slow way through chamber after treasure-strewn chamber. Jeffrey struggled against his professional training, managed not to spend too much time cataloguing what he was passing. But he couldn't help giving out the occasional gasp or groan, yearning to pick up and carry along. Now it was Sergei's single-minded scramble that urged them along. The man knew much better than he what loomed behind them.

The long passage finally narrowed, then narrowed once more, until they left the treasure behind and moved into a dank, foul-smelling tunnel lined with the slime of ages. The tunnel then dead-ended, the solid rock wall before them offering no clue, no hope. To the right was a small door with an ancient iron clasp rusted shut. To the left a second door, this one bearing a newer padlock.

A thought struck Jeffrey hard enough to overcome any natural logic. His heart in his throat, he knocked softly on the left-hand door.

Behind him Sergei hissed a question, warning, and curse all in one.

"Hello," Jeffrey called softly, sweating heavily. Then he waited.

From behind the door a very small, frightened female voice said in English, "Who's there?"

• • •

Yussef had no idea whatsoever how to address a man of the Consul General's rank. So he chose to rely upon haste.

"Jeffrey Sinclair is my friend." Or was, if he was too late. In which case there remained no harm in hurrying for the treasure's sake.

"I would like to call him a friend as well," the Consul General of the United States replied solemnly in good Russian. "He has spoken of his friends from the Ukraine as good people, people upon whom I would be confident to rely."

Yussef nodded, taking the measure of the man's tone, deciding now was the time to go with the feelings of his friend. "Jeffrey Sinclair is in danger."

"Ah."

"Possibly worse." In a few words Yussef related what had transpired that day. The Consul General stood alongside a tall, lanky, blond-haired young man who listened with singular intensity. When Yussef had finished, the Consul General turned and spoke in quick, sharp bursts to the man, who was already dialing furiously on the security desk's telephone.

Yussef felt himself draw his first full breath since driving by the guesthouse. The Americans reacted with the speed and precision of which he had heard. Here indeed was hope.

The Consul General turned back to Yussef. "I must return to my office for a moment and give instructions to my staff. We will try to call in further assistance. I must ask you to wait here. There is a strict policy of not allowing non-screened personnel beyond this point. You wish for something?"

"Go," Yussef urged. "I have a lifetime to drink and eat. My friend has perhaps only a few moments."

•   •   •

It was indeed the strangest gathering in Yussef's entire existence. But he would be forced to wait several days before realizing fully what awaited him and the Consul General as they drove into the Markov palace's main gates, followed by two carloads of marines. Taking all but one of the consulate's contingent of soldiers off duty and into civilian clothes was why they had been slightly delayed in arriving.

Standing on the palace's front steps was an Orthodox priest in flowing black robes and long, gray-flecked beard; a gray-haired gentleman in Western suit with a small gold cross in his lapel, and Ivona with Bishop Michael Denisov. Below this group was a phalanx of hard-faced men, some in uniforms, others not. Yussef stiffened at the sight, suddenly terrified for all concerned, but was stilled by the Consul General's calm explanation, "Some of these are friends of mine from the KGB. We called and asked for their assistance. The others I do not know."

"Friends and allies," Yussef replied, knowing a flood of relief as more and more familiar faces came into view. Crawling around the house's vast perimeter, leaning from upper-story windows, calling out to others unseen, were a number of allies, Ukrainians all. Those along the perimeter had armed themselves with short iron rods taken from the warehouse collection. They watched all who arrived with danger-

320

ous eyes. But there was no sign of Jeffrey Sinclair.

The Consul General climbed the stairs alongside Yussef, made brief introductions, heard the report from the architect, which confirmed both Jeffrey's arrival and the Chechen thugs' empty-handed departure. The KGB chief and the Ukrainians' appointed head man then reported that the house had been thoroughly searched. Numerous times. And nothing had been found. No sign at all.

An alarm sounded by watchmen at the front gates sent forth a score of running, shouting men. A pair of cars roared away on screeching tires, followed by racing figures, weapons held high. The KGB gathered at the base of the steps watched with evident approval, offered applause when the grinning men returned through the gates.

Yussef held out the crumbled note, said, "Jeffrey claimed to have found the treasure here in the palace."

"Impossible," the young KGB officer replied. "I have personally been all through the manor. The grounds as well."

Yussef asked the officer, "Could your men escort me back to the guesthouse? There is an old woman who just might know the answer. But there are men outside the doors who will wish to keep us forever apart."

• • •

The rust-frozen old clasp was proving infinitely harder to pry open than the newer padlock.

Jeffrey's hands were slippery with sweat as he hacked at the stubborn bolt lock with a two-foot-long, jewel-studded Byzantine cross. The floor at his feet was flecked with gold chips and thumbnail-size rubies shed by the impromptu tool.

Behind him, Sergei held their last remaining candle stub aloft and nursed a serious gash on his other arm, the result of a misplaced blow. Farther down the passage, a violently shivering Leslie Ann Stevens, wrapped in a packing blanket taken from a group of late Renaissance silver goblets, sat on a chest holding a set of ornamental medieval daggers chased in solid gold. She was supposedly keeping guard, but Jeffrey guessed the young lady was so deep into shock and sheer exhaustion that she was scarcely aware of anything about her.

He was growing increasingly frantic. The hammering was proving both futile and extremely painful. His hands ached, his fingers were so lacerated by the sharp-edge jewels that his blood formed a sticky glue under his grip. And he was making no visible progress at all.

In anger and frustration, he slammed the cross down with all his might and broke it in half. He was almost glad to see it over and done with.

Then the last candle flickered and died.

Leslie Ann Stevens let out a low moan.

He was standing in the darkness, listening to Sergei fumble with his lighter and wondering what on earth they could do to get the blasted door open when a sound at the far end of the tunnel stopped his heart. Sergei hissed a Russian oath. Leslie Ann gasped a series of terrified oh-oh-ohs.

Jeffrey closed the cell's door, fumbled with numb fingers for the shattered padlock, set it in place as best he could. Knowing it was futile. Knowing they were trapped in a dead end. Knowing they were facing death, but not knowing anything else to do. "Move back behind the bales. Quick. Sergei, give us light. Hurry."

Then the ringing voice of hope and freedom. "Jeffrey! Jeffrey Sinclair! It's Stan Allbright! Are you down here, son?"

CHAPTER
40

Father Anatoli glanced at the floor and said quietly, "My brothers, we do not stand upon treasure."

"What rests beneath us," Bishop Michael agreed, "is a powder keg. A bomb ready to destroy us all."

It had been the Consul General's idea. Why not, he had suggested, place the three churchmen as joint administrators over the task of storing and dividing the treasures? The other groups, he had continued, could take joint responsibility for guarding it.

The groups had agreed with an alacrity born upon relief. After all, they had experienced decades of enmity and distrust and bloodshed, and only a few hours of this new fragile peace. It was a peace, they realized, based upon a most urgent need. A stronger and more solid footing was required for so great a treasure.

"The truce that surrounds and protects us," Father Anatoli said, "is more fragile than a single thread. It remains only because of the greater threat that still lurks outside. We must work to cement it while we still can. A quarrel between us would therefore be disastrous."

The three of them—Father Anatoli of the Russian Orthodox Church, Bishop Michael of the Ukrainian Rites Catholic Church, and Reverend Evan Collins of the Saint Petersburg Gospel Fellowship—sat together on upturned packing crates in the upstairs formal parlor of the Markov winter palace. Their conference was lighted by a pair of naked bulbs set to either side of the great mahogany entranceway.

"If we cannot work in trust with one another," Bishop Michael agreed, "how can we hope to stem the tide of conflict that will soon rise among the others?"

"And which already threatens the very life of this nation," Reverend Collins added.

"It would be a horror," Father Anatoli declared, "to see our returned fortune become the reason for further bloodshed. Better we had never found the treasure at all."

"But we have found it," Bishop Michael countered. "And with it has come a great responsibility."

"But the risk. There is wealth enough to destroy us all if we cannot unite."

"Or to heal many wounds," Reverend Collins said, "if we can."

"It is as you say," Father Anatoli acceded. "Yet our churches are so different, and conflict so familiar."

"Then let us look beyond the churches," Bishop Michael urged, "and join as brothers in Christ."

Down the hall from their own chamber, the moods of the other leaders were being shown in great bellows of argument and discussion as guard stations and duties and schedules were hammered out. The three church leaders sat in silence for a moment, listened to the shouting men and their strong oaths, and knew how easily the oaths could become curses, the words become blows.

"Too many of my people search for the salvation of a past that never was," Father Anatoli declared. "Some want the monarchy, which they declare was benevolent and beloved by all the people. Others want the Communists back in power and say they really didn't do so badly after all. Others say the church must rise back to the power of old, be the *only* church and the soul of the Russian nation." He sighed. "Such lies we tell ourselves. Such fables we feed our hopes upon."

From outside the manor came watchmen's shouted reports, ringing around the yard every three or four minutes, echoed from within the palace by their fellow guards. And for now, within their chamber, all was quiet, all was honest, all was openhearted harmony.

"At times I feel that running a church here is like fishing in heaven," Reverend Collins confessed. "Not a week passes that I don't have at least a couple of people come in and ask, can you help us grow? Can you teach us more?"

"Yet how many of them come to you because of the Gospel," Father Anatoli countered, "and how many because you are from the West?"

"I would be the first to admit," Reverend Collins agreed, "that many of those entering our doors do so because they associate us with *success*. With *wealth*. They assume we Westerners have all the answers because we have made our system work while their own has failed. But that, too, is a problem. They see no wrong in our Western society. They accept the New Age cults and the get-rich ministries just as hungrily as they do the Gospel."

"My people also drift very easily," Bishop Michael confessed. "Today it is Mass, tomorrow a Protestant revival, the next day a liter of vodka."

"When I am faced with this in my own congregation," Reverend Collins offered, "I remind myself that a newborn baby cannot be expected to stand up and run. It is still in diapers. It makes mistakes. It needs to be held and fed and loved and coddled."

"There is great wisdom in what you say," Father Anatoli murmured. "Great wisdom."

"When Hezekiah was a twenty-five-year-old king," Bishop Michael interjected, "he reversed a two-hundred-year-long trend by demanding that the Israelites return to worshiping their Lord. The priests, under this young king's instructions, tore down every heathen shrine in the country. They cleaned the pagan altars from the high places. They purified the nation. Hezekiah then declared a seven-day period of worship. And so many came with sacrifices that at the end of this time the priests returned to the king and said, we must have more time; give us seven days more. The people donated so much money that it was left in heaps outside the temple."

He looked at each man in turn. "In my heart of hearts, I believe that the same miracle could occur here, if only we were to join together and offer the Lord's message in a spirit of His divine love."

"And yet, and yet," Father Anatoli murmured, his gaze sorely troubled. "What can I say to those of my church who do not agree with the concept of brotherhood among Christians?"

"What we should say to everyone in every church who thinks this way," Reverend Collins replied. "Tell them that throughout the New Testament, we are declared joined to one another. A body of believers. The bride of Christ. A hint of the divine in earthly form. I think we owe it to our Father to behave as He commands, don't you?"

"Indeed," Bishop Michael agreed. "And yet, within my own church at least, the greatest problem is where to draw the line between Christian and heretic."

"But who are we to judge what is and is not a part of the body?" Reverend Collins replied. "The Book of Proverbs states that God truly despises someone who sows discord among those God loves. Who here on earth has been given such perfect judgment that he or she can say who in God's eyes is among the fold? And if there is not the power of perfect judgment, why would anyone wish to take such a risk?"

His dark eyes filled with penetrating strength, Father Anatoli observed, "You have thought of this at length."

"I have had to face within myself the desire to judge," Reverend Collins replied somberly. "To be perfectly honest, I don't agree with many of your practices, or in some respects even with your concept of Christ." Evan Collins shook his head. "But to argue about it, or judge you, is just to make matters worse. As soon as the battle is started, even by thoughts that are never uttered, the war is lost."

"I feel I have waited all my life to hear such words spoken," Bishop Michael said.

But Reverend Collins was not finished. "The truth of Jesus Christ I would defend to my dying breath. My whole life is based upon His gift of salvation. But I must continually be on guard to separate my own restricted perspective from His divine and eternal truths."

"And how do you do that?" Father Anatoli asked.

"By remembering three things at all times: that I am human, that I could be wrong, and that I most certainly don't know everything."

"My brothers," Bishop Michael told them, a gentle smile playing upon his features. "Last night I dreamed that the white roses of heaven were unfolding and sending their petals down to fall in invisible drifts upon this scarred and hurting earth. People were being healed, shadows were being banished, and hope was being restored."

"Our people need our help," Father Anatoli declared. "And there is only one answer we can show them. Love and harmony in the name of Jesus Christ. Unity beneath the glorious banner of our Lord."

There were sober nods around the circle. "If we are to concentrate on the ones in need and not on the problems of an earthly existence for our churches," Reverend Collins agreed, "then we must show in our lives what we promise they will find within their hearts. The everlasting peace of Jesus Christ."

"We must build a shelter for our people's suffering hearts," Father Anatoli went on. "We must work as one to erect a home filled with light and hope, a palace large enough for all believers. One strong enough to withstand the bitterest of winter winds."

"The only answer," Bishop Michael urged, "the only way forward, is mutual forgiveness."

"By living the teachings," Father Anatoli agreed, "of our Lord Jesus."

They stopped at that, shocked into stillness by the boldness of their words.

CHAPTER
41

Prince Vladimir Markov put down the telephone receiver, and was pleased to find that his hands were not shaking.

From his place at the desk, the same desk which had passed from father to son for seven generations, Markov gazed at the blue-upon-blue of cloudless sky meeting deep Mediterranean waters. The sweet scents of jasmine and lemon blossoms drifted in through tall open windows. Beyond the glass-fronted French doors, the veranda table bore a sterling silver coffee service, a gift to his grandfather from the czar himself. A brilliant white umbrella protected the wrought-iron table from the afternoon's warmth. His chair, from which he had been drawn by the general's telephone call, was at its customary place by the outer wall, so that Markov could sip his coffee while watching a bustling Monte Carlo prepare for evening.

Markov did not return to his coffee, however. He looked out toward the horizon with eyes that saw nothing, took in nothing, and reflected upon all that was lost. All that was placed beyond his grasp, and would remain so forever.

It was good of General Surikov to telephone. He had called to report personally about the developments, and to say that they were coming. Despite the man's many faults, Markov decided, Surikov had the mark of a gentleman.

Prince Markov unlocked the bottom right-hand drawer

to his desk. His hand hesitated over the box containing his great-grandfather's set of matched dueling pistols, then settled upon the letter resting beside it. Gently he pulled out and flattened the single sheet. Although the page was yellowed and brittle with age, the Cyrillic handwriting was fresh and strong and certain, as though written only the day before.

The letter had been sent by his grandfather, universally known as the old prince, to Markov's own father, several weeks before the Bolsheviks overran Saint Petersburg and overthrew the czarist government. It was the last word his father had ever received from any of the family:

My dear son:

I know it is not your habit to listen to advice, especially from me. I also know that you shall go your own headstrong way no matter what I say. Yet I beg you to honor an old man's request on this one matter, if on nothing else: Do not ever collaborate with the enemy, no matter what they may offer.

From what I can see of the gathering storm, these thieves are attempting to hide within the cloak of legitimate authority. They intend to steal all we have—our lands, our homes, our titles. They may then find themselves robbed of their own power to govern. When they realize this and show weakness, you may be tempted to negotiate with them in hopes of restoring yourself to power. Do not do so, my son. Do not forsake your soul to these evil ones. They will repay you with nothing but empty promises.

If you were to try and collaborate, the day will come when you shall displease them. Make no mistake, my son. With such people, it is inevitable that displeasure or jealously or enmity will occur. When that happens, they will kill you.

Understand this, and you understand an essential difference between a man of honor and such men as these—they have no respect for human life. None whatsoever. Their only answer to a problem is to kill. To destroy. To annihilate.

Do not allow yourself to be sucked into the maelstrom, no matter how strong the temptation. In the end it will destroy you, unless you choose to become like them, which is itself a destruction worse than death.

As the Good Book says, you cannot serve two masters. Remain loyal to who you are. Do not taint our family's great name with the walking of false paths. The thieves will never return us to power, nor offer you the glory they might claim. Even when everything earthly is lost, hold steadfast to the truth.

And so, my son, may the good Lord keep you and yours.

Farewell

Carefully Markov refolded the letter and drew out the embossed teakwood box. He hefted the cold metal, was mildly surprised to find it far heavier than he expected, and knew a moment's regret that he had never been granted an opportunity to meet the old man.

CHAPTER
42

That night Ivona returned to her room, exhausted by the day and defeated by the internal voices that called to her with deafening intensity. Once in bed, her mind would not cease its restless searching.

She wanted so much to condemn Jeffrey. He and his ways went against everything she had ever known or believed. Yet she could not. The bishop had accepted him since the very beginning, despite her strongest disapproval. And Jeffrey had returned this trust by accomplishing the impossible.

Ivona had accepted work on this investigation because the bishop told her to. It had been her duty to set aside her doubt, no, more than that, her *certainty* that the church's treasure was lost and gone forever. To do the bishop's bidding was her life's work, even when doing so had been an exercise in dangerous futility.

Here again, Jeffrey had proved her wrong.

Then there was Yussef. *Her* Yussef. He had turned to this Western stranger with questions she had waited a lifetime to hear him ask of her. Why? Why had he turned to Jeffrey and not to her? Why was it so?

Even more disturbing, why did she herself feel this answering call within her own heart?

The very foundations of her world were being shaken with violent intensity, and she felt utterly helpless in the face of such a storm.

Always before, she had simply assumed that the bishop and the priests, the *good* priests, were the ones to have a close relationship with God. They read all the holy books. They lived holy lives. They worked in holy service. They acted as God's holy emissaries. She *expected* them to have such a deep spiritual life.

How was it, then, that such a divine spirit dwelled within Jeffrey when he prayed? He was none of these things, not even a part of the holy church. Yet her own basic honesty would not allow her to deny what she had seen, what she had felt, both within the man's actions and within the man's words. And to admit that this spirit existed within him challenged her to find it also for herself.

Finally she slept, and dreamed of a funeral. A funeral long over, yet still continuing. The friends and the mourners and the incense and the priest and the flowers and the tears were all gone, yet still the funeral went on. Still she was there, and somehow she knew she had been there for a very long time.

The funeral van sat in an empty field under a leaden sky. It was nothing more than a rusted hulk, without wheels or windows or doors, locked into place by an anchor of weeds.

There beside the coffin sat her husband. Only it was not he, but rather a young boy who looked sadly out through the hearse's window frame. At the sight of her, he started guiltily and turned back to his place beside the coffin. As he turned, he aged, resuming what she knew was the position she had forced him into for the past forty years, forced to sit and wait with her without ever understanding why, or what she herself was waiting for. Yet he loved her too much to leave. So he continued to sit, trapped in a funeral that had lost all meaning to everyone, including herself. And in the process he had become an old man, stooped and bent and defeated.

Her attention was caught by another person standing a few paces away, and with a shock she recognized herself. Her back was to the hearse and her husband. She stood in such rigid, unbending anger that vines had wound their way up around her legs and body and bound her to the earth, just as they did the ancient van. With her anger blinding her, she had not even noticed that she too was trapped.

Ivona walked around to the side of the van, but the distance was great, so great that even as she walked her husband continued to shield her from seeing the coffin. Faster she walked, and faster still. Still she could not see around her husband. Suddenly she was running, and as she ran she realized she was fleeing, pursued by all the wasted years and all the chains of anger.

With that flash of realization the coffin came into view.

And it was empty.

She stopped, shocked into frozen stillness by the sight of that vacant coffin. Ivona understood then. She *understood*.

She mourned years lost, and hurts caused her by an uncaring world. She was angry with the apathetic way life had treated her. She had used her sorrow as a weapon to punish the world for her loss. Especially her husband. And her God. And herself.

And for nothing.

There was only one answer. Only one solution. She flung herself down before the empty coffin, and she wept. She wept for the youth which was no more. She wept for the years that had been lost. She wept for her husband, and for herself. She wept for the anger she had harbored against her God.

A hand came to rest upon her back. The hand of her husband. And somehow, at the same time, the hand of her Lord.

The calm, gentle motion was enough to awaken her. And as she sat upright, her face washed by the same tears she had sobbed in her dream, she realized that, somehow, all was forgiven.

Ivona rose from her bed, knowing a wisdom and a need that left no room for slumber. It was time to extend the hand of forgiveness here on earth.

CHAPTER

43

The next morning Jeffrey arrived at the American consulate to find Casey waiting for him at the front door. "How are the paws?"

Jeffrey raised two bandaged hands. "Not bad. Your doctor did a great job."

"Good to hear. Come on up, the CG's waiting for us."

As Jeffrey entered the Consul General's office, Allbright rounded his desk as usual, hand outstretched, only to drop it and say, "Guess that's not such a good idea."

"They're a lot better than they look," Jeffrey said. "Mostly just scratches."

"What about your friend Sergei?"

"Fifteen stitches in his arm, and almost hugged to death by his grandmother when he got back home."

Allbright smiled. "The old lady's given me and Casey a standing invitation to come and eat with them any time we like."

"You should take her up on it; she's a great cook," Jeffrey said. "How is Miss Stevens?"

"Left for Berlin last night as scheduled. Sedated, of course, but otherwise in good shape, all things considered. Our base doctors should have her back on her feet in short order. They've unfortunately had quite a bit of recent experience treating released hostages and kidnap victims."

338

"A tough sign of troubled times," Casey offered.

"You said it. Here, take a seat, both of you. Can I get you anything?"

"I'm fine, thanks."

"Your reservation took a bit of arm twisting. As you know, most planes to and from the West are booked solid these days. But we managed to get you onto the midday flight for London." Allbright glanced at his watch. "We'll drive you out, of course. Probably should plan to leave here in a half hour or so; that'll give you time to pack."

"Thanks a lot," Jeffrey said, his spirits lifting dramatically.

"Don't mention it. The least I owe you is help with moving up your departure date and maybe an explanation."

"You don't owe me anything," Jeffrey replied. "As a matter of fact, it seems to me I'm the one who owes you a life."

"Well, let's just put it down to one friend helping another, how's that?"

"Fine," Jeffrey said. "Thanks."

"I'd still like to fill in a few gaps," Allbright added. "But before we start with that, would you like to call anyone and let them know you're coming in early?"

"If it's no problem."

"What's the use of being a Consul General if you can't throw your weight around every now and then? Just give Casey as many numbers as you can think of. It improves your chances. Sometimes the operator hits with one, sometimes with another."

"Modern-day Russian roulette," Casey offered.

"Right. In the meantime, let me give you some of the background to the situation we've been facing here."

Situation. Having almost been killed by one gave the word an entirely new meaning. Jeffrey handed three telephone numbers to Casey. "Thanks a lot."

"No problem. Be right back."

"Okay, let's back up about six months," Allbright began. "Early this year, a senior KGB official was accused of staying in office after he was offered retirement, not out of patriotism or some misguided fervor for Communist ideology, but to get rich. He used the only existing network of contacts the nation had, the Party power structure, to swing assets and deals his way. His efforts came to light when one of his former KGB associates, now working with our buddies in the new anti-crime squad, linked his activities to one of the most powerful mafia clans in Russia."

"Your friends and mine," Casey said, reentering the office. "The Tombek clan."

"Word has it that this is just the tip of the iceberg," Allbright continued. "As the scent of wealth grew, so did the number of KGB bosses clamoring for a piece of the action."

The phone chose that moment to ring. "That'll be your call," Allbright said.

Jeffrey sprang from his seat, accepted the receiver, shouted a hello, and heard Alexander's voice through the static.

"Jeffrey, what a delightful surprise. I hope you are not calling because of bad news."

"Everything's fine," Jeffrey said, looking down at his bandaged hands, thinking back over the previous twenty-four hours, feeling weak with relief. "Really. How are you doing?"

"I am very glad to report that I continue to progress on almost a daily basis. The doctors are quite pleased, so much so that they are actually puffing themselves up with pride, as if they were solely responsible for my recovery and I was simply along for the ride. But there you are. Human nature, I suppose."

"Are you at your flat?"

"Yes, of course. Where did you think?"

"I gave the operator a string of numbers, and yours was the one that came up. I was just wondering if you were already back in the shop."

"Ah, I see. No, my dear boy, I am still taking my leisure at home. Although I must admit that I have begun strolling down to the shop as part of my daily constitutional. Not to interfere, you understand. Your lovely young bride has managed things quite well in your absence, I am happy to say. Even the count has granted her his official seal of approval."

Jeffrey turned toward the back wall so he could hide his tired smile from the two gentlemen. "I hope I still have a job when I return home."

"Don't even joke about such matters. There is much awaiting you. Gregor called this very morning to ask if you might be able to arrange another trip to Cracow in the near future. When do you expect to return?"

"That's why I called. My work here was completed early," Jeffrey replied. And, he added to himself, almost permanently. "Please, if you would call Katya and tell her that my flight should be arriving late this afternoon."

"She will be delighted to hear this," Alexander assured him, "as am I. But you sound quite exhausted. Are you certain everything is all right?"

"Everything is fine," Jeffrey replied. "I have a lot to tell you."

"I shall look forward with great anticipation to hearing every word."

"I can't get over how much better you sound."

"Yes, and grateful for every moment of life and relative good health left to me," Alexander replied, then added, "And for the pleasure of good friends."

"Good friends," Jeffrey agreed, and hung up.

"Our buddies in the anti-crime squad are averaging a new discovery every other day," Casey told Jeffrey as he drove them toward the airport. "The latest was a state research institute that set up a private company, then placed the former local KGB leader as president. The institute sold this new company one hundred state-of-the-art computers for pennies. The company then turned around and resold the hardware for three thousand times the purchase price. The senior directors of the institute split the profits."

"People on the street call such deals 'nomenklatura privatization,'" Allbright explained. "Who has money these days to buy the factories going up for sale? The list is limited to only three groups—foreigners eager to buy on the cheap, Russian mafia seeking to go legal, and the old Communist Party elite using funds they stashed during their heyday."

"And it is looking more and more like the lines separating the Party and the mafia are disappearing," Casey said.

"Exactly. Now that their Communist Party power base is dissolving, the former bosses are scrambling like rats from a sinking ship, grabbing for anything that might keep them on top. The mafia is making money hand over fist right now, what with the breakdown in laws and security. Maintaining connection with the old Party bosses is a logical step to becoming legitimate."

"In other words," Casey summed up, "It's a real mess."

Jeffrey sank back into the cushions, interested in the discussion but distracted by thoughts of the last few hours. The farewells with Yussef, Sergei, and Sergei's grandmother had proven more difficult than Jeffrey had expected. There had been a few tears from the old lady, a round of back slaps and numerous farewells from both men. Jeffrey had found himself making promises of another trip very soon just to get out the door.

But nothing could have prepared him for Ivona's goodbye.

She had taken him aside and with downcast eyes had solemnly thanked him for his gift of wisdom. Those had been her words: a gift of wisdom. Jeffrey had been so surprised he had actually kissed her cheek.

"Right now," said Allbright, "this collection of KGB, former Party bosses, and mafia is gathering power with auctioned factories, and the people are again being crushed under the same old weight, now bearing a new name. And that means there are lots of angry, disaffected people out there. Every day, the public's hatred for all this chaos is mounting. It is a powder keg with the fuse tamped and burning."

Jeffrey asked, "So why doesn't the government do something?"

"Because their hands are tied. You see, the current parliament was elected under the old Communist scheme, where the local Party dominated everything and opposition was outlawed. Given the circumstances, it is amazing that even a third of them are backing the government's proposed reforms, which they are."

"Which leaves two-thirds of the parliament against them," Jeffrey deduced.

"Not necessarily. One-third, yes; the hardliners go all purple at the sound of the word reform. But another third, the pivotal group, is made up of the people smart enough to realize the old Communist system doesn't work, but frightened by the thought of change."

"It's sort of like driving with one foot on the gas and the other on the brake," Casey explained.

"Which pretty much sums up the government's position right now," Allbright agreed. "In order to keep the hand-wringers from bolting, they have been forced to give up control of several key ministries, including defense."

"And security," Casey added.

"So, in regard to a lot of things, the government is simply powerless. This is one of those cases where we just have to hope that the tree of democracy will take root, and with time a good pruning of all these dead branches will be possible."

"And you think that will happen?"

"I'd sure like to think so. Right here, right now, we're watching the biggest economic upheaval the world has witnessed since the Industrial Revolution. The largest country in the world is trying to go from complete anticapitalism to capitalism in one fell swoop. And they're doing it! But people keep pointing to unsolved problems and shouting out gloom and doom with these great voices, while the grass of change grows quietly.

"Look," he continued. "Eighty-five percent of Saint Petersburg's economy depended on the military-industrial complex. Now the military isn't buying *anything*. So local companies are trying to go from tanks to toasters without investment capital. I've seen the result. You want to buy a three-hundred-pound toaster?

"But you know," he went on, "nature can take a squirmy little worm and turn it into a butterfly. So can they. They've just got to close things down, break them up, then rebuild. And it is happening."

"But how fast?" Jeffrey asked.

"Yes, that's the million-dollar question," Allbright agreed. "Can they do it before the people lose patience?"

"What do you think?"

Allbright was a long time replying. "After the Germans were defeated in the First World War, the country suffered this awful time of economic hardship. When historians look for reasons why the Nazis came to power, they point to this horrible depression and hyperinflation, and they say, 'Look, see how bad things were? The Germans would have accepted just about anything to get food back on the table.' But for a few people, myself included, this just doesn't hold water. A lot of other places have suffered bad economic times and held on to democracy and basic principles of human justice. No, I think it was a bad economic struggle tied to something else, something just as big. The people faced a *vacuum*."

"In leadership," Jeffrey suggested.

"Not just leadership. Deeper than that. You see, the first World War didn't just destroy the country's industry; it defeated an entire value system. In those chaotic days after the war, the Germans had nothing to cling to, no basis for hope or confidence. Then the Nazis came along and filled this vacuum with hate. And on that hate they rebuilt a nation's pride."

Jeffrey thought it over. "Seventy years of Communism swept out overnight could produce a pretty good vacuum."

Allbright nodded grimly. "Our biggest hope is the Russians' own patience. They just might be able to see this through. Watch Russians standing in line for bread in the dead of winter, and you get some idea of how much patience these people really do have."

"Seems to me there might be a better source of hope than that," Jeffrey said quietly.

Allbright grew still. "You're talking about religion?"

Jeffrey shook his head. "I'm talking about faith."

"Hard to see how," the older man replied doubtfully. "It would be nice, I admit. I even have enough hope left myself to have asked the three churches to oversee the distribution of that recovered treasure. And maybe, when we are talking about just a few people, it might work. But with all the nation's churches?"

Allbright gave his head a doubtful shake. "The Protestants argue with one another, and some accuse the Orthodox of not being Christian at all. The Orthodox respond by urging all Russians to treat the incoming Protestant missionaries as heretics. Then they both look down their noses at the Catholics. And the Catholics don't like much of anybody except themselves. Long as you see these different churches at one another's throats, I doubt you'd find many people around here who'd agree that religious leaders could find their own hats, much less answers to a nation's problems."

"I wasn't talking about religion," Jeffrey repeated, his voice still quiet. "I was speaking about faith in Jesus Christ. The one hope eternal."

Allbright examined him for a long moment before replying, "Something tells me it's a shame we don't have more people like you around here. People able to look to the heart of the matter and lay it out in plain words that plain people can understand."

* * *

The plane lifted up through the layer of clouds and on into the endless blue. Jeffrey leaned back in his seat with a very tired sigh, extremely glad the Consul General had made the travel arrangements for him. He wanted nothing more at that moment than to be home.

He picked at the bandages wrapped around his hands and looked out on the brilliant cloudscape. Tracers from earlier aircraft stretched out like long white ribbons across the sky.

Fatigue turned the previous hours and days into a jumble of conflicting memories. He drifted into sleep, only to be jolted awake. He opened his eyes to find the stewardess leaning over him, asking if he cared for food. He did not, but accepted anyway. He thanked her as she set down the tray, refused her offer of something to drink, and turned his face back toward the window.

His eyelids drifted downward once more, weighted by the stresses and strains of the past days. This time he slid smoothly into welcome rest. His final waking thought was of Katya.

Acknowledgments

"The mind-set of the times threatens to strip our faith of symbols, rituals, dramas, mystery, poetry, and story, which say about life and God what logic and reason and rationalism can never say. Instead, we attempt to analyze and explain God. Scripture becomes mere religious information, and faith simply the progressive realization of moral or 'religious' goals. From this perspective we cannot expect anything but flatness. One-dimensional faith, like a tent with only one peg, easily collapses. Yet, we Americans tend to secure our faith primarily with the one peg of logical thought."

> Reverend Lynn Anderson
> (Church of Christ)
> *If I Really Believe, Why Do
> I Have These Doubts?*

Throughout the journey of this novel, I have been constantly humbled by the gentle hospitality of people whose hearts were open to our Lord, and by the smallness of my own world. I hope I have managed to convey some of this spirit in my work. The writing of this book has coincided with Isabella, my wife, beginning graduate studies in theology at Oxford University.

Despite the strains of studying in this area for the first time (her previous studies have been in law and international relations), Isabella has continued to walk with me through the formation of this book, helping out at every turn. Truly, this work was completed in large part because of her loving assistance and bountiful wisdom.

Because of the importance of these dialogues among churches, all discussions on matters of doctrine and faith were taken verbatim from interviews I had with respective priests, bishops, and ministers. I have done this in hopes that people interested in becoming more involved in evangelistic efforts within the former Soviet lands—and make no mistake, help is desperately needed—might perhaps gain a bit more insight into the current religious culture.

United States Consul General to Saint Petersburg, Mr. Jack Gosnell, has spent more than twelve years serving his country in Russia and China. His knowledge is simply immense. It was a great privilege to work with him. His overview of the political and economic situation facing Russia today was both succinct and extremely perceptive. We are indeed fortunate to have a gentleman of such talents representing us in this volatile region. I would also like to thank his lovely wife and most talented staff for their gifts of assistance and hospitality.

While in Saint Petersburg, I was granted the opportunity to speak at length with a member of the nation's Foreign Ministry. I did so with the understanding that I would not name him. But I would nonetheless like to offer my very sincere thanks for the perceptivity and depth of analysis he granted me.

Vladimir Gronsky is editor of the International Department of the *Leningrad Daily News*. At the conclusion of my visit to Saint Petersburg, I was faced with the daunting task of pulling together the results of almost fifty interviews. Mr. Gronsky assisted me in rising above the mass of facts and related experiences, and searching out the overriding themes. With his honest advice as guidance, I was able to establish certain tenets that became central points in this story's development. I am indeed thankful for his patient aid.

H. Kozyritskiy is the Mayor of Sestoretsk, the region running from northern Saint Petersburg to the borderlands. In a discussion that was slated for fifteen minutes and ran to over two hours, he outlined with frightening honesty the economic trials facing his region. If Russia is able to overcome the challenge facing it today, it will be in no small part due to the unsung efforts of men like him.

Reverend Allen Faubion and Reverend Larry Van Tuyl are pastors at the International Church of Saint Petersburg. For those traveling over, Sunday services are located inside the Concert-Theater Complex at 39 Nevsky Prospekt. (This was altered in this book to a location used by another Western group giving services only in Russian, as the story required a more permanent location.) I would like to offer my heartfelt thanks both for the excellent information granted to me in our discussion prior to the service, and for the most inspiring sermon. May the Lord richly bless them and their work.

Dr. Karl Keller, pastor at the Walnut Grove Lutheran Church in British Columbia, was a leader with Christian Embassy, and traveled with a group of Canadian Christian businessmen on a goodwill mission to Moscow and Saint Petersburg. They had high-level meetings within the national and city governments, and with military officials. I am very grateful that Dr. Keller was willing to take the time from his mission work to stop and share with me both his experience and his findings. Several of his observations have been worked into Reverend Collins' discussions.

The story of Alexander and Gregor's escape from Poland at the end of the war was drawn from the experiences of my wife's uncle, Marian Tarka. He was a member of the Polish Home Army, or AK, and when the Russians arrived and fellow members began to disappear, he had the idea of escaping into the Red Army. The story is his save for one fact; he survived his interrogation, and remained with the Red Army until discharged, while his friends made their escape into the woods and joined the AK and eventually left Poland. The route up through Scandinavia to London was one used by a large number of escapees in the turmoil before the Soviet's Iron Curtain was firmly fixed into place.

The story of Zosha's escape from the trek headed from the Warsaw Uprising to the German concentration camp is also true. It is the story of my wife's aunt, Dusia Tarka, who escaped due to the courageous efforts of one young man, who slipped in and out of the line of German soldiers to save as many young people as he could. She never even learned his name.

Ryszard Litwicki was taken from his home in Lvov by the Germans to work at forced labor in Berlin, where during the bombing campaign he worked in a bomb depot. I am grateful that he survived the experience, and was willing to speak of his upbringing in what now is western Ukraine, and then was the area of Poland known as Galicia.

Eugenia Krajewska is secretary to the Father Superior at the Marian Fathers monastery outside London. When she was eleven years old, she and her family were deported from Poland to a logging village just south of the Arctic Circle in European Russia. This life story made the chronicle of Ivona Aristonova's tragic past. It is very hard for us as Americans to fathom the suffering caused to literally millions of people by Stalin's policy of amalgamation and relocation, what was commonly referred to as Russification. Her story is in no way exceptional, and stands as a testimony to a tragedy that we as free men and women must strive never to permit to surface again.

* * *

Some time ago, Reverend John Wimber spoke to the Holy Trinity Church in Brompton, England, on the desert experience. The section in this book that began with a reference to the sixty-third Psalm was drawn from his magnificent teaching.

Each year, bookstore owners from across the nation join together for the Christian Booksellers Association annual convention. This year, Dr. Joe Aldrich spoke at the Sunday service. His address was on the need for harmony among the body of believers. Great inspiration, as well as considerable material for this book, was drawn from the gentleman's well-spoken wisdom.

Reverend Alec Brooks is formerly President of the Bethany Fellowship, with responsibility for their worldwide missionary program as well as the Bible college. Currently he is teaching Theology, Marriage and Family, and Developing A Christan World View at this same college, and remains a member of the advisory board. He was most helpful in gaining a solid perspective on how an evangelical missionary pastor might view the Orthodox church—his words formed the discussion Jeffrey had with Reverend Evan Collins on the issue of icons. Alec has been a good friend and most helpful guide over the years. I am grateful for the opportunity to grow from his wisdom.

The gentlefolk at Christies auction house continue to show remarkable patience with the presence of an author with no possibility whatsoever to purchase any of the items he hovers around. I am especially grateful for Amelia Fitzalan-Howard's surprising eagerness to offer hospitality, wisdom, insight, and answers to what I am sure appeared to be an unending stream of questions.

Her Majesty Queen Elizabeth recently opened an exhibition in Buckhingham Palace of antiques and paintings collected by one of her forebears, King George III. I would like to extend my thanks to the staff who prepared both the exhibit and the excellent brochure. They proved an invaluable source of information for the period from which many of the antiques in this book were drawn.

The story of Communist Party and KGB bosses secretly attempting to establish a Party-controlled mini-economy for no other reason than greed is true. I would like to thank the BBC's Panorama news team for their excellent coverage of the story, and for supplying me with most helpful documentation as this book was being developed.

A very special thanks must be extended to two leaders of the Russian Orthodox Church, Metropolitan Anthony in London and Metropolitan Ioann in Saint Petersburg. They were most kind in their offers of assistance and contacts. In both cases, I was an unknown American Protestant who simply wrote and asked questions. In both cases, I was answered with open-handed kindness. Thank you.

Bishop Kallistos, of the Ecumenical Patriarchate in England, is author of numerous books and articles on orthodox faith. I found his book *The Orthodox Church* to be a wonderful introduction both to the history and the present-day status of this church. I am also most grateful for the hours he so willingly shared with me. His kind assistance went far beyond discussing with me such painful subjects as KGB infiltration into the Russian Orthodox heirarchy. He was also most open in sharing what Christian faith means to a Russian Orthodox, where it parallels the Protestant faith and where it diverges. He is a kind and Spirit-filled man, whose assistance added greatly to the work on this book.

Diakon Vsevolod Chaplin, personal assistant to the Patriarch of the Russian Orthodox Church in Moscow, outlined a number of current issues facing the church in Russia today. He was open and frank about the trials besetting the church, both from within and without. He discussed the church's historical perspective to evangelical movements and the impressions of today. He then made introductions for me, both with the senior bishops and Metropolitans in Russia and with the Orthodox community leaders in Great Britain. This book's attempt to portray the Orthodox church's position with authenticity stems in large part from his very kind assistance.

Father Archimindrit Simon is personal assistant to the Metropolitan Ioann of Saint Petersburg. He was an extremely erudite individual, who helped to place the current problems and issues facing the Russian Orthodox community in simple, understandable terms. This was no small feat, as everything besetting the church today is a legacy of that which has come before. He and all his staff were burdened with the work of ten. I am indeed grateful that he would nonetheless take an entire morning to educate me.

Bishop Michael Kuchmiak is head of the Ukrainian Eastern Rites Catholic Church for all of England, Wales, Scotland, and Ireland. I was humbled by his willingness to rearrange extremely busy schedules to talk with me in depth about his church and the crisis it faces today as it emerges from forty-five years of illegality and persecution.

Marina Karetnikova is a deacon and lay minister in the Baptist church of Saint Petersburg. She is also a teacher at

the newly opened Bible college in that city. She was extremely helpful in granting me a living history of the Russian Baptist movement and of the courage and faith dem-
onstrated by its believers through these tremendously
difficult times.

Father Graham Woolfenden was trained as a "Biritual"
priest, meaning that he was most familiar with the Eastern
Rites churches, as well as with the differences between them
and the Catholic liturgy. He was most helpful in granting
me this essential overview required before in-depth research
could be started.

Valerie Morozov is Director of Education of the Bibles for
Everyone Society of Russia. Their primary purpose is twofold: to supply Bibles in modern Russian and other Soviet
tongues and to teach Bible classes to school-age children.
Their number of classes has increased from ten in 1989 to
one hundred thirty in 1992. They currently operate classes
in foster homes, orphanages, hospitals, and reformatories. I
am very grateful for his taking the time to discuss the situation facing them as they try to set up classes inside former
Communist-run school systems, and for the overview of
Christianity in modern Russian society. They are in dire
need of both teaching aids and financial support. Anyone
interested in assisting them should please contact: Valerie
Morozov, Bibles for Everyone Society, %Bethany House Publishers, 11300 Hampshire Avenue South, Minneapolis,
Minnesota 55438.

• • •

In my own search for spiritual growth and growing wisdom, there have often been points where the way ahead has
seemed filled with questions. If anyone faces such times, and
seeks the advice of one who has spent a lifetime walking the
spiritual path and helping others to do likewise, I would
strongly suggest they write: Reverend Paul McCommon,
%Bethany House Publishers, 11300 Hampshire Avenue
South, Minneapolis, Minnesota 55438.